This first edition
is personally signed by the author:

Ryn Sear

BAEN

TIGER BY THE TAIL

BAEN BOOKS by JOHN RINGO

PALADIN OF SHADOWS:
Ghost · *Kildar* · *Choosers of the Slain* · *Unto the Breach* ·
A Deeper Blue · *Tiger by the Tail* (with Ryan Sear)

TROY RISING:
Live Free or Die · *Citadel* · *The Hot Gate*

LEGACY OF THE ALDENATA:
A Hymn Before Battle · *Gust Front* · *When the Devil Dances*
· *Hell's Faire* · *The Hero* (with Michael Z. Williamson) ·
Cally's War (with Julie Cochrane) · *Watch on the Rhine*
(with Tom Kratman) · *Sister Time* (with Julie Cochrane) ·
Yellow Eyes (with Tom Kratman) · *Honor of the Clan* (with
Julie Cochrane) · *Eye of the Storm*

COUNCIL WARS:
There Will Be Dragons · *Emerald Sea* ·
Against the Tide · *East of the Sun, West of the Moon*

INTO THE LOOKING GLASS:
Into the Looking Glass · *Vorpal Blade* (with Travis
S. Taylor) · *Manxome Foe* (with Travis S. Taylor) ·
Claws that Catch (with Travis S. Taylor)

EMPIRE OF MAN:
March to the Sea (with David Weber) · *March to the Stars*
(with David Weber) · *March Upcountry* (with David Weber) ·
We Few (with David Weber)

SPECIAL CIRCUMSTANCES:
Princess of Wands · *Queen of Wands*

STANDALONE TITLES:
The Last Centurion
Citizens (ed. with Brian M. Thomsen)

TIGER BY THE TAIL

A KILDAR NOVEL
CREATED BY JOHN RINGO

BY JOHN RINGO &
RYAN SEAR

TIGER BY THE TAIL

This is a work of fiction. All the characters and events portrayed in this book are fictional, and any resemblance to real people or incidents is purely coincidental.

A Baen Books Original

Baen Publishing Enterprises
P.O. Box 1403
Riverdale, NY 10471
www.baen.com

ISBN: 978-1-4516-3863-9

Cover art by Kurt Miller

First printing, January 2013

Library of Congress Cataloging-in-Publication Data

Distributed by Simon & Schuster
1230 Avenue of the Americas
New York, NY 10020

Pages by Joy Freeman (www.pagesbyjoy.com)
Printed in the United States of America

10 9 8 7 6 5 4 3 2 1

To every man and woman in the U.S. Armed Forces.
Standing tall in the face of adversity,
Serving with commitment, courage, and honor.
America owes each one of you
a debt it can never fully repay.

And, as always:
For Captain Tamara Long, USAF
Born: 12 May 1979
Died: 23 March 2003, Afghanistan
You fly with the angels now.

Acknowledgments

Thanks to Bill Fawcett, for giving me the shot in the first place, and to John and Toni for believing him. And a big thanks to my wife K. L. H., who put up with my many late nights in the basement office.

TIGER BY THE TAIL

CHAPTER ONE

On a moonless, tropical night, Vanel Kulcyanov sat motionless on the deck of a battered, thirty-five-foot fishing trawler, doing the hardest thing he'd ever done in his life—waiting.

If not for what he was about to do, he would have been mesmerized by the endless South China Sea around him. Until five days ago, he had never been more than ten miles from home. But the valley of the Keldara in Georgia, in the Caucasus Mountains of Eastern Europe, was thousands of miles away. Now he was on the other side of the world, where palm trees grew everywhere, rain fell every day, and to even think about moving was to sweat.

The eighteen-year-old thought his training had been hard. He thought the endless PT, weapons training, live-fire exercises had been hard. He thought the particular nightmare of specialized underwater operations training had been very, *very* hard. But all that was nothing compared to right now, awaiting the order to begin tonight's mission. *The American song is right*, he thought. *Waiting* really *is the hardest part.*

Vanel was entering real combat for the first time tonight, and the anticipation was rattling his normally calm nerves. It wasn't that he was afraid—well, a small part of him was, for only an utter fool or madman did not fear battle. But he had made his peace with it, and whatever fear was in him now resided in a far-off corner of his mind.

An even greater fear was spurring him on now—the fear of not measuring up to his people's expectations. The blood of countless Keldara generations flowed through his veins, stretching back to his people's Varangian roots. Over the centuries, that had been blended with the very best warriors the Keldara could find to lead them. The idea of not carrying their proud warrior culture into the twenty-first century was inconceivable, and Vanel was going to make sure that he did not fail the rest of his team, his family, or the Kildar.

Unlike many of the Keldara, who weren't comfortable around large bodies of water, Vanel felt as home in or on it as he did on dry land. The qualifications needed to be accepted into Yosif's team were among the highest of all the Keldara units, and again he felt a swell of pride at being accepted into the elite of the elite.

He stared out over the glass-smooth waters at their target, a small cluster of lights five hundred meters away. He itched to be there already. To be doing what he'd been trained to do, what he had been *born* to do—his part to guarantee that his team's role in the op would be executed flawlessly, so that the next stage could be achieved. But they had not received the go order yet. So, Vanel and the rest of his team sat. And they waited.

The problem was that the only thing to do while waiting was to think. Vanel could go over the plan again, but he already knew it like the back of his hand. Every part, every task that the men beside him would execute to reach and take their objective was burned into his brain. And once that had been committed to memory, all that was left was to think about the many things that could go wrong.

To prevent that, he checked his gear one last time. Weapons, first and always—the sleek, matte-black HK416C rifle slung across his chest, the .40 caliber Sig Sauer P229 with integral silencer on his right hip, and his Gerber Mark II double-edged combat knife in a horizontal belt sheath at the small of his back.

The compact HK416C was practically brand-new—Vanel had only received it three weeks ago. He'd fired about two thousand rounds through it and trained enough to fieldstrip, clean, and reassemble it blindfolded before the trip. The Keldara version of a SEAL team had been using the HK MP5A2, but the Kildar hadn't been happy with the 9mm's range and knockdown power. After evaluating the variant 5.56mm carbine rifles available, he'd grudgingly settled on the 416C as their replacement instead of the M4A1. It had several advantages over the Colt carbine, including a more durable barrel, a rotatable butt plate on the retractable stock, an ergonomic handgrip on the forestock, and a folding front sight.

The two most important differences between his new rifle and the MP5A2 were the improved range and penetration of the 5.56mm round. Along with the best rifle, Mike had gone with the best ammunition he could find. Every team member carried Mk 262 bullets with a 77-grain Sierra MatchKing round. The bullets were manufactured by Black Hills Ammunition, and designed for long-range engagements of up to seven hundred meters. While it would be unlikely that the swim-ops team would engage an enemy at that range, it was definitely better to have the option and not need it than the reverse. The bullet also demonstrated consistent improved yaw characteristics at up to three hundred meters, increasing the possibility of target takedown.

All this came in a German-designed and built fire-selective assault carbine that could be shortened to just over twenty-two inches long. The screw-on suppressor at the end of the barrel added another eight inches. Last but not least, it could be fired without completely clearing the barrel of water—which the team would most likely end up doing at some point. The Kildar wasn't thrilled about using two different ammunitions for their primary and secondary weapons, but as he had also said more than once, if any member had to draw their pistol in combat, they were already in deep shit.

Next was equipment. First, Vanel checked his waterproofed radio and transceiver. Then came the gray and black Evolution closed-circuit rebreather system with its Vision electronics package to maximize breathing mix and scrubber efficiency. Other equipment included his fins, full-face mask, including the MUM-14 submersible night vision monocular, depth gauge, bulletproof vest, weight belt, and buoyancy vest. Everything was in order and positioned for maximum accessibility, no rattle, no clank. Optimized to ensure that the mission would go smoothly and by the numbers. But all of the specialized gear wouldn't have mattered. If the Kildar had ordered him to strip, put his knife in his teeth, and swim to their target naked, Vanel would have dived overboard in a second.

Of course, that was assuming that the mission would actually *begin* sometime—Vanel took a deep breath and began running over the specs of the target vessel in his head. Noticing his team leader, Yosif Devlich, watching him, Vanel nodded curtly.

"Sir?"

"How are you doing, Vanel?"

"I am ready, Leader." He rubbed his chin, which was just beginning to sprout a few hairs. While he had the same white-blond hair and clear blue eyes like the rest of his siblings, Vanel had not inherited the typical massive Kulcyanov build. He was a few centimeters shorter and although well-muscled, he was also much leaner than his brothers. But the All Father had seen fit to bless him with seemingly endless stamina—he could run or swim for hours without tiring. "I would very much like for the mission to start."

"Good, good. Soon enough," Yosif said with a nod.

"Leader?"

"Yes?"

Vanel hesitated, hoping the others wouldn't tease him for what he was about to say.

"About our call sign—"

"Thank the All Father—I thought I would have to be the first one to ask," Edvin Kulcyanov, Yosif's second-in-command, said.

"Oh, All Father," Yosif answered with a sigh, then shook his head.

"I understand it is from some TV show, but..." Vanel continued tentatively.

"I asked Martya the same question when we received the new call sign. I still don't get it because I haven't seen the show," Yosif replied.

"Yes, thank you, Leader—It's just..."

"We're named after a whore..." Edvin said.

He was interrupted by the radio.

"Firefly to Team Inara, report."

"A *whore*..." Edvin repeated, shaking his head ruefully.

"Inara One," Yosif replied, clearly trying not to sigh. "Go...I think all the good names were taken."

"Even *Oleg's* team is named after a girl," Devlich said. "Jayne. A girl's name, yes? Inara Two, go."

"Vil?" Dima Mahona said. "Zoe is a girl's name, yes? Inara Three, go."

"And why Washing and Book or whatever?" Devlich said. "These make no *sense!*"

"Inara Four, ready," Vanel said.

"I am looking this up," Dima said, pulling out his combat pad. "There's an app for that..."

"You are *not* looking this up," Yosif said. "We are in the middle of a mission."

"And the mission name? Eh? I mean, Operation Goat-Fucker was both a tribute to Father Ferani and about capturing a *haji* goat-fucker. That I could understand. But..."

The last member of the team checked in, then Vanel heard the order he'd been waiting for all his life.

"Team Inara, commence Operation Joss-Whedon-Is-A-God."

"Affirmative," Yosif replied with another sigh. The Kildar had been insufferable ever since finding some failed American TV show. He kept promising to "hunt down some Fox exec and show him the meaning of pain."

Yosif signaled the first man to slip into the water. The next man followed after a five-second delay to let the first one clear the insertion area.

When his time came, Vanel felt his mask to ensure the seal was tight all around and his oxygen mix was flowing. He checked his rebreather computer to ensure that all systems were green and checked his fins to ensure they wouldn't catch or slip. Then he slid over the gunwale into the blood-warm waters of the ocean.

He sank down, achieving neutral buoyancy at thirty feet below the surface. As his sweat was washed away by the ocean water, Vanel saw the other members of his team through the glowing green of the night vision monocular. The view was a little disorienting, but he adjusted as best as he could.

When the team was assembled, Yosif led them on their one-klick swim to the target, compensating for the ocean currents to insure that they reached their target on time.

A suitable warm-up for tonight, Vanel thought. His blood sang in his veins as he kicked forward, matching his teammates' pace perfectly as they headed out into the tropical night.

"Team Yosif is away. More New Meat heading into the grinder." Bullet-headed former SEAL Master Chief Charles Adams watched the tramp freighter the Keldara team was heading for through infrared binoculars.

"Is that concern I hear in your voice, Ass-boy?" Mike Harmon, Adams' boss, another retired SEAL, leader of the Keldara Mountain Tigers Special Operations Group, didn't lower his infrared binoculars either. Shorter than Adams by a few inches, he had short brown hair, direct brown eyes, and a broad-shouldered, solid physique. "After Florida, we agreed that Yosif's team could use some real field training, and I can't think of any place better than here."

"Here" was off Pulau Mangkai, an island near Malaysia in the Anambas Archipelago. It was near the infamous Strait of Malacca, which separated the Malay Peninsula from Sumatra. The strait had been one of the world's busiest shipping passages since the seventh century, when the Srivijaya Empire, based at Palembang, Sumatra, expanded its influence to Java and the Malay Peninsula.

It controlled the strait for the next seven centuries, benefiting from highly profitable trade with Chinese, Indian, and Arab merchants.

When Srivijaya declined in the mid-thirteenth century, the Malacca Sultanate rose to power, aided by taking control of the strait. It was vanquished by the Portugese nobleman and naval tactician Afonso de Albuquerque in 1511. Portugal ruled the area for a strife-filled one hundred and thirty years, until the Dutch conquered Malacca in 1641. The Anglo-Dutch Treaty of 1824 saw Malacca become a vassal of the British Empire. This lasted until 1957, when Malacca joined other Malay states to form Malaya and together with Sarawak, Sabah and Singapore, formed the nation of Malaysia in 1963.

Throughout it all, the strait saw ships carrying everything from glassware, camphor, cotton goods and textiles, ivory, sandalwood, perfumes and gemstones back in the day to oil, coffee, cheap Chinese toys and expensive electronics today. And all the older stuff as well.

When pirate activity surged early in the twenty-first century, the Malaysian, Indonesian, and Singaporean navies stepped up their patrols of the strait, cutting hijacking in half over the last few years. The pirates didn't stop working, they just moved their operations elsewhere. Like off Mangkai Island. All of this made them the perfect training targets for Yosif's underwater operations team.

"Hell, no," Adams said. "Every man among them can chew thunder and shit lightning. They will take the objective and reduce it to a bag of smashed asshole if so ordered. I am still a bit puzzled, however, why you didn't rate Vanel higher after my recommendation."

Mike and Adams were "team buddies," a bond far far stronger than family, from their SEAL days. After a short stint on the teams Mike had switched to being an instructor for most of his SEAL career. When he did go back to the teams there had been an "issue" that saw him out on civvie street with sixteen years of training to be the deadliest human being on earth and not many other skills. Adams, on the other hand, had taken the usual route of promotion through the teams, eventually rising to master chief. They'd reconnected a few years later, when Adams and his SEAL team had gone into Syria to rescue Mike. Mike had gotten seriously wounded while executing a one-man holding action against an entire commando battalion to rescue forty-nine kidnapped American women.

When Mike had settled in the valley of the Keldara a few years later, he'd called up Adams—by then retired and looking to escape four ex-wives—to help train the local "militia" in small arms combat and tactics. Adams had come over, loved the place almost as much as Mike did—the landscape, women and beer were all spectacular—and had been living there ever since. He had Mike's back every second, but that didn't mean he was afraid to question "The Kildar's" orders when he felt it was appropriate.

"It's not for lack of talent. The kid swims like he's got gills instead of lungs, you put him through BUDS yourself, and with a bit more practice, he might be almost be as sneaky as me someday."

"So where's that 'but' I'm waiting for?"

"Well, I don't call you Ass-boy for nothing. Vanel will earn his stripes soon enough. I instructed Yosif to put him on point tonight."

"Works," Adams grunted.

"Once he gets through this, we'll know where he goes from there. And you know the best way to get blooded—"

"—is to get bloody. Hoo-yeh."

"Hoo-*yah*," Mike responded. There was an accent difference between east and west coast SEAL team battle-cries. "Hoo-yeh" or "hoo-yay" was east coast, the more laid back "cooler" "hoo-yah" was west coast.

"Surfer Dude."

"Ass-boy."

They might have been BUDS buddies but once a SEAL always a SEAL. Whichever coast.

Adams kept his eyes on the small freighter the Keldara team

was approaching. Every so often, however, he'd move the field glasses just enough to check his boss out of the corner of his eye.

Mike had gone through hell and back in the last couple of months. Their last mission near home, involving a missing scientist and enough WMDs to wipe out most of Europe, had gotten FUBAR fast. In the end, the Keldara been forced to pull a 300 and eradicate about four thousand Chechens with only a hundred of their own in the shit. The enemy force had been stopped, no doubt. But the price the Keldara had paid was high, both in blood and a lot more.

The casualties had been high—Sawn, Padrek, Kiril, Father Ferani, and many others—

—*Gretchen*—

That one Adams knew Mike was still coming to terms with, although he was much better than he had been immediately afterward. His love, Gretchen Mahona, had been killed during the fighting, and her loss had put him out of action for weeks. Even the threat of a whole cargo container of VX nerve gas shipped Stateside by Al-Qaeda terrorists hadn't been enough to rouse him. The Keldara team sent to Florida, led by Adams and their intel chief, Patrick Vanner, had been caught in an ambush meant for Mike. Adams had taken five rounds in the chest and Vanner had been in a coma for a week. That's when Mike had come back to his old self. And he had come back with a vengeance, dismantling the terrorist operation with a precision and lethalness that was fucking scary, even for the Kildar.

Afterward, Mike had returned to his normal self, more or less. Adams, however, had resolved to keep a close eye on him for, well, as long as it took for him to be assured that Mike was truly back to his hell-bent for leather ways.

The master chief wasn't concerned that Mike wasn't up to the task of planning or running the op. It had taken a lot of persuasion to convince Mike not to lead the underwater team, and Adams still wasn't sure the Kildar wasn't about to gear up and go after the assault force. No, the master chief was more concerned about his boss's *mental* state. His concern wasn't that Mike was crazy—it helped to be a little crazy, especially if you were a SEAL. Not crazy in the get-you-bounced-out-of-the-service-by-failing-a-psych-eval. No, Mike was crazy in the sense of doing whatever it took to complete the mission; like tucking himself into the wheel well of a jet plane and flying across the ocean to Syria, for example. *That* sort of crazy was the good kind.

The kind of crazy that, when presented with the opportunity to buy a rural Georgian village and assume the mantle of Kildar, essentially ruling a bunch of farmers descended from the ancient Varangian Guard, made Mike ask, "Where do I sign?" He had immediately set about transforming the pre-Industrial Revolution village, turning it into a modern agrarian farming community that also brewed one hell of a beer. He had also turned the local boys into the hardest-fighting militia the likes of which Europe—or perhaps the world—hadn't seen since World War II. *That* sort of crazy was the really good kind.

No, the mental state Adams was concerned about was that of a commanding officer sending men into battle again. Mike, Adams, Vanner, and the one hundred had certainly vanquished the Chechens, although at a high cost. Hell, Adams hadn't seen such a new crop of barely bearded Keldara warriors since he'd first signed on. The question in his mind—which he'd had to ponder long and hard before he'd even admit to thinking about it—was had the Kildar finally exorcised those demons that had hounded him ever since Gretchen?

It was a simple truth: as the Kildar, his responsibility extended to everyone in the valley, all the families, every man, woman, and child. Each one would gladly lay down his life for Mike, Adams, or any of his brethren in a heartbeat. And Mike was the sole person accountable for giving them the orders that would put them in harm's way. Never mind that to the Keldara, combat was like breathing, or that they were the very best Adams had ever seen. The point was that Mike was the one who was ordering them to go and possibly get their asses shot off. Adams knew he tried to maximize their chances with the best training, intel, and equipment they could get, but sometimes, things went wrong.

But that won't happen tonight, he thought, sneaking another peek at Mike. Everything was running shipshape. The team was away, the first objective was about to be taken, all was in order—

"I suggest that you spend more time observing your team and less time eyeballing me." The Kildar still hadn't lowered his binoculars.

"Affirmative. You could have let them use the torps to get there, you know."

"Oh my *God*—when did my master chief turn into such a pussy? Next you'll want to carry each one there on your back. This is *advanced*, live fire training. If the Yosifs prove they can handle this, they might be able to catch a ride next time out."

Adams returned to monitoring the freighter. A one-kilometer swim in calm water, even adjusting for the ocean currents, should take the team roughly fourteen minutes in full gear. Adams kept his eyes glued on the freighter that served as the enemy's perimeter guard, waiting for the signal that they'd arrived.

The concept behind the closed-circuit rebreather system went back almost four hundred years to 1620. That was the year Dutch inventor Cornelius Drebbel first heated potassium nitrate to release oxygen for the crew of his oar-powered submarine. The heat also turned the potassium nitrate into potassium oxide, which absorbs carbon dioxide. Drebbel had inadvertently created a working rebreather system more than two centuries before a single-person system was invented.

The first practical rebreather, designed for escaping submarines, was produced around 1900. The Dragër rebreathers were mass-produced and used by Germany in World War II. The U.S. Navy had its own expert in Dr. Christian J. Lambertsen, called "the father of the frogmen," who ran the first rebreather class for the Office of Strategic Services at the Naval Academy in 1943.

Although a variety of modern closed-circuit rebreathers (CCR) had been developed since, they all operated on the same basic principle: a gas-tight loop, consisting of sealed components, providing a breathable mix of oxygen and a diluting gas, such as nitrogen, to the diver. The mouthpiece—or in the case of Team Yosif, their full face masks—was connected to tubes conveying inhaled gas to and removing exhaled gas from the diver and into a counterlung, or breathing bag, which held the expelled gas. The loop also contained a scrubber containing sodium hydroxide to remove the exhaled CO_2, as well as a valve that allowed the injection of gases, including oxygen and perhaps a diluting gas, from a separate tank into the loop, and another valve that permitted the venting of gas from the loop if necessary.

Although early models required the diver to keep track of and adjust his own oxygen mix, twenty-first-century models used solid-state sensors to monitor the oxygen-nitrogen mix. It sent this information to a microprocessor that controlled the oxygen-delivery system, ensuring the optimum mix was delivered to the diver with every breath they took.

The advantages of the closed circuit rebreather system were longer dive time (up to three hours), lighter equipment (since the bulk of the gas was pure oxygen that was mixed with nitrogen as needed, instead of the heavier oxygen-nitrogen mix), less decompression time (since inhaled nitrogen was kept to a minimum) and, most important for Team Yosif, no telltale trails of exhalation bubbles to mark their progress. The main disadvantage of standard rebreathers was that the diver couldn't go much deeper than forty feet below the surface. Since the oxygen in the tanks was unpressurized, it would be affected in the same way that a human would as they descended. It would compress under the pressure, making it more difficult to draw a breath. Tonight, however, that wasn't an issue for the infiltration team.

Vanel, Yosif, Edvin, and the rest of the team reached their objective in eleven minutes, thirty-nine seconds. The target vessel was a nondescript small coastal freighter, about 170 feet long and anywhere from forty to sixty years old. Its once-maroon hull was covered with a mix of barnacles and large patches of orange rust that were slowly spreading toward the deck. The railing on the port side was bent in two places, with an entire section missing at the stern. Its exhaust stack was pitted and bent, and thermal scans had revealed that the engine was barely functioning, probably just enough to keep the batteries charged. Its anchor chains were also covered in rust and algae. But since it was the lookout post for the largest group of pirates in the area, it didn't have to go anywhere.

The team had trained on a matched vessel for the past two days, until they knew it inside and out. After the boat piloting issues the Keldara had run into in the Florida Keys, they'd also spent some time learning how the engine worked and how to pilot the damn thing—just in case they needed to get it running.

The team had received up-to-the-minute intel on the boat guards' slipshod patrols. They knew that, despite facing the direction an enemy would typically approach from, the rear port quarter stood unguarded a minimum of twenty minutes out of every hour. They had reached the boat seven minutes after the most recent guard had flicked his cigarette over the side and ambled back into the crew quarters.

Yosif's head popped out of the water, followed by Vanel's. The two men listened for any noise from above for a few seconds, then Yosif nodded to his teammate. Readying his neoprene-clad grappling hook, Vanel propelled himself half out of the water with his fins. At the height of his lunge, he tossed the small hook up at the railing. It caught the lower horizontal rail with a barely audible *clunk* and snugged tight. Vanel tugged on it, then put his full weight on it and nodded.

Receiving the go sign from his team leader, Vanel wrapped the line under his shoulders to secure himself, then removed and secured his rebreather and fins. Switching his mask over to breathe outside air, he began climbing hand-over-hand toward the deck. He was less than a meter away from the railing when he heard a hatch undogging and creaking open. Vanel froze on the line, listening to the approaching footsteps getting louder as someone approached his position.

"Sitrep on Yosif?" Mike asked, still scanning the ocean like the binoculars were surgically attached to his head.

"The team has begun their insertion—shit, there's a pirate on the rear quarter. Four's dangling with his balls in the wind about a meter below the tango. Yosif has the ball." Adams watched for a few seconds to see how Yosif would call it. Their primary goal was to preserve stealth for as long as possible while taking the ship. So far, so good. "Wouldn't even know he'd almost gone down on the last op."

Yosif had been part of the team that had accompanied the Kildar to recover the VX gas. Unfortunately, he had been exposed to it when one of the boats they'd been chasing had run aground and broken up. Yosif and Sergei had injected themselves with the counteragents, atropine and pralidoxime. The secondary effects of both were bad, but much better than the slow, painful death promised by the nerve agent.

Yosif had run though the entire gamut, according to their doctor: "hot as a hare, blind as a bat, dry as a bone, red as a beet, and mad as a hatter." He'd suffered through a fever, flushed skin, photophobia, decreased sweating, dry mouth, dehydration and hallucinations. Although he had gutted it out and finished the mission, he also had been on restricted duty for two weeks. Their medic had cleared him for return just before they had left for the South China Sea. This was his first time back in the field since Florida.

"I expected nothing less from him," Mike said. "But confirm Lasko is on top of the situation."

"With pleasure."

Five hundred yards east-northeast of the old trawler, Lasko Ferani sat in the lap of luxury. The two-hundred-foot yacht he was on was almost as stable as being on land. Well, not quite, but certainly close enough for what he was about to do.

"Firefly to Blue Hand, over."

"Blue Hand."

"Confirm target."

Lasko didn't move from the reticle of the ATN 4-12X80 Day/Night scope mounted on the Barrett .50 caliber semi-automatic rifle he was using for tonight's operation. After extensive target shooting, this was the first field use of the switchable scope, and so far, he was impressed. It had a 1000-yard bullet drop compensator (he still figured his sightings on the fly, and so far the scope had matched him ten-for-ten) with interchangeable cams for six calibers—including the .50—a 1000-meter rangefinder, and an illuminated reticle with eleven light settings.

What Lasko liked best was that he could convert it from daylight shooting to night vision in less than fifteen seconds with a simple swap of the eyepiece. There was no change in eye relief, and he could keep the scope zeroed at all times. It was just about perfect.

"Target is confirmed."

"Hold visual, and do not fire until ordered."

"Affirmative." Steadying his breathing, Lasko settled his reticle on the man leaning on the railing more than a thousand meters away. This wasn't nearly as difficult as other shots he had made. Certainly nothing like shooting the engines of a cigarette boat traveling at sixty miles per hour from a chase helicopter, just taking one example.

With each exhalation, calm enveloped him, until there was nothing but the ready shot and his finger ready to squeeze the trigger. The slight movement of the ship he was on, the slight movement of the ship his target was on, the negligible wind, round drop, his breathing, his heartbeat; all were calculated and factored into his bead on the target.

In the next few seconds, the man would be dead, one way or another.

Vanel clung to the line as a match flared above him. A moment later, he smelled harsh local tobacco burning. A shadow fell over him, and he saw a man leaning against the railing and looking out to sea—right above his head. A droplet of sweat fell off the pirate's hand onto Vanel's facemask. If the guy glanced down or noticed the small grapple against the railing, the mission would be blown before it had even started.

Not if Vanel had anything to say about it. He clicked his tongue in the back of his throat once, querying his superior officer as to what he should do. The answer came back immediately.

"Hold position. Terminate only if sighted."

Great. Nominal for the mission but not his preference. Keeping a firm grip on the line with his left hand, Vanel slowly, very slowly, reached for his suppressed Sig. Undoing the snap in time with a wave slapping the ship's hull, he drew it just as slowly. He kept his feet planted on the rusting hull, careful not to scrape any flakes of metal off. He raised the pistol, aiming just under the target's chin. A hit there would ensure that the subsonic bullet would do the most damage, and more importantly, prevent the pirate from crying out.

Vanel held his shooter's position, waiting until he heard the order to fire. Five seconds...ten seconds...fifteen seconds. But until he got the word, he aimed and waited as the unsuspecting man smoked his cigarette above him.

CHAPTER TWO

Adams gave his side of the ocean one more sweep, then lowered his binoculars. Vanner's intel team had assured them that there wouldn't be any Indonesian Navy patrols or commercial traffic in the area tonight. However, eyes in the sky only went so far compared to boots on the ground—or in this case, on deck.

Since the operation they were about to commence could involve a fair amount of heavy ordnance, Mike had wanted to make damned sure there were no local entanglements. Sure, he could have made a call and gotten his connects in D.C. to help clear the way if it had come to that. It wasn't like they didn't owe him a favor or ten. And then there was a cache of records in the basement of the *caravanserai* that included some interesting stuff on Indonesian politicians. But rather than getting wrapped up in red tape, the Kildar preferred to do it the old-fashioned way. By scanning the horizon and making sure no one was heading toward them.

Of course, the state-of-the-art radar that had been installed in—and cost more than—the battered trawler they were using gave them backup far beyond the horizon. Add the equally powerful unit in the yacht serving as their HQ several hundred meters away, and a UAV overhead and they were covered six ways from Sunday.

The only problem was, as they all knew from hard experience, it was that seventh god-damned way that always bit you in the ass. Raising the binoculars to his eyes again, Adams checked on the freighter insertion team.

"How's he doing?" Mike asked, still scanning the ocean around them.

"So far, so good. All that guy has to do is look down, and he gets himself a bullet in the brain."

"Yeah, or he heads back inside and gets one a few seconds later. Ironic, isn't it, how close this guy is to buying it, and he doesn't have a goddamn clue."

"Yeah, and us with ringside seats, so to speak." Adams' jaw worked. "A bit different running the show from out here, eh?"

Mike didn't reply, just nodded.

Adams was about to scan the starboard side again when his attention was drawn by a commotion on the deck of the old freighter. A pair of pirates dragged a struggling, sobbing man down from the bridge onto the main deck. Adams noticed that Mike's field glasses had also turned toward the action on the distant ship. The pirate above their man glanced briefly at what was going on, but soon returned to staring out into the night

"Fellow pirate, or hostage from the last ship they hit?" Mike asked rhetorically.

"Hard to tell." Adams watched the kneeling man plead with his captors, obviously begging for his life. "Should the team intervene?"

There was a second's silence, and Adams knew Mike was weighing the pros and cons of having his team risk exposing themselves and allowing their targets to possibly raise the alarm versus saving one man. As he opened his mouth to reply, one of the pirates thrust his *parang* into the prisoner's chest, impaling him on the short, curved blade. He pushed the still living man off his weapon, dragged him to the edge of the deck, and kicked him into the water.

Mike's jaw worked. "Make sure Inara gets aboard before the sharks come."

"Works." Adams contacted Yosif. "Inara, you are go."

▲   ▲   ▲

Cheok Yi Jung drew hard on his cheap, Korean cigarette as he stared out over the dark water, cursing his luck. *Stuck on the damned watch boat while everyone else gets happy-happy!*

The *lanun* were celebrating a major haul, spoils from a freighter that had netted them almost twenty thousand U.S. dollars, a fortune in these waters. Many of the pirates had wanted to go to Singapore or Malaysia to blow it, but their leader, Yeung Tony, had insisted that they stay off the grid. So they had brought their booze, drugs, and prostitutes out to their hidden base and the party had begun in earnest a few hours ago.

But Jung was marooned out on the watch freighter as punishment for almost screwing up the entire job. He had been the *tekong*, or driver, responsible for keeping the small boat steady next to the large freighter. The *lanun* would stand ready with their climbing poles, made of bamboo stalks with a mangrove root lashed to the top end to form a hook. When the boat drew close enough to the target's stern, the *tekong* keeping it steady in the rough wake, they'd hook the railing and scramble up the bamboo to the deck. Five could climb the tough bamboo and get aboard in a dozen seconds, razor-sharp *parangs* clamped in their teeth. From there, they would seize the bridge, round up the crew, rob them and loot the safe, and get the hell off. The whole operation could be done in under five minutes if the pirates knew what they were doing. And Yeung's crew definitely knew what they were doing.

However, once the assault had begun, a rogue wave had broadsided Jung's skiff, sweeping it away from the freighter just as his lead men had latched on with their poles. Two men had been left dangling in midair, but scrambled up to the deck before they could fall overboard.

Not only did Jung forfeit his additional share of the loot—*tekongs* usually got extra pay for their hazardous job—but he was stuck out here for the night, all because of something that wasn't even his fault.

Jung listened for a moment, hearing the faint shouts and squeals of the girls, mixed with tinny, throbbing K-pop, drift out over the water. A door creaked open to his right, and he glanced over to see a pirate—he couldn't tell who—drag a captured crewman onto the deck. As the man pleaded for his life, his tormentor stabbed him in the chest, then threw the body overboard. Jung knew the killer might be the next one to die—Yeung Tony had been wanting to expand into kidnapping for ransom, but it was hard to release a dead body back to its family. *It's still better than the mainland.*

He had grown up in the slums on the outskirts of Kuala Lumpur, Malaysia's capital city. At night, he and his sister would climb the tallest tree in their neighborhood and stare at the bright lights of far away downtown, dreaming about what it must be like to live there. With both parents dead from cholera, they had spent their days foraging in the streets, picking through garbage and shoplifting on the rare occasions they could sneak into one of the tiny shops along the dirt road.

Jung had killed his first man when he was twelve, stabbing a gap-toothed Malay who was trying to rape his sister. They'd fled the tin-roofed neighborhood he'd known all his life and headed into the city, where things were even worse. One day, Jung had woken up to find his sister simply gone, as if the city had swallowed her whole. With nothing left and nothing left to lose, he'd joined one of the local street gangs, and quickly turned to piracy. After a few years, his childhood memories had blurred, until it seemed like this had always been his life. At least here he had a place to sleep, and friends to watch his back. Even Tony was a fair leader—although Jung was still pissed about losing his extra share *and* missing the party.

Taking one last drag from his cigarette, he flicked the butt into the water and turned to go. As he did, his leg bumped the railing, and his ragged shorts caught on something sharp.

What the— Jung bent over to look at the small, four-pronged grappling hook, each tine covered in sound-deadening neoprene. It was latched onto the railing hard—as if it was supporting something—or someone—below.

Straightening, he turned toward the bridge, opening his mouth to scream a warning to the rest of the crew. As he sucked in a breath heavy with ocean salt, he sensed something moving behind him before everything cut to black.

▲   ▲   ▲

On the luxury yacht *Big Fish*, Patrick Vanner, former Marine and head of intelligence for the Keldara, rubbed his temple and took a sip of his strong, black Indonesian coffee. *Nothing like fresh roasted—as in picked off the vine less than forty-eight hours ago.*

"Are you all right, Patrick?" Greznya, his top intel puke and new wife, watched him with a concerned expression on her gorgeous face.

"I'm fine—just a bit of a headache, that's all." At least he hoped that's all it was. The three bullets he'd taken on the blown Florida op occasionally still made their aftereffects known. Sporadic headaches were the most common, but he'd been suffering some haloing in bright sunlight, which could usually be counteracted by dark sunglasses and limited exposure. The downside was that he didn't get to watch Greznya sunbathe as often as he would have liked. Out here, that was practically a crime.

Taking another sip of coffee, he stood and surveyed the room.

"Status report?" he asked his team.

"Team Yosif has reached the target and has engaged the enemy. Team Jayne reached their LZ twenty-one minutes ago and is moving into position. Lasko is on overwatch above us, and the Kildar and the master chief are observing on the trawler," Greznya reported.

Vanner nodded. They'd soundproofed the large cabin, but if the Keldara sniper went green, they'd still hear the reports of the Barrett twenty feet overhead.

"General ship traffic on radar quiet. Nothing approaching within ten nautical miles," Irina said.

"Monitoring of communications on naval and law enforcement bandwidths also ongoing—nothing urgent to speak of," Daria said a moment afterward.

"Communications of commercial vessels in the area also quiet. Nearest AIS is over two hundred klicks. It would seem that everyone is avoiding area," Greznya, who was pulling double-duty, said.

"Given all the pirates migrating here in the past few years, I can't blame them." Vanner nodded in satisfaction, then clenched his teeth as a bolt of pain shot through his temples. While the Keldara men had all been tasked as front line fighters, the women were put on fire support and intelligence gathering details. They handled both equally well, with Irina, Daria, and his beloved Greznya—none of them more than twenty-one years old, and all staggeringly beautiful—managing multiple information feeds on a local and regional basis. "How's the translator program coming along?"

"Operating at seventy-eight percent efficiency. It appears to be taking longer to assimilate the local dialects."

"Unsurprising, since there's probably hundreds in the region alone. All of the raw pickup will be great for our database, though."

After their op in the criminal city of Lunari, in Albania, and the difficult op in Florida, Vanner had realized that they really needed a translate-on-the-fly program. No, even more than that; they needed something that could take in multiple streams of raw verbal data, create its own dictionary for each language, and extrapolate for dialect, slang, etc. Not only did it have to handle what was being said now, but scale to incorporate the inevitable shifts in language from year to year, including business terms, street slang, specialized terminology, and anything else that might come up in the future. Although Vanner was proficient in eight languages and knew enough to get by in a half-dozen others, often the amount of raw data the girls could pull was way too much for one person, or even a team, to process efficiently.

They had been tweaking a suite that handled most of what they needed, but it been dealing primarily with European Romance languages over the past few months. The Kildar's East Asian op had fit perfectly with Vanner's desire to expose the program to languages with no relation to the cluster that had developed on the European continent. After this, he'd have to hit Africa and South America, and maybe some of the indigenous tribes north of the Arctic Circle—assuming any were left—and he'd have a near complete library of the major languages around the world to tap into. *And then comes the app*, he thought with a grin, *but first steps first.*

Vanner sipped his coffee. "Maintain overwatch. Holler if anything interesting happens out there."

▲   ▲   ▲

As the pirate fell, Vanel scrambled up the rope one-handed. When he got a grip on the railing, he climbed over, keeping his pistol trained on the body sprawled on the filthy deck. The subsonic 9mm bullet had made a neat hole that now leaked a mix of blood and clear fluid from the back of the pirate's head.

There was an odd, metallic taste in his mouth, and every sense felt heightened. He saw everything, smelled everything, felt everything. The slight movement of the rough deck under his feet. The stink befouling the crotch of the dead man's rough shorts, overpowering his rank body odor. The last wisp of cigarette smoke leaking from the man's open mouth. The clarity of the empty deck through his night vision gear. Vanel had never felt more alive. There was no guilt, no fear, no hesitation, only the thrill of executing his mission. After confirming his kill, Vanel holstered his pistol and unslung his carbine before reporting in. "Inara Four on deck. One tango down. Deck is clear."

"Roger." Moments later, the other five team members had climbed up and assumed their positions, holding until Yosif gave the orders to move. Three seconds later, two men had stashed the body and were heading to the engine room to secure it and sweep forward. The second pair was opening the door that lead amidship, and Yosif and Vanel were climbing silently to the bridge.

On the narrow catwalk, they paused outside the door, listening for any sign of conversation or awareness of them from the small, dark room on the other side. Their surveillance had indicated anywhere from two to four pirates manned the bridge at any one time.

Pulse hammering in his ears, Vanel heard the engine room team report in. "Engine room is secure. Ready to cut power on your mark."

Yosif glanced at Vanel, who raised his H416C and nodded. *Ready.* Reaching for the door handle, the team leader replied, "Three . . . two . . . one . . . *mark.*"

Inside the bridge, the console lights winked out. The second they did, Yosif turned the handle and pushed the door open. Hand back on the stock of his silenced rifle, he entered and turned right, advancing along the wall.

Vanel entered the door and went left. Immediately he encountered two pirates, one in the battered captain's chair, the other standing next to him. The standing man was just turning to the black-clad, masked figures that had burst in.

Vanel put a three-round burst into each one's chest, controlling his carbine's recoil and keeping his sight locked on. His shots dropped the nearest man to the floor and made the sitting victim slump back into the chair. Neither made a sound as they bled out, filling the air with the coppery tang of blood. He heard the metallic cough of Yosif's weapon on his right, but didn't take his eyes off his two tangos.

Not seeing any other motion or targets in the room, Vanel carefully stepped through wisps of gunsmoke toward the bodies. He cleared their hands, then signaled that his side was cleared and safe. Yosif confirmed the other side was clear and checked on the rest of the team. Yosifs Two and Three had taken out four tangos while sweeping forward to the bow. Yosifs Five and Six had cleared what appeared to be a crude crew quarters, dispatching three more pirates, for a total of eleven tangos down so far.

Sixty seconds later, the two below teams had finished clearing the entire rest of the ship. After receiving reports from both, Yosif contacted the trawler. "Kildar, this is Inara Leader. First objective has been secured, eleven tangos KIA, no casualties on team, over."

"Roger that, Kildar and master chief are en route."

Yosif and Vanel headed down to the main deck to form up with the rest of their team and greet their leader. As they waited for the other ship to approach, Vanel took a look at what they were about to deal with in the second phase of the operation. He'd seen it in the photos, but taking it in for real was something else entirely.

"Father of All, what have they done out there?"

After deploying the back-up insertion team to reinforce Team Inara, Mike and Adams had gotten in a Zodiac inflatable equipped with a noiseless electric motor and sailed to the trawler. Climbing up the rope ladder that had been lowered for them, The two men stood on the bridge, which had been cleared of bodies, and scanned the pirates' base two hundred fifty meters away.

"That is one helluva feat of kludging," Adams said of the haphazard tangle of boat parts, tin sheets, cargo containers and driftwood that made up the enemy headquarters. It sprawled in all directions, built with little rhyme or reason, with crude rooms tacked on wherever they were needed. Rope bridges, some as high as thirty feet off the ground, connected several areas to one another, while the dock area was a mass of skiffs, crude rafts, and even bright blue chemical barrels, all lashed together to make a slowly undulating platform. Raucous Asian dance music blared over the water, and bright lights illuminated crude balconies where the pirates smoked, snorted, or shot dope and enjoyed the attention of local hookers. "Usually pirates are hit-and-run, with no fixed HQ. These guys must be pretty goddamn confident to build all this out here."

"Yeah." Mike focused on the blue barrels dotting the dock area. "Hopefully those barrels are either empty or still sealed. Don't need any of our guys exposed to any chemicals in the water."

"You want to change the insertion?" Adams asked, finger on the transmit button of his radio.

"No, they should be all right. It is part of the night's work, after all. Just make sure everyone cleans up really well afterward—no telling what they might catch in or out of the water."

Adams grunted agreement. "Too damn bad we couldn't get a girl on the inside. I know Katya was practically begging to get out there for recon."

"Yeah, but as a round-eye, she would attract way too much attention. Even with her capabilities, it would have been too risky for her to feed us any intel. Also, it would have been too difficult to school her in the not-so-niceties of Southeast Asian prostitution quickly. That said, it does make me wonder about the possibility of acquiring some Asian women for future jobs on this side of the world. Our talent, while very good, just doesn't blend in well enough here."

"Of course, sometimes that can be an advantage, too," Adams pointed out.

"Yeah, maybe in the cities, but not out here."

The radio clicked, and Mike answered.

"Go for Mal."

"Simon here," Vanner replied. "Team Jayne is in position."

"Roger that." Mike scanned the pirate base one last time, spotting a strange conglomeration of heavier metal, what looked like welded steel plates on a high point above the base, overlooking the entire small harbor. Near as he could tell, it looked almost like a small bunker. *What the hell is that?* His senses twitched, that feeling that something wasn't quite right kicking in. He clicked his transmit button. "Order all teams to switch to AP ammo. Team Jayne to begin flanking assault in five minutes from my mark. Team Inara, deploy to secure dock area."

"Roger."

"Gonna be a bitch and a half to clear all those damn little rooms and cubbies," Adams remarked.

"Yeah, but it makes for excellent close-quarters and broken terrain training," Mike said. "Besides, these fucks shouldn't prove to be that much of a challenge. Ideally, they will all be too drunk, stoned, fucked, or any combination of the three to mount an effective defense in the first place."

Adams grinned mirthlessly. "Well, that is why we let them party before moving in, isn't it?"

His rebreather and fins back on, Vanel and the rest of Team Yosif had debarked from the trawler to the Zodiac. When the go order came, they had all swapped out their magazines as ordered, entered the water again, and headed for what passed for the dock area.

Three minutes later, Vanel's head broke the surface, which was covered by a thin film of oil and other noxious chemicals. Wiping his facemask with a gloved hand, he decided to keep breathing from his tank while scanning the floating material for tangos. He had already removed his night vision goggles to avoid being blinded by the ambient light.

The next few seconds were the most critical part of establishing their beachhead. Six of the swimmers were on the left side of the dock area, with the other six inserting on the right. If any were spotted, they risked being caught on open, unstable ground between the pirates and the water.

Vanel shucked his rebreather and fins again, grimacing at the acrid, chemical taste of the air around him. Slowly, silently, he hauled himself onto a dugout boat lashed to two barrels. His black wetsuit blending with the shadows, Vanel began low-crawling over the uneven terrain. His goal was the first row of rough buildings, about fifteen meters away. There he would clear the area and provide cover for the rest of his team as they advanced.

Halfway over, a door made from a corrugated tin sheet burst open and a half-dressed man and woman staggered out. Whooping and shouting, the pair headed for the main dock, their feet thumping on the wooden planks.

Vanel slid into the water, ducking behind a nearby barrel. The triangular space was barely large enough, but he managed. "Inara Four to Leader."

"Go, Four."

"One tango and a female are on the dock five meters away." Vanel peeked up just enough to see the two sharing a bottle of something as the man began groping the half-naked woman. "Cannot reach target without possibility of detection. What are your orders?"

There was a slight pause. Vanel waited patiently, figuring Yosif might be kicking this up the chain of command. They tried not to harm innocents whenever possible, but Vanel doubted the Kildar would allow the presence of one whore to compromise the entire mission.

"Can you terminate tango and subdue the woman without detection, Four?"

"Yes." Vanel had been figuring out exactly how to do this while waiting for an answer.

"Roger, you are go."

"Roger, Four out." Taking a deep breath, Vanel ducked under the water's surface and began pushing himself toward a narrow, open space by the dock. Forty-five seconds later, he broke the water again just enough to grab the side of the crude dock. Above, he heard soft grunts and a rhythmic motion that made the boards creak. Drawing his pistol, Vanel cleared the barrel and action. Gripping the edge of the dock with one hand, he hoisted himself up, supporting his body with his left arm while extending his pistol toward his target.

The two were huddled together, the woman sitting on the man's lap while he rocked back and forth. Her head lolled on her shoulders in what was mostly likely a drug-induced stupor as the pirate thrust into her. Vanel took in the sight even as he drew a bead on the man's temple and squeezed the trigger.

The bullet made a neat entry hole just above the pirate's eye. It took a fist-sized chunk of bone and brains with as it blew out the other side of his skull. The man flopped to the deck while the woman stared at her suddenly limp john. Before she could react, Vanel was kneeling beside her. He brought the butt of his pistol down on the back of her neck, knocking her out. After rolling the dead pirate's body over the side, he secured the unconscious woman's hands and feet with zipties and improvised a gag from a strip of her threadbare mini-skirt.

"Tango is down and woman is secured. Continuing insertion."

"Roger."

Holstering his pistol, Vanel readied his carbine and crept to the narrow path leading to the first row of shanties. Other than the two romantics, all of the activity seemed to be coming from higher up. Regardless, they were going to sweep and clear as they went, to prevent any nasty surprises from appearing in their sixes.

Reaching the first hut, Vanel gave his night vision a chance to readjust after the brightness outside before peeking into the interior. Seeing no one, he signaled the rest of the team to sweep forward and ducked inside, clearing the room from left to right.

The floor of the stinking hovel was covered in sleeping mats, filthy clothes, empty beer bottles, and the remains of crude meals. Vanel held his position until the rest of his team had rejoined him.

"Team Jayne is in position and ready to begin their sweep," Yosif informed his squad. "Let's move out."

CHAPTER THREE

"The boy is good."

Having watched Vanel take out the pirate and subdue the woman on the dock, Mike nodded at Adams' remark. He kept his field glasses trained on both teams as they began their sweeps of the lower huts, occasionally panning up to that reinforced slab of steel above everything. "Chief, make sure Blue Hand is zeroed in on that piece of armor up top."

"I was wondering about that thing myself. Think we got trouble?" Adams asked as he opened a channel to Lasko.

"Don't know. Could be the king pirate just likes to sleep in more protection than his lackeys. We'll keep an eye on it as the op develops."

"Lasko's already zeroed in on it as one of his secondary targets." Adams returned to watching the teams clear the first level. "So far, so good. You know what that means."

"Yeah—it's bound to go to hell sooner or later. Wait, let me make sure. 'What's the worst that could happen?'"

"Oh, you evil bastard."

Flanked by Yosif, Vanel crept from hut to hut, making sure each one was empty. On the last one, he pushed aside a ragged blanket and almost took a *parang* to the chest. He managed to turn the blade aside with the barrel of his HK and push the defender off him. With a shout, his attacker leaped forward, blade raised to chop his skull in half.

Vanel lined up his carbine and triggered a three-round burst into the man's chest, dropping him in his tracks. Hearing movement inside, he pushed forward to see a blanket still swinging from someone ducking through a back exit, their footsteps slapping the ground as they fled. With Yosif right behind him, Vanel cleared the exit, making sure no one was waiting to ambush them, then took off in pursuit.

Though Vanel was short and muscular instead of tall and broad like his kin, the walls of the narrow alley brushed his shoulders, making him twist sideways and trot down the winding path. Rounding a corner, he glimpsed the runner scrambling up a chain dangling off a tugboat prow that had been wedged into the trees.

The man was pulling himself onto the deck as Vanel and Yosif both shot at him. The bullets chopped into wood and sparked off the metal hull as the man rolled to cover.

"All Father's Beard!" Vanel hissed as he exchanged magazines. "I know I hit him!"

Yosif radioed back to base for orders. "Kildar said continue our sweep forward. Rest of the team will clear pieces below."

"Roger." HK ready, Vanel began creeping forward again, alert for any noise or movement.

Yeung Tony leaned back and watched a young Chinese prostitute prepare his *batu kilat*, vaporizing the methamphetamine in a glass pipe that concentrated the fumes. She offered the pipe to him and Tony inhaled the pungent chemical smoke, eager to chase the white dragon again. While he did that, he forced the girl's head down between his legs.

As the meth entered his lungs, then his bloodstream, he grinned at the heightening of his senses as he adjusted the signature purple doo-rag on his head. The drug made everything around him crystal clear, like his eyes had just switched into high definition.

From the whores fucking him and his men on the large, improvised balcony below to the riches strewn around his room, cash
and designer clothes interspersed with high-end electronics, like
the 65-inch LCD television mounted on one wall, he saw it all.

He *ruled* it all.

An average-looking man, half-Malay, half-Korean, Tony wasn't
the leader of this group because of his strength or ability with a
weapon. Rather, it had been his skill at planning hijackings and
his uncanny ability to figure out where the local authorities were
patrolling that had cemented his leadership. It had also helped that
he'd killed the last two challengers to his position, both securing
his rule and establishing his ruthlessness.

Now numbering seventy-five strong, his group roamed the seas
around the Archipelago with impunity, his teams striking three
or four ships in a night. With much of the region's attention still
focused on the Straits of Malacca, Tony knew it was only a matter
of time before the authorities began patrolling farther east. But he
didn't expect that to happen for at least another few months. In
the meantime, he and his people would enjoy the fruits of their
labors. And the profits from selling the box they'd recovered from
the last boat should enable them to expand even more. It might
even allow them to bribe someone inside the port authority to
pass along information on desirable shipments. Inhaling another
hit, Tony leaned back, letting his mind drift to fantasies of leading a pirate army to plunder the seas with impunity.

His dreams of bigger and better things were interrupted by two
sergeants, both grim-faced, entering his quarters. Between them
was one of the *lanun*, holding a blood-soaked bandage to his thigh.

"*Penambuh! Dajal-dajal hitam-bertopeng!*" the wounded man
babbled in Malay.

The mention of killers and black-masked devils, along with the
creeping paranoia instilled by the drug, put Tony on high alert.
Knocking the whore aside, he pulled up his pants and stood.
"Might be special forces fucking with us. Radio the lookout ship
and see if any suspicious boats are in the area."

"We're trying, but cannot get a reply—"

"*Taik!*" Tony punctuated the Malay profanity by spitting on the ground. "Goddamn Indonesians might be here already! Get everyone up and armed, *now*! Get on the quad and shoot anyone out there that's not us!" He pointed at his other sergeant. "You, get the boat ready!"

As he spoke, the chatter of automatic weapons fire exploded in the compound. As his second sergeant ran out the door, Tony scrambled for the room behind his living space, dragging the prostitute with him. "Come on, whore!"

In here was more loot from their heists—high-end electronics, from LCD televisions, Xboxes, and Playstations to a full-size arcade game, more designer clothes, and paintings, leather furniture, and artwork taken from luxury yachts. Ignoring all of it, the pirate leader grabbed a set of night vision goggles and put it on his forehead. He ran to an unmarked box, one meter long by half that deep and wide, that seemed to be a complete piece of smooth, olive-green metal with no seams, just two metal handles.

Drawing a pistol from his waistband, Tony grabbed one end of the case and pointed the gun at the whore. "Pick it up, or you die!"

The girl grabbed the other end and hauled ass after him. Tony left through a side opening, making sure he was in darkness before he positioned the goggles over his eyes and turned them on. He then headed down a dark, narrow trail into the jungle, tugging the box and the prostitute behind him.

Fifteen meters below the chattering AK-47, Vanel heard updates over his radio as the operation shifted into high gear.

"All units, this is Mal. Engage enemy at will."

"—Team Jayne is moving to engage—"

"—Inaras Two and Three have cleared lower level and are moving to support positions—"

"Inara Eight—encountering moderate fire—moving to flank—"

Yosif and he kept moving higher up the pirates' base, taking out all targets of opportunity. It helped that the shooting was confusing most of the drunk or drugged pirates, making them easy prey.

Covering each other's advances, Vanel and Yosif mowed down three clusters of the enemy before they even knew what hit them. A brief transmission from Yosifs Two and Three, saying they were coming up behind the Leader and Four, made the two Keldara smile at the doubling of their firepower.

The pair was heading for the next group of ramshackle buildings when bullets began chopping splinters from the wall next to Vanel. He ducked back around the corner, but not before taking two rounds in his body armor. The impact made him gasp, but a quick check showed the bullets hadn't penetrated. The left side of his chest did feel like it had been hit with a hammer, though.

Tracking the wild rounds back to their origin, Vanel gave the shooter another moment to empty his magazine. The moment the lead stopped flying, he poked his carbine around the corner and fired two bursts at where he had last seen the muzzle flashes coming from. The position stayed silent afterward.

Hearing more gunfire right behind him, Vanel didn't turn to check on his leader until a loud crash shook the boards under his feet. He glanced back to see the mangled body of a pirate on the ground a few meters away, bloody bullet holes pocking his upper chest.

"Fuckers are dropping from the sky now!" With a grin, Yosif motioned for Vanel to move out. Rising to his feet, he was about to round that corner again when the night was shattered by the thunder of something much larger than an automatic rifle.

"Quad .50!" Adams was on his radio, watching as the emplacement tracked any movement and the four barrels spit death. "Sonsabitches got their hands on a quad!"

"I love firepower," Mike said. "Except when it's on the other side."

This shooter, however, was either wounded or high, as he seemed to be firing indiscriminately, the big rounds chewing up anything they were aimed at, building, the pier, pirates—and coming way too close to the Keldara on the ground.

"Blue Hand, take him out!"

On the *Big Fish*, Lasko exhaled and fired in the millisecond between two heartbeats. The SLAP-T round would have easily pierced the double-walled steel ship plate protecting the gun emplacement, except it didn't have to. The Keldara sniper had aimed for the narrow slit through which one of the bottom barrels protruded. The large, armor-piercing bullet mangled the ammo box and cored through the mount. Even after penetrating all that, it still had enough kinetic energy left to rip through the gunner, tearing him almost in half.

The quad mount fell silent for a few seconds, but its three remaining guns starting firing again.

There is a world of difference between getting shot with a 7.62x39mm round and a 12.7x99mm, or .50 BMG round.

Assuming the average AK shooter does manage to hit you, which is unlikely past 150 yards, if the bullet flies true, it will penetrate and make a good-sized hole in its target from which much blood will flow. If it tumbles during flight or on impact, the wound cavity and subsequent injury will both be much worse. Add the possibility of fragmentation to all of this, and the 7.62 is a definite manstopper, no doubt.

The .50 caliber round, being three times larger, can cause much more horrific damage to the human body. If it doesn't yaw, the target simply ends up with a larger hole in their body, which can be survived given prompt medical attention. While the round does not automatically tear a limb off if it hits one, it will mangle whatever it does hit into uselessness, and provides one-shot kill capability just about every time.

Multiply that power by four, and Team Yosif had almost stepped into a gruesome whirlwind of lead death.

Every team member immediately sought cover no matter where

they were. Once they were hidden from sight, Yosif and Vanel tried to get a vector on the gun to take it out. Unfortunately, it was high up and well protected, both by the slope of the earth and the large piece of freighter hull someone had hauled up and installed as armor. The gunner inside stitched rounds into anything even remotely moving in his field of fire, blasting his own people, tree branches waving in the wind, blowing apart crude huts. Basically, if it moved, he shot at it until it didn't anymore.

Against that overwhelming firepower, the swimmers' only choice was to hug cover and wait for divine intervention. That came in the form of Lasko's single .50 caliber round, which accomplished as much as the Quad gunner had done with twenty to thirty rounds at a time.

When the deafening roar of the Quad .50 fell silent, Vanel and Yosif hauled ass, hustling to what they hoped was a better firing position. The other two team members hadn't joined them yet, so it was their two carbines against a vastly superior weapon.

They had just reached their new position when the Quad .50 started up again. Apparently the new gunner was not high, for long bursts immediately started hammering near them, making both men hit the deck. Large bullet holes punched into the wall behind them, the impacts shaking the wooden floor. The bullets flew so fast and furious that the top half of the metal wall behind them fell onto the two Keldara. Although they could have moved, the two men stayed right where they were, knowing that trying to free themselves would invite the gunner to perforate the wall and themselves with a hundred or so rounds.

"Inara One to Firefly, request supporting fire on the following coordinates, over!" Yosif shouted over the din of the heavy machine gun emplacement.

"Given enough time, those guys would probably kill all of their own people, however..." Adams watched the emplacement fall silent again as Lasko shot the second gunner through the same hole, but a few moments later it started booming yet again. The Yosif team had been using the lulls to try to flank the big gun. Unfortunately, they couldn't get enough of an angle to clear it before it started up again.

"Mal to Team Jayne, what is your position?" Mike asked.

"This is Jayne Leader. We are above the encampment and can see both teams pinned by heavy fire."

"Make sure that quad never shoots again."

"Affirmative."

Oleg Kulcyanov stood approximately one hundred twenty-five meters away from the crippled but still devastating heavy machine gun emplacement. With the rest of his team watching for tangos, he brought what looked like an oversized shotgun to his shoulder and aimed through the M2A1 reflex sight at the thundering Quad .50.

Mike had been looking for a suitable weapon system for the man-mountain that was Oleg for some time. A M249 SAW, while certainly impressive, seemed to be simply a waste of his capability to project direct fire support onto a target. Even the modern, kick-ass M60E4 just didn't seem to be enough of a weapon for his primary team leader, difficult as that was to believe.

Mike had been weighing the pros (overwhelming one-man firepower) and cons (realistic amount of ammo that could be carried and overall weight) of a chain gun right out of *Predator*. That was before Colonel David Neilson, the Kildar's executive officer and lead trainer, had informed him about the updated Milkor automatic grenade launcher. The U.S. Marines had ordered mods on the three-decade old weapon that had brought it into the twenty-first century with a vengeance. Since even Mike couldn't get his hands on an XM25 system yet, the MGL-140 would have to serve, and in Oleg's hands, it was doing that quite well; it was both easy to use and devastatingly effective.

Staring through the infrared sight that also compensated for drift, Oleg lined up his reticle on the emplacement and sent two high explosive anti-tank rounds at the target in less than two seconds. The HEAT rounds obliterated the remaining guns, as well as the pirate shooter, in an explosion that echoed off the jungle and out over the water. The blaze of flame that erupted from the emplacement sent fire fifteen feet into the air, and the impact flattened three huts around the destroyed gun.

"Jayne Leader to Mal, target has been eliminated, over."

"Come on in and clean up the rest."

"Roger."

"Patrick?"

"Yes, Grezyna?"

"Raven has picked up a small boat that has left the north side of the island, and is heading out to sea."

"What?" Vanner rose and walked to the screen. It wasn't that he didn't believe his wife, but they had been over the sat shots of the island with a fine-toothed comb and hadn't found any sign of a hidden harbor or cave large enough to hide a boat. Sure enough, a boat was heading out to sea. All he could ID was that it was an open, center-console fishing boat with twin outboards. "Any guess as to where it's headed?"

"It's not very large—perhaps twenty to twenty-five feet long. It is moving at approximately forty miles per hour on a heading of zero one five degrees. Open ocean that way. Your guess is as good as mine."

"The Kildar will not be pleased that someone managed to escape the perimeter." Vanner hit his transmit button. "Mal, this is ... Simon ..."

"—of course I want the cigarette brought around ... no, Badger and I will handle this one personally ... Roger that," Mike said.

Still tracking the various Keldara teams' progress, Adams turned to find Mike wearing a shit-eating grin.

"Feel like doing a bit of boating tonight?" the Kildar asked.

The master chief raised an eyebrow in unspoken query.

"Apparently some pirate with more guts than brains is trying to leave our op still breathing."

Adams' other eyebrow raised as he slowly shook his head. "You were just dying for a chance to take that sucker out, weren't you?"

Mike shrugged. "I'm not going to deny it. I had been looking forward to seeing what the riceburners could do out here, but damned if we could find any. Ah well..."

Five minutes later, Mike was at the helm of a '97 38-foot Fountain Fever named *Red Hot*, with the rare twin Merc 525 SC engines and a new Hardin exhaust. He'd picked it up cheap through the same liquidator in the Philippines who'd supplied the trawler and the training freighter. After a thorough search to make sure there were no drugs hidden onboard, they had been using it as a pleasure craft on the typically glass-smooth ocean.

Now he was cruising at sixty miles an hour through the clear but dark night while Adams navigated their intercept course. The FLIRs eliminated the issue of vision, other than adjusting to maintain a constant on the horizon. They had two Keldara aboard, Vil Mahona and Danes Devlich, both of whom had also gone along on the Florida op, and could handle the boat in a pinch. The only real problem was that Mike was motoring through waters that were charted, but not known to him personally. Running aground on a reef out here could be not just embarrassing, but fatal. The sharks here were both belligerent and numerous, the apex of a vicious food chain that wouldn't mind chowing on humans if they got the chance.

Mike had left cleanup of the island to the Keldara teams already ashore. He had also notified Vanner to get the yacht in gear and follow them. However, it wouldn't arrive on scene for another hour at least, and they were going to catch up with the pirates well before then.

At least the boat rode like a dream, slicing through the calm water and responding deftly to the wheel. After the pounding he'd taken on the Atlantic during the Florida mission, Mike had almost forgotten the sensation of running calm water with the wind in his hair.

"Mal, this is Simon."

"Go, Simon."

"You are approximately seven hundred meters away from the target. We grabbed a UAV shot of the boat, and they have some interesting-looking cargo on board. These guys probably unassed with the really good stuff."

"Are you suggesting we should take them alive if possible?"

"The thought had come up, especially if they can give us any information on where that box came from or how they got it."

"Works. Will let you know how it turns out." Mike turned to Adams. "Our runners are trying to leave with something interesting. Try to take at least one alive."

"Roger that. They should be visible near the horizon due north," Adams shouted.

Even as he said that, Mike spotted movement on the horizon and opened up the throttle, making the cigarette boat surge forward.

"Got 'em. I am a leaf on the wind..."

"Wrong character, dude."

Yeung Tony pounded the arm of his chair as he watched his island hideout shrink toward the horizon behind him. *Everything gone, all in a few minutes!*

The worst part was that he didn't even know who had done this to him—but he was damn sure gonna find out. *No one* destroyed his operation and sent him running into the night without paying for it!

The whore was piloting the boat while Tony and his lieutenant scanned for signs of pursuit. She had indicated that she could handle it when he'd asked with his pistol, leaving him and his man free to watch the surrounding ocean.

Tony's gaze returned to the olive-green box on the floor of the twenty-five-foot boat, which he had anchored among the huge mangroves that grew on the island's north side, perfectly camouflaging it. They'd carried the box along a hidden trail he had carved out himself, narrowly missing another team that had been coming in from the west side, lead by a giant, masked man dressed in black with a huge fucking gun in his hands. Seeing him had let Tony know that whoever had come for him and his crew definitely wasn't local, which puzzled him. *Who the fuck are those guys? Private ship security out for payback? Mercenaries hired by the Indonesian government?*

"*Pemimpin!*" Yeung's man, who had also been watching the island through a pair of night-vision binoculars, pointed due south. "*Kami yang diikuti!*"

Grabbing the glasses from the other man, Tony scanned the waters to the south and saw a larger boat rapidly approaching. "*Taik!*" He tossed the binoculars back and grabbed his AK-47. "Faster!"

Their boat leaped ahead, but it was obvious that they weren't going to outrun their pursuers. *No matter*, Tony thought as he knelt at the rear of the crew compartment and waited for their enemy to come within range. *Time to make the fuckers that destroyed my life pay!*

"Got movement on the target." Adams had his M4 aimed at the boat about three hundred meters away. "I think they've spotted us."

"In that case." Mike throttled back a bit and readied the one million candlepower spotlight. "Vil, disable their engines."

The Keldara sighted on the stern of the boat with his M4 and squeezed the trigger. Three rounds smacked into it, and the engines immediately began to miss, then died a few seconds later.

Shouting and automatic weapons fire began coming from the pirates' boat, but Mike quickly swung them out of range of the AKs. "We don't really *need* another boat right now, I suppose."

"Especially one without a working engine," Adams replied.

"Anyone here speak Chinese?" Mike shrugged when they all shook their heads. "Didn't think so. I don't even think Anastasia does. Simon?"

"Yes, Mal?"

"Give me a short, phonetic command to surrender in Chinese and Korean."

There was a brief pause before Vanner relayed the commands in both languages. Mike picked up a megaphone.

"Drop your weapons and surrender, or we will open fire!" He repeated it in Korean, and got another volley in their general direction as the only reply.

"Now they're pissing me off." Mike grabbed his M4. "Master Chief, Vil, Danes, let's see what we all can do to persuade the good folks over there to surrender. Remember, try to take at least one of them alive."

"With pleasure," Adams replied as he sighted in on the other boat. "Purple doo-rag." He squeezed the trigger, and three hundred yards away, the man with his head covered by a purple kerchief dropped. "Only wounded. Swear."

"Okay, you wanna play?" Mike said as he took aim. "Receiver of the AK held by the man next to him." He held the M4 steady, exhaled, and fired. The loud cursing drifted over the water to them as the man found himself holding a useless hunk of metal and wood.

Over the next few minutes, the four shooters carefully and precisely wounded the opposition while taking exactly no success-ful return rounds. They followed this up by putting several holes into the boat's hull. This was more difficult than it appeared, as it took a few rounds to insure that the hull was penetrated at the correct angle to let water in. The boat was listing to port when the two bloodied men and what looked like a young woman held up their hands and allowed the Kildar's boat to pull alongside.

The three pirates were brought aboard, thoroughly frisked, and their hands and feet secured with zip-ties. Mike had the two Keldara haul the mysterious green box aboard as well, and left the damaged boat to sink into the vast depths of the Pacific Ocean.

CHAPTER FOUR

"Now *this* is interesting."

Mike was clustered with Adams, Vanner, Greznya, Vil and Danes around the strange green box.

"Anybody seen anything like it before?"

"It's a green rugged conditions shipping case," Adams said. "Seen a million of them in my time."

"Well, duh," Mike replied. "What I don't get is why there's no markings on it at all. That should mean it's not military, since they stamp things every which way. But it *screams* high-level military hardware of *some* kind." Mike bent over, examining a pair of odd, round holes, one on the upper left and one in the upper right corner of the front of the case. He was pretty sure those were the lock mechanisms, but there was no identifying name or any real way to get an idea of what they were up against. "I don't remember any keys. Adams?"

"I'm getting old but not that old," the former SEAL said. "No keys."

"Where's Creata?" Vanner asked Greznya.

"Off-watch."

"I think we're going to need her expertise." Creata, also known as Mouse, was one of the smallest Keldara women. Out of all of Vanner's intel girls, she was the best at figuring out any sort of lock or device, mechanical or otherwise. She was also a very efficient killer when necessary. Mike had found that out during the Albanian op, when he'd found her standing over a thug she had sliced in half with the laser drill she had been using. Creata had blown his head off, then gone back to popping the safe door without missing a beat.

"I will get her." Greznya disappeared below deck.

Mike radioed Yosif. "Inara Leader, this is Kildar, what's your sitrep, over?"

"Inara Leader to Kildar, perimeter is secure. We have captured eighteen tangos, with forty-four KIA. Three wounded, none killed on our side. Team Jayne is sweeping the rest of the island for anyone hiding, over."

"Roger that, good work. Police all weapons and collect anything recoverable, then set charges for complete demo and standby for further orders."

"Roger, Mal."

By the time Mike had finished his conversation, Creata was kneeling in front of the box, with a miniature borescope in hand. She threaded the end into one of the holes and nodded.

"The box is secured with two disk tumbler locks. They are most likely Abloys, or, considering where we are, possibly Solexes."

"What're those?" Adams asked.

Creata straightened up, took the position of "parade rest," cleared her throat and looked into the distance.

"A disc tumbler lock or Abloy Disklock is a lock composed of slotted rotating detainer discs," Creata stated, didactically. "Instead of pins that are manipulated by a key, these contain a series of small metal disks in a row. Each disk is cut in a distinct pattern so that part of it, anywhere from ninety to as much as two hundred seventy degrees, is missing. When the proper key, which is cut on two different axes, is inserted and turned, it rotates the disks like the tumblers of a safe, lining them up correctly and opening the lock. Because there are no springs, the lock cannot be bumped. It also cannot be picked by normal means, as there is no way to access and manipulate the disks without a special tool."

"Which you have, I trust?" Mike asked, trying not to grin.

Nielson had been cracking down on the military etiquette lately and all the Keldara were going around like brand new jarhead nuggets. Mike figured it kept the colonel happy and didn't seem to be interfering in operations.

Creata cocked her head as she regarded the Kildar.

"It would not do much good at home, now would it?"

Mike grinned. "Absolutely not."

"I have not had opportunity to work live on one of these yet. I've had the class but that is different. What I do know is that they take a *long* time. Best to bring it downstairs, where I can work undisturbed."

"Vil, Danes, you heard the lady. Move it out," Mike said. "When you're done, start going over your AARs with the master chief."

"And what will you be doing in the meantime?" Adams asked.

Mike's lips peeled back in a wolfish grin. "I'm going to go have a chat with those pirates to find out what they know about what they stole. Vanner, I'll need translation capability."

The intel chief hefted his Toughbook laptop. "I figured you would."

On the rear deck, Mike studied the three prisoners. Each had been secured to chairs, their hands and feet zip-tied to the metal arms and legs. Some kind soul had even treated their wounds.

"Let's see . . ." He pointed at the woman. "Prostitute, I'm guessing." He switched to the halting Chinese Vanner had prepped for him. "Speak English?"

Shaking her head, the woman let loose a stream of rapid-fire Cantonese; at least, Vanner assured him that's what she was speaking. His laptop recorded her words and parsed them into cohesive, if a little disjointed, English that Vanner fed to him.

"Working near Pemangkat . . . hired to work on island for a few days . . . attacked by base . . . wait a minute, base was attacked by gunmen. He—" She nodded at the man in the purple doo-rag, who scowled and looked away, "—made me go with him," Vanner reported.

"Why were you piloting the boat?" Mike asked.

"He say he shoot me if I do not."

"Okay." Mike drew his pistol and pointed it at her face. "What do you think I'll do to you if you don't tell me what I want to know?" He sighed, lowered the pistol and looked at Vanner as there didn't seem to be a translation. "Hello?"

"Working on it," Vanner said just as the laptop spit out a string of Cantonese. "Oops."

"What?" Mike snapped.

"I think it just said, 'Your dog is a fruit.' Hang on..." There was another stream of Cantonese and he nodded. "There. Got it. Gah. I hate Chinese. 'Of the moment are considerations of future actions of a negative form.' Seriously?"

The girl looked away from the .45's muzzle, which must have seemed huge, and spoke even faster.

"I swear...that is all I know."

"Don't have a huge amount of street cred in Southeast Asia." He holstered his sidearm and walked over to the shot caller. "Guess we'll have to improvise." A part of him regretted the necessity, another, darker part him did not.

"You have no idea who I am, do you?" he asked the pirate leader.

The guy spat a strange language back at him.

"What's he saying?"

"Just a moment." Vanner tapped keys. "Looks like he's Malaysian. He's said, 'I don't know what you are talking about...you Americans...This is illegal...You cannot do this to me...' Pretty much repeating variations of the same stuff."

"Yeah, too bad no one here gives a shit about what I'm going to do to you in the next few minutes." Mike walked over to a toolbox and took out a claw hammer, tucking it into the back of his shorts. Hauling a small, study metal table with him, he went back to the man and set the table down next to his chair. Flipping out his lock blade, Mike cut the pirate's right hand free. He slammed it down on the table, then pressed the blade of the knife to the man's wrist, holding it diagonally, so if the guy moved he would slash his veins open. "I know you can't understand me, but I'm sure you can grasp the concept of holding your arm really still. Vanner, give me, 'where did you get the green box?'"

The only answer he received was the man spitting in his face.

Mike tore off the man's shirt with his free hand and wiped his cheek. Dropping the filthy shirt, he drew the hammer and smashed it down on the pirate's pinky finger. The pirate screamed in agony and whipped his hand out from under the blade, scraping skin and opening a long slash as he cradled it to his chest.

"One down, nine to go," Mike said. "Translate that."

Breaking the rest of the fingers on the leader's hand elicited no new information. It had, however, put him into shock by the time Mike started working on his palm. It did have the desired effect on their other male captive. He was now leaning over to get as far away as he could from his maimed leader and the crazy American working him over. For now, Mike was content to let the poor bastard sit there and think about what would happen to him when it was his turn.

The woman was more of a mystery. She sat with her head down, eyes closed. Mike had let her be for now; he knew she could hear what was going on.

He tossed the bloody hammer onto the small table. "This guy's done for now. Get a medic out here to treat him and clean this up. Make sure he stays alive."

"Hey, Kildar, check this out." Vanner was sitting behind his laptop with the monitor facing away from the other two prisoners.

Mike walked over. "What you got?"

Vanner kept his voice low as he replied. "While you were busy, I put my tweaked voice stress lie-detector program through both of the conversations you just had. The meat there—" He waved at the slumped pirate. "—he's telling the truth, he doesn't know shit about shit. The girl, on the other hand, I've gotten several hits off her that tell me she's hiding something."

"No shit?"

"I'm not sure *what* it is, but there's definitely more to her than she's telling."

"Two mysteries in one night? And here I thought our little training cruise was going to be fairly straightforward." Mike straightened to regard the Chinese woman. "She looks like she might even clean up well. I'd rather not leave any marks on someone who may be sticking around, yet I want to know what she knows." He tapped his cheek as he pondered, then snapped his fingers. "Water, water, everywhere; nor any drop to drink."

Vanner looked at him quizzically. "It has been a while since I've read Coleridge, but I'm not sure how 'Rime of the Ancient Mariner' fits this situation."

"Don't worry, you will." Mike hadn't taken his eyes off the woman. "And she definitely will by the time I'm done."

Although waterboarding was only brought to most of the modern world's attention in the past decade, it has been around for more than four hundred years.

The technique goes back to the sixteenth century and the Spanish Inquisition. The Catholic inquisitors used a variety of it, known as the *toca*, or *tortua del agua*, as an interrogation and punishment device. It popped up around the world in the intervening centuries; the Dutch used it during the Amboyna Massacre in 1623. Variations were also used as punishment in American prisons, notably in Sing Sing and in the South, during the nineteenth century. It was used by the American military during the Spanish-American War; the "water cure," as it was called then, was privately espoused by President Theodore Roosevelt, although he spoke against it in public. Both the Japanese and German armies used it in World War II. The U.S. generals banned its use in Vietnam, although the Vietnamese used it on each other with impunity. Variants of the technique also appeared in Chile, Northern Ireland, and South Africa. Elite branches of the U.S. military still use a mild form of the technique during their SERE training to prepare soldiers for what they might encounter in enemy captivity.

Wherever and whenever it was used, the common agreement was that waterboarding was an efficient and quick way to break someone. CIA officers who submitted themselves to the procedure ended up capitulating in an average of fourteen seconds. Even Navy pilots and SEALs were exposed to waterboarding during SERE training. Adams was somewhat famous in the NAVSPEC community for having broken his restraints and nearly choking one of his "interrogators," a tabbed SEAL instructor, to death. They had to break his fingers to get him to let go of the guy's throat. Interrogators preferred it because of the rapid results it achieved, and because it didn't leave any marks on a victim—on the outside, at least.

Mike was planning to use it now for those exact same reasons. He had modified a reclining deck chair and table into a platform that now held the quivering woman, her arms and legs tied down again. Vil and Danes each held one of the chair's arms, so they could adjust its angle as the Kildar required. He had a medic standing by, and had requested that a pulse oxymeter be attached to monitor the level of oxygen in her blood. This would ensure that she didn't pass out or even die from the technique. Just in case she suffered a heart attack from the stress about to be put on her body, he'd also had the defibrillator from the ship's medical stores brought up and prepped. Mike didn't expect it to go that far, but he wasn't taking any chances either.

The pirate captain had been moved below deck, his wounds being tended. The second man, however, still had a ringside seat to what was about to happen.

Mike looked at his two men. "Vil, Danes, you ready?"

Both Keldara nodded.

Mike leaned over the woman, who stared at him with fear-filled eyes, and read aloud the message he'd worked out with Vanner.

"I know that you are hiding something. Tell me what it is, and this will stop at once. If you do not tell me what I wish to know, it will continue until you answer my questions. Do you understand?"

She babbled in terrified Cantonese, which Vanner translated.

"She wants to know why you're doing this to her. She's just a whore, and she doesn't know anything about the green box. She seems to be telling the truth about the box, but she's lying about something else."

"Here's the truth, honey," Mike said, bending over to look her in the eyes. "First truth: You're hiding something. Little black box says so and the little black box don't lie. Second truth: I want to know what that is. Because it affects my operation and I'm an intensely curious person. Third truth: I may do good things but I am not a good guy. I am a very very bad man. So I am going to enjoy this. You are not. Fourth truth: You can tell me what I want to know which is well, everything in some sort of coherent order, or I can pass my free time finding it out. I'll enjoy finding it out. It's a great hobby with fun for the whole gang. But the moment that you tell me what I want to know I will, with great reluctance, stop hurting you." He waited for the translation then cocked his head to the side. "Last chance. Want to tell me what I want to know?"

She looked him in the eye then shook her head defiantly.

"All right, I gave her a chance. Hook her up."

The Keldara medic cut open her shirt and attached leads to her chest from an automatic emergency defibrillator, then rigger-taped an O_2 sensor to her middle finger.

When the medic was done, Mike readied the canteen of ocean water. The salt water would irritate the lining of her nose and throat, increasing her discomfort even more.

"Let's give her a drink and see what happens. Vil, Danes, raise her feet until I say stop."

The two Keldara began lifting the end of the chair until it was at a fifteen-degree angle to the deck with her head at the bottom, while Adams clamped a cloth over her face and nose. Gripping her chin, Mike positioned the canteen and waited until she exhaled, then began pouring a steady stream of water over her nose and mouth.

There was a surprised splutter, then a hideous gurgling sound interspersed with muted, choking noises as she was forced to ingest liquid instead of air. Mike gave it a ten-count, then stopped, watching as she coughed and choked. There was a gagging sound, and water sprayed out through the cloth as she tried to clear her lungs. More Cantonese could be heard through her sobs.

"What do you want? Why are you doing this to me?" Vanner translated in an emotionless tone. "Other stuff nonessential. Not enjoying this, boss."

"Got it." Mike gave her a few seconds to catch her breath, then bent down to her ear again.

"All you have to do is answer my questions. Why are you here? Why did the pirate take you with him?"

"I—I don't know—I'm telling you, I'm just a whore—"

"Wrong answer." Mike secured the cloth and began pouring again. This time he got to eight before she choked, spluttered, then started to convulse.

"She's vomiting! Turn her!"

The two Keldara lifted the chair, and Mike moved the table away and cleared the cloth so they could flip her face-down. A thin stream of bile drooled from her mouth, and she gasped for air, hanging by her restraints from the chair, her wet hair hanging in front of her face.

Mike let her go until she had calmed down, and was quietly sobbing.

"Second part," Mike told Vanner. His intel chief displayed more phonetic Cantonese on his laptop as MIke squatted down. He pushed the curtain of hair aside to look into her face.

"That is awful, isn't it? All that water...it feels like you are about to drown. All you have to do to make it stop is tell me what you are doing here, and it will, I promise. Just answer my questions, and this will all end."

Her teeth chattering, the woman gasped out a short, choppy reply.

"I don't know what you want," Vanner translated. "Please stop..."

"I am afraid we cannot do that." Mike stood and motioned for the Keldara to set her back on the table. "How's her oxygen level?" He asked.

"Steady at ninety-three percent," the medic replied.

"Let's go again." The cloth was placed over her face, which was a bit harder this time, as she tried to whip her head back and forth until Adams restrained her. In return, Mike gave her a fifteen-count of water this time. When he let up, her convulsions were much harder, her arms and legs straining against her restraints as she flopped on the chair.

"Shit, she's defibrillating! Let her go, boys."

"No heartbeat detected..." the box chimed in slightly Swedish-accented English. *"Charging...Stand clear...Defibrillating..."*

The woman's back arched as the current shot through her, then she collapsed back on the chair, screaming as she expelled the liquid from her lungs.

"—ENGLISH! I SPEAK ENGLISH! JUST STOP, PLEASE!"

Mike nodded to Vanner and the others.

"See how easy that was?" He wiped her face off. "So, you've understood everything we've been saying?"

"Yes...I learned at nun school...in Pengmankat."

"If you don't want more, tell me what I want to know."

"I do not know what is in the box, I swear!" the girl gasped, clearly trying not to cry. "Yeung Tony was told about it from a man he met in Phuket. The man told him it was being smuggled north, and if he could get his hands on it, the man would pay well, more money than Tony had ever seen. Tony found out what ship it was on and sent his men to grab it. They did, and he was about to contact his buyer when you people showed up and started killing everybody."

"And you are absolutely sure you do not know what's inside the box?" Mike casually raised the canteen over her head again.

"NO! No, please, I swear!"

"Who's the buyer?" Mike asked then raised the canteen again as she paused.

"A dealer named Arun Than. Yeung was to sail to Hong Kong once he had the box, and Than would contact him to set up a meeting."

Mike had been checking Vanner's read of the woman's story, and the Marine gave him a thumbs-up.

"All right, we're going to keep you with us for the next few days. You'll be in a cabin, but be under guard the entire time, so don't try anything stupid, or else what these guys'll do to you will make all this seem like child's play."

Mike was mostly bluffing—as far as he knew, the Keldara didn't go in much for torture. Vil and Danes, however, were both very solid, muscular examples of the Keldara male, and looked menacing enough that he was pretty sure she wouldn't try anything.

"Take her below and let her get cleaned up." The two warriors escorted the staggering woman below deck, half-supporting her with one hand on each arm.

"You're sure that stress detector program is on the level?" Mike asked.

"Well, there's a plus or minus three percent variance," Vanner said with a shrug. "But overall, it's been right ninety plus percent of the time."

"Even on non-English speakers?"

"I've been testing it on the Keldara over the past few weeks," Vanner said. "The guys are pretty bad at lying—they show up right away. The girls, of course, are much more skilled, and Katya is damn near an artist. Whatever Jay has been teaching her, it's working."

"That's a scary thought," Mike mused. "What's that saying about the female of the species being more deadly than the male?"

"Ah, Kipling. Well, I don't know about more deadly, but certainly more skilled at deception. Although, so is Jay, so it's not clear it is gender-based."

Mike thought of the sociopathic rage Katya concealed under her beautiful face, just waiting to strike at the right target with her deadly fingernails. He thought of Creata calmly standing over the dead Armenian, a smoking pistol in her hand. He thought about the rumor he had heard of one of the Mothers during the battle against the Chechens, and what she had done with an enemy soldier's heart. He had never learned whether there was any truth to that rumor, mainly because he never wanted to know if it *was* true.

"Don't ever underestimate a woman, Keldara or otherwise, on her lethalness—trust me, you'll lose every time."

"I am married to Greznya, sir," Vanner replied.

"Point," Mike said. His radio beeped. "Mal, this is Locki. I have opened the box."

Mike exchanged a glance with Vanner.

"I thought she said it would take some time."

His intel chief shrugged. "I've found that when Creata puts her mind to something, she's a lot like Scotty on *Star Trek*—always under-promising and over-delivering."

A minute later, they both stood in one of the first level salons. Adams and Creata were also there, gathered around the box.

"I thought you said that opening the box might be tough, Creata?" Mike asked.

"I thought so, too. But once I understood the basic concept, it went faster than I'd expected. There are no other secondary locks or traps involved." She stepped back. "As a prize of battle, the honor of opening it is yours, Kildar."

"Thanks, I think." Visions of poison gas or a simple explosive booby trap went through his mind, but Mike reached for the lid and lifted it.

The box was cleverly hinged along the back, with the seam between the top and bottom hidden underneath a ridge of metal, which was why it had escaped detection. The inside was completely filled with a single piece of dark gray packing foam. Mike reached for it and removed it, revealing—

"Computer boards?" he looked up at Vanner. "*This* is their treasure?"

Vanner leaned down to examine them, then looked up at the Kildar.

"If these are what I *think* they are, they're just about priceless. We need to set up a Skype call with Doctor Arensky."

CHAPTER FIVE

As days go, Colonel Bob Pierson thought, *I've had worse.*

The Office of Special Operations Liaison, or OSOL, handled all sensitive special operations outside the United States. They assisted operator teams that needed intel, a favor, or that had just gotten into a jam they couldn't handle on their own. OSOL also briefed the higher-ups on what was going down when necessary, then relayed new orders to the operator or team in the field. It was staffed twenty-four/seven by higher echelon officers, and could perform just about any service an operator needed done ASAP or sooner.

Pierson's shift had been remarkably quiet; so much so that he thought he might be able to get out at what was approximately a normal shift-end time. He also knew the approximate odds of that happening, as it was an old maxim in intel analysis: *the longer things remain quiet, the bigger the shit storm that's coming down—*

And just like that, the secure phone rang. With a resigned exhalation, Bob picked up the receiver, immediately shifting from slightly tired officer to perfect, precise, professional soldier.

"Office of Special Operations Liaison, U.S. Army Colonel Robert Pierson speaking, how may I help you?"

"Go scramble," a familiar voice on the other end said.

Bob did so and leaned back in his chair. He knew the caller on the other end well, and also knew that his plans for a quiet, uneventful evening had been shit-canned the moment he'd picked up.

"Aren't you supposed to be on vacation, Mike?"

"Yes, and here in the land of tomorrow it's eighty-nine degrees and sunny. How are things in your neck of the woods?"

"Well, they had been quiet until you called. Otherwise it's about forty-five degrees and raining salamanders. I'm sure this isn't a social call, however."

With Mike, it never was. Bob had first "met" him during the Syria op, and had been Mike's handler on the D.C. end of things ever since.

"Is it ever?" Mike briefly outlined what he and his Keldara had run into, including the loot they'd picked up from their captives.

Bob blinked twice.

"Is Vanner absolutely sure about the cargo?"

"We checked with Doctor Death. They're the real deal. My question is, what the hell am I supposed to do with them?"

"That is a good one. Just sit tight and let me inform some people who need to know right now. I'll get back to you as soon as I can."

"Works. I'll be around."

"Okay. I'll be in touch the second I know what The Man wants done."

"You're taking this that high?"

"Not my call. But somehow I have a feeling that I'll be visiting a certain big white house before the night is over."

"Good luck. Jenkins out."

Bob hit the disconnect button, then dialed a number that went straight to the National Military Command Center.

"This is Colonel Pierson in OSOL. We have a situation."

Two and a half hours later, the President, dressed in an immaculate tuxedo, held up a hand.

"Wait a minute, let me get this straight. Computer chips that run a nuclear power plant were found in the possession of ocean pirates off Singapore?"

"Yes, sir. As improbable as it sounds, that is the situation in a nutshell," Pierson said. "However, to clarify, they are not simply computer chips, but the motherboards that are the brains, if you will, of a nuclear reactor."

The President rubbed his chin.

"Bob, I know Mike's intel is on the level. If he says he's got 'em, then he's got 'em. But frankly, this sounds like the opening of a James Bond film."

The rest of the cabinet secretaries and chiefs of staff all smiled or chuckled politely, then their expressions grew serious to match the President's.

"Do we have any intel on a missing shipment?" he asked.

"Nothing has come across my desk in the past two weeks regarding missing or stolen nuclear reactor operation boards," the head of the NSA said. "Whoever lost these is keeping it very quiet."

"Before we get any deeper into this, Mr. President, are we waiting on the NRC chair, or are they not going to be involved in this?" the DCIA asked.

The President exchanged a glance with his secretary of defense.

"Let's just say they have enough on their plate monitoring current nuclear activity in the U.S., never mind the rest of the world. Post-Fukishima, they're far too busy implementing the new safety protocols mandated for all reactors around the nation to be involved with something like this."

The President activated a large monitor on the wall, which showed a picture of the boards in their formerly secure case. The image had been sent as part of a heavily encrypted transmission from the *Big Fish*.

"What do we know about the shipment itself?"

All heads turned to the secretary of the Department of Energy. He turned to his deputy secretary, who cleared her throat.

"Preliminary analysis has determined that the chips are of Chinese manufacture. Working with the CIA, we have traced them to the Semiconductor Manufacturing International Corporation out of Shanghai."

"There's a familiar name," NSA snorted. "They'll manufacture anything to turn a buck."

"Given China's very strong interest in becoming a world leader in generating nuclear power, we—" the deputy secretary nodded at the CIA director, "—found it odd that the company would be exporting chips when there are dozens of planned pressurized water reactors either on the drawing board or in early construction stages in China itself. It stands to reason that the company would be ordered to produce chips for its own country's needs first, and then sell to other nations only after the internal market was satisfied."

The CIA director took up the narrative. "Therefore, we figure that the chips were being sold on the black market by someone high up in the Chinese government, perhaps a high-ranking military officer. That would explain the lack of official markings on the box, as well as its integral high security."

"Not that high, if one of the Keldara could open it," the secretary of defense muttered.

"Apparently you weren't in the loop on their Italian job," the DNSA said, shaking his head.

"However, the transport information was apparently leaked, and the illegal shipment was hijacked."

"Where were the chips supposed to be heading?" the President asked.

"At this point, we have no idea," DCIA replied. "Even with the chip manufacturing programs throughout Southeast Asia, there's no shortage of countries that might want these. My geeks tell me the architecture is a nightmare. Pakistan, India, Indonesia, North Korea, and even such faraway places as Mongolia, Kazakhstan, or Iran, any of them could be a potential buyer. The bottom line is that someone high-up in China is providing vital nuclear reactor technology on the black market to whoever's got the cash to pay for it." The director let his gaze play around the room. "I don't think we need to go into the potential problem this could lead to regarding refining weapons-grade nuclear waste into useable material for the manufacture of nuclear weapons."

"No, you don't. I've already got that coming out of my ears regarding Iran as it is." The President had turned to stare at the innocuous-looking boards nestled in their foam beds. "All we'd need is Pakistan or North Korea getting their hands on them."

"But, Mr. President, the purchasing country would still need a reactor to put the boards into. Surely, these are relatively worthless without the proper facility," the deputy secretary said, incurring a glare from her superior.

"It's a point," the President said.

"Sorry, should have covered that point at the beginning," the secretary of energy said. "These chips can be used to modify just about any PWR into a fast breeder. And it's pretty much impossible to tell without a very close inspection."

"O . . . kay," the President said. "Yes, that should have been in the very initial brief. Next question: Options?"

The Joint Chiefs didn't even bother to exchange glances.

"With relations with China growing more tenuous by the month, as well as current OTEMPO, inserting American assets, military or otherwise, into this situation is disrecommended," the CJCS said. "We jointly recommend it would be best to use on-site resources to identify, analyze, and if possible, action the supply chain series. However, no action plan should be engaged that might compromise Chinese sovereignty or social integrity."

"Of course," the President said with a slight smile. "And the fact that it's a Georgian group rather than American makes it deniable if the Chinese do get upset."

"There's that," the DCIA said. "I'd rather not put our assets on it, either, sir. Support if necessary, yes. Agents actively involved . . . Not so much."

"Colonel," the President said. "It says here that Mike had discovered the identity of the person who was supposed to be purchasing the boards from the pirates, correct?"

"Yes, Mr. President."

"All right then, see if he can arrange a meeting with the buyer and follow the chain to whoever's on the other end. It's bad enough

China owns two-thirds of our country as it is. The last thing we need is to have them supplying state-of-the-art, build your own nuclear weapons, reactor control materiel to anyone with the cash to buy it."

"What about securing the chips, sir, or at least replacing them with dummies or rendering them inoperable? I mean, if they were to somehow get out of this Mr. Jenkins's hands—what's so funny?" the secretary of energy asked upon seeing smiles and even chuckles coming from the joint chiefs and the CIA head.

The President smiled in genuine sympathy.

"I'm sorry, Tom, the humor is unintentional. Since you haven't been involved with previous operations where Mr. Jenkins's expertise has been utilized, let me assure you; he is *very* skilled at retaining sensitive materials. My only worry is that he'll use them to install Georgia's next nuclear power plant in that fortified valley of his."

The President rose from his chair, signaling the end of the meeting.

"Thank you for coming in on such short notice, and keep me posted on your progress regarding this matter. Now, if you'll excuse me, I have to get back to the State dinner before the South Korean president and my wife both start wondering where I ran off to."

Thirty-seven minutes later, Pierson was back at the OSOL office and on a video link with Mike.

"So, what does The Man want done with these?" Mike asked. He appeared to be drinking a beer.

"How does tracking down both the buyer, and if possible the seller, sound to you?" Pierson asked.

"I dunno, how much is it worth to you?" Mike asked.

"Seriously?" Pierson said. "These are bad pieces of electronics going to bad people."

"Anastasia needs new shoes," Mike said, referring to his Russian harem manager. "These ops don't pay for themselves, you know."

"I know, I know. Send us a bill," Pierson said, trying not to wince. "Usual rates?"

"For you? Buddy rate, definitely. Only two and a half costs. If it was Vlad I'd have him pay through the nose. I'm still pissed about his Excellent Georgia Adventure. It would be good to give the boys a more in-depth tour of Southeast Asia anyway." He chuckled. "They are going to shit a brick when I take them into Hong Kong. And I'll practically have to put Adams on a leash while we're there."

"Just try not to make too big a splash there, okay? The CJCS got all diplomatic and buzzword bingo trying not to say, 'We really, really don't want to piss off the Chinese over this!' And let me know if the trail leads you to mainland China, all right? We'll definitely want to alert the higher-ups before you set foot there."

"Don't worry, Bob, I plan to keep this a sailing tour."

"Good. Is there anything else you need at this point?"

"Yeah, let the Marshals know we'll be keeping *Big Fish* for a couple more weeks. If you've never been on one of these, you've got to try it. It's got everything you need, and then some, all at your fingertips. I'm still trying to figure out how I can get ahold of one of them without shelling out eight figures. Our beer sales are good, but not *that* good."

Pierson grinned. The luxury yacht had been confiscated by the DEA from a major Miami drug lord only three weeks earlier. It had been very courteously loaned out by the U.S. Marshals from the Central Governmental Surplus Repository in Hollywood, Florida. After the Keldara had blown through during the VX op, the Marshals had bent over backwards to extend whatever service they could to the Kildar or anyone remotely associated with him.

"I'll let them know tomorrow morning—I'm sure they'll nod politely and say thanks for the update."

"If you really want to screw with their heads, tell 'em I said we'll try to patch all the bullet holes. Jenkins out."

"Pierson out." Bob shut down the Skype, hoping he wouldn't be hearing from Mike for a few days at least. *'Cause if I do, there's no telling what kind of trouble he'll be bringing with him . . .*

"So that's the long and short of it," Mike announced to his senior officers. Adams and Vanner sat in brown leather chairs around the mirror-polished teakwood conference table. Neilson was teleconferencing in on a secure satellite feed from the valley of the Keldara. "We'll be staying in South China Sea for the next several days while tracking down the interested parties. The floor is now open for questions or action items."

"Is there anything you'll need from home? Air support, equipment, more ammo?" Neilson asked.

Mike looked at Adams and Vanner, both of whom were nodding. He pointed at Vanner first.

"If we're going to be moving to twenty-four/seven operations, I could use a few more intel girls. Especially if we'll be accessing multiple countries at once."

"You just like the idea of the girls walking around in those itty-bitty bikinis," Adams said with a snort.

"Hey, since I'm a happily married man, *you* should be thanking *me* for this. Besides, it's hardly my fault the Georgian summer is so short that if you blink, you miss it entirely."

"All right, three more girls will be on the way within twelve hours. Anything else?" Neilson asked.

Mike caught Adams' stare.

"Yes, Ass-boy?"

"We're running low on beer."

"You guys are lucky," Nielson said. "Mother Lenka just finished a batch. Since everyone did so damn well on the op, I am sending you a few cases of the *really* good stuff. The girls and the quill will be heading out this evening via our usual airline. They should be there in about sixteen hours, give or take. We'll arrange with Vanner for transportation from the nearest port. Kildar, anything else you can think of?"

"No, we're good for now. From what I heard from on high, I get the feeling they would like us to keep a pretty low profile on this one."

Vanner snorted this time. "They do understand how we typically operate, right?"

"Hey, Disney World was still standing after we were finished, remember?" Mike said.

"Nope, I was way too busy recuperating at that island paradise you'd set up," Vanner replied.

"Exactly. Anyway, this should be primarily a littoral mission. We will reevaluate if it goes in-country anywhere, however."

Adams stretched and put his interlaced hands behind his head.

"Another week or two on this floating pleasure palace. If I thought there was a God, he'd be smilin' down on me for sure."

"Everyone's passports are in order, correct? I do not want any red tape if we're stopped by navy, coast guard, or customs."

"Everyone's papers are in order, but how do you expect to explain the thirty sets of Level IV body armor and fatigues, not to mention the heavy weapons?" Vanner's tone was only half-joking. "Hell, the force we've got could probably overthrow one or two governments around here without too much trouble."

"You've got waivers for all the nearby governments," Nielson said. "I'll get started on clearance for others. Singapore is always a stickler about this stuff but I've got friends in low places. However, the Kildar has a point. You can have anything up to and including a nuclear weapon, and with the right clearance all that a customs guy will do is shrug 'cause it's waaay over his pay grade. On the other hand, one itsy bitsy mistake on your passport and they're all over your ass."

"All of that stuff will be kept strictly out of sight any time we're near port. The boat is clear on paper, and I can call in the diplomatic big guns if I have to. Vanner, you'll have command while we're ashore, and any pirates thinking they can take this ship will be in for a nasty surprise. Anything else?"

"We are thin on regional intel," Vanner said. "Right now the girls are scrambling to put together packages for the Keldara but we could really use someone from the area as a local guide."

"Second that. I even got a guy in mind. Local I worked with in Taiwan a few years ago. Member of the Marines, and served in what they call their Amphibious Searching Unit of the Republic of China Marine Force."

"'Amphibious Searching Unit?'" Vanner asked.

"Swim-ops. I won't call them SEALs but they make noises. And they are pretty good. Up to GROM standards."

"Okay, see if you can get in touch with him. Vanner?"

"I also know someone who might be able to help us out. Former jarhead named Jace Morgan. Marine Force Recon officer who headed one of the first Marine Special Operations Teams when they were formed in '06. He served all over the Pacific, including living with the Montagnards in the Highlands of Vietnam. After he left the service, he moved to Singapore, and been there ever since. Speaks a lot of the major regional languages, and can get by in most of the others."

"Sounds like either could work. Each of you get in touch with your respective prospects, and we'll get them out here for an interview while we head to Hong Kong. Unless there are any other issues to deal with—" Mike rose from the table. "—I am going to have a little chat with our female captive, see if I can bring her around to our side. After all, we'll need her to help set up the meeting with this Arun Than."

"Ah, maybe we should let someone else talk to her first," Vanner said. "I mean, it's highly unlikely she's going to be very forthcoming with the man who just waterboarded her."

"Actually, that experience usually makes detainees more cooperative, but I'm willing to try another approach. Who did you have in mind?"

"I thought Katya might be the best choice. You know, ex-hooker to current hooker. She can probably relate, having been through something very close to this, and could probably make a better connection with our captive. On the other hand, I suppose you could try to see if the pirate leader himself would set the meet."

Mike's lips peeled back in a wolfish grin. "No, your way works just fine. However, I will go extract the contact intel for this guy in Hong Kong. Go tell the boys and girls what's going on—I am off to talk to a pirate again."

"Aren't you forgetting something?" Vanner asked.

Mike turned back to him, a puzzled look on his face.

"You better go put Katya on the clock."

"Oh . . . right."

"With any luck, she might even be decent this time," Adams said.

Mike stepped out into the red-gold light of the rising sun washing over the *Big Fish's* bow. A lone woman was lying on her back a few meters away, dressed in Serengeti aviator sunglasses and three triangles of white cloth than barely covered her amazing tits and tight, toned ass. Her blunt-cut blond hair was tousled and damp, as if she'd just taken a shower, and she had earbuds in, listening to something on her iPhone. Her lips were moving, but he was damn sure she wasn't singing along with a song.

Mike blew a breath out between his lips. Ever since the Florida op, Katya had seized every opportunity to parade around in hardly any clothing, even back home. When he'd tried to call her on it, she had simply told him that she was working on something called "self-aware body image," and that Jay, their resident spymaster, had given her the assignment. Mike had confirmed this with Jay, and grudgingly allowed it to continue, despite the constant distractions it caused.

When she heard him approach, Katya raised herself up on her elbows and stared at him. While looking like she was posing for the cover of a swimsuit magazine, she was the farthest thing from a model there was. Behind those shades were the cold, flat eyes of a born sociopath. Mike warned every new man away from near her, unless the poor bastard wanted to become a eunuch. But her mind was diamond-sharp, and the biological additions a black-box American medical lab had made to her last year had turned her into a hell of an undercover operative in certain situations. And the one thing Mike knew for certain about Asians was that they always went crazy for blondes . . .

"Morning, Katya. Enjoying the trip so far?"

When she removed one earbud, Mike could hear the tinny noise of what sounded like a Chinese language lesson coming from it.

"If by that you mean being bored out of my skull, then yes, I am having a wonderful time, thank you."

"Glad to hear that, because I've got a little job for you."

"Finally. Where and when?" she asked.

"Right now works, and it's right here on the boat," Mike said. "I assume you are aware of the three prisoners we brought on board last night?"

"They were all the rest of the girls could talk about. What about them?"

"One is an Asian prostitute. She was close to the pirate leader, and probably heard things he talked about with his men. I want you to get close to her. Find out what she knows."

She lowered her sunglasses enough to regard him over the rims.

"What? Did the vaunted Kildar charm not do the job?"

"Not after I waterboarded the bitch three times."

"So, you want me to be nice to her—the good cop to your psychotic one?"

"Something like that."

"Me?" Katya said, looking at him over her rims again.

Mike thought this might be the first time he'd ever seen her on the verge of real laughter.

"I realize that most people would consider me psychotic for assigning you the 'good cop' position, but—"

"What are my parameters?"

"Drug her, fuck her, slap the shit out of her, whatever way you feel will work best. There is a time limit, however—we're bound for Hong Kong, and should be there in about fifty hours. I want everything she knows by the time we go ashore."

"Fine. Jay said I should practice my interpersonal and interrogation skills anyway. This seems like a good place to start." She tapped a perfect, white tooth with a French-manicured nail. "It will be good to pretend to be something other than a whore for once. The usual rates will apply, of course."

"Of course."

Katya rose gracefully to her feet and brushed by Mike in a cloud of coconut bronzing lotion and papaya body spray.

"I'll let you know how it goes."

▲   ▲   ▲

So close! So fucking close!

In the bathroom of her plush stateroom, the prostitute Soon Yi leaned over the marble sink and tried not to throw up any more bile. Her stomach was already empty from the waterboarding. Only her intense training and self-control had allowed her to clean up in the shower afterward without suffering flashbacks.

As she stared at herself in the mirror, that same self-control allowed her to not smash it to pieces. *I only needed an hour or two to get the box back until these fucking* gwai-los *showed up and started killing everybody!* She was just about to make her move to kill those idiots and set up the meeting with Than herself. She had even caught a break when Tony had kidnapped her and tried to escape on his boat. But the damn round-eyes had come after them again. Now she was outnumbered, unarmed, and on a luxury yacht on a westerly heading. The only solace she could take from everything that had happened was that she was still fairly close to the green box.

Taking another deep breath, she took stock of her situation. *The guards seem sharp enough, if a bit—simple,* she mused. *Seducing one may be my ticket out of here... at least they look cleaner than the pirates. But I still need to gain access to the box itself.* She had been left on her own for a few hours, probably to let the isolation and hopelessness of her situation sink into her psyche. But if her captors thought she'd play her part that willingly, they were in for a surprise...

Wrapping herself in the thick, white, terrycloth bathrobe—for a prison cell, the accommodations were great—Yi tied the matching sash around her waist. That they'd allowed her to have it was interesting—it meant that her captors didn't consider her to be any kind of threat. *Perfect.*

She walked back to her cheap dress, which was hung over the back of the gilded chair near the make-up desk. Taking it into the bathroom, she turned on the hot water to cover any noise she was about to make. While the mirror fogged over, she felt along the lower hem for a small break in the material. Finding a tiny loop of metal there, she pinched it between her fingers and leaned close to the running water, then began speaking clear, distinct Mandarin.

The small microphone implanted in her lower mandible picked up every word. It used the conduction of her own body's electrical field to transmit her words through the antenna in the dress hem, which was powered by tiny batteries that were also sewn into the material. The burst message was boosted using the yacht's radar array, transmitting to a satellite that relayed it back to her handler at the Second Bureau in the Ministry of State Security in Beijing.

"Black Chrysanthemum reporting."

"Proceed," the calm voice on the other end ordered.

Soon Yi gave a terse summary of what had happened since she had hooked up with the pirates twenty-four hours ago. She included names and descriptions of the primary captors, everything she had seen so far. "Many speak with a strange accent, probably Slavic-inflected. Speculate that they are Eastern European mercenaries, hired by a shipping company to eliminate piracy. Their leader was very—insistent about learning whether I had any connection with the target."

"Acknowledged. Did you volunteer any information?"

"No. Cover is still intact."

"Good. Is your primary subject still alive?"

"Unknown at this time."

"Is the target still intact?"

"Unknown at this time. Will attempt to find out. What are my directives?"

"Primary mission is still to acquire information on buyer and seller of the box and its contents. New secondary mission is to gather intelligence on your captors through whatever means you deem necessary, including personnel files if possible. Report in every twenty-four hours if possible."

"Understood. Black Chrysanthemum out." Soon Yi released the antenna and left the bathroom. Tossing the dress over the back of a chair, she sat on the bed and leaned back against the suede headboard, feeling a wave of tiredness wash over her. The bed, covered in clean, white sheets and a down-filled duvet, looked very inviting. Her head was sinking toward it when a firm knock sounded on her door.

Quickly she mussed her hair and scurried into the corner of the bed against the wall. "Who's there? What do you want with me?" she called out in a fast, shrill voice.

"My name is Katya. I would like to speak with you, if that's all right."

Yi's eyebrows rose at this, and she let the silence drag out a bit before replying.

"All—all right." She made sure she was wearing her cheap slippers as she tucked her legs underneath her.

The door clicked and opened, and a beautiful young woman stepped inside. She was dressed in a black pencil skirt and matching jacket over a cream blouse, with smooth, long legs ending in a pair of matching designer heels—real Jimmy Choos, if Yi were to guess. Her naturally blond hair was smoothed and pulled away from her face, and she stared at Yi through a pair of dark tortoiseshell glasses framing light blue eyes.

"Good, I see that you have had a chance to use the facilities." Her English was good, if a bit clipped and formal, as if it was not her native tongue. Turning to the open door, the woman spoke to the tall, handsome man outside in a language that sounded vaguely Russian, but wasn't. *Definitely Slavic*, Yi thought. Shaking his head, he started to reply, but she cut him off and made a shooing motion at him with her hand. He closed the door, leaving the two women alone.

The woman walked to the makeup desk, pulled the chair out, placed it in the middle of the room, and sat down, crossing her legs. She looked at Yi for a few seconds, then smiled.

"As I said outside, my name is Katya. What is yours?"

"Yi—Soon Yi." She kept playing her role of terrified prostitute, and cowered in the corner of the room.

"It is a pleasure to meet you, Ms. Yi. You must be hungry. Can I get you anything to eat or drink?"

"Who are you? What do you people want with me?"

"I am the executive assistant to the Kildar—"

"Kil-dar." The word didn't come naturally off Yi's tongue. "The man who—who—" She shook her head and let a tear trickle down her cheek. Even with her training, it wasn't entirely acting.

"Yes. It is complicated," Katya said with a nod. "What has been done to you was regrettable—"

"But you work for that *hun dan*! What are you, another whore, just better-dressed?"

"I suppose one could compare the relationship to that of a prostitute and her pimp, although I am much more highly compensated," Katya said with a shrug. "How the Kildar chooses to conduct his business does not impact how I choose to conduct mine. The important thing right now is that he has decided to keep you alive for the time being."

"Why?"

"Because he thinks you know more than you are telling him." Katya uncrossed her legs and sat back in the chair. "He has sent me down to find out if that is true." She shrugged her elegant shoulders. "So far, I am not seeing very much to justify his reasoning."

"What? Are you saying he will have me killed if I do not give him something?" Yi hugged her knees to her chest, partly to show fear, and partly to keep her shoes close to her hands. "What does he want from me?"

Katya leaned forward slightly. "He says that you mentioned that you heard the name of the person Yeung Tony was supposed to contact in Hong Kong. Any more information on this Arun Than, or on Tony himself, would help us—and you—tremendously."

"I—I don't know that much. Tony just said that Arun Than was the guy who would make him and his pirates rich. That's all, I swear."

"That is not very much at all. I do not think the Kildar will be very pleased with this." Katya rose and walked to the end of the bed, making Soon Yi do her best to meld into the wall. "Relax, I'm not going to hit you." She sat on the edge. "This may be hard to believe, but I know exactly what you are going through—I have been where you are right now."

"You—you really were a whore?"

The blond woman's smile grew tight.

"Yes. Stuck in a brothel in the middle of nowhere, I had to spread my legs for whatever man walked through the door." Her expression softened. "After a while, you start thinking of yourself as worthless...just a hole for a man to stick his dick into and pay your pimp, who might give you just enough to survive until the next day. I have been there and I have done that. When the opportunity came for me to make a better life for myself, I took it, even though there were aspects of it that—displeased me. That still displease me. However, that same opportunity is before you right now, Ms. Yi. If I were in your shoes, I would strongly consider taking it before it is withdrawn."

"But I do not know anything about that box! Please, you have to believe me!"

Katya stared at her for a long minute, then blew out a breath.

"I believe that you believe what you are saying—but I am not sure that the Kildar will. Let me go talk to him, see if I can get you some more time. I'll come back and talk to you again in a couple of hours. In the meantime, let us get you some food, all right?"

Yi didn't reply, only nodded. Katya rose and walked to the door. She opened it, then turned back.

"Please, think about what I said. We will talk again in a little while." Then she left.

Soon Yi stayed where she was, evaluating the conversation. "Katya" had said all the right words, made all the right overtures to try to draw her into her confidence. A run-of-the-mill prostitute would probably been convinced, but an operative with Soon's training wasn't.

Despite everything she had said, despite probably telling the truth about her past, very little of her emotional appeal had ever reached the blond woman's eyes. She was a stone-cold killer, through and through.

She may even be deadlier than this Kildar, Soon Yi realized, and began thinking about how she could give them enough information to keep herself alive a while longer.

"Nice outfit," Mike said when he saw Katya in the command room. "How'd it go?"

"So-so. Greznya is running the conversation through Vanner's voice stress scanner for analysis, and I want to review the interview at least once before I go back in."

Katya tapped a white tooth with a nail, pondering something before continuing.

"She cleaned herself up. Most data on waterboarding victims indicates a high percentage have a deep aversion to any kind of running water immediately afterward." She removed the glasses and handed them to Daria. "I am interested in seeing how the recording from these compares to my implant. It seems they can be used for everyday surveillance without detection. Would be good in sunglasses, too."

"We will get on that," Vanner said.

"Cottontail," Mike said, making her turn toward him. "What is your take on her?"

"She is definitely more than she seems. I am just not sure exactly what that is yet. I said we would feed her, and that I would talk to you to buy her some more time. Put the Oxystim in her drink. I suggest fruit juice to mask the taste. I will give it about ninety minutes to digest, then go in to let her know that you have graciously allowed her to live until morning, but that you expect results tomorrow, otherwise she will be shark bait. That should do it, no?"

"It's a good start. I'm just really curious what the hell this bitch is hiding. Vanner, make sure someone's watching her room twenty-four/seven. I don't want to miss anything."

"Yes, Kildar."

CHAPTER SIX

Jace Morgan had been just about everywhere in this man's world, from above the Arctic Circle in Siberia to the deep jungles of Africa, and on every continent in between. He thought he'd seen just about everything too, but the situation he was currently heading into was one of the strangest ones he'd ever encountered.

It had started with a call out of the blue from Patrick Vanner, asking if he was available for ten to fourteen days' work around Southeast Asia. Figuring the intel specialist needed security or bodyguard work, Jace had checked his schedule and said sure, where and when.

"'When' is right now, and at the moment 'where' is a yacht currently sailing on the South China Sea toward Hong Kong." Vanner had e-mailed him a first-class ticket from Singapore to Tan Son Nhat International Airport in Ho Chih Minh City. An escort there would take him to the helicopter that would ferry him out to the boat.

"Works for me," Morgan had replied. Checking his ticket, he saw the flight left in three hours. Fortunately, he always kept a light duty bag packed, and he had grabbed it, flagged down a motorcycle taxi, and headed for the airport. He'd lost an hour and fifteen minutes to the packed streets, and made it through security with ten minutes to spare.

The eighty-five-minute flight had been uneventful; it was only when he landed that things had started to get a bit—unusual.

He was met by a spectacularly beautiful young woman, with eyes so deep blue Jace thought he might drown in them if he wasn't careful, and lush brown hair braided into a single, thick rope that was draped over one shoulder. She was damned young—if she was twenty, he was a Thailand whoremaster—and was holding a small sign with "J. Morgan" on it.

Jace walked up to the young woman, his six feet, three inches making her look up at his face.

"That's me."

"A pleasure to meet you, Mr. Morgan," the young woman said in accented English, but didn't extend her hand. "My name is Martya. Our pilot would like to get underway, so unless you have any more luggage to pick up . . . ?"

"I'm ready to go."

Martya looked around before leaning closer to him.

"Are you not carrying?"

The former Recon Marine kept his face deadpan.

"Weapons, drugs, or both?"

"Oh, I am sorry . . . I am not quite used to the language—"

"It's all right, Martya, I'm not carrying anything." He wasn't crazy enough to try either, particularly in Singapore, where the drug laws made America's look like a slap on the wrist.

"Is good. Follow me, please."

"With pleasure." Carrying his bag easily in one hand, Jace followed the slim girl out of Terminal Two, through the airport, and out the main entrance door, into the heat of an early Vietnamese fall. Outside the main building, she headed toward a cluster of hangars well away from the main runways. "Our helicopter is over here."

"I'm right behind you." Quickening his pace, Jace easily kept up with the smaller girl as they headed for a Eurocopter AS355 helicopter that was warming up as they approached. Another woman, dressed in cargo pants, T-shirt, and aviator sunglasses, stood at the passenger door, obviously waiting for the pair.

"Any trouble finding him, Martya?" she shouted over the din

of the whirling blades. The slender girl shook her head as she climbed aboard.

"Copilot Tamara Wilson, former U.S.M.C! Pleased to meet another jarhead!" she shouted.

"The pleasure's all mine!" he yelled back.

Tamara jerked a thumb at the passenger compartment.

"Climb aboard, I'll stow your bag."

"Can do!" Jace said as he stepped up into the rear of the aircraft, where his next surprise was waiting.

There were two other girls besides Martya inside, each as beautiful as she was. One was a stunning tiny blonde with perfect, milk-white skin who introduced herself as Xatia. The one beside her was freckled, but her skin tone, along with curly, bright-red hair, suited her emerald-green eyes perfectly. Her name was Tsira.

Besides a small seat for him, every other square inch of the passenger compartment was taken up by several cases of beer, a brand called Mountain Tiger. Jace had heard of it; some Eastern European microbrew, apparently selling like crazy in the States. Practically impossible to get in Southeast Asia, however.

"Everything all right back there, Captain?"

Jace looked toward the cockpit to see another woman on the stick. She was short and trim, with all the right parts in all the right places. He must have been staring, because her lips compressed into a thin line.

"Something wrong with the view, Captain?"

Jace scrambled to put on a pair of headphones. "No, ma'am, everything looks great from back here. I'm just wondering when I get to meet Auric Goldfinger."

Tamara had gotten into the copilot's seat in time to hear his remark, and both she and the pilot chuckled.

"Yeah, the Kildar gets that kind of reaction a lot. Don't worry, Vanner will fill you in when we get there."

"It hadn't even crossed my mind," he replied. *Especially not with this view.*

The two women completed their preflight check, and the

helicopter lifted off smoothly and headed south, leaving the city behind and shooting forward over the endless South China Sea.

Settling back to enjoy the ride, Jace tried not to ogle the bevy of gorgeous babes surrounding him, which was hard work. They were also doing their best not to look at him, conversing in a language that sounded similar to, but not quite Russian. His list of questions for his old friend Vanner, however, was growing longer with each passing nautical mile.

What the hell is he mixed up in? he thought. *And if this is who he's working with, why the hell didn't he contact me sooner?*

"Patrick, the helicopter with the girls and Mr. Morgan is inbound. Kacey estimates they will be landing in approximately five minutes," Greznya reported.

"Sweet," Patrick said with a nod. "I can't wait for him to see the place and meet the Kildar. Hey, Adams, whatever happened to your guy?"

The master chief, who was enjoying a bottle of Mountain Tiger while sprawled on a couch, smiled lazily.

"It turns out that he wasn't available for what we needed. But he has something that the Kildar will like very much."

He refused to say anything more on the subject, even when pressed. Vanner just shrugged and joined Greznya on the aft deck, which had been reconfigured into the helipad. A few minutes later, the Eurocopter came into sight and passed over the fantail, looping around to approach from the aft for a gentle landing. Kacey Bathlick, the pilot, powered down the rotors, and the three female and one male passengers disembarked.

"Jace! Over here!" Vanner trotted out to meet his buddy, clapping his back in a hug. "How was the flight over?"

"Man, Singapore Air's got nothing on these women!" Jace nodded at the three girls, each of whom smiled and nodded shyly back as Grezyna herded them inside. "You have *got* to tell me what you're working on."

"All in good time, buddy. First, why don't you give me a hand?"

Vanner walked back to the passenger compartment. "Grab a case or two—let's get these babies on ice."

Jace set his duty bag on top of two cases, picked them up, and carried them inside, trying not to gawk at the luxury yacht around him. The *Big Fish* was decked out in teak and white leather everywhere he looked. At least, everywhere that wasn't taken up by unsmiling, solid, oddly good-looking men every few yards.

"Hand those off to Vanel and Edvin—thanks, guys," Vanner said. "Come with me into the conference room, and we can catch up a bit. Greznya, please let the Kildar know our guest has arrived."

Jace couldn't help watching the young woman's lush curves and pert backside as she strolled away, and let out a low whistle.

"Careful—that's my wife you're ogling," Vanner said with a huge smile.

"No shit? Jesus H. Christ, congratulations, man! When did you get hitched?"

"That . . . is a very long story, most of which you don't have the need-to-know," Vanner said with a slight grimace. "This situation is . . . decidedly odd. But most things involving the Kildar are."

"That's the second time I've heard that name. Patrick, what in the hell's going on here? Since when do you work for a Bond villain?"

Vanner led him into a plush room that had a long, oval table in the center, surrounded by several leather swivel chairs, each with an executive stationary set in front of them. A sweating bucket of beers on ice sat on the table.

"Drink first, answers second."

Jace grabbed one of the bottles—it was another Mountain Tiger. He frowned at the wax seal on top, then grabbed a letter opener and carved the wax off. Uncorking it, he took a drink and almost gasped as the golden liquid hit his tongue.

"Goddamn, that's good!"

Vanner nodded from his seat at the end of the table.

"It should be. That's the real deal—the best-of-the-best Mountain Tiger beer, straight from the valley of the Keldara, in the Caucasus Mountains."

"Okay, let's see...Kildar, Keldara...wait a minute. I have heard of these guys. Are you working with those kick-ass fighters from Georgia? Something about pretty much putting paid to the last of the big Chechen militias? What are they looking for, an in-depth tour of Southeast Asia?"

Vanner leaned forward and opened a bottle of Mountain Tiger for himself.

"Close. Here's what I can tell you..."

Ten minutes later, Jace leaned back in his chair, drained his bottle, and set it on the table.

"Okay, let me see if I've got this straight. Sometime during the Byzantine Empire, a group of marauding Celts, for lack of a better term, was captured by the Byzantines and turned into the personal guards of the emperor. They were sent to what is now Georgia, to manage a remote tax post, and settled in this particular valley. The Empire falls, as they all eventually do, but no one tells the Varangians, who stay where they are and become farmers. They keep their customs and religion alive, and one of those involves the Kildar, a foreigner who's their landlord-slash-warlord. These warrior/farmers have since been living in that particular valley for the past fifteen-odd centuries, until your Mr. Jenkins came along and starts rapidly bringing them into the twenty-first. Now he's got roughly a company of 'security specialists' under his command, and, shall we say, helps out certain interested foreign powers when asked nicely. The women are gorgeous, the men are handsome, they're all hardcore, and they brew a helluva beer. That about sum it up?"

"Look, I know how it all sounds—I wouldn't have believed it myself if I hadn't seen some of the stonework in the *caravanserai*. Well, that, and heard the lyrics of their songs during their festivals. They're the real deal all right, and the Kildar...Well, it's the best job I've ever had, and that includes working for Uncle Sam."

"It all sounds way too crazy to believe." Jace nodded at the empty bottle. "However, I've only had one of these, and you've never been a good liar. Therefore, I can only assume that when the impossible is removed, whatever remains, however improbable, is the truth."

"You got it, Sherlock. So, you interested?"

"Uhm, beer, girls and killing bad people? Hell, *yes*. Assuming I pass muster with your—Kildar, is it?"

"Right."

Just then the door opened, and Vanner and Jace both stood up as an unassuming-looking man entered. He was fit, but fairly average-looking, standing about five-foot-ten, with brown hair and brown eyes. His demeanor, however, was that of a man who knew what he wanted, and would do whatever it took to get it done. Jace respected the type, as they were vastly preferable to the other kinds of commanding officers he'd encountered during his tours—mostly either REMF limp-dicks or ass-kissers; or ROAD pussies just marking time 'til they were back in the world.

"Mike Jenkins, this is Jace Morgan," Vanner said.

Jace held out his hand, which Mike took in a firm grip.

"A pleasure, Mr. Morgan. Patrick's been telling me a lot about you."

"I hope I can live up to the hype. Seriously, it's good to be here, and thank you for the opportunity, sir."

"Have a seat." Mike watched Jace as he sat. "Not fond of the high-and-tight, huh?"

Jace swept his straight black hair back off his forehead. "It was the only thing I didn't love about the Corps. Besides, why advertise my former profession that openly?"

"Point. I trust Patrick's been filling you in on some of the details of our operation."

"Only what I need to know at the moment, sir. I assume more details will be forthcoming if we come to an agreement."

"Correct. What do you think about the duty we'd like to hire you for?"

"Just to make sure I understand the mission parameters, you're looking for a guide to the general region, someone fluent in the languages, customs, tribes, politics, and everything else. I've spent time in just about every country in the region, ranging as far south as Australia and far north as Mongolia. I'm fluent in Mandarin, Cantonese, Burmese, Hmong, Japanese, Thai, Malay, and Vietnamese. I'm passable in Samoan, Lao, Wu, Min, Montagnard, and Tagalog. Area dialects will be catch-as-you-can, since even tribes living next to each other may have almost completely different pronunciations. Don't even get me started on real village dialects. Most of them are completely different languages. Those . . . *nobody* knows all of those."

Mike raised an eyebrow. "And I thought Vanner was a polyglot."

"It's a gift. And I'm half-Indonesian, thanks to my mother."

"Works." Mike's jaw worked as he consulted his iPad. "Your personnel file looks great—Marine Corps Expeditionary Medal, Navy and Marine Corps Commendation Medal, expert across the board shooter. Four tours with Fourth Force Reconnaissance Company out of Okinawa before the unit was deactivated, mainly in Southeast Asia."

"Yes sir, both white and black ops."

"Very good, as we have been known to pop a few caps when the need arises. With Vanner's recommendation on top of that, I'd say you're perfectly suited for the opening. The offer is twenty-five thousand dollars, plus expenses, and tax-free, for approximately two weeks' work. Bear in mind that we keep very odd hours, so you'll probably spend most of that time on duty. What do you say?"

"On board, sir."

"Then welcome aboard, both figuratively and literally," Mike said, holding out his hand. "Vanner may have mentioned that from time to time I've had the opportunity to do certain favors for the U.S. Government. The details of any previous ones are unimportant, but you've probably seen YouTube videos on us."

"Yes, sir, particularly the op near Russia. I'm looking forward to meeting the members of your team. Those are some kick-ass SOBs."

A peculiar expression crossed Mike's face, but it was gone in an instant.

"Good. We're doing another favor for Uncle Sam right now, babysitting a package as it heads to its final destination. The contents are specialized computer boards, which is all you need to know at the moment. We have about two days before we make

Hong Kong—have to swing by Ho Chih Minh City to offload the helicopter. I suggest that you use that time to get familiar with our people and draw your weapons and gear. Vanner will fill you in on any other questions you may have."

"Of course, sir, but I doubt all of that will take two days. What can I get started on in the meantime?" Jace asked.

"If you're that eager, why don't you review the in-country briefings that are going to be distributed to the Keldara for their details and accuracy? You can coordinate with Patrick and the girls on those as well. Also, what do you know about the black markets in the region?" Mike asked.

"I'm most current on Singapore and China in general, particularly Hong Kong, but I know people who know people. Tell me what you're looking for, and I'll see what I can find out."

"We're supposed to be meeting with an 'Arun Than' in Hong Kong. I'd really like to know everything about him before we reach port," Mike replied.

"Understood. I'm on it."

"Good, I look forward to the briefing. Patrick, when you see Adams, send him my way and tell him the position's been filled."

"I will, but he'll probably find you first. Said his guy wasn't available, but he had something else you'd want to know about. If we see him, I'll boot him in your direction."

"All righty." Mike stood up and nodded at both of them. "Time to go talk like a pirate. Or at least to one."

Jace and Vanner both stood as well. Once the Kildar had left the room, Jace turned to Vanner.

"Hey, did I put a foot in it by mentioning Russia? I mean, that footage that made the Internet was almost as unbelievable as your story about the Keldara."

"That op was a hard one," Vanner said with a shrug. "We lost a lot of good people on it. Don't worry about it—you couldn't have known."

"Acknowledged. Either way, I have the feeling that life is going to get a lot more interesting."

"You don't know the half of it. So what's up with you? Not happy transferring back to First CivDiv?"

"Yes and no. It's the old saying all over again: when you're in the shit, all you want to do is complete the mission and get out, and when you're out, all you think about is when can you go back in."

"Spoken like a true leatherneck. Come on, let's head below and get your 782 gear," Vanner said.

"It'll be good to get my hands on an MEU again. Maybe you guys even have a Kimber model for me. Think we'll be needing anything heavier?"

"Hard to say at the moment. You prefer an M4?"

"You know I can use it, but I prefer a shotgun with a mixed load for anything in the bush. Benelli's fine, or a Mossberg or Remington if that's not available."

"Let's go see what we got. On the way, I can tell you the bad news about most of the girls..."

Vanel was walking down to the impromptu mess hall that had been set up for the Keldara, intending to get his meal and eat up on the main deck. Along the way, he passed Vanner talking to a tall man with jet-black, shoulder-length hair and dark blue eyes.

"And here's one of them now. Vanel Kulcyanov, this is Jace Morgan. Jace will be working with us while we're in the region."

Vanel shook the taller man's hand.

"Is pleasure to meet you, sir."

"You too, Vanel." The two men continued on their way, and Vanel continued on his. His next surprise, however, almost took his breath away—literally.

"Hello, Vanel," a soft voice said on his right as he entered the mess hall.

"Xatia?" Vanel stared the small girl for a few seconds before closing his gaping mouth. "What are you doing here?"

"Sergeant Vanner requested more intel girls to come here. When volunteers were asked for, I said yes."

"Oh...of course." Vanel tried to get himself under control.

He'd known other girls were inbound, but not why, although he should have put two and two together. He certainly hadn't expected Xatia to be one of them.

"Is something wrong?" the girl's lush lips compressed in the cutest pout he'd ever seen. "You do not seem happy to see me."

"No! I mean, no—I am, uh, very pleased that you are here. It is, um, very good to see you..." Aware that he was babbling, Vanel jerked his head toward the mess hall. "I am going to get something to eat. Would—would you care to join me?"

"I cannot, Gretznya is going over current operations with us—oh no, I should have already been there! Do not worry, I won't tell anyone you were the reason why I was late!" Before he could reply, the short, shapely girl turned and ran down the hall, leaving a dumbfounded Vanel staring after her.

"That is quite all right! You could tell anyone you wanted..." His words trailed off, and Vanel felt a blush heat his cheeks. He glanced around, hoping no one had seen him just make a complete fool of himself. His heart pounded, and blood rushed through his ears. The feeling was as just as intense as combat, but for a completely different reason.

Vanel had had a crush on Xatia Mahona ever since he had first laid eyes on her, when she was five and he was six. From that moment on, he hadn't looked at another girl. They had grown up together, and for the past year he had been working up his nerve to begin the request for her betrothal. Two things stood in his way; first, he had wanted to pass his first test of combat. The farming he knew like the back of his hand, but he had wanted to face and conquer the test of blood.

The second one was much more difficult; facing Xatia's parents, particularly Mother Mahona. With any luck, his parents would talk to hers, and he wouldn't even have to be present. That was how it had been done for generations, and who was he to mess around with tradition?

Shaking his head, Vanel walked into the mess hall to find two other members of his team, Yosif and Marko, sitting before full plates. While the Keldara families often ate together, the Kildar had mandated that while on operations, especially ones with a flexible timetable, food should be available at all times for team members. And the chef that had come with the *Big Fish* was very adaptable. Although many of the Keldara were open to trying new foods, they also appreciated a taste of home—even if it wasn't anything close to what their own Mothers could cook up.

"Glad to see you could leave your cover long enough to join us, new fish," Marko teased. Yosif's and his encounter with the shack wall was already fodder among the teams, with them already suffering a good amount of ribbing.

Vanel simply shrugged as he joined them.

"Was not our fault reinforcements were too slow to help us to finish the sweep. We simply made ourselves comfortable while waiting for you."

Marko snorted, while Yosif smiled at the comeback.

"Have you heard the news?" the team leader asked.

Having just taken a large bite of his *golubtsy*, or stuffed cabbage roll, Vanel shook his head.

"We are to stay in this area for at least ten days, maybe even a fortnight." Yosif looked around to make sure no one else was listening. "I even heard from Daria that we are heading to Hong Kong."

"Where's that?" Vanel asked.

"Former British colony city that was 'given' back to China in 1997. Check the e-mail on your tablet, it's all in the summary the girls worked up. Also, there is a new officer on board—"

"Yes, a Jace Morgan," Vanel said. "I was introduced to him in the hallway by Sergeant Vanner." He tried not to look too pleased by the surprised expressions on his teammates' faces. Instead, he took another bite of the cabbage roll. *Not even close to Mother's,* he thought.

"*You* met him?"

Vanel swallowed his food and nodded.

"I am sure the sergeant was simply being polite."

"Anyway, you are supposed to please review the data and let

me know if you have questions. You can also follow up on your iPad if you wish."

"Of course." The other two kept talking, but Vanel's mind was whirling with the possibilities. *Ten to fourteen days more on boat... with Xatia!*

A broad smile spread across his face as he took another bite of the cabbage roll, suddenly not minding its taste in the least.

Wiping blood from his fingers with a towel, Mike handed the wet cloth to Dmitri as he left Yeung Tony's room, his blood boiling.

Usually interrogations were pretty easy. Since the subject only had to live long enough to give up the necessary information, there were no restraints on how far Mike could go to extract said information. The Albanians and Russians had been pushovers—a couple of shots to a knee or elbow with a sledgehammer or pistol, and they cracked like walnuts.

But Yeung Tony was proving to be another story. Unfortunately, Mike did need him alive for now, since it would be impossible to set up a meeting with Arun Than by himself. Without Tony to vouch for him, they'd get nowhere. Unfortunately, the Malay also seemed to have figured that out, and was being as difficult as possible without getting himself killed.

Mike had been working on the pirate for the last hour, trying to make him more cooperative, but after a soldering iron applied to several areas, improvised tooth extraction, and several other persuasion techniques, the fuckhead was still resisting. He'd given up everything—*except* how to contact Than.

Taking a break, Mike stalked down the corridor of the yacht, figuring he'd go visit Tony's whore. Maybe she would see reason where her boyfriend did not—and even if she didn't, he would have a hell of a time trying to convince her.

As Mike walked through the corridors of the opulent yacht, greeting various Keldara as they passed, he began cooling down. To the point where he decided a change of plan was in order. He called the kitchen to get an update on a very specific dinner for two he'd ordered earlier that afternoon. Then he went to his stateroom, shit, showered, and shaved, and threw on tan linen slacks, a black silk button-down shirt, and woven deck shoes.

When he received word that the meal was ready, Mike told them where to deliver it, and strolled down to where Soon Yi was being held.

Oleg was on duty there, and stiffened to attention as Mike approached.

"Oleg."

"Kildar."

A rattle made Mike look down the corridor, where a crew-member, pushing a wheeled cart, approached. "Right on time. I am going inside to interrogate the prisoner."

The big man was already unlocking the door. The service person stopped at the two men. "Everything is here as ordered, sir."

Mike nodded. "Thank you. I'll take it from here."

A frown crossed Oleg's face as he took in the place settings, covered dishes, and bottle of wine chilling in a bucket of ice. "...Kildar?"

"Yes, Oleg?"

"All this is necessary to interrogate the prisoner?"

"There's a saying back in the States; if you can't dazzle 'em with brilliance, then baffle them with bullshit."

A blond eyebrow raised at the phrase. "Surely that is not what you are serving to her—"

Mike chuckled. "Hardly." He lifted the largest cover to reveal a succulent roast duck in orange sauce, with Chinese five-spice added for a bit of kick. "Katya told me she didn't touch any of the food or drink we gave her earlier. Simply put, yesterday we tried hard, now I'm trying a—softer approach."

"Very well, Kildar." Oleg opened the door for him.

"Thank you." Mike paused in the darkened doorway. "There will be no need to open this door unless I specifically order you to, understood?"

Oleg nodded.

"Yes, Kildar."

He slipped inside and closed the door, hearing the huge Keldara lock it from the outside. Mike stood with his back to the entrance for a moment, letting his senses adjust to the room. Shapes began to materialize in the gloom—a sheet-covered form in a corner of the bed, a chair in the middle of the room. Sounds came to him as well—the most important one being the steady breathing of the person in the bed.

Mike was ninety percent sure she was faking it.

Anyone who lived on the streets developed a subconscious awareness of their surroundings almost immediately. Those who didn't, died—it was that simple. Soon Yi had been around the block, and Mike was sure she had awakened the moment the door had opened. The big question now was would she come at him soft or hard. If he'd broken her with the waterboarding, she would be soft. If not, she'd come at him hard. If Mike had been a betting man, he'd have said hard.

Time to remove the option, he thought. Mike hit the lights and wheeled the cart into the center of the room. He saw the sheet tremble a bit, but she didn't move.

"I know you're awake under there, so you might as well come out. I brought dinner." Mike removed the cover again, letting the heavenly fragrance of roast duck waft over to her. Smaller dishes held saffron rice and an array of fresh tropical fruit.

Slowly, Soon Yi's head emerged from underneath the sheet. "What are you doing?"

"I'm going to eat. Why don't you join me? There's plenty here, and you must be starving by now." Grabbing the wine from the ice, Mike examined the gewürztraminer with a cocked eyebrow. He would have preferred a beer, but the chef had politely but firmly insisted on pairing the wine with their meal. He checked underneath the table. There, as instructed, was a second bucket filled with iced bottles of Mountain Tiger. With a shrug, he tore the foil off the bottle, then began uncorking it.

"No . . . I mean, why are you doing this?" she asked.

"Because I'm hungry." Freeing the cork with a *pop*, Mike filled both wine glasses. He set the bottle back down in the bucket and grabbed the chair from the makeup desk. Setting it down, he picked up the carving knife and fork and pointed with the knife at the edge of the bed across the tray from him. "Come. Sit. Eat."

Without waiting for her to move, he began expertly carving the duck breast. It was quite easy, since the meat was falling off the bone. "Maybe I will keep the chef onboard a while longer," he muttered.

Even while carving, Mike was aware of the woman as she slowly crawled to the edge of the bed. She was wearing a short, dark blue silk robe that had been among the clothes they had supplied her with. He heard her pick up the butter knife that was part of her place setting, exchange it for the fork, then exchange that for a pair of chopsticks.

"Wise decision." He looked up, making her flinch, and smiled. "Shall I serve?"

She stared at him through slitted eyes. "You eat some first."

Mike shook his head. "It's the same food for both of us—here, I'll show you." He picked up her wine glass and took a mouthful, screwing up his face as he did.

"See—you did poison it!" she accused.

Mike swallowed with an effort. "No—" He coughed. "—it's just *much* sweeter than I'd expected." He extended the glass. "And I'm still standing. Try it."

She took the glass and sniffed at its contents, then tentatively sipped it. Her face also screwed up into a cute little frown, as the front of her robe slipped open a bit. "You are right, far too sweet. I don't suppose . . . you have any beer?"

Mike raised his eyebrows. "A girl after my own heart." He removed the wine bucket from the cart and replaced it with the bucket of beers from underneath. He carved the wax off and removed the cork, then offered her the bottle. "This should be more to your liking."

She drank, slowly at first, then more deeply, her eyes widening as she swallowed. "That is—incredible!"

"Careful now, don't go crazy with it," Mike warned as she tipped the bottle up again.

"Why not—it will probably make what's going to happen next more bearable," she said when she'd lowered the bottle again.

Mike had been opening his own bottle of Mountain Tiger, and looked steadily up at her. "Well, since what's happening now is dinner, I think we'll be able to manage that without too much difficulty, right?"

Her eyes flicked to the food. "Again, you first," she said as she took another swig.

"Fine by me." Picking up her plate, Mike filled it with duck breast in sauce, rice, and slices of fresh papaya, mango, pineapple, and star fruit. He cut the breast with his fork, speared a piece, and brought it to his mouth. "Damn...that is good." He tried another bite with some rice, and enjoyed it even more. "I think I've changed my mind. You can watch me eat all of this instead."

She licked her lips—a sight Mike appreciated. "Perhaps—since you seem to be all right—I will have some."

Mike offered her the plate, which she took and set back down on the cart. She picked up her chopsticks again, and her gaze rose to meet his. "Enjoy."

She smiled briefly at that, then attacked her plate with vigor. Mike ate sparingly, making sure to keep her plate full as well as the cold beers coming. After three helpings—of everything, including the beer—Soon Yi dropped her chopsticks, sat back on her elbows, and belched.

She giggled and covered her mouth with a small hand. "You probably think that is rude."

Mike shook his head—Jace had given him a crash course in Chinese table etiquette. "On the contrary, I believe that means the food was good, right? I'll have to let the chef know."

Soon Yi pushed herself back up just enough to grab her latest beer. "Who *are* you?"

Mike smiled. "Just another crazy round-eye, that's all."

She smiled back, then frowned in mock annoyance. "Who has enough men and guns to take pirates down in their home waters? Who has—" she lifted her beer bottle, "—enough connections to bring in the beer that's being sold on the black market for two hundred pesos per bottle? You're anything but a crazy round-eye..."

"What about you?" Mike asked. "You don't seem like the typical Southeast Asian streetwalker. And why'd you try so hard to hide the fact that you speak English?"

Soon Yi shrugged. "What did you expect—the biggest pirate group in the area..." she took several swallows of beer, then belched again. "That no one in their right mind would screw with, all taken apart like...like..." She drained the bottle and set it on the cart with a *clank*! "like it was a child's fort made of pillows. If any of my regular customers find out I speak English, they think it means I think I'm somehow better than them. It makes them mean. If I told you that, I thought it would get me killed."

"And now?" Mike asked, raising his own bottle to his lips.

"Now...I have the chance to thank you for sparing my life..." She rose off the bed, the short robe hanging open as she came around the cart, pushing it aside to sit in his lap. "Now you want Asian delight?" she asked as she rubbed his chest, then began unbuttoning his shirt with deft twists of her fingers.

"Well, I'd be lying if I said the thought hadn't crossed my mind—" was all Mike could say before she kissed him. Her mouth was hot and sweet, the spice of the duck sauce mingling pleasantly with the tang of the Mountain Tiger beer.

Caught off guard for a moment, Mike recovered quickly, darting his tongue between her lips. She opened her mouth wider and welcomed him in as her hands finished unbuttoning his shirt. One spidered its way down his chest and stomach, heading for his fly, while her other hand held the back of his head in place while she kept kissing him.

Mike's hands were anything but idle either; he barely had to touch the robe before it fell off, revealing the rest of the taut, athletic body that had been hinted at on the deck the night before. Despite being Asian, she had small but full, round breasts with small nipples. He grew even harder at the sight, but restrained himself.

"You want me love you long time?" she whispered in his ear.

"Sure, but without the broken English cliché," he replied.

"You'd be amazed at how that turns on American tourists," she said.

"Who said I was an American?" With that Mike grabbed her tight ass with both hands and stood up, lifting her with him. Soon Yi gasped in surprise and threw her arms around his neck, while her legs snaked around his waist. The silk robe slipped down around her waist, but he made sure to keep it with them as he walked toward the bed.

"You have that kind of look about you . . . like you expect everyone else to submit to your demands . . ." She whispered in between nibbles on his ear.

"Oh? And would you?" He asked as he set her down on the silk sheets.

"Since you could kill me and feed me to the sharks, and no one would know, it would be in my best interests, too . . . ohh . . ." her voice became more breathy as Mike used the robe to massage her breasts. Rubbing first one, then the other with the smooth silk, making her arch her back as her nipples stiffened under his expert attention.

"Well, you've seen how bad I can be . . . I think I'll show you just how good I can be too . . ." Mike kept up the silken massage while his other hand gently explored between her legs. She moaned more loudly and spread them wider.

Mike didn't need any more of an invitation. Sliding down, he began flicking at her pussy with his tongue, just enough to tantalize her without giving any true satisfaction. And all the while, he kept caressing her firm, high breasts through the sheer silk. He knew from experience how aroused a woman could get from that, and judging by Soon Yi's quickening moans, she was just as susceptible.

Soon Yi responded immediately, pressing his head down between her silken thighs while squirming with delight as he lapped her. After a few licks up, down, and from side-to-side, Mike curled his tongue into a U-shape and teased out the swollen bud of flesh he knew was there. He teased it unmercifully, alternating sucking on it and blowing across it. He drew it back and forth, in and out until she fairly screamed with pleasure, but hadn't come yet.

After several intoxicating minutes, during which his tongue was about to go numb, she pulled away and sat up. "My turn." Pulling him upright, she laid a trail of hot kisses down his chest to his pants, where she unbuttoned him and drew his pants down, maneuvering around the definite bulge there. Mike was pleased at his foresight in not wearing any underwear.

"Mmm." Stroking his erect shaft, she played with the tip of him, flicking her tongue out to play with his head the way he had played with her before. One of her hands massaged his balls as skillfully as if she was holding a pair of Baoding balls, while the other worked his shaft like, well, like a pro, to be perfectly honest. But that didn't mean Mike wasn't enjoying himself.

Before he could say anything, she leaned forward and placed her wet lips on the head of his cock. Undulating her neck, she cradled his head with her tongue while varying the pressure of her lips around it. The feeling was unlike anything he had ever experienced, and Mike almost lost himself in the rush of pleasure she was giving. However, he brought himself back from the edge to keep an eye on her, although she was making even that very simple act very difficult.

She took him deeper into her mouth, and soon Mike found himself being blown quite expertly. Although he would have expected that her rather small mouth wouldn't have been able to handle him, she deep-throated him with relative ease, only gagging once before settling into a natural rhythm. She even played with his tip, sliding it around her cheeks before going down to the base of his shaft. He let her go for another few minutes, and even let her talented tongue work its magic on his balls for a bit, swirling all around them.

Even though Mike was enjoying the hell of of it, after his brief lapse of concentration earlier, he maintained situational awareness of her at all times. That was one of the ways he could delay his orgasm for as long as he wanted. Her "seduction" of him was what made this whole scenario even more exciting—he knew this sexy Asian whore was anything but a prostitute, and given what he had done to her earlier, he figured she'd probably like nothing more than to kill him if she ever got the chance. That adrenaline high, mixed with the sex, was a combination he couldn't beat with a whip—although maybe he'd try that next time.

He did, however, make her work for it. About the time he figured she might get lockjaw, he gently pulled out, every inch of him tingling. His erection was still strong, and he tapped the tip of his dick on the swollen lips of her pussy. She pushed her hips off the bed, arching to meet him.

"Please ... please ..." she moaned.

After sheathing his member, Mike used his tip with near-surgical skill, inserting it just far enough to widen her lips, then pulling out again. The movement was just enough to excite the vulva and cause an almost overwhelming desire in any woman for the rest of him. He had played this game with several of the local girls, and it never failed to drive them crazy. One of them had even chased him out of the bedroom, still stark naked, when an incursion alert had forced him to interrupt their sex session before he was really able to get started.

This time, however, he would be practicing a variation of *coitus interruptus*, although not for the usual reason. He alternated his strokes, gradually going deeper inside her, although he was careful to keep the pressure on her clit and labia. Since she had stimulated his head so well, it was now numb for all intents and purposes, allowing him to ride her for as long as he wanted.

However, he kept up his odd thrusting, first shallow, then deeper, alternating them, but not settling into any sort of typical rhythm that she could enjoy. Indeed, she groaned and moved her hips in frustration as he continued tantalizing her, but Mike was just as determined to prevent her from enjoying this at all.

Finally, Mike had had enough, although to judge from Soon Yi's excited moans, she could have gone all night. He slowly withdrew from her one last time, then reared up and left the bed, leaving her gasping and staring at him in shock.

"Where—where are you going?"

"This has been delightful, but I'm afraid there are other matters aboard ship that require my attention." Mike pulled his pants back on and zipped up. "But don't worry—" he said as he pulled his shirt on. "—I'm sure I'll see you again."

And with that, he grabbed the cart, wheeled it out the door, and was gone, leaving a puzzled—and very frustrated—Soon Yi behind.

After her second encounter with the Kildar, Soon Yi had wrestled with the turmoil of emotions coursing through her.

Out of everything that had happened, the sex with the Westerner was actually the least of her worries. She had been raped while still a teenager, by one of her countrymen almost a decade ago. He had never been caught. Oddly, and although she knew it made no sense, she sometimes felt like she owed that man her thanks. Since she would never be considered properly marriageable after that, it had been a big reason for her entering the intelligence service.

Along with that, her father had been profoundly disappointed in her, as they had taken the risk of violating China's one-child policy to replace their son, who had been killed in a traffic accident, Instead of the replacement son they craved, they had a daughter instead. Soon Yi was raised in an environment that created a classic closet narcissist; craving acceptance and affection from men, but unable to reciprocate in kind. As she was also very intelligent, once she recognized this, she did everything she could to erect a wall between herself and her emotions, suppressing them in order to excel at her job, the only thing left that gave her any satisfaction.

None of this made what she and the American had done any more acceptable, but Soon Yi justified the act as part of her duty. She had played the swallow before, and had seduced more than one man on other assignments when necessary. It was simply part of what she needed to do to complete her mission—just like posing as a prostitute to gain access to Yeung Tony had been.

Because of that same iron-hard commitment, she had excelled

during her training. Her dedication to cold reading and analyzing a subject were what had allowed her to see through Katya's attempted ruse. Now she applied those same skills to what she had just participated in. That, however, was where she was encountering cognitive dissonance.

First and foremost, she wasn't sure who was seducing whom. This "Kildar" had exhibited all of the classic signs of arousal and commitment—at least in the act itself—but his leaving before his achieving climax—or at least giving her one—was unprecedented, at least in her experience. There had been nothing wrong with her technique. There never was—every man she had set out to conquer had succumbed to her charms with ease. Which made this man all the more puzzling.

And the second issue—which she was loath to admit to herself— was that he had been good at what he did... *damn* good. Even now there was an itch deep inside her that was begging to be scratched. And there was really only one way to do that. One of the reasons Soon Yi was such a good operative was her complete divorcement of the act of sex from any emotion whatsoever. But that was before she had encountered someone like this Kildar...

Soon Yi went to the shower to clean up, disturbed by the thoughts that kept running through her mind. If her control found out what had happened, he would accuse her of becoming emotionally involved, and have her removed from the mission.

The very idea is ridiculous! she thought. *He's just another* gwai-lo— *a talented one—but another one nonetheless. My mission is clear. It is obvious he enjoys the sexual relationship, and that is what he shall continue to receive in order to deepen the relationship, such as it is.*

As she thought, Soon Yi had unconsciously moved the shower wand down between her legs. Now, switching it to pulse, she let the jet of water stimulate her already sensitive parts until she shuddered and leaned against the wall, gasping as her orgasm overtook her. And although Mike's face rose in her mind, she banished the vision of him just as firmly, replacing that with her evaluation of him based on what she had seen—and experienced—of him so far.

He is used to dominating, to being in control. He enjoys it, enjoys causing fear in others—men, women, it doesn't matter. So, how would he react to someone who resists him more—vigorously?

Afterward, she cleaned herself up and reported in to headquarters. The conversation was brief:

"This is Black Chrysanthemum reporting. I have initiated a sexual relationship with the mercenary leader."

"Does he suspect anything?"

"No, he is very—single-minded. He still believes that I am just a prostitute who was involved with Yeung Tony."

There was a slight pause on the other end, which struck Soon Yi as odd. "I have received information from my superior regarding this new development in your mission."

"Yes?"

"Not only are you to maximize your relationship with this 'Kildar,' and report any information you discover, but you are also under orders to ensure that no harm is to come to him."

"I—I understand." Soon Yi could not fathom why that particular order had been given, but then again, it did not matter. It had been given, and she would carry it out to the best of her ability.

"What is the status of the package?"

"They want me to try to convince Tony to set up the meeting with his contact in Hong Kong. I imagine that they are going to attempt to sell it there."

"Remain attached to the package at all costs. Again, maintain the relationship with your secondary target, and ensure his safety. We will ensure that the proper authorities are notified of your presence once you arrive in the city."

"Understood. Black Chrysanthemum out."

Soon Yi broke the connection, then quickly stripped the antenna and batteries out of her dress. Looking around for a suitable hiding place, she ran the antenna around the edge of the mirror, and hid the sealed batteries deep inside the bar of soap they had given her. Once that was done, she went to bed, still trying to banish the errant thoughts about the *gwai-lo* Mike Jenkins out of her mind . . .

CHAPTER SEVEN

Whistling with good humor, Adams strolled down the hallway toward Mike's stateroom the next morning. Seeing the open door, he rapped knuckles on the doorjamb.

"Hey Ass-boy, you got a minute?"

Behind his small desk, Mike looked up from his tablet.

"Sure, come on in."

Adams walked in, grabbing another chair and setting it in front of the desk before plopping himself down.

"Met the new guy. He seems all right, even for a jarhead."

"Well, you still get along with Vanner, right?" Mike asked with a smile. "Anyway, since Force Recon's done the most cross-service training out of all the spec ops, I expect he'll be able to keep up and then some. Whatever happened to your guy?"

"That's what I wanted to talk to you about." Adams leaned forward in his chair. "It seems Liu got out of the military two years ago, and into something much more lucrative."

The beginning of a frown crossed Mike's forehead.

"I'm listening."

"Turns out he's head of security for the largest import company in Hong Kong. If it can be brought into China and sold for a profit, they want it. I also found this article on the Internet that says beer is the number one alcoholic drink over there."

Mike's frown grew larger.

"Wait a minute—*you* actually researched something? On the Internet? You know that involves computers and stuff, right? Why do I feel like I should be worried about that?"

"Okay, okay, I actually had one of the girls pull the info together, but that's not important. What is important is that I set up a meeting with my buddy, take him a couple six-packs of Mountain Tiger, he kicks it up the chain, and boom! We gain entry into a huge new market for our beer."

Mike expression made him look like he'd just been pole-axed.

"You? You? *You* want to negotiate a Mountain Tiger distribution contract for *China*? That seems like it falls a bit outside your qualifications."

"Not quite, see, here's what I was thinking—"

"As I recall, didn't you fall asleep the one time you sat in on a meeting about the brewery?"

"*That* wasn't my fault—I had been informed there was going to be a tasting session."

"And didn't Mother Lenka end up chasing you out of the brewery with a stick?"

Adams spread his hands in a "what-can-you-do" gesture. "You know Mother Lenka. She overreacts to everything..."

"And would this negotiating involve, say, roaming around Hong Kong getting drunk, laid and probably gambling...? Sort of like, oh, *VEGAS*? You do remember Vegas, right? Oh, wait, no you *DON'T* remember Vegas *at all*... And when you're drunk you're the *WORST* negotiator in the *WORLD*..."

"I won't be negotiating anything, so you can relax on that front. We just have the girls whip up a quick packet of information on our products—hell, they can probably e-mail one to us from home. I give it to him, along with contact information for the brewery, and Mother Lenka or someone back home who handled the negotiations in Vegas can take it from there."

"Let me repeat. Hong Kong. You do realize the Keldara have *never* been to a city like that. That I'm going to need all of my guys present and frosty to keep them in line. Although, expecting you to be present and frosty under those circumstances is the real silliness."

"Yeah, but that's what you brought this Morgan guy onboard for, right?"

"Not really—he's supposed to be regional intel, not oversee a team. He just got here, and none of us save Vanner really know him. Yes, he looks great on paper, but does he still have the skills? You never know that kind of stuff until the shit goes down, and if he doesn't, it's too late."

"Yeah, I know. But even then, you take care of yourself, too—as you've proven time and time again." Adams shrugged. "When it comes down to it, Mike, I'm a door-kicker and ass-whipper, pretty much in that order. Give me a hard target to take down, and I'm your man. But riding in limos to meet black marketeers in fancy hotels and talk about computer boards, not so much. This way, I can also get something done while you're out chasing your intel."

"If you were planning to beat your friend into working with us, then yes, you're the perfect guy for the job. But I'm still having a hard time wrapping my head around you selling our beer."

"Hell, Mountain Tiger's so good it practically sells itself. All I'm doing is sitting down with an old friend and giving him an opportunity to make his company and ours some money."

"I was really counting on your ugly mug being there to ensure that this Arun Than guy doesn't try to double-cross us."

Adams shrugged. "Just take Oleg—he'll do just as well in the hardass role as I would, probably better."

"Promise me this is *not* going to turn out like Vegas."

Adams stared back at him, the picture of innocence.

"Of *course* not. SEAL's honor. This is a simple meeting, in, out, no muss, no fuss."

"Yeah . . . don't forget I know all about the honor of a SEAL when it comes to furlough." Mike narrowed his eyes, as if trying to see inside his master chief's head, before nodding curtly. "All right. But you *will* stay in touch. If the shit goes down, I expect you to double time it back if I need you."

"Aye aye, Captain Crunch."

Soon Yi was dressed and sitting at the edge of her bed when Katya returned at mid-day. This time the blond woman wore a more relaxed outfit of navy slacks and a white, short-sleeved blouse.

"How are you this morning, Ms. Yi?"

"I am—all right. I have considered your proposal, and I think that I may be able to help your—Kildar."

Katya's elegant eyebrow arched in surprise. "Please continue."

"I believe that I can convince Yeung Tony to work with your people."

Katya nodded. "How?"

"We were—closer on the island than I had revealed at first. I—I did not want that to become known to the Kildar, for fear he would further torture me to force Tony to tell him what he wanted to know." Soon shook her head sadly. "It wouldn't have worked, of course."

Katya shook her head. "Probably not. So, why do you think you can persuade him now?"

"Because I believe I can appeal to Tony's self-interest. If I may ask, what were you planning on doing with the three of us once you had gotten the information you are seeking?"

"Most likely you will be turned over to the authorities in Hong Kong, who will deal with you as they see fit."

"That is something I am sure Tony would not like at all. Please, let me speak with him. If I can offer your guarantee that you will not turn him over to the Chinese authorities, I believe he will do as you ask."

"I will discuss this with the Kildar. I will be right back." Katya turned and walked out of the room, closing the door behind her.

"What's your take on this?" Mike asked after Katya had filled him in on the conversation.

"I do not see the harm right now," Katya replied. "After all, your methods do not seem to be gaining you very much, are they?"

"Little fucker's durable, I'll give him that. I've got all the information I need, but he refuses to make the call to Than and set the meeting for his 'new personnel.'"

Katya rolled her eyes. "I cannot say that I blame him, since you probably plan to kill him the moment that is done."

"The thought had crossed my mind." Mike turned to the third person in the room. "Jace, your thoughts?"

"The black market in Hong Kong—hell, all of Southeast Asia, for that matter—operates on equal parts trust and distrust, if that makes any sense."

"Just like everywhere else in the world," Mike replied.

Jace nodded. "You will definitely need Tony breathing to confirm a meeting with Than. If he gets even a hint that something's not right, he'll disappear, and you won't have a dumpling's chance at dinnertime of finding them. Unless Vanner feels he can set up an audio suite of Tony's voice that will sound authentic, which is hard enough for another speaker. Not to mention any computer program will have a lot of trouble parsing vocal tone and inflection. Since he's disposable anyway, if you give Soon Yi the ammo of seeming to bargain for his life, she may be able to pull it off."

"And we still have not come up with anything on this woman other than her hooker story, right?" Mike asked.

Katya shook her head. "Correct. If she has a jacket, it is very well hidden."

"Crap. I could really use some leverage on her, instead of the other way around." Mike looked from Jace to Katya and shrugged a shoulder. "Set it up. Jace, work with Katya on this, watch the hooker as she talks with Tony. Let me know how it turns out." He turned back to his iPad.

Katya turned to the tall man. "Follow me."

"Yes, ma'am." Jace left the stateroom and walked behind the short, blond woman in silence. She didn't make small talk, and Jace didn't try either—along with the off-limits edict on the intel girls, Vanner had also warned him about Katya. *Too bad, as she is fucking gorgeous*, he thought while watching her hips sway under her slacks.

"You are better off keeping your mind off my ass and on the job at hand," she said without turning back.

Jace smiled in return. "I'm pretty good at multitasking when necessary." His attempt at humor only earned him a wintery glare. "Damn. Is it me, or did it just get fucking chilly in here?"

"It is definitely not you."

They headed through the ship until they came to a bedroom door guarded by a huge Keldara. He had a young face and hair so blond it was practically white. Jace nodded at him—he was still trying to learn all their names—and got a stolid nod in return.

Katya turned to him. "We are here. You will be additional security. I am sure you can act the part of a big, hulking American, right?"

"If pressed," Jace replied.

"We will escort her to the pirate's room and go from there. Keep your mouth shut. I will do the talking," Katya ordered.

"Affirmative."

"Stay right here. Open it, Oleg."

The man-mountain unlocked the door and Katya went inside. There was a brief conversation, leaving Jace alone with the Keldara. He scanned the big man quickly, not raising an eyebrow at the prosthetic foot. He'd known several operators who were just as deadly minus one limb. Sometimes they were even more so, as opponents tended to underestimate them.

He nodded at the room. "Is she always like that?"

A frown crossed the giant's face as he considered the question. "She works for Kildar. Answers only to him or Jay. Is much like Caucasian viper: deadly if provoked, so best to always approach with caution. I do not spend any more time around her than necessary."

"Good to know."

The guard nodded.

There was movement from inside the room, and a small Chinese woman emerged a moment later, followed by Katya. The prisoner barely glanced at either of the two men before dropping her gaze to the floor.

"This way." Keeping a firm grip on the other woman's arm, Katya marched her past the door guard. Jace fell into step behind the two women as they proceeded to the aft section, where the engine noise was muted but noticeable.

Katya took the Chinese hooker to a door guarded by two Keldara. She snapped a command at one of the guards, who unlocked and opened the door. The mingled stink of sweat, piss, and blood drifted out of the room.

"*Bundun!*" Soon ran inside the room. "Could one of you release him, please?"

Jace threw a questioning glance at Katya, who nodded. Taking out a SOG Spec-Elite folding lockblade, he flipped it open and stepped inside.

The stink was much stronger, combined with an underlying odor of burned flesh. The room was almost bare, containing only a chair and single bed. Although a tarp had been spread out underneath the chair; rusty, dark brown spatters marked the carpet and walls. A narrow doorway led to a tiny bathroom that had been stripped of any accouterments, and contained only a sink, toilet, and shower stall.

The prostitute was bent over the man, murmuring something Jace couldn't quite hear. "Step away, and keep your hands where I can see them," he said in Mandarin. She moved aside, and Jace got his first look at the captive.

The pirate was a fucking mess. His face had been severely battered, with his right eye swollen completely shut, and one ear missing, replaced by a stained red bandage. Trickles of dried blood crusted his mouth, and one side had a sunken look that Jace recognized as being caused by several missing teeth. He bent to cut the zip-ties restraining the man in the chair, freeing his feet first, then his arms. When he cut the last one, the Malay nearly fell over.

"Get out!" Soon Yi hissed. "He won't listen to me if any *gwai-los* are here!"

"Don't try anything stupid," Jace warned as he headed for the door.

"You're not staying in there?" Katya asked as he walked into the hallway. "What if she tries to kill him?"

"She wouldn't be stupid enough to off her meal ticket." Jace shook his head as he closed the door. "You said you guys are willing to try this her way; it's best to let her do it how she wants. He's already been brutalized by other men, and if he's seen relying on a woman to save him now, it just emasculates him further. Besides, you have the room wired for cameras and sound, right?" He continued off her nod. "So, if she can get what you want in private, what does it matter if she's watched or not?"

"I don't trust her, that is what matters. We shall see." Katya turned to the door and crossed her arms.

"Yeah, I bet you get that feeling a lot." Jace did the same with his arms and leaned against the wall.

The moment the door closed, Soon Yi's demeanor altered completely.

"Come on, come on, get up!" Appearing to care for the beaten pirate, she roughly hoisted him up, slinging an arm over her shoulder as she half-carried, half-dragged him to the bathroom. Yeung Tony's head lolled on his shoulders as he moved.

"What...what's going on?" The words were muffled, partly from his swollen jaw, partly because he was half-conscious.

Still holding on to him with one arm, Soon turned the cold sink tap on with the other. "What's going on is that you're going to set up this meeting with Arun Than for the *gwai-lo!*" she hissed.

"What are you—"

Before he could finish, she bent him over and plunged his head under the tap. The pirate twisted and tried to squirm away, but Soon Yi had twisted his other arm up to his shoulder blade. It was the one the man had worked on with the hammer, and she noted the broken fingers had been expertly splinted and bound. After ten seconds, she let him up.

"What the fuck are you doing?" Tony gasped after spluttering and choking for a few seconds.

"Trying to save your worthless life, dog," she muttered into his ear, just above the running water. "Just do what they say and set up the damn meeting."

"Why should I do that? So that *setan* can put a bullet in my head? Why are you here? Are you working for them now?"

Soon twisted his arm higher, making the man gasp in pain. "I'm working for myself, no one else. If you give them what they want, I can ensure that you will not only get off this boat in one piece, but you'll be extradited to Indonesia, or maybe even back to Malay, rather than standing trial for armed robbery and murder in China—"

"What? What are you talking about? Why wouldn't they try me for piracy?"

"Because, you stupid pig, China doesn't have any antipiracy laws! Instead, they try a person for the related crimes committed during an act of piracy. You stand trial for those multiple counts of kidnapping and murder, and you won't get a slap on the wrist—you'll go to prison for life if you're lucky, or receive the death sentence if not. But take their offer, and I can get you out of Hong Kong and into an easier court to the south."

"How the fuck are you going to do that? Who are you?"

"That's not important. What's important is how badly you want to live."

Soon kept him bent over the sink for a few moments, letting the thug think his situation through. After a few seconds, he nodded. "All right. I'll do it."

"And not a fucking word to any of the *gwai-los* or I'll feed you to the sharks myself. Just smile and do whatever they say, you got it?"

Tony nodded again, then jerked as Soon tore a strip of cloth from his tattered shirt.

"All right, let's get you cleaned up a bit, so it looks like I actually took care of your worthless ass." She began wiping the dried blood and snot off his face. After a few minutes' work, she led him back to the chair and sat him down. "Remember, no bullshit, no funny business. Set the meeting, and tell them both you and I will be there. I'll handle it from there."

Cleaned up, Tony seemed to have gotten a bit of his fire back, even as beaten as he was. "Why should I trust you?"

"Because you do not have any other choice." She turned from him, walked to the door, and knocked. It opened to reveal Katya's unsmiling face.

"He will make the call," Soon said.

A few minutes later, Jace, Vanner, and Katya were all hunched over a computer, trying to watch the conversation between Soon Yi and Yeung Tony.

"Can you remove the running water?" Jace asked. "With them talking in the bathroom, I can't see her lips move. Not that I'd be able to read them speaking Mandarin or Cantonese anyway, but I also can't hear shit over it."

"We're trying, but she wasn't speaking very loudly in the first place, so the water's drowning out their conversation. We're lucky we picked up anything at all," Vanner replied.

"Wait a minute. Tony is speaking normally there." Katya replayed a snippet of the feed. "What did he just say?"

Jace listened to it twice more to be sure.

"He's asking her what the fuck she's doing. He sounds surprised. An odd reaction, particularly if they're supposed to be as close as she claims they are."

Katya glared at the frozen picture of the woman on the monitor.

"Something about this woman is not right, but I cannot put my finger on it."

"Maybe you should chemically interrogate her," Vanner suggested.

Katya shook her head.

"That is too unreliable. If she is another operator, she will have been taught how to nullify the effects. And besides, she has gotten us what we wanted. I will simply keep a close eye on her during the operation." She smiled tightly. "It looks like the Kildar will have me on retainer for a few more days." Katya headed for the door. "Keep trying to wash the audio, and send me the best version you can get."

Jace exchanged a look with Vanner, both men sharing the same thought: *Oh, boy.*

A few hours later, Jace walked down the hall to the Kildar's office. The door was ajar, and he heard two voices inside; Mike's, and another woman's. It sounded like a logistics meeting, but from the flow of the conversation, it seemed that the young woman was doing most of the talking, with the Kildar providing "yesses" and "no's" when appropriate. Jace stood a respectful distance away, and waited for them to finish.

A few minutes later, the door opened and a tall girl walked out, maybe twenty years old if she was a day, and just as model-gorgeous as the rest of them. "Mr. Morgan," she said as she passed him in the hallway. Once again, Jace had to almost pinch himself at the scenario he'd found himself in.

Fuck, what's her name? Vanner had introduced her to him earlier as the Kildar's administrative assistant. As with all admin personnel, Jace figured he'd better get it right, or he'd be screwed in the future—and not in a good way.

"...Hello, Daria," he got out just in time as she walked down the hall.

"Come in, Captain. Something I can do for you?" Jace walked in to find Mike wiping a smile off his face.

"Something humorous come to mind, sir?"

Mike shook his head once.

"No, it's...I just realized with your rank, well, 'Captain Morgan.' I'm sure you got enough hell from your fellow team members."

"It was all in fun, sir—and it did get me more than a few rounds of free drinks. But everyone on my teams was always mission-first and foremost."

"Of course. What did you wish to see me about?"

"I have that update on the Chinese black market operations, including a focus on Hong Kong. I can send the file to your tablet if you wish, or we can go over it here and now."

"Send me the report, but why don't you give me the highlights right now. In particular, is there anything we need to be concerned about going into the city?"

"Yes, sir. The primary issue will be the firearms. Hong Kong has very strict gun control laws, with heavy prison sentences for anyone convicted of possessing an illegal firearm."

"Well, ours are legally obtained and licensed, as far as that goes."

"Yes, as a militia in Georgia, you're fine. In Hong Kong, not so much."

"But let me guess—criminals in the city have little to no problem obtaining black market guns whenever they wish."

"Like most of China, just about anything can be obtained if a person is willing to pay the price. Depending on the sort of officer or bureaucrat we encounter, we might be able to bribe our way out of a simple possession charge. But if we are caught pulling the trigger, getting away with it will be almost impossible. Given your connections with the U.S. government, if we are detained on a weapons-related charge, kicking this to higher-ups could be as much hindrance as help—"

"Particularly when the red tape starts spinning. The Chinese would love that; semi-rogue American ex-military running amuck in Hong Kong. I'm very aware of the bureaucracy issues. Along with news coverage, that's one of the things they pay me very well to avoid whenever possible. I only bring in the big government dogs in a situation that I cannot handle, or I suspect might spin out of even my control. Not that that ever happens, of course."

Jace smiled and nodded.

"Regarding our meeting, it looks like the on-site team will have to go in soft, with the assault team held in reserve nearby," Mike continued. "Besides, there are plenty of ways to obtain guns from the other side—sometimes even while they're carrying them. Anything else?"

"Not so much. As we are foreign tourists, we are supposed to report to the police within twenty-four hours of our arrival. However, I expect that you will want to forgo that little request."

"You expect right."

"Okay then. As to your other request: Arun Than. Not a lot to say about him on the record. He's what's called a fixer in local parlance: he brokers deals between parties looking to buy and sell for a cut of the payment. Usually he never holds anything for either party, just serves as the go-between. He's well connected throughout the entire Asian region, from Shanghai to Mumbai, and points north and south as well. He can move just about anything: currency, gems, gold, merchandise, cigarettes, even vehicles. His latest claim to fame was organizing the transport of a brand-new fifty-foot cigarette boat from the western side of China to Shanghai by truck, with absolutely no record of it ever happening. Everyone I've spoken to vouches for him, says he's a stand-up guy who will deal straight with parties on both sides of the transaction."

"And here I thought there was no honor among thieves," Mike said.

"Yeah, well, that and ten yuan will get you a cup of green tea in Shanghai. The most important thing to remember, sir, is that *mianzi*, or 'face' counts for a lot in this area of the world."

"I am aware of that."

"Of course, sir, however, what you may not be aware of is just how much of an Asian's very psyche is tied up in both it and *guanxi*, their version of social networking, which works very differently than for us Americans. For example, they might say 'yes' to a request, or defer it to a superior, although their manner and body language might be clearly saying 'no.' That means that the request isn't going to happen, but they feel the relationship is worth keeping enough to at least pay lip service to whatever is being asked for."

"I understand that the Chinese and Japanese almost never say 'no' straight out."

"Exactly. They'll tell you just about anything else, from 'we will take that under consideration' to 'I'll have to discuss this with my superiors' or 'that may not be very convenient.' The reason I'm bringing this up now is that I have heard that you are, well—the best way to put it is direct when you want to get something done."

"My reputation is preceding me again. Yes, since I find it's often the best way to handle a situation."

"Yes, sir, and in many cases I would agree. After all, we Marines are also typically not known for our delicate cultural sensibilities." Jace grinned. "However, Recon does things a bit differently. That's why we were so successful here during the Vietnam Conflict compared to other branches of the military. From General Tony Zinni's experiences as part of the Marine Advisory Group in country to his work during operation Provide Comfort after the first Gulf War, our mindset has always been to learn from and work with an indigenous populace whenever possible."

"Which I agree with completely," Mike replied. "Typically, I am polite as long as they are. When they are not, neither am I. Satisfactory?"

"Yes, sir."

Mike nodded. "All right. I'll take a look at your report, and let you know if I have any other questions."

"Yes, sir." Jace started to rise, then hesitated.

"Something else on your mind?"

"Yes . . . permission to speak freely, sir?"

Mike frowned. "Granted, and next time you don't have to ask. What's up?"

"It's about that pirate. He was worked over pretty good."

Mike leaned forward and rested his elbows on his desk. "Do you have a problem with my methods?"

Jace shook his head. "Not at all, sir. While I was pulling the market report, I also did some digging on him. Assault, armed robbery, drug smuggling, rape, kidnapping, sex slavery—that fucker would do anything to turn a buck. By the time I was finished, I was ready to go down there and spend some quality time with him myself."

"'Quality time.' That's good. So, what's the issue?" Mike asked.

"I was simply wondering what the chain-of-command is on that sort of interrogation."

"Ah." Mike leaned back in his chair. "All interrogations of any kind are carried out by me. I decide what degree of force to use and when to apply it. While I lead from the front, and would never ask anyone under my command to do anything that I wouldn't do, neither will I ask anyone to do something they are unwilling to do. In my experience, interrogations, particularly ones of that nature, often fall into that category. Are we clear?"

"Perfectly, sir."

The Kildar leaned forward again, his expression as dark and cold as a Georgian winter.

"Besides, if I asked anyone else to do it, I would deprive myself of the pleasure, and that is something I simply will not do. The bottom line, Captain, is that I'm not a nice man. I just play one on TV."

"Understood, sir."

And just like that, the darkness vanished, and Mike was his regular self again.

"All right then, let me know if there's anything else you need."

"Not at this time, thanks."

"Glad we had this little chat."

CHAPTER EIGHT

A little more than ten hours later, the *Big Fish* dropped anchor three nautical miles away from Victoria Harbor and the city of Hong Kong. Jace, Adams, Katya, and several of the Keldara stood on the starboard side, staring at the illuminated skyline glowing like a beacon of civilization in the darkness.

"Father of All…" Vanel breathed. "It lights up the entire night sky."

"It is amazing…to be so bright from this far away," Grenzya said.

"Hong Kong…you will never find a more wretched hive of scum and villainy," Jace said, earning shocked looks from the Keldara.

"How can you say that about something that looks so beautiful?" Martya asked.

"Often it is the most beautiful flowers that are the most deadly," he replied. "Like most major cities around the world, Hong Kong looks great from a distance, but once you get closer, its true nature becomes very apparent."

"Jesus, Morgan, don't scare 'em before we get there," Adams muttered. "It's just like any other big city."

"Sorry, Master Chief, but that's where you're wrong. The city-state of Hong Kong has played by a different set of rules than the rest of China, and the world, for that matter, for decades."

Jace's words were closer to the truth than anyone, including him, knew. Loosely translated as "fragrant harbor," the port city had been an anomaly ever since the British East India Company's first visit in 1699. Trade between Great Britain and China had quickly flourished, with the city rapidly growing as a result. Trade imbalances and deteriorating diplomatic relations over the next one hundred forty years had led to the First Opium War in 1839–42. The resulting Treaty of Nanking had ceded Hong Kong Island to the English in perpetuity, and the Brits had immediately founded Victoria City on it. The Second Opium War, fought from 1856–60, saw Kowloon Peninsula and Stonecutter's Island taken by Great Britain under the Convention of Peking. In 1898, Great Britain negotiated a ninety-nine-year lease of Lantau Island from China, making it a British port throughout much of the twentieth century, save for four years of occupation by the Japanese from 1941 to 1945.

After years of discussion, Hong Kong was returned to the People's Republic of China in 1997, ending 157 years of British rule. The transfer came with the understanding that the city would be administered as a "Special Administrative Region." This meant Hong Kong would retain its own laws and much autonomy to govern itself, except in matters of defense and foreign policy, for at least fifty years after the transfer.

In the fifteen years since, the city had solidified its place among the premier metropolises of the world. It had also weathered its share of problems, including economic scares like the 1997 Asian financial crisis, and health scares, such as the bird flu outbreak, also in that year, and the SARS crisis of 2003.

Constrained by its land boundaries, the city had expanded upward instead of outward, and its glittering skyline held the Keldara—and more than a few of the staring Americans—enthralled. But Jace was determined to make sure that everyone going into the city was aware of the dangers lurking beneath its bright, shiny façade.

"If I were you, I would probably treat this one step below tango territory. Hong Kong is a city built on commerce, but that doesn't mean it won't take care of its own. Not to mention chew up and spit out any *gwai-lo* that tries to interfere with it."

"What is that word, sir?" Vanel asked.

"It's a derogatory Chinese term for any outsider," Jace said with a slight grin. "It literally means 'white ghost.' You don't want me to get into a two-hour explanation of the secondary cultural meanings including, 'unimportant' and 'going to be gone long before anybody cares about its complaint.' Note the use of 'it,' which is a good way to think about how most Chinese view foreigners in general, as in, 'doesn't really exist,' 'foreign devil to be screwed over by superior Chinese intellect,' and 'somebody to sell shoddy silk, spices, and tea to because they're too uncultured to know the difference.' By the way, that's exactly how they viewed your Byzantine employers and what they called *them*. Two thousand years ago.

"It is unlikely that anyone would say it to your face, but don't take it personally if you happen to hear it. Make sure you review the primer I sent out about the strict firearms laws in the city. Hopefully, no one will have to use or even show them. Always keep your passports with you in a secure place, as the pickpockets here are very slick. Remember, even as foreign citizens, you are bound to obey the city's laws whenever possible. Hopefully we'll be in and out before we're even supposed to register with the police."

"Register with the *police*?" Adams said. "Is it mandatory?"

"Yes. And since we're skirting it, we should be gone before anyone notices. Just keep your wits about you, and you'll be fine. Just keep in mind that Lucas must have been to Hong Kong. As Obi-Wan said: 'You'll never find a more wretched hive of scum and villainy. We must be cautious.'"

Catching the confused glance between Vanel and Martya, Jace shook his head.

"Jeez, Adams, haven't you shown them *Star Wars* yet?"

They had approximately twenty hours before the meeting, and there was still a fair bit to do. Daria had handled accommodations and vehicle rental in the city, but had run into a potential logistics snag.

"Wait a minute, the hotel we're meeting Than at is where, exactly?" Mike asked.

"The Ritz-Carlton itself is on floors 103 to 118 of the International Commerce Center overlooking Victoria Harbor. The meeting is set up at a private room at Tin Lung Heen, a Cantonese restaurant on the 102nd floor."

"Great, that severely limits our access and egress points if we have to unass in a hurry, or even worse, get out ahead of a building lockdown," Mike said.

Daria was unfazed by this development. "According to the conversation between Mr. Than and Yeung Tony, he was most insistent—apparently it is the only place he will meet customers when he is in the city."

"Wonderful, a fixer with five-star tastes," Mike grumped. "Could he get more public? Whatever happened to meeting in a shady bar or dark alley? Since we don't have any choice, we'll play it his way. At least I should be able to get some decent dim sum. What about appropriate clothes? I wasn't expecting to be heading anywhere with a dress code on this trip."

"Two pairs of slacks, two short-sleeved shirts, and two sport coats should be waiting for us at the Royal Pacific Hotel and Towers, along with our rooms. I also took the liberty of having an assortment of clothes tailored for the Keldara who may be appearing in public as well. Two suites, one for operation staging, and one for running surveillance, are also reserved at the Ritz."

"Works. So, I'll be wearing the short-range earpiece for communication with my back-up, assault, and Vanner's team. What else?" Mike asked.

"The surveillance pen will also be ready, so that we'll be able to see and hear what you're seeing and doing. Given where the meeting is being held, Captain Morgan has suggested that all of the meeting team and backup go in unarmed, unless someone wishes to take something that is undetectable for all intents and purposes. Sergeant Vanner has proposed keeping backup weapons in the comm suite, and the captain agreed, a bit grudgingly, it seemed. If anything goes terribly wrong, the assault team can be summoned. Other than Soon Yi, whom do you expect to accompany you?" Daria asked.

"With Vanner heading the surveillance team, Morgan and Katya can man the outer room. They will appear to be on a date. Oleg will command Team Jayne in the van in the garage."

Daria nodded, making notes. "Initial estimates based on the blueprints and schematics give them a three-minute access time to the room, assuming we will be able to access and override the elevator controls. If they must take the stairs, it will be at least seven minutes."

"And then they'll be almost too pooped to fight, not that they still wouldn't. Let's not go all *Mission: Impossible* here," Mike said. "This should be a simple sit-down and discussion of the future transaction, maybe a little negotiation. If Oleg and the boys are needed, then something has gone seriously FUBAR."

"Of course, Kildar."

"One more thing. Have we heard from Adams recently?" The master chief had headed out for his meeting with his buddy several hours ago.

"Nothing yet."

"That's what worries me." Mike rubbed his chin. "Try to raise him, will you? I just want to be sure that he's not tearing through the city."

"If he was, I am sure that the news stations would pick up the story," Daria said.

Mike shook his head. "That is *exactly* what I do not want to happen."

Mike and his teams had checked into their rooms at the Royal Pacific in the early morning, trying to be seen by as few people as possible. He'd gotten confirmation that Vanner and the girls were almost set up in their own suite at the Ritz, and would be up and running well before the meeting that night. Mike had them download all of the necessary hotel floor plans to the operation teams, then tried on his clothes for the evening's op. The olive-green sport coat, cream button-down shirt, and taupe gabardine slacks were all superbly tailored, and the entire outfit was half the cost of anything he could get in Europe. He tried on the Italian, woven brown leather deck shoes and surveyed himself in the full-length mirror. *I wonder how they would do with digi-cam fatigues*, he thought.

With a few hours to kill before the pre-op briefing, he decided to go for a run along the harbor. Life on the *Big Fish* was great, but Mike never wanted to leave land behind; laps on the ship just weren't the same. After making sure Soon Yi was secure in the adjoining suite, he left the hotel and headed south on Gateway Boulevard, passing the Gateway Towers, a multilevel shopping mall called Ocean Center, then the Marco Polo Hotel, followed by a bland white commercial building called the Star House. Mike passed the Tsim Sha Tsui Pier on his right, then hit a public pier that extended west into the harbor and east along the shore. The walkway, named the Avenue of Stars, was decorated with bronze statues and red and gold monuments highlighting China's great actors and directors.

Not giving any of those a passing glance, Mike was also careful to avoid the many tourists reading and taking pictures of their favorite actors and actresses. Instead, he enjoyed the view of the vast harbor that surrounded the small peninsula on three sides. Passing the Hong Kong Museum of Art on his left, he turned that way to cut through the Salisbury Garden and head back into the city. Guided by his smartphone, he navigated the crowded streets, heading steadily north by northwest until he wound up passing the International Commerce Center.

The modern building, completed just last year, was a tall, gleaming rectangle of glass, with triangular-cut corners at its base. Cars and people swirled around it in a flurry of constant motion, with well-dressed men and women entering and leaving in a steady stream. As he ran past, Mike noted the underground vehicle entrances, as well as the general layout of the surrounding streets and buildings. Although Vanner would have all of this covered with maps and photographs, for Mike there was never a better substitute for boots—and eyes—on the ground. The fact that he could get in his daily exercise while doing a sneak and peek was even better.

By the time he passed the ICC, he'd worked up a decent sweat—no doubt the extra humidity had a lot to do with that. Although he could have kept going for another hour, he decided to head back, grab a shower, and go over the site plans and general op schedule once more.

Back at the Royal Pacific Towers, he slowed to a walk and entered the gleaming gold-mirrored building, passing the chrome sculpture of jumping dolphins out front. They'd gotten him a plush "Towers Harbour" suite, which was much better than the bare-bones places Mike had stayed while on business in Eastern Europe. There was a separate parlor area that looked out onto the harbor, with an in-wall flat-screen television, luxurious desk and leather-backed chair, minibar, and all of the standard furnishings. The bedchamber was long, with the soft king bed in the center facing a row of three-quarters windows that gave the guest a panoramic view of Victoria Harbor, not that he had given it more than a cursory glance upon walking in. The beige carpet was thick and soft, and the room had simple, clean lines, with cream walls, a slightly vaulted ceiling and modern, black lacquered nightstands on either side of the bed.

The marble bathroom off the bedroom was well appointed, with a tub and separate shower stall. As Mike approached the bathroom, he heard water splashing. A short, crumpled dress lay on the floor, next to a pair of well-worn slippers by to the door.

What the hell? Keeping his hands at his sides, but ready to strike, he eased up to the door, then shoved it open and burst inside. He got a view of a huge pile of bath suds and a startled yelp as a small figure almost disappeared underneath the mountain of bubbles.

"What the fuck?" He stepped over to the side of the tub, knelt, and plunged his arm into the bath, encountering hot water and slick, warm flesh. Grabbing what he thought was an arm, he hauled up a dripping, soapy, buck-naked Soon Yi, who coughed and blew out a puff of soap as she cleared her mouth.

"What the hell are you doing in my room?"

"I was in the junior suite next door." She shrugged her slim shoulders. "It was easy to pick the lock. When I saw this tub, I knew where I was spending my time until you returned." Still dripping water, she stared at him. "Besides, I thought that maybe … you and I could continue where we had left off last night."

"Continue?" Mike frowned and made a mental note to have the outside guards sweep prisoners' rooms every fifteen minutes in the future. He was just lucky he hadn't had any sort of weapon in the room, otherwise this might have turned out much worse.

He crossed his arms. "I was pretty much done last night, but go on." Seeing her athletic body clean and dripping wet, however, was making him want to do things to her all over again.

"Well, Yeung Tony probably didn't tell you *everything* we did together." She grabbed the washcloth off the rack and slowly began wiping the bubbles from her body, giving him a tantalizing peep show as more skin was uncovered.

Mike narrowed his eyes. "Don't tell me you're a sub?"

Soon shook her head, making drops of water splash onto him. "Not quite. But sometimes I do enjoy being overpowered and taken. Tony was good—but judging by last night, I think you're much better. In fact, I was wishing you hadn't left so suddenly, not when things were just getting really interesting. But you're here now, so we can pick up where we left off. However, I am going to make you work for it—"

She had been wiping down the valley between her breasts, when suddenly she whipped the wet cloth at Mike's face. He ducked it, but upon coming at her found she had grabbed a towel and thrown that as well. Batting it aside, he reached for her arm, but his fingers slid off her slick skin as she smeared a handful of suds into his face.

Mike stepped back, trying to block the doorway while clearing his eyes. The bathroom wasn't large, but Soon was very nimble, and when he felt a touch on his left arm, he reached in that direction, only to come up with empty air. Hearing a mocking laugh behind him, Mike wiped the rest of the soap off and emerged from the bathroom to find a large shape sailing through the air straight at his head!

Ducking, he heard porcelain shatter, and turned to see one of the lamps that had been beside the bed lying in pieces on the floor. He looked up to see Soon lifting the other one off the nightstand on the far side of the bed. She raised it above her head, glaring at him.

"Put it down *now!*" he ordered.

"You will to have to make me—" she heaved it at him, but Mike was ready this time and caught it. Dropping it on the bed, he stepped onto the mattress and charged after her as she ran into the parlor.

He had barely cleared the doorway when he found the desk chair lying in his path. Leaping over it, Mike felt his head brush the ceiling. He came down on the other side and took in the room at a glance. Soon had darted around the loveseat and stood staring at him, naked and magnificent.

Mike was equal parts enraged and engorged. He'd never had a woman who enjoyed foreplay like this—subs were his normal sexual taste, but this was just as big a turn-on as anything he'd ever experienced. He took one step forward. "There's nowhere to run. You will not make it out that door."

"Then I will just have to fight you," she said, raking her nails across the back of the couch. Her ferocity excited him even more. For the first time, he wasn't in total control of a scenario, and although it felt strange, this game of cat-and-mouse was also sublimely pleasurable.

Mike took another step forward, stalking her, trying to freeze her in place with the most predatory glare he could muster. "You are going to pay for resisting me."

"Only if you catch me first, and that will not be easy." She tensed at his next step as Mike weighed his options. *Around, over, or through?* Around the couch would let her go the other way to escape. Over, and she might be able to duck away from him and reach the other side. That left—

Mike's next step took him right in front of the furniture. Soon Yi started to move, but before she could take a step, Mike picked up the couch and flipped it onto its back. Now Soon Yi was the one caught by surprise. She had started to dart left, but was forced to dodge the moving couch. With her cover gone, there was no place left to hide. Instead of fleeing, now she lunged at Mike, both hands going for his face.

This straight-on attack had no chance of working. Mike grabbed both her wrists and pivoted, using her momentum to fling her around him. Staying with her, he pushed her into the wall, then trapped her with his own so she couldn't get free. He couldn't remember the last time he'd been this hard.

Even with her wrists pinned and her body trapped, Soon Yi still tried to fight back, craning her neck forward and snapping at Mike's nose. He reared back and glared at her.

"That is not going to fly." He dragged her back into the bedroom and, still holding both her arms, stripped a pillow of its case and gagged her. "That should take care of your mouth until I want it open again."

He marched her back into the parlor and over to the desk, which he cleared of its phone, lamp, leather blotter, pad of paper, and pen set with a sweep of his arm. Bending her over the lacquered surface, he kept her hands above her head while forcing his knee between her legs. She tried to head butt him, but he just took the blow on the crown of his head, then backhanded her so hard that his knuckles tingled. Soon's eyes rolled back as her head lolled on her shoulders.

He forced her thighs apart and stuck two fingers deep inside her. She was incredibly wet, whether from the bath or the fighting, Mike didn't know and didn't care. She shuddered at the impaling, and he thrust them even deeper, rubbing the middle of his fingers against her clit as he withdrew them, then pushing harder inside to reach her cervix. A moan escaped her gritted teeth as he thrust in and out faster.

That gave him enough time to get the condom out and sheath himself. He didn't waste time on any preliminaries, just thrust his way inside. All he was knew was that by his third thrust she had wrapped her legs around his waist and ragged little gasps of pleasure were coming from her gagged mouth. His mouth was busy as well, sucking hard and biting at her nipples and breasts.

Mike worked her over for a solid ten minutes, until she was trembling all over. But he still didn't let her hands go, nor did he untie the pillowcase. Instead, he simply pounded the fuck out of her for a long time. After a while, he turned her around, bent her over the desk again, and took her from behind, which excited him even more as she grasped the edge and screamed into the gag.

The pounding she had taken had left her pussy swollen and dripping, and he gripped her tight little ass with both hands while he fucked the resistance right out of her. She cried out as he varied his penetration, sometimes fast, sometimes slow, her sounds just turning him on even more.

Mike felt like he could fuck her forever. He didn't even need to slow his thrusts or think about anything else to slow his own climax. He had reached that state of almost but not quite light-headed euphoria where he could go literally for hours without losing his erection. It was almost like he was outside himself, watching his body fuck the Chinese whore, and yet he could feel every exquisite sensation . . . and it was god-damned incredible.

After a few minutes of that, he grabbed the armless desk chair and set it upright, then sat down in it. Pulling her off the desk, he sat her down on his dick and began thrusting again, making her rise up off him with every pump of his hips. Soon grabbed his shoulders hard enough to draw blood and threw her head back, whipping her hair back and forth. After a minute, she reached for the gag, but he slapped her hand away.

"No! Only I do it!" he ordered.

She nodded, then got off him and turned around so he was penetrating her from a different angle. Mike knew this position well—he could easily get her off a half-dozen times, since the head of his cock was hitting some of the most sensitive spots in the vagina.

Grabbing her by her short hair, he pulled her head back. She sucked in a breath, and arched her back, trying to relieve the pressure on her spine. Mike wasn't having any of it, however, and kept the pressure on while he began pumping again. Before long, she was screaming, and he was howling right along with her.

But he only allowed her three shaking, screaming orgasms before he let himself come, then pulled out. After all, he always wanted to leave them wanting more....

Breathing hard, he stood over her as she tried to rise from the floor. "You've got thirty minutes to get yourself cleaned up and presentable. Try anything against me in that time, and you will regret it."

She began crawling to the bathroom while Mike picked up the desk phone, which was off the hook and beeping incessantly. With his pants still down around his ankles, he picked it up and called the front desk. "Yes, this is Mr. Jenkins in Suite 1802. I'm afraid there's been some damage to the furniture in here..."

Jace let out a low whistle as he escorted Katya into the marbled lower lobby of the Ritz-Carlton, on the ninth floor of the 484-meter-tall International Commerce Building, the tallest skyscraper in the city. "This Than guy sure knows how to live."

He'd packed smart casual, and was wearing a black linen button-down shirt under a wrinkle-free tan sport coat, chinos, and leather slip-ons. He wore a borrowed dark pair of Tom Ford sunglasses, and had smoothed his black hair back into a small ponytail, looking like a man striving hard to be at least one step above Eurotrash.

On his arm, Katya drew admiring stares with every step she took. Her stunning body was sheathed in an off the shoulder, wine-red cocktail dress that ended well above the knee, with matching high heels. Her blond hair was upswept in a French twist, and a pair of oversize Donna Karan sunglasses in a matching red frame completed the effect of a sophisticated French or German woman out with a man she might have just picked up and brought back to her hotel.

"It all seems designed to distract and confuse people," she replied.

"More like be astounded at how the one percent get to live," he replied with a grin.

"Don't let the trappings fool either of you—remember that we are here on business," Mike said in his ear.

"Yes, sir." Jace let his smile fade as he casually checked their six one last time.

Typically, the Kildar was all business. Walking a few yards ahead of Jace and Katya, he kept Soon Yi close to him with a firm hand on her elbow. The Chinese hooker was dressed in a light-blue linen summer dress with sandals on her tiny feet, and looked unusually animated and glowing.

Jace let the Kildar reach the elevators first. Katya and he would follow a minute later, giving the impression that they were two separate parties going to the same restaurant.

Mike and Soon were met by a lovely young female staff member. "Tin Lung Heen restaurant, please," he said.

"Of course, sir." The woman led Mike and Yi into the elevator and pressed the button for the 102nd floor.

Jace faced away from anyone who might have been watching and subvocalized, "Team River to Mal, do you copy?"

"Loud and clear, River One."

"Team River to Firefly, do you copy?"

"Read you loud and clear." He heard Vanner's voice in his ear. "Got your date on line as well. Everything's working perfectly."

The blond woman exhaled. "I bet Vanner loves to watch—everything."

Jace let a bit of frost edge into his voice. "I heard he almost got killed during the Florida op. Doesn't sound like a desk-sitter to me."

"Maybe that was his problem, too much watching and not enough doing."

Jace dropped the chill several more degrees. "Fortunately, that won't be an issue here."

Katya eyed him coolly. "Your loyalty is—admirable."

"No, it is well-earned, on *both* sides. No one I'd rather have covering my back in the shit. Come on, we're up."

Another lobby attendant approached them, and Jace named their destination. They were escorted inside, the doors noiselessly closed, and he felt the familiar drop in the pit of his stomach as the elevator ascended.

"This is a fast one," he said, mostly to calm Katya, who looked a bit uneasy at the rapid ascent.

She shrugged off his reassuring hand. "I am fine."

Turning away so the attendant couldn't see his face, Jace said. "Team Jayne, sitrep?"

Oleg's deep voice filled his ear. "Team Jayne is in position. Everything is quiet down here."

Everyone was in place: the assault team was secure in the parking structure underneath the building. Vanner and two of his intel girls had the best positions; in a full suite on the 105th floor, coordinating audio and visual for all of the teams and the Keldara on the boat. All they needed now was for their guest to show . . .

When they exited the elevator, Jace hid his smile at Katya's smothered gasp at the restaurant before them. It was a set in a long, rectangular room on one side of the building, its high ceiling nearly lost in the dimness above. The main room was lit by a large wooden candelabra that resembled a wagon wheel, with a couple dozen white-shaded lights casting a soft glow over the diners. On their right was a black stone wall split horizontally by a narrow window. Through it, the chefs could be seen working their culinary magic. Just past the maître d's station on their left was a black lacquer shelf that stretched from floor to ceiling. It contained at least fifty small spaces, each filled with a small ceramic jar, and matched an equally tall wine rack at the far side of the room. Beyond the tea shelf was a row of floor-to-ceiling windows that ran the length of the restaurant, giving the diners a spectacular view of Victoria Harbor and Hong Kong at night. The air swirled with exotic, inviting scents, from the aroma of roasting fish to the spicy tang of what Jace was sure was barbeque sauce. Despite his being on point and sweeping the area, his stomach grumbled at the smells.

Jace spotted Mike and Soon Yi being escorted to their private room. He stepped to the podium, placing his hands casually on the edge, just like an imposing American would. "Mr. Morgan and guest for 7:45."

"Of course . . . Mr. Morgan, right this way." The maître d's step was hesitant as he led them into the room. This was probably because Jace and Katya had been last-minute additions on the normally full reservation list. That also meant that someone was going to be upset that their reservation had been bumped, but it couldn't be helped—there was no way Mike was heading into that room without backup nearby.

The maître d' led the couple to a small table near the center window. It was straight across from the corridor leading to the private room, Jace noted with satisfaction. He made sure to take the seat with a view of the podium by the simple expedient of pulling the other chair out for Katya. They had an even more amazing view of Victoria Harbor here, with the neon and white lights of the buildings contrasting with clusters of smaller lights on the various boats traveling the waterway. The maître d' left them with menus and his wish for an enjoyable evening.

A waitress appeared the second the maître d' left and set down water glasses. "Would you like tea to start, or something from our bar?"

"What would you prefer, my dear?" Jace asked Katya, hiding his smile behind his menu as the young woman tried to parse the selection of white, black, scented, green, and oolong teas.

Finally she looked up to almost glare at him. "Whatever you recommend will be fine, I am sure."

"We'll start with a pot of the fifteen-year Puerh, please." Jace had never tried the fully fermented black tea, but figured now was the perfect time.

"Katya, dear—" was all he got out before a loud voice in his ear made him wince slightly. Jace didn't need to look over to see an older man with a silver-haired woman protesting loudly over his missing reservation. The maître d' attempted to handle the incident, promising them a table the moment one opened up. His soft voice was clear to Jace, thanks to the short-term bug he had stuck under the front edge of the podium.

"What?" she asked, snapping him back to the events in front of him.

"I suggest that you smile, otherwise onlookers might think you're not enjoying yourself."

"Who said I was?" Even as she spoke, Katya turned on a smile as incandescent as the lights outside. Jace sensed the shift in the tables around them as men and women both couldn't help looking at the gorgeous young woman and her date.

"That's more like it—I think."

The beautiful woman sniffed. "I should be in there, not that Chinese whore. I am . . . better equipped to deal with this situation."

"No doubt the Kildar was worried that your beauty might distract our target too much." He glanced up from the menu again as he heard the words he was waiting for.

"I have a room reserved for 8:00 PM under the name Than."

"Yes, sir, the other members of your party have already arrived, and are waiting for you. If you will follow me, please."

"Speak of the devil, our target's here." Jace said to Katya as well as the surveillance team.

"Copy that. Patching you to the Kildar now," one of Vanner's intel girls said.

"Go for Mal."

"River One here. Than has just arrived, and doesn't look too bothered by the fact that you got here first."

"Good. Let's see what he thinks once he meets me."

Returning to his menu, Jace let his eyes flick up just enough to see the slender Asian being escorted to the private room where the Kildar and Soon Yi awaited him. He made sure he had a clear line of movement to intercept Than if the fixer decided to leave early.

The waitress returned with their tea, and asked if they were ready to order. Exchanging another glance with Katya, Jace rattled off a quick dim sum order, including pork and shrimp dumplings with caviar; Wagyu beef potstickers, light on the black pepper; baked abalone and goose puffs; and the barbeque trio for two. She nodded and departed, just as Arun Than walked into the room.

Jace already had his smartphone out, and turned it on to see the picture of the view from Mike's surveillance pen. It was a good look at the Thai fixer in the middle of a large empty space. It revealed a man somewhere in his late-forties or early fifties, long and lean, with close-cropped black hair edged with silver at his temples, and alert, dark brown eyes. He was dressed in a tailored, cream summer-weight suit, complete with a Windsor-knotted tie. His body language was relaxed but watchful. However, he obviously wasn't pleased with the change in plans.

"You are not whom I am scheduled to meet here," Than said, standing behind a chair on the far side of the table.

"Yeung Tony's plans changed at the last minute," Mike said with no introduction, apology, or flattery. "However, he advised me to go in his place, and to confirm what I am saying, not only have I brought Soon Yi, whom you apparently already know, but I can put you in touch with Yeung Tony himself to confirm that everything is all right."

Jace watched a smartphone appear at the bottom of his screen and slide across the table. Than looked at it, then back up at Mike, who smiled. "Just press the green key."

Arun Than picked the phone up and touched the screen.

Jace watched his smartphone intently. "Okay, here we go. Let's hope Tony's convincing enough."

"I expect he will be," Vanner replied.

The microphone in the pen was excellent, and Jace heard every word from the other phone. "Hello?" Tony said in Cantonese.

"Hello. What happened to you?" Than said, watching the small screen while speaking at it.

"In case you are wondering, this is not a recording. It is the evening of September thirteenth, and the Hong Kong cricket team split a pair of matches with India earlier today. I regret that I could not meet with you, however, urgent business detained me near Malaysia. However, Mr. Kildar has agreed to serve as my representative in this matter. I trust that you will extend him every courtesy, as you would with me."

"I—will. Are you all right?"

"I am fine. I look forward to the completion of our business, and to seeing you personally soon."

"As do I. In that case, good night."

"Good night to you as well."

On the *Big Fish*, Yeung Tony leaned away from the smartphone he'd been using to talk with Arun Than. "Okay, I did what you wanted, now get that goddamn thing away from my head."

Vanel didn't move until he'd gotten the okay from Daria. Only then did he remove his silenced pistol from the back of Tony's head.

"You did very well, Mr. Yeung." Daria removed the smartphone and made sure the call had been disconnected. She also closed the two laptops they had been using. One had contained the script that Tony was to tell Than. The other one was a translator program that transcribed Tony's words as he spoke, as insurance against him trying to warn Than. The girls had disguised the worst of his injuries with artful make-up, leaving the thug with a puffy-looking face, but in the dim light of the room, it would have been hard to notice.

Vanel had been crouched behind the pirate, his pistol out of sight from the videophone. He walked around the small room, always conscious of their prisoner in case he made any move to escape.

Daria paused in her work, pressing a finger to her wireless headset. "All right, the meeting is proceeding. Get him back to his quarters."

Danes and Vil came in and waved for the pirate to come with them. Vanel was the last person out of the room, and grabbed a laptop to carry back to the intel room.

"Daria, a question?" he asked as he followed her through the ship.

"Yes?"

"If I had been forced to shoot the pirate, what do you think the Kildar would have done once the other man had realized he was dead?"

A smile crossed her face. "Oh, I am sure he would have improvised something suitable."

The Asian stared at the smartphone for a long moment, then set it on the table as he pulled his chair out. Only when he was seated did he take out a handkerchief, wipe the phone clean, and slide it back toward Mike. "It would seem that you have the advantage, Mr.—Kildar?"

"Don't assign him too much importance, Arun. Mr. Kildar is simply a mercenary hired by Tony to make sure that I got to the meeting."

Jace's view of Than shifted to the right, and he figured Mike had turned to look at the woman, probably not too happily, either. The pen camera shifted back to the Asian.

"Very well, Soon, although I am surprised that Tony would trust such a sensitive package to you."

"The best disguise is often to hide in plain sight. But we didn't come here to discuss my qualifications, we came here to do business."

The first round of appetizers arrived at their table, and smelled great. Katya poked at hers with a dubious expression.

"Trust me, you'll love it," Jace said, popping the fragrant pork and shrimp dumpling into his mouth without taking his eyes from the screen.

"Show him," Soon said.

The pen turned to the wall as Mike reached down to the floor beside him and picked up a small metal case with a combination lock. Turning it toward the black marketer, he flipped the catches and opened the lid, blocking Jace's view of what was going on.

"Damn it." Jace said under his breath, then raised his voice. "Mike, we can't see what's happening."

"Can't be helped...he's looking the board over right now," Mike replied, the words coming from the back of his throat sounding a little odd without being shaped by his lips or tongue.

A minute later, Mike closed the case and Jace watched Than nod. "It is genuine."

"Of course it is. Did you doubt it?" Soon snapped.

"Of course not, my dear. However, given the—" His eyes flicked to Mike before returning to her. "—alterations that have occurred so far, it behooves me to not simply accept anything at face value any more."

"Perhaps this will set your mind at ease: the board is yours to take with you, as a token of my good will." As she spoke, Mike resettled the board into the case, closed it, and pushed the case toward the other man, who was regarding Soon Yi from under one elegant, arched eyebrow.

"Most kind of you."

"That kindness only goes so far. Since you're satisfied with the sample of the package, it's time to show us the promised payment."

"Of course." Than reached into his jacket pocket and pulled out a small velvet bag, about the size of his fist. He set it on the center of the table. "Feel free to examine them. I have a loupe, if you have need of one."

"Why not—mine's in my other bag, anyway." Soon had taken the pouch, with Mike turning to watch her. Accepting the jeweler's loupe, the petite woman opened the drawstring and gently poured the contents out onto the table.

"Whoa..." Jace whispered.

Katya swallowed her mouthful of abalone and goose puff and

chased it with a gulp of tea to avoid choking. "Are those what I think—"

"They certainly are." They both stared at the screen as a small stream of rubies, sapphires, topazes, and emeralds cascaded onto the table. Each stone was already cut and polished, their myriad facets flashing an expensive rainbow from the overhead lights.

"Than is fucking connected, to be able to get his hands on that many gemstones. He must know major people in Thailand to move that many rocks."

Soon had expertly screwed the loupe over one eye and was examining stones at random. After looking at four or five, she raised her head, removed the loupe and handed it back to him, and nodded. "They are acceptable."

"So pleased to hear it. The amount you have is one-quarter of the agreed-upon payment. Now, let us discuss the particulars of the delivery of the balance of the shipment, as well as the rest of the payment due—"

Jace lost the rest of Than's words, as his attention was drawn to a loud discussion at the maître d's station.

A mountain of a man, as tall as Oleg, but easily twice as wide, jabbed a thick forefinger into the waiter's chest as he leaned forward. Dressed in a slightly rumpled black, pinstriped suit, He carried an ivory-topped, black Malacca cane, and had curly, black, shoulder-length hair, and the broad, flat nose and brown skin marking him as Samoan.

"Uh-oh, I think that may be trouble. Look over casually, then back at me," Jace told Katya, who was about to turn to the discussion.

The giant's words came clearly to Jace's ear. "—you will take me there right now! Otherwise you'll be taking the express down to the ground, and it won't be by elevator. You have three seconds to decide."

He was flanked by two burly men stuffed into off-the-rack, shiny suits, both of whom seemed more than ready to pound the smaller man into one-hundred-ten pounds of tuxedoed pulp.

"Mal, we may have a situation in the main dining room." Even as Jace spoke, the man and his two thugs followed the trembling maître d' toward the corridor leading into the private room. "Correction, three large and angry-looking men are heading your way, ETA five seconds. What are your orders?"

CHAPTER NINE

Issako bin Sunia was royally pissed off.

So pissed off, in fact, that he hadn't been able to finish his light dinner of *oka*, raw shark meat prepared sushi-style and served on the back of a nude whore; *lu'au*, a stew of taro leaves, onion, and coconut milk wrapped in taro leaves and slow-cooked over a fire; and his favorite, *sea*, a Samoan delicacy made from the insides of an ocean slug. Issako had his *sea* created specially for him by his private chef, using a traditional recipe that was almost one hundred fifty years old.

But today, all of that normally delicious food had been like ashes in his mouth. Every succulent mouthful was bland and tasteless once he had received the news that the shipment of computer boards had been stolen from his thieves who had stolen them from the military ship in the first place.

Until that point, Sunia had been congratulating himself on the perfect crime. Bribing a lowly quartermaster's assistant to switch two boxes, he had looked forward to receiving the fat payment promised once the real boards had been delivered to their new destination.

Instead, he'd received word that the transport boat had been attacked by pirates near Mangkai Island, and the box lost. He had spent every waking minute afterward, along with a large amount of cash, finding out who had taken his shipment and where they were now.

It had taken bribes, favors, and threats to all kinds of people; from lowly street thieves all the way up to the possibility of a war with a subgroup of the Luen *triad*, but Sunia didn't care. He had to get that box back at all costs. Everything he had fought for and scratched out of the glittering illusion that was Hong Kong teetered in the balance of the next few minutes.

And if Issako bin Sunia was anything, he was a survivor. He had clawed his way out of the slums of the capital city of Alpa, on the island of Upolu, at the age of eleven. Taking to the sea, he had learned the freighter trade sailing the Pacific and Indian Oceans. But he had saved every scrap of currency he could beg, borrow, earn, or steal, all with one goal in mind—Hong Kong.

Five years later, he had landed at the port city and swore an oath that he would either make his fortune there or die trying. That had been twenty years ago. Now his increased girth—with muscle slowly turning to fat over the past several years—tailored silk suits, and the chauffeured Rolls Royce Silver Phaeton that transported him around the city showed how far he had come.

Unseen by anyone but the women he slept with, but just as important, was his completed *P'ea*, the intricate, geometric tattoos that every adult Samoan aspired to have. Once he had carved out a secure niche in the Hong Kong underworld, he had returned home and had the best tattoo artist in the nation complete the patterns from above his knees to his lower stomach.

And now it was all in danger of being snatched away. All because his own men couldn't fend off some two-bit pirates and protect the most valuable cargo they'd ever been entrusted with! For the tenth time, Sunia cursed himself for not following his instincts and doubling the guard on the box.

Now, he restrained himself from throwing the maître d' across the room with one huge arm, and brushed by him to reach for the door of the private dining room. Twisting the handle, he threw it open and strode in, followed by his two less massive but still very large bodyguards, both of whom drew their pistols as they entered.

"Nobody move!" The scene Sunia interrupted wasn't what he'd expected. The private room was oddly large, with the ceiling at least two stories off the floor. An exit sign dangled in midair, pointing to another door at the back of the room. Three people were seated around a square table, a man Sunia recognized, a woman he did not, and a third one who came as a complete surprise to the huge Samoan.

"Hey, this is a private meeting—!" the third man started to say.

"Shut up!" *A white man? Who is this fool?* Issako almost dismissed the woman, except that she looked like she had just swept something off the table into her lap. "Everyone put your hands on the table! Anyone pulls a gun and they die!" He studied the unassuming-looking foreigner for a second. The brown-haired man's adam's apple bobbed like he was gulping in fear. The gangster glared at him in even more furious anger before turning on his competitor.

"Arun Than! I should have known you were dipping your fingers into my business!" Issako spat in Cantonese.

The tall Thai spread his hands, as if trying to implore the huge Samoan to realize his mistake. "I have no idea what you are talking about, Mr. Issako. Yeung Tony contacted me three days ago saying that he had a very valuable package he needed to sell. He did not volunteer where it had come from, nor did I ask—"

Issako cut him off by slamming his large fist on the table. "I do not care what was said! The box is mine, and I will have it back right now!" he thundered. Spying the small case on the table, he grabbed it and flipped the catches. Opening it, Issako's face darkened even more when he saw a piece of his lost prize within.

The white man shrugged. "Hey, I don't care who buys it, as long as your money's good—"

Issako cut him off as well. "I told you to shut up, *pukio*! You and this *pa'u mumuku* are already dead, you just do not know it yet!" Snapping his fingers, he switched to Cantonese. "Search all of them, and then take them out the back way. I will question each one myself—in private."

He saw the white man swallow again as he was made to stand and suffer the indignity of being searched by Sunia's henchmen. The second one took his time with the Chinese woman, who grimaced but stayed silent as he pawed at her breasts and between her legs. He turned to his boss and tossed him a velvet bag with a leer on his face.

"They are all clean. The whore was hiding this."

Sunia opened the bag and smiled at the glittering fire of the gems inside it. "This is more like it," he said in English again. "All right, let's get the hell out of here."

"Team River, hold your position," Mike said in Jace's ear as the Samoan and his two goons disappeared down the hallway. "Team Jayne, you are green. River One, do you recognize the new guy?"

"Yeah, he's a local gangster named Issako Sunia. Samoan, mid-level player in the Hong Kong underworld. Usually deals in cigarettes, drugs, women, or cars—high-tech stuff isn't his M.O. Your box must be worth quite a bit if he's willing to stray this far outside his comfort zone—"

Jace was cut off by an angry shout. "Translate," Mike ordered.

"...He's pissed at Than for muscling in on his action. He's going to take all of you to a location where you can be interrogated in private. Shall we take them out?"

"Negative, too much collateral nearby to risk it. Follow us and cut off their escape route. The assault team will take the three tangos in the garage. I want Sunia alive. Copy that, Jayne Leader?"

One hundred and five stories below the restaurant, Oleg Kulcyanov wiped his sweating brow as he listened to the Kildar's orders. The air-conditioning in the van had been on when they'd entered the underground parking structure, but the five-man squad had been sitting for a half-hour with the engine off, and it was getting more than a bit ripe now.

"Understood, Kildar," He said into his headset. "Three tangos incoming with you and the girl. Eliminate the others, but take the one called Sunia alive. Firefly, we need photo identification of the one who is not to be killed."

"Isolating and sending to you now," Vanner replied. "Also sending their projected route down to the garage to you."

Oleg felt his pocket vibrate and pulled out his smartphone to see a texted photo of a large, curly haired man in a black suit and carrying a cane. "ID received." He waited to get the route the gangsters were taking the Kildar out, his eyes widening in surprise. "Team Jayne taking positions now."

Oleg clapped their driver on the shoulder. "Givi, they are heading to another parking area. Get us there now!"

"They're moving the Kildar and Soon Yi out the back. Come on." Jace rose and strode toward the passageway, scanning left and right in case anyone tried to detain him. No one got in his way, and he reached the door to the private room without incident. "Are they clear, Firefly?"

"Yes, River One, everyone has left the room."

"Copy that." Even with the confirmation, Jace turned the handle, shoved the door hard, and slipped into the room fast, going down the right side wall while searching for any tangos. He saw Katya moving down the left side without being told, checking under the table and everywhere else while closing in on the fire exit door.

"No alarm. They must have disabled it." Jace turned to Katya and found her slipping off her heels. "Good girl."

"I did not fall off goddamn turnip truck yesterday!" she hissed back.

"Right, sorry. Where are they now, Firefly?"

"Five floors down and moving fast," Vanner replied. "No one's hanging back—they're all *di di mau*ing out of there."

"All right, we're in pursuit." Jace slowly eased the fire door open and slipped into the bare, concrete stairwell. He could hear the slap of multiple footfalls several floors below. He let Katya enter behind him, then quietly closed the door. "Let's go."

Just as he was about to descend, he heard a hiss from the landing above them. Waving Katya to stay back, Jace edged to the middle of the landing and peeked up.

Standing at the top of the stairs was Creata, holding two pistols with their muzzles pointing skyward. She flipped the guns in her small hands and held them out butt-first.

"Hell, yes!" Jace leaped up the stairs and grabbed the pair of SIG-Sauer P229s out of her hands. "Thank *you!*" he whispered.

"Is nothing," she whispered back, drawing two spare magazines from her pocket and handing them over. "Go help the Kildar."

"We're on it." Jace's leather-soled slip-ons made little noise as he crept back down the stairs. He gave Katya the other pistol and spare magazine and together they began descending after the Kildar and the gangster holding him hostage.

They caught up to within three floors of the group. Then it was all about staying both silent and out of sight of the group ahead of them. That, and trying not to get dizzy going around and around and around the endless squares of steps...

"Problem, Oleg," Dmitri Devlich, Oleg's second, said from the passenger seat as they approached the ramp leading up and out of the parking structure.

"What now?" Oleg swiveled around to look through the windshield at what their driver was pointing at.

"Sign says to go left only, when we need to turn right to reach other parking space. Is short distance—"

"Then go right. That is no problem at all." Oleg turned back to making sure the other three members were ready to go. The van swerved into a hard right turn, pushing the massive Keldara against the wall. A horn blared from straight ahead, and for a second the entire interior of the van was filled with blazing white light. Then Givi cranked the wheel hard left and they were plunged into the relative darkness of another ramp leading down.

"I think the driver of that oncoming car thought it might be a problem," Givi said with a chuckle.

"Oleg?"

"What now, Dmitri?"

"We are not tenants here, correct?"

"Of course not! Why do you ask such a question?"

"Because—" The driver pointed to the automated gate blocking their entrance into the garage, and the small box next to it. "—only tenants can enter here."

"Father of All!" Oleg pressed on his earpiece. "Firefly, this is Jayne Leader. We have a barrier to the garage, can you override?" He listened for a few moments, then looked back at the gate. "That is good point."

Opening the door, he got out and ran to the bar, trying to ignore the hot, still air and the stink of exhaust. Bending under it, he lifted up with his legs, mustering all the force he could into wrenching the bar upward.

It was no contest. With a squeal of protesting gears and a flash of sparks from the control box, the gate flew skyward. Oleg held it up long with one arm and waved the van through with the other. Once they were clear, he let the gate go, ran for the passenger door, and jumped in.

"Firefly, this is Jayne Leader. Problem eliminated. We are moving to intercept now."

Jace had been tracking the floor numbers as they descended, and held up a fist when they reached the third floor, making Katya stop behind him. He strained to hear what was going on below—there was a muffled conversation, then what sounded like a door opening.

"Firefly, where is Team Jayne, over?" Jace asked.

"Team Jayne is in position," the same intel girl—Jace thought her name was Xatia—said. "Close off rear escape route now."

"Roger." Jace waved Katya over to the left side of the stairwell, and he took the right side. Without words, he told her to cover the right side, as she would have the better point of view, and he would cover the left in a crossfire. Together, they silently continued down after their boss.

Oleg smiled as he shrank into the shadows of the nearby concrete wall. He was not thrilled to be working in the city; it was hot, noisy, and stank like nothing he'd ever smelled before, not even the annual pig slaughter back home. However, the one thing he did like about doing urban ops was the incredible amount of cover available.

Scanning the deserted parking lot, even he couldn't see where the rest of his team was concealed. The dozens of cars around, not to mention the thick concrete columns and sloping ramps, afforded plenty of protection. He might have even been able to bring the MGL-140 without anyone being the wiser. *But surely that would be overkill*, he mused.

The stairwell door the team was arrayed around creaked open. "Jayne Leader to Team, stand ready. Targets are coming out."

Four radio clicks answered him.

"Jayne Leader, this is Firefly. Team River is in position behind targets, over."

"Roger." Oleg sat between two cars, a silver Mercedes-Benz sedan and a black BMW coupe, and steadied his HK416C, with the stock fully extended and snugged into his shoulder. Eye to the sight, he watched the operation unfold.

One of the hired thugs came out first, pistol at his side, sweeping right and left, looking for any signs of life. Oleg grinned; the man would find none. Sure enough, after a few seconds he waved the rest of the party forward. The Kildar came out next, with Soon Yi on his heels, and Arun Than emerging last. They were followed by a very large man in a black suit and carrying a black cane under one arm, and the silver case in the other. He had shoulder-length, curly black hair, and was followed by another man who was obviously more hired muscle.

"Targets designated. Curly hair is to be taken alive, repeat, alive. Execute."

▲   ▲   ▲

In the shadows underneath a chromed out, canary-yellow Humvee H3, Givi Kulcyanov watched and waited, silenced pistol held in both hands ahead of him.

With no way of knowing how professional the guards accompanying their target were, each team member had selected the cover that made the most sense for his assigned position. Since Givi was to be the closest to the target door, he figured they would be the most observant in checking the spaces between the cars around the concrete entranceway. But Oleg doubted that they would take the time to do even a cursory sweep under the cars themselves, and he was right. Even if they had, two bullets to the face would have been their only reward, giving the Keldara the element of a much different kind of surprise.

Upon hearing the order to begin the operation, Givi rolled left. The moment he was clear of the vehicle's underbody, he got to his feet, but stayed bent over, concealed behind the Humvee's bulk.

Three ... two ... one, he counted in his head, then took a step forward and aimed around the corner at his designated target.

There was silence for a few seconds after Oleg's order, then the ripping-cloth-and-metal sound of four silenced pistol shots echoed through the garage. One moment the two bodyguards were walking, the next they had dropped out of sight, taken down by chest shots from less than five meters away. The shooters had positioned themselves and aimed their shots so as not to risk coming close to the Kildar, the woman, or Than. As Oleg watched, each Jayne member emerged from their hiding place, cleared the pistols from the dying men's hands, and finished each with a shot to the head.

Meanwhile, Mike was working on the big guy. He'd stripped him of his cane and disarmed him when the Samoan had gone for his own pistol, breaking his arm in the process. As the big man clutched his useless limb, Mike toppled him with a heel kick to the knee. The gangster howled in agony as he rolled on the ground, trying to clutch his ruined leg with his remaining hand.

Oleg kept watching from his vantage point as his team members reported in. "Jayne Two, clear."

"Jayne Three, clear."

"Jayne Four, clear."

"Jayne Five, clear."

The stairwell door opened again. Oleg swept his rifle over to cover it, then lowered his weapon as Jace and Katya emerged from the stairwell. Standing, the big man went to meet them, still keeping an eye out for other tangos or civilians.

Having relieved Sunia of the case, Mike was kneeling on the big man's chest, holding a silenced pistol to his forehead. Oleg noted with satisfaction that the rest of his team had come out to both cover the remaining tango and ensure that neither Soon Yi nor Arun Than tried to slip away. Hearing a slight squeal of tires, he glanced at the concrete ceiling of the level above, trying to figure out if the vehicle was coming their way. Keeping one ear on it, he turned back to cover the Kildar as he interrogated the wounded man.

"—no time for bullshit or games. You got one chance to tell me what I want to know, or I splatter your brains all over the floor. Who's the buyer for the control boards?"

Sunia spit his words out through gritted teeth. "I do not know exactly who they are—all I know is that the package is supposed to go to Myanmar! Contact would be made once it arrived!"

"Bullshit! Who's your goddamn contact?"

"It was set-up—through third parties—for everyone's protection!"

Mike thumbed back the hammer on the Sig. "Maybe you'll talk better through another hole in your head—"

Mike's threats were interrupted by the Vanner cutting in on all frequencies. "All teams, this is Firefly! Armed men driving toward you. ETA fifteen seconds!"

"Grab him, Oleg! This fat fuck's going to answer my questions!"

Oleg had just slung his rifle and was bending to grab Sunia when the glare of high-beam headlights washed over everybody, accompanied by the squeal of tires. He looked up to see a Toyota

4Runner speeding toward them. Two gunmen popped out outside the passenger window and rear driver's side window. They began firing long bursts from their stubby submachine guns as they closed. Tongues of orange flame spat from the muzzles as bullets sparking off the concrete all around Mike and his people. Even above the echo of the submachine guns, Oleg heard the squeal of spinning tires, and suddenly smelled burning rubber.

"KILDAR!" Oleg whirled around and lunged for Mike, who was already leaping out of the truck's path. It was less than ten yards away when the Team Jayne van shot out of its parking space and smashed into the driver's side front fender. The impact shoved the higher truck into the nearest row of luxury sedans and SUVs. The 4Runner tipped over, sending the gunman on the driver's side flying into the air. He slammed head first into the concrete roof and fell in a lifeless heap in the middle of the lane.

The van's passenger door slid open, and Dmitri, Oleg's second-in-command, shouted, "Come on!" He was still taking fire from the wrecked Toyota, the bullets making popping sounds as they punched through the van's metal sides. Apparently some of the reinforcements had survived the crash.

Shrugging off his rifle, Oleg ran to the rear corner of the passenger side. He made sure his weapon was ready before ducking his head around the corner to get a glimpse of the shooter. The bloody driver was standing on the wrecked truck, visible from the waist up, firing at the driver side of the van. Oleg aimed and fired a three round burst just as the man saw him and tracked over to shoot. The rounds took the driver in the throat and head, spraying blood on the concrete wall behind him. Triggering his weapon in a useless burst skyward, he fell back, then sagged out of sight.

"Oleg, get inside, we're unassing right now!" the Kildar ordered.

"Have not collected target yet!" the huge Keldara replied as he scanned for the wounded Samoan, who seemed to have disappeared.

"Belay that and get in here *now*!" Mike said.

The Jayne team leader had just turned to head for the open

passenger door when the squeal of tires alerted him to a potential new threat. Oleg turned to see a chopped and lowered bright-green-and-blue Honda coupe accelerate toward him, its lights catching him in their halogen glare as a pistol extended from the driver's window.

Bringing his rifle up to his shoulder, Oleg braced himself and began putting short bursts through the car's windshield. His first shots hit left of center, where he figured the driver's chest would be. He was correct, as the car swerved immediately after he starred the glass. Oleg kept firing, hitting the center right windshield as well, then going back to the left, alternating with each burst. The car jerked again, sideswiping a few more luxury SUVs and sports cars. It finally shuddered to a stop a few yards away from the huge Keldara, its engine dying with a final wheeze. Oleg waited for anyone to dare to come out, but no one moved in the smoking, bullet-ridden car.

He whirled on his prosthesis, ran for the passenger compartment through the hanging clouds of gunsmoke, and climbed inside.

"Where is curly-hair?" Oleg asked as he slammed the door closed.

"Lost him in the fight!" Mike said. "Forget him. Dmitri took a round."

Only then did Oleg notice that the American, Jace, was behind the wheel. The rest of the team was all crowded into the rear of the van, giving Givi just enough room to examine Dmitri's red-stained shoulder. Each probe brought no sound of pain from the warrior, although his face was tight, and his gaze stared somewhere far off in the distance.

"It is not good. The bullet missed his vest and broke his shoulder blade. Fragments of both the round and bone are still inside. He will need an operation. But he is in no immediate danger of bleeding out, at least."

"All right, we'll get that fixed ASAP." The Kildar peered through the cracked rear window. "No sign of pursuit. Slow it down a bit, Jace."

"Dmitri was lucky he only took one round; the outside of this door looks like Swiss-fucking-cheese. That's gonna raise our profile a bit," Jace said as he pulled around a turn. "There's the exit."

"Don't stop for the gate—we barely did on the way in," Oleg advised.

Nodding, Jace began pressing the gas pedal down to ram their way through when a large, blocky black vehicle appeared out of nowhere, cutting off their escape route.

"Hold on!" Slamming on the brakes, Jace threw the van into reverse and looked back, only to curse in frustration. "What do you want to do, Kildar?"

Mike was also looking at the second heavy-duty S.W.A.T. truck that had just rolled out to block their six. Both vehicles were disgorging heavily armored Hong Kong special unit officers armed with automatic rifles. "First, nobody move." He leaned around Jace to see the same thing happening ahead of them.

In less than twenty seconds, the van was encircled by a ring of lethal-looking cops, all aiming assault rifles at the van. Two of the helmeted, masked officers parted for a short, paunchy Asian in a rumpled, tan, summer-weight suit and a salt-and-pepper crew cut to approach. He walked up to the driver's door and rapped his knuckles on the cracked window, which shattered into hundreds of fragments at his touch.

Jace smiled at him. "What seems to be the problem, officer?" he asked in flawless Mandarin. He held his pistol with the hammer back below the window, ready to shoot the polite cop in the face if he was had to. Since the only realistic outcome of that was a swift death, he *really* hoped he wouldn't have to shoot the guy.

The officer's own smile was tight as he held up his identification card and badge. "My name is Lieutenant Fang Gui, Criminal Intelligence Bureau, Hong Kong Police. I understand that a gentleman named Mr. Mike Jenkins is inside this vehicle, and that he was a witness to a rather unfortunate accident in a lower level of this parking garage. I would like him to accompany me to our station to answer a few questions. He is not under arrest, and will be free to leave the station at any time. However, his cooperation in this matter would be most appreciated."

"Just a moment, please." Jace turned and translated the information to Mike, who peered around the seat at the man with a puzzled frown. The Kildar looked back into the cargo compartment of the van. Filled with heavily armed Keldara, a prostitute, and a black marketeer, it stank of blood, sweat and burned powder. Despite what had just gone down, all of them—even Dmitri— looked ready to go if he gave the order.

"Stand down, all of you," Mike said in Keldara before turning back to the police lieutenant.

"Okay, let's go."

CHAPTER TEN

"I do not fucking believe this!"

An hour later, Jace watched in incredulity as Mike was politely shown into an interrogation room. He was followed by the officer who had stopped them in the International Commerce Center's underground parking facility.

The last sixty minutes had passed as if in a dream. Not only were Jace, Katya, Soon Yi, Arun Than, and the rest of the Keldara not arrested, they weren't even made to get out of the battered, shot-up van. Instead, Mike was allowed to debark, with Jace and Katya accompanying him, and they were all taken under guard to the May House skyscraper, in the Wan Chai District on Hong Kong Island. There, Jace and Katya cooled their heels in a hallway while Lieutenant Fang was speaking with the Kildar. They had both been perfunctorily searched, and were clean, having left their pistols in the van. The police had missed their camouflaged earpieces, and had even left them their cell phones.

Katya slouched in the hard-backed plastic chair. "So what is the problem? We are not under arrest, correct?"

"Keep your voice down," Jace muttered out of the side of his mouth as two officers walked past. "That *is* the problem. Nobody is under arrest after a run-and-gun battle, along with at least four premeditated murders, which is what those self-defense takedowns would look like to the HK cops? I haven't even counted the several charges of assault and battery, not to mention a pair of kidnapping offenses once they talked to Soon Yi and Arun Than. By all rights we should be headed to China Ferry Terminal, and then a short trip to Stanley Prison to await our 'trial.' That we're being treated as actual witnesses, or even guests, means the HK Police have something else in mind for us."

Jace's earpiece crackled, then he heard Vanner's voice. "Team River, this is Firefly, over."

Jace pulled out his cell phone and leaned over it, elbows on his knees, pretending to be engrossed in something. "This is River One. Before continuing, I cannot guarantee there are not ears on us."

"Understood, but I wouldn't worry about it," Vanner replied. "We are all clear of the op building. The room was sanitized. Your current position is on the eleventh floor of the May House building, correct?"

"Correct. How's Dmitri?"

"He's in surgery right now. Thanks for the tip on that doctor, it made that situation a lot easier. Are you getting anything from the pen camera?"

"Shit! In all the excitement, I forgot to check." Jace thumbed through his screens until he found the picture of the police lieutenant reading some papers. "Got it. I can't believe they didn't confiscate it."

"Do you have sound?"

Jace turned his phone's volume up, and heard the rustle of the page as the lieutenant turned it. "Yeah."

"All right, I'm going to try using your phone as a boosting antenna so I can pick up the signal. We're a couple blocks away, but I can't get a solid fix on the Kildar's position. This may drain your piece's battery faster."

"Great." Jace saw activity on the screen and watched as a third person entered the room. "Must be the officer who serves tea and takes notes. Whatever you're going to do, do it fast—they're about to start."

Jace hadn't finished talking before the lieutenant started with the date. "Lieutenant Fang Gui of the Hong Kong Criminal Intelligence Bureau, speaking with Mr. Michael Jenkins, an American citizen—" Glancing at Mike for confirmation, he continued off the other man's nod, "—currently living in the country of Georgia. I am taking his statement regarding his witnessing of a traffic accident in the underground carport at the International Commerce Center, One Austin Road West, Kowloon, Hong Kong. Let the record show that Mr. Jenkins is not under arrest at this time, nor is he suspected of any unlawful activity."

Jace's brows rose at that. *What game is this guy playing?* "Was he blind? Surely the garage had security cameras?"

"They did, but we circumvented them once we knew where Sunia was going," Vanner said in his ear. "No sense having everyone watching what was going on down there."

"Right." Jace returned his attention to the screen, where Lieutenant Fang was offering Mike a beverage. He chose coffee, while Fang opted for tea, and said something to the lower-ranking officer as he rose to fetch the drinks.

"What was that?" Katya asked, having slid over to watch as well.

"He said, 'take your time.'" Jace's frown deepened. "Now we'll learn what screws are about to be turned, and how deep. Firefly, are you receiving?"

"Roger, although it comes and goes."

"I'm sure Mike will fill in any gaps."

The lieutenant regarded Mike steadily as he talked. "First of all, thank you for agreeing to come to our office, Mr. Jenkins."

Mike's stare was just as steady right back at the man. "You extended an invitation that I really couldn't refuse."

"Quite. Now that we are alone, I wish to speak to you about Issako Sunia."

"Never met the man."

"Your protestations or denials are of no consequence. As I said, you are not under arrest."

"So, I could just get up and walk out of here," Mike replied.

Fang's eyes narrowed. "You could. However, I doubt that you or the rest of your companions would get very far."

Mike leaned forward. "You do not want to play 'threaten the foreigner' with me. Believe me, it won't work."

"Your name is not unknown to us, Mr. Jenkins." The lieutenant smiled thinly. "You and your people have quite a reputation among certain intelligence circles. I know that the governments of several countries—powerful countries—handle you very delicately after a particular action in Albania. However, no one, including my own government, is willing to say why." He consulted a piece of paper on the table. "This is the answer I received from my superiors after a standard inquiry about you. Quote: 'Mr. Jenkins is considered a good friend of the Chinese people, and every courtesy should be extended to him at all bureaucratic and law enforcement levels.'"

He set the paper back down and regarded Mike. "Are you aware of what you have to do to be considered 'a friend of the Chinese people'?"

"Not generally, no."

"Neither am I. In fact, I've never even seen such a communiqué until this one arrived. Whoever you are, you have very powerful friends."

Mike simply shrugged.

"Do I need to know what he's talking about?" Jace whispered.

"No, and for your sake, hope that you never do," Vanner replied.

Fang continued. "Then there is that matter of the incident in the mountains of Georgia. It has been described as an incredible stand of your people against an overwhelming force of Chechens. Your side was victorious in yet another mysterious mission, this time earning the thanks of Russia, I believe."

Mike's jaw worked, but he shrugged again. "Your point?"

"So, I am aware of who you are, whom you know, and what you can do. I have no desire to let this particular situation spin any more out of control any more than it already has." Fang rubbed his chin. "This may be difficult to believe, Mr. Jenkins, but I am trying to work with you, not against you."

"So far, the only evidence I've seen of that is that I'm not in jail, another thing you do not want to happen. If you really are on the level, why don't you tell me what the hell is going on, and why two tac-assault teams just happened to be hanging around the mall in the ICC while I was there."

"Fair enough. You happened to stumble into an ongoing investigation of Mr. Sunia and his activities in the city. We have been amassing evidence to arrest and subvert him in going after other triads and gangs in Hong Kong. The package that he was so desperate to obtain drew him to the attention of the Counter-Terrorism and Internal Security Division, which has been liaisoning with my department regarding this recent development."

"Right. So, if he has the package, you can go arrest him, case closed."

Fang's smile this time was as cold as Mike's when he was on mission. "Unfortunately, it is not so simple. Possession of that particular material is a grave crime, both here and in the People's Republic of China. Without naming any names—" He cocked his head at Mike, "—we know who currently possesses that material. We need to learn who in China has high enough clearance to have access to it, as well as to whom are they selling it. With Sunia no doubt lying low after the—accident—in the carport, there still remains the problem of keeping the package moving along to its final destination."

Mike blinked. "Am I hearing you correctly?"

"I believe so." Fang consulted his watch. "In approximately five minutes, we will be releasing Mr. Than with our profuse apologies for detaining him. Once that is done, we will release you shortly thereafter. We would like you to contact him and set up a time and place to complete your exchange. Once that is done, we will step in to arrest Mr. Than, having seen him accept the stolen materials, and continue our investigation from there. You will be free to continue on your way, and would have the thanks of the Hong Kong police, and its government, to take with you."

"What about the incident in the garage?"

"We're already spinning it as a shootout between two rival gangs, with no mention of any foreigners involved. The local newspapers are filled with such stories on a regular basis. The public will accept that, and it will fade away soon enough."

"All right, let Than know, and us as well." Mike rose to leave.

Fang rose as well. "Then you will assist us?"

"I didn't say that. It will help me if you put it out that we were held overnight, but released due to lack of evidence. After that gets around, I have to talk to Than and see if he's even willing to still deal with us after all this."

"I am sure that Mr. Than and you will come to some kind of arrangement. You are both businessmen, after all." The police officer's mouth quirked up in a wry smile. "Besides, if everything else fails, you can always mention that you most likely saved his life tonight."

"Yeah, and not just once, either."

Fang extended a business card. "Call me when everything's ready."

Mike took it with a cool smile. "I still haven't agreed to do anything for you."

Fang's smile mirrored his. "But I have every confidence that you will make the right decision."

"...and that's it in a nutshell, Bob," Mike said. "Uncle Sam is definitely not the only ones interested in these chips."

"Of course not. The fact China's tracking them doesn't surprise me at all. However, I am surprised at how fast they got on to you."

"Supposedly they were already tracking the guy who had stolen the chips in the first place. He hunted us down as we were talking to Than, and the Hong Kong PD came along for the ride."

"Do you buy that story?"

"It's as plausible as anything else China puts out in the press," Mike replied. "Of course, given that business in Armenia, I'd imagine they want to keep an eye on me, too. Still, if you guys have anything on this Fang Gui, I'd love to see it."

"I'll see what I can turn up." Pierson jotted the name down, then leaned back in his chair and rubbed his temples. "This Myanmar intel, how sure are you about it?"

"The guy I talked to really wanted to keep breathing, so I'd say it's a solid lock."

"Okay. And before I go talk to everyone again, remind me what I said about letting me know if you were going to China?"

"Hey, Hong Kong is not mainland China. If anything, it's the bastard child of a three-way between the motherland, the U.S., and England. When you said 'China,' I thought you meant let you know if we were dropping into Beijing or Shanghai."

"I did mean that. But I also meant anywhere *near* China. Things are precarious enough between us and them without any official entanglements—like a Hong Kong police lieutenant taking such an interest in you and your Keldara running around the city."

"If it makes you feel any better, we were as surprised as you were."

"It doesn't really. You have to admit that it sounds damned fishy that they just 'happened' to be on the scene in time to talk to you."

"I freely admit that. We're already working on a way to get out from under Fang's thumb. Answering to one master is enough for me, thanks."

"We do pay well—not that I'm saying you're in it just for the money, either."

"Yeah. I mean, that is nice, assuming I survive long enough to collect." Mike grinned. "But since I'm already up to my ass in alligators over here, is anything outstanding in the PRC you want me to handle? Should we drop in on the Premier?"

"As tempting as that sounds, do not even joke about it—even over a scrambled line."

"See? I knew you hadn't lost your sense of humor over this."

"Not yet," Bob grumped. "Talk to me after I inform the brass about this—it'll probably be a much different story."

"Myanmar? They used to be called Burma, right?"

"Yes, Mr. President. The military junta changed the country's name from the 'Socialist Republic of the Union of Burma' to

'Union of Myanmar' in 1989," the CIA director said. "They had been controlled by a military junta for more than forty-nine years. In 2008, they began transitioning to a democratic government through a constitutional referendum. Their first free elections were held in 2010."

"Much of the media still refers to the country as 'Burma' to delegitimize the change," The NSA director said with a roll of his eyes.

The President nodded. "Right, right—the secretary of state visited there recently, and we announced the exchange of ambassadors. It is my hope that Myanmar can be an example to the more repressive regimes in the area. That includes its much larger neighbor."

"Yes sir, but from what we've seen, the country still has a ways to go. There is some concern some several quarters, including members of Congress, that Myanmar is simply putting a new face on the old regime." The CIA director referred to a paper in front of him. "These issues begin with the 2010 elections, which many nations and the U.N. claimed was fraudulent. However, since then there have been several pro-democratic advancements made. These include the release of Aung San Suu Kyi, the opposition leader, from house arrest and allowing her to run for a seat in the national Senate, which she won handily."

"Right. She's the one I gave the medal to, right?"

"Exactly, sir. They also released more than six hundred fifty other political prisoners, created a National Human Rights Commission, enacted tighter regulation of their currency, passed new laws that permit labor unions and strikes, and relaxed the government's censorship of the press."

"That all sounds good to me. So what's the problem?" the President asked.

The DCIA continued. "Reports from well-placed sources inside the country show that the military is still actively moving against several indigenous groups. Their tactics have included rape, genocide, and other terrorist acts. As I'm sure you recall, the U.S. government passed the Burma Freedom and Democracy Act in 2003. This act bans all imports from Burma, bans the export of financial services to that country, freezes the assets of certain Burmese financial institutions, and extends the visa restrictions for Burmese officials in our country. The BFDA is renewed annually, most recently during this past July. Although the U.N. and we have requested proof of demonstrable gains in democratic procedure, such as the establishment of an independent judicial system, they have not been able to supply any evidence, or even shown meaningful progress yet. My point is that Myanmar could improve its status with the U.S.—and the world—if they were to make true steps toward government reform instead of just lip service. The full report is available for your review if you wish."

The President waved a hand. "That's another matter. Right now, the nuclear control boards heading there means what exactly?"

The NSA director cleared his throat. "That is a good question— for starters, Myanmar doesn't even have a nuclear reactor."

"What?" This came from the secretary of defense.

"There had been plans announced for them to purchase a reactor and build it with help from Russia back in 2000. From what we've seen, there hasn't been any movement on it since 2007," the DCIA said.

"So, why are they going there?" the President asked. "Is the military planning to sell them to another nation?"

"We're exploring several possible scenarios—one of them being that the military may have constructed an underground reactor in secret, possibly with help from North Korea," the NSA director replied.

"Okay, let's operate on that hypothesis. The chips come in, the reactor goes online, and?" the President asked.

"And perhaps Myanmar moves closer to processing yellowcake uranium for its own nuclear weapon. Or producing waste for dirty bombs," the DCIA said.

The NSA director held up his hands. "To what end?"

The DCIA was more than ready for him this time. "While ostensibly democratic, Myanmar, or Burma—whichever you fucking want to call it—is still in a vary fragile state. Hundreds of thousands of refugees are going to be returning to their homeland over the coming months. They will further strain a nation already under pressure from decades of mismanagement and underdevelopment. This doesn't take into consideration the numerous indigenous groups in the country—including the Han Chinese, Va, and Kachin—all of whom were involved in anti-government fighting as recently as 2009, and who probably do not share the current government's goals. The military may wish to try to threaten them into cooperating. They may even plant evidence of nuclear activity among them to create a plausible reason to crack down even harder—"

The President interrupted. "Surely those groups were fighting the junta government, not the current one?"

"Yes and no. The Myanmar Army is still involved in actions against several groups even today. The fact remains that there are groups both inside and outside the current government that may wish to foment unrest to advance their own goals. This may possibly include members of the former junta itself, as we're fairly sure there were several high-ranking generals who had to be persuaded to cede power. If they can create the right circumstances, I'm sure they would love to seize control again."

"Could this be part of some kind of power play by one of Myanmar's neighbors to bring them under another nation's control?" the President asked.

"China was the obvious puppet master, however, given what Mike told us about the Hong Kong police's involvement, it seems doubtful—" Pierson began.

"Unless they're running a misdirection op, pretending to be in the dark while orchestrating the whole damn thing. It wouldn't be the first time it's happened," the DCIA broke in.

"Yes, except China had been the junta's primary weapons supplier for years," The SecDef replied. "With them on the decline, that leaves a hole in their market, apart from supplying the government army with weapons. But they still have access to Myanmar's emerging trade markets, which will be hungry for goods and services. The country is also very rich in natural resources, which their eastern neighbor will badly want. China would gain more from a stable government that's eager to trade than another coup that could lead to civil war."

"What about India?" the President asked.

"First, Bangladesh lies between both nations. Their relationship with Myanmar is tenuous at best, owing to the quarter-million Burmese Muslim refugees in country," the DCIA said. "As for India, they're still struggling with trying to lock down their eastern border with Myanmar, which has been a major corridor for drugs, guns, and counterfeit currency. A fence was begun to block all one thousand nine miles of the shared border in 2003, and its construction has continued ever since. Land disputes and indigenous protests have slowed the progress. Bottom line, India has enough on its plate with Pakistan to take any real notice of its much poorer neighbor to the east."

"Walling off the border, eh? If they ever get it finished, let me know if it actually stops crime over there. Maybe I can use it to placate those idiots in Congress that want to wall off Mexico." The President sighed. "As a fan of democracy wherever it takes root, we want to make sure Myanmar stays that way, correct?"

The DCIA adjusted his rimless glasses. "Yes, sir. The country is part of our ongoing plan to show the Asian nations that a democratic government can flourish in that part of the world. Also, if everything goes well, we could have an excellent bulwark against China—"

The SecDef snorted. "Myanmar won't risk antagonizing its largest neighbor, which could crush it like a bug within forty-eight hours of a border incident. Your pipe dream will never come to pass."

"Regardless, anything that risks destabilizing it could set back our plans in the region for years or longer. Maintaining their democratic government is paramount to creating the possibility of an Asian Spring—" The DCIA pinned the SecDef with a steely glare. "—which we could actually plan for, unlike the never-forecasted Arab Spring."

The SecDef was about to retort when the President raised a hand. "Gentlemen, please—now is not the time to look backward." He turned to Pierson. "We'll let Mike follow the bread crumbs into Myanmar, and see what he uncovers. Does he have a plan for getting away from the Hong Kong police?"

Pierson nodded. "If I know Mike, he has several. I just hope they don't involve automatic weapons or explosives."

"So do I. Let him know he still should maintain a low profile in the area, okay?"

"Absolutely, Mr. President."

"So, now we have to worry about the HK police breathing down our necks while trying to get Than to take us up the chain to the next link in whoever's running these damn boards around Southeast Asia."

Mike had convened his senior officers in the conference room. He had patched in Nielson from home, and included Jace Morgan for obvious reasons. One seat was conspicuously empty.

"But Fang said that his orders are to extend you every possible courtesy," Jace said. "Typically the Chinese are very big on following orders from their superiors, so they shouldn't be that much of an issue."

"Yes, but as a certain ex-Marine Recon operator paraphrased recently, we are pilgrims in an unfamiliar land. If we are going to set up this meet, I want all avenues and angles triple-covered before we move forward," Mike replied.

"Roger that. Speaking of covering our angles, where's Adams?" Nielson asked. "Or do I not want to know?"

"That is a goddamn good question." Mike shot a look at Daria, who shook her head.

"All attempts to contact him have gone unanswered. The good news is that there have been no reports of a foreigner with his description in the news in the last twelve hours."

"Assuming we don't have to break him out of jail, I will skin him alive when I next lay eyes on him. Keep trying to raise his

AWOL ass." Mike took a deep breath and shook his head. "What did you come up with on Fang?"

"His jacket is pretty bare bones. Born in Beijing, both parents still alive and live in the city. He received high marks in all schooling. Studied law enforcement in college and graduated at the top of his class before his transfer to the Hong Kong police force, where he's been for the past fourteen years. The one oddity is that he transferred through the Special Duties Unit, the elite paramilitary force similar to the American Delta Force. He was there for two years, then transferred out to the Criminal Intelligence Division, which is very uncommon, as most SDU officers remain with that department until they retire. He has received high marks from all his superior officers. Has also received two commendations for bravery, once for saving an infant child during a bomb threat at a local shopping center, and the other was talking a hostage-taker into surrendering after nine hours of negotiations."

"Sounds like a straight-up cop to me—except that he's got his finger in this whole stolen computer boards thing, which sounds like it's outside his AOE," Mike said.

"He did say he was liasioning with Counter-Terrorism—maybe they've got the inside track on this," Jace offered.

"Maybe, but something still doesn't sit right about HK police involvement in something that's obviously bigger." Mike turned to Jace. "How are we coming regarding Than?"

"Better than I expected," the ex-Recon Marine replied. "I had to burn a favor or two, however, once word got out that Sunia was MIA and that I had a part in that, my credibility went up a notch or two. Apparently the big man had been tearing up the streets and his friends while looking for his lost package." Jace slid a smartphone across to Mike. "The programmed number in there is where Than can be reached for the next four hours."

"No time like the present." Mike picked it up and dialed. The other end rang three times before it was answered. "Mr. Kildar, I presume?"

"Correct." The pause stretched out, with Mike intending to let it go as long as necessary. When dealing with criminals and not having the upper hand, he firmly believed that whomever spoke first lost.

"Will Soon Yi be joining us?" Than eventually asked.

"No. I am handling this from now on. I understand that you were released from the Hong Kong police several hours before we were."

"And?"

"Well, when a man sets up what should be a nice, quiet meeting to discuss moving some merchandise, but ends up getting busted and grilled by the police, he starts to wonder who the fuck set him up."

"If you are implying that I had anything to do with your predicament last night, may I remind you that I was taken in right alongside you."

"Which matters how? I'm sure deals are cut in this city between people like you and the police every day—" Mike saw Jace's eyebrows rise in surprise as the Thai interrupted him.

"However, that insult to my integrity I will not tolerate. If you are aware of anything about me, Mr. Kildar, you will know that I have never worked with the police in any capacity. Also, one might ask the same about yourself. After all, the meeting was originally changed on your end. Who is to say that our mutual acquaintance wasn't arrested and didn't give up both of us in exchange for a more lenient sentence?"

The phone's speaker was loud enough for the rest of the room to hear Than's indignant reply. Mike raised an eyebrow at Jace, who nodded. "Point. All right, let us assume that we are both being played here. During my—interview, the officer mentioned that the Hong Kong police had been watching this Sunia guy for a while."

"That would make sense, particularly if he had graduated from running American cigarettes to more sensitive items. It is possible that you and I both got caught in their very broad net. However, I distrust the coincidence."

"That makes two of us. The fact remains, though, that we still have the rest of your merchandise, and you still have the rest of our payment."

This time the pause was one of surprise. "You...still wish to proceed with the original deal?"

"Hell, yes. I don't want to hold on to this shit any longer than necessary. But I also can't just chuck it overboard either, as appealing as that sounds right now. I don't know about you, but I have overhead that *must* be paid, or the men who come to collect that make that fat Malay fuck look like a fluffy black kitten."

A dry chuckle rasped from the phone. "That I understand perfectly, Mr. Kildar. I, too, have incurred expenses on this job that will need to be settled soon. Given our current situation, however, how would you propose handling the exchange?"

"I'm working on that right now. Let me contact you in two hours with particulars."

"How can you be sure that it will be secure?"

"Let's just say I am taking precautions for uninvited guests. Believe me, I have no plans to visit the May House again. Two hours."

"Very well. Pending what you tell me, I will decide then."

"I will be in touch." Mike cut the connection. "Jace, find us a meeting place on the harbor suitable for not only Than and myself, but also the Hong Kong police."

"You don't ask for much, do you, Kildar?" Morgan replied as he pushed his iPad forward. "If everyone is amenable, I suggest the Shekou Container Wharf, in the industrial port of Chiwan. It's got cranes and shipping containers galore there. Of course, the HK police will have to close it down for a while..."

Vanner raised an eyebrow. "How did you know that's what he was going to ask for?"

Now it was Jace's turn to grin. "Would you believe ancient Chinese secret?"

"No."

"Okay, how about I went through every aspect of a drop, from the most public place to the most secluded, that was still accessible by both land and water? If the Kildar had asked for something in the woods or the mountains, or in the heart of the city, I would have had the optimum site for each one ready to go."

"Better not give away all your trade secrets, Jace," Mike said as he picked the tablet up. "I won't see any need to keep you on the payroll."

"Ah, but in a city of more than seven million people, knowing exactly *which* site to use is what you pay me for. This place is perfect. With enough warning, you could hide a small army there and no one would ever know it."

A smile crossed Mike's face. "I'll settle for a couple squads of Keldara."

CHAPTER ELEVEN

The container wharf at Chiwan was exactly as Jace had described it. A large concrete and asphalt wedge that jutted into the harbor off the Nanshan District in Shenzen, it held rows and rows of brightly colored shipping containers stacked next to each other. Between the rows were lanes that could easily be turned into death traps by positioning a couple of shooters atop the containers at both ends. Cargo ships were docked at several cranes, but at the insistence of the Hong Kong police through the Customs and Excise Department, no offloading was happening for the next two hours, despite the increasingly incensed complaints of the dock master.

"It's perfect," Mike had said upon getting a look at the overhead view courtesy of Google Maps. Then he had spent most of the next several hours either coordinating the various teams for the op or on the phone to Arun Than, Fang Gui, and anyone else who factored into what was going down that night.

Eleven hours later, everyone was in place. Only one person was unaccounted for, and he was causing Mike more than a bit of discomfort. "Any word from Adams at all?" he asked as he stood on the jetty next to the black water of the harbor.

"No," said Daria. "Repeated calls and texts have all gone unanswered."

"Shit. Daria, next time we're in the States, remind me to talk to that certain hospital in Virginia about a permanent tracking implant for him."

"Yes, sir. Should this be done with or without the master chief's knowledge?"

"Without is probably better. Once we pull this, we're gonna have to unass from the city immediately, with or without him. Jace, any word on your end?"

"I let everyone I could think of know to keep their eyes open for him, including a few people at that distribution company he'd mentioned. No one's heard anything about either of them. But the word's out that you're looking high and low for him, so hopefully he'll get wind of it." He stroked his chin. "Too bad you couldn't just microchip him, like a dog or a horse."

"Yeah, but those are passive—you'd still have to go out and find him. Regardless, I'm going to have to put him on a very short leash for the rest of this trip," Mike muttered. "Okay, everyone in position?"

"Team Firefly is online," Vanner said.

"Team Inara is in position," Yosif replied.

"Team Jayne is in position," Oleg said.

"Remember, Jayne Leader, they must be left alive. You copy?"

"Copy . . . Mal."

"Better check in with the locals." Mike switched to his second mike. "Lieutenant Fang, do you read?"

"Yes, Mr. Jenkins. Again, I must repeat my superior's misgivings about the conditions you demanded in order to set up this operation. From the location to the command structure, it is very . . . unorthodox, to say the least."

Mike grined at Jace as he hit the transmit button. "What can I say, Fang? I'm just a lowly *gwai-lo* here, with all the baggage that entails. However, I did get Than to agree to the meet. You'll get what you want, and everyone will go home happy."

"That remains to be seen, Mr. Jenkins."

"Then just keep watching." Mike cut the connection and turned enough to catch Jace watching out of the corner of his eye. "You do realize that what's about to go down may make you unable to return to the city for a few months...or years."

Jace shrugged. "No worries. Like I told the others, I've never been all that fond of Hong Kong. It's actually fitting that my last look at it will probably be a cargo dock."

Mike was about to reply when headlights flashed at the other end of the main corridor. "Firefly, sitrep?"

"Two SUVs coming in—apparently Than's trust only goes so far," Vanner said.

"I don't blame him, I wouldn't trust me either in this situation. Going on-air now." Mike switched over to Fang's frequency. "Than's coming in. Make sure none of your people moves before I give the signal, or the whole thing will be blown, copy?"

"Yes, Mr. Jenkins. Just get Than to take delivery of the chips, and we will handle the rest."

"Stay tuned." Mike muted that mic and hit the one for his men. "Everybody ready. Go on my mark."

Two radio clicks answered him.

Eighty feet above the ground and hidden under a white tarp, Lasko lay atop the cab of a container crane approximately one hundred fifty yards away from the meeting site. As soon as they had confirmed the meeting site, he had been tasked with infiltrating the wharf and finding the best vantage point to oversee everything. The cab of the ship-to-shore crane gave him an unobstructed, one-hundred-sixty-degree view of the entire area, including the harbor.

Since the range was much shorter than usual tonight, Lasko had chosen a 7.62mm M110 Semi-Automatic Sniper System rifle with a 20-round magazine and external suppressor attached. He was using it straight out of the box, including the Leupold 3.5X10 daytime scope—with all of the halogen mounted floodlights around the perimeter of the area, the place was bright as day. The only way anyone would be able to detect him once he began shooting was by tracking the angle of the shots back to his place of concealment.

Lasko peered through his optics, setting up the rhythm of his shots should he have to take down multiple targets quickly. While he lamented the idea of leaving targets alive, that was what the Kildar had ordered, and so it would be.

"Three, four, five..." he counted under his breath as the two SUVs drove toward the Kildar and Jace. He then moved his reticle onto the policemen who thought they were concealed around the area. "...six, seven, eight..."

Wedged in between two shipping containers, Oleg hit his radio. "Team Jayne, report."

Five clicks answered him. Oleg nodded, satisfied that everyone was in position.

They had been assigned the most difficult part of the operation; once the police team had dispersed to its various positions, they were to maneuver into a position to cover them as well as the exchange on the wharf.

This time Oleg would be providing cover, not cover fire. He snugged the MGL-140 up to his shoulder and aimed at the open space where the SUVs were pulling to a stop. Less than three hundred yards—he'd have to arc it to make sure the grenade armed and landed within the target zone, otherwise he'd be launching metal paperweights...

Jace had done enough of these kinds of meetings to know the drill. Stand relaxed, with hands in plain sight, but be ready to move for both his weapon and cover in a heartbeat. Despite the friendly sounding conversation over the phone, Than wasn't messing around this time. A small army of hired thugs emerged from the Cadillac Escalades. They were professional enough, setting up a perimeter around Mike and Jace that cut off any exit except by diving into the harbor, and communicating with each other by radio. Jace checked the hiding places of the police he'd spotted so far—if any were seen, this op would turn very bloody in a heartbeat.

Only when they were sure the site was secure did the rear passenger door of the second SUV open, and Arun Than emerge. Flanked by two of the bodyguards, he approached the Kildar and Jace. One of the men walked toward Mike with a portable metal detector, but was intercepted by Jace, who shook his head. The hardcase looked back at Than, who held up his hand.

"Than," Mike said.

"Mr. Kildar." The Thai fixer nodded to his men. "More overhead for what is turning into a very expensive meeting."

"Not my call, and I am sure it was not yours either."

Than regarded the pair. "I do not see a case with the rest of my purchase nearby."

"That's because a slight problem has arisen." Keeping his hands away from his sides, Mike stepped closer to the other man. "Are you sure you weren't followed?"

"I had decoy cars head out from several of my places of business at the same time. Another added expense."

"Well, they weren't good enough. Don't look around or react in any way now, but the Hong Kong police are already here."

Than's eyebrows rose, but he betrayed no other outward reaction. "There is no way they could have hacked my communications. Have you lured me out here to betray me, Mr. Kildar?"

"Of course not," Mike snapped. "You trusted me enough to come out here, and I'm holding up my end of the bargain. I'm also going to get your ass and mine out of here in one piece. However, you will have to do what I say when I—"

Mike was cut off by the sound of automatic gunfire erupting from the rearmost SUV, which was answered by weapons fire from several points around the yard. A moment later an amplified voice ordering everyone to drop their weapons and place their hands on their heads echoed off the container walls around them.

The moment he heard gunfire, Jace had drawn his Brügger & Thomet MP9 machine pistol. Then he rushed Than, taking him to the ground as the two bodyguards were felled in the initial volley.

"What the hell happened?" Mike snapped.

"Police might have gotten made! Or we got sold out by someone inside the force!" Jace shouted while checking for threats in their immediate vicinity. So far, the hired goons were exchanging fire with the cops, but no one was coming toward them—yet.

He glanced back at the Kildar, who was in the dirt and barking orders into his lapel mike.

"Jayne, go! Inara, stand-by for extraction!"

"Team Jayne, execute."

With four squeezes of the trigger, Oleg sent four grenades sailing toward the designated target zone. When they hit, they began pluming clouds of dense, gray smoke over the area.

Although he was itching to advance and back up his team, he knew he needed to stay where he was, just in case the police had their own back-up for the men on site. Reports from his people began filtering in:

"Jayne Three, my two targets are down."

"Jayne Five, both targets neutralized."

When the shooting had started, Jayne Four, Gregor Ferani, had risen from his hiding place atop a stack of containers and eased over the side into a narrow alley. Reaching out with his right hand, he pushed against the opposite container and hand-walked his way down to the ground.

Completely occupied with exchanging fire with the gunmen in the yard, the pair of Hong Kong policemen ten yards away never heard him land. Shaking his head, Gregor rolled a flash-bang grenade right under their feet. He stepped around the corner of the cargo container, mouth open, hands over his ears. The grenade went off with an ear-splitting crack and bright flashes a second later.

After all, the Kildar said incapacitate them—not that they had to be unharmed, he thought as he moved to his secondary position, searching for more prey.

▲   ▲   ▲

With Dmitri out of commission for the time being, Givi had been field-promoted to acting second in command. Jayne Two also had a pair of policemen to subdue, and Givi, who was only a few centimeters shorter than Oleg, chose a more direct route.

He also climbed down from his elevated position to the roof of the bottom-most container, his hands gripping the edge and his feet on the ledge formed by the roof. Then he inched his way over until he was right above the two men.

When Oleg's smoke grenades detonated, Givi had simply stepped into space. Two hundred ninety-five pounds of Keldara and gear hurtled down at the unsuspecting pair of men. He slammed into both of them, his forearms smashing down on their shoulders, knocking the pair to the ground. One was out cold, but the other tried to get up. He was swiftly put down by a rap of Givi's rifle butt to his head.

"Jayne Two, targets cleared."

Atop the cabin, Lasko aimed and fired, aimed and fired. His rubber bullets incapacitated every person he aimed at, both police and gangsters alike. The whoop of a siren behind him made the laconic sniper pause a moment. He keyed his headset even as he reached for a magazine of high-velocity rounds, just in case.

"Kildar, police reinforcements are approaching from the water. What are your orders?"

"Disable them as well, Blue Hand. No fatalities!" Jace heard Mike yell into his mic.

Even with the smoke and Team Jayne's elimination of much of the police team, rounds were still coming much too close for Jace's comfort. He had gotten Than behind their SUV, which had been peppered with rounds from the police, rendering it undrivable. The remaining shooters on Than's payroll were more interested in saving their own skins. One of them dove into the second SUV and backed it up to try and escape the wharf.

"We have to get to cover—" he shouted just as more bright

lights lit up the end of the narrow road. He poked his head up long enough to see another riot control vehicle pull onto the wharf. "Jesus, did Fang bring everybody in the building with him?"

A smoke grenade burst in front of the advancing armored truck, but didn't slow it. The ugly black vehicle accelerated toward the SUV. Its armored prow smashed into the target vehicle's rear hard enough to send it careening to one side. The SUV smacked into a row of containers and bounced off with a crumpled front grille and fender, and no sign of the fleeing driver inside.

"Blue Hand, target police vehicle to disable, repeat, disable!" Mike ordered. A moment later, the left front tire on the riot vehicle deflated with a bang. The one behind it went next, but the big truck kept approaching. "Shit, they got run-flats on it!"

"Where's the gems?" Jace shouted at Than.

"They're safe, but you'll never see them unless you get me out of here!" the Thai shouted back.

"We're working on it! Get to the other—" Jace's order was cut off again by the armored vehicle crunching into the other SUV, hitting its rear corner hard enough to buckle the frame as it shoved the smaller vehicle aside. The riot truck also dispersed much of the smoke, making Mike, Jace, and Than visible to the remaining police.

"Jayne Leader, pop smoke on my position!" Mike called.

Meanwhile, Jace drew a bead on the riot vehicle. He knew there was no hope of penetrating the armor, but he would provide as much of a distraction as possible to allow the Kildar and Than to escape.

"I'm open to suggestions, Kildar!" he yelled.

"Wait—say again!" Mike frowned as he pressed his earpiece and listened. "Oleg says there's a—large truck heading our way very fast!"

Sure enough, the honk of an air horn could be heard at the far end of the wharf. For a moment, everybody turned to look at what was coming down the pike.

Barreling along at top speed, a tractor-trailer truck swerved into the road from the street outside. For a moment, its right side lifted off the ground, the truck careening forward on its left wheels before slamming heavily back down again. The horn blared again, and the truck's twin smokestacks belched out black smoke as it picked up speed, its bright lights blinding everyone.

"Who the hell—?" Jace began, but was stopped by Mike.

"Only one man can make that kind of entrance."

The truck's air horn blared yet again, and sure enough, Jace caught a glimpse of a manic-looking Adams behind the driver's wheel. "You gotta be shitting me..."

"Nope. All teams, all teams, unass on my mark. Get ready," Mike said to Jace and Than.

"Where are we going?" Than asked.

"Just follow us," Jace replied, tensing to run.

"Jace, make sure you collect Adams," Mike said. "Than, you're with me."

"Okay, but I still don't under—" the fixer started to say.

"No time. Jayne, evac plan Sierra Foxtrot, now!"

A second later, bright flashes and loud explosions sounded at several different places throughout the wharf. Plumes of black smoke jetted into the air around the perimeter and throughout the containers themselves. The entire jetty was quickly covered in a thick haze.

"Wait for it!" Mike said.

Spotting the trouble riding up his rear, the driver of the riot control vehicle had tried to turn to face the seemingly out-of-control truck. Before he could get all the way around, the semi broadsided him.

The impact sent the six-wheeled vehicle skidding toward the edge of the wharf.

"Inaras scatter!" Mike broadcast the moment he saw where the APC was headed.

The driver tried accelerating out of the way, but he was too late. The riot vehicle hung up on the edge of the concrete platform as its left wheels pitched off the surface, then the semi shoved forward harder as Adams floored the gas pedal. The semi's engine screamed as it forced the APC into the water with a huge splash.

"Go go go!" Mike said, running for the water as well. "Team Inara, assist police out of vehicle, then evac from area."

"Come on, Than!" Jace grabbed the Thai and hauled him with toward the edge of the wharf.

"Where are we—wait—you're not serious—"

"JUMP!" With Mike beside him, Jace dragged the fixer into Victoria Harbor. Behind them, a series of blinding pyrotechnics erupted throughout the wharf, raining sparks and smoke down on the remaining policemen and hired thugs.

When the smoke and fireworks cleared a few minutes later, there was no sign of Mike, Jace, Arun Than, or any other foreigners.

Well, except for one.

From his perch high above everything, Lasko watched the whole operation go down, shielding his eyes when the fireworks went off to preserve his sight. He had disabled the police boat by hitting its stern with a trio of shots that had killed the engine, and clucked his tongue when his regular bullets had not stopped the police vehicle. He also saw the riot truck's team appear in the water and get picked up by a raft deployed from the drifting police boat.

His next hour was spent observing many policemen go up and down the entire wharf, taking photographs, talking to the other officers who were there, and generally reconstructing what had happened. That made the Keldara pause, as he figured someone would eventually figure where the shots from overhead had been coming from, but as he watched the activity through his scope, no one seemed to be bringing that particular aspect up.

As the HK police scurried around, representatives from the container port came over and got into what looked like a heated discussion with Lieutenant Fang and several of his men. From what Lasko could tell, it seemed to be about when the wharf would be reopened to ship traffic again. The bickering voices even got loud enough to carry to his location.

While watching the argument, Lasko heard a quiet voice in his ear. "Blue Hand, prepare for extraction."

"Affirmative. Extract in two minutes." Lasko folded and stowed his tarp and slung his rifle after removing the suppressor and covering the scope. After making sure no one was looking in his direction, he began climbing out onto the long boom of the idle crane. At the very end, he tied off a loop of Edelrid Cobra 10.3mm rope to the lowest bar, pulled on climbing gloves, and radioed in. "Blue Hand ready for extraction."

A black Zodiac raft with a silent electric motor zipped out from behind a docked cargo ship toward the crane. Timing his descent, the Keldara sniper fast-rappelled down until he hung a meter over the water.

The Zodiac slowed just enough for him to drop in and untie the knot, allowing him to collect the rope. At the tiller, Vanel twisted the throttle and turned the raft around as Marko kept watch on the men farther down the wharf.

In seconds, the three men disappeared back into the night.

CHAPTER TWELVE

"While your methods are highly unorthodox, Mr. Kildar, I must say that I cannot fault their effectiveness," Arun Than said.

He was sitting on the rear deck of the *Big Fish*, dressed in a white linen short-sleeved shirt and trousers, and drinking a cup of *cha-dam-ron*, strong black tea sweetened with sugar, no milk.

Across the table from him, Mike sipped a cup of strong black coffee. "I was a bit concerned that you might try to resist once you saw we were going into the water. However, once the divers got to you, everything went as well as it could."

Once in the water, Mike, Jace, Than, and Adams had all been met by Inara team members, who gave them each buddy mouthpieces and escorted them from the operation area to a large Zodiac they had waiting four hundred yards past the operation zone. The moment the four men were onboard, the raft had zipped back to the yacht. They had waited for the rest of the teams to join them, including Lasko, Vanel, and Marko, who rendezvoused with the thirty-five-foot tender vessel five miles out. Once everyone was aboard, they had gotten underway, and were currently enjoying the sunrise while heading out into the South China Sea as fast as the twin Cat 3606 engines could propel them.

"I hope the clothes that were selected for you are comfortable,"

Mike said. "It was too bad nothing could be done about your suit. Again, we'll make sure a replacement is sent to you."

The lean Thai shook his head. "Since this is the second time my life has been saved by you and your people, I think it is I who should be offering you a gift."

Their conversation was politely interrupted by Daria, who led Tsira and Martya onto the deck. The latter girls were each carrying a covered, silver serving platter. "Gentlemen, breakfast is served. Mr. Than, as we were unsure as to what you would prefer, we took the liberty of having our chef prepare what we understand to be three traditional Thai breakfast foods."

Tsira set her tray down and removed the top, letting Than inspect the offerings. "*Chok*, our classic rice porridge. *Khao khai chiao*, an omelet with white rice. I see you even included the typical chili sauce and cucumber slices. And *khao tom*, or rice soup, this one looks to be made with shrimp." He leaned back in his chair and smiled at the ladies. "Well done, it all looks delicious. You will join me, of course, Mr. Kildar?"

"Call me Mike." The Kildar picked up his fork and knife as Martya set down a large tray, laden with his traditional eggs, steak, bacon, home fries, and toast. Noting his guest's appreciative gaze, Mike motioned for him to dig in as the girls left. "There's plenty here, so feel free."

"Thank you." Than stabbed a piece of bacon from Mike's tray and added it to his meal. "Although I appreciate your staff's enthusiasm, I haven't eaten any of this in years. Not since I was scratching a living out in Bangkok. My tastes run to more Western fare nowadays."

"From what I gather, you've come a long way since then." Mike said as he popped a slice of steak into his mouth.

"Some would say yes, some would say no. What I do not have, it would seem, is the connections that you have in places like Hong Kong." Than ate a bite of his omelet, chewing thoughtfully. "For example, if you do not mind my boldness, just how did you know that the police were waiting to arrest all of us?"

Mike cleared his throat. "I had not been quite as forthcoming about that in our previous conversations. I have a highly placed informant in the Hong Kong Police. When they learned of my detainment two nights ago, they got me released shortly after Lieutenant Fang let you go. I figured we were being followed anyway, and that was confirmed late yesterday afternoon. That was the reason I needed to get you and myself away from the police in a fashion that would prevent any effective pursuit."

"Which seems to have worked very well indeed. However, I would guess that the heavily armed men that you have at your disposal would also prevent the authorities of any nation from asking too many questions." Than leaned forward. "You cannot be just a simple mercenary hired for Soon Yi's protection. Just who are you exactly, and why are you here?"

Mike sipped his orange juice. "That, Arun, is a long story for another time. For now, let's just say I brought some of my people down here to do some specialized training, and have stumbled onto something that certain groups want me to look into further."

"How artfully vague." Than nodded and smiled as he continued eating.

"Trust me, you really do not want to know any more." Mike finished his steak and started on his eggs. "Besides, like you said earlier, I'm sure you have skeletons in your closet that you'd prefer your clients don't know about either."

The Thai's brown eyes twinkled as he nodded. "Oh, more than you can count. Since I expect to be a guest on your yacht for a few days, perhaps I'll even share one or two. Asia is a fascinating region in many ways. But for now, let us finish our meal and then conclude our business, yes?"

"Of course. But to avoid any misunderstanding, you are my guest while you are aboard this vessel. My only request is that you do not approach the bridge, or attempt to enter any of the staterooms that are guarded by any of my men. Oh, and the young ladies aboard are not for recreational purposes. Other than that, you have the run of the rest of the ship."

"You are most kind. Regarding your women, delightful though they appear, my proclivities do not extend in that direction. Rest assured that no one here is in danger of receiving any unwanted advances. Your men, while handsome, tend to run a bit too—defined for my taste."

"Fair enough."

"In the meantime, I might as well deliver to you the rest of your payment." Than began unbuttoning his shirt, revealing a wrinkled, still-damp T-shirt underneath. "Just a moment while I . . . take this off."

"Would you like some privacy?" Mike asked with one eyebrow raised.

"No, it will just take a moment. Besides, it will be good to have this clammy thing away from me." He removed the shirt and pulled the T-shirt off over his head. Mike noticed that the undergarment didn't behave like a normal shirt—it flexed oddly, as if made of a thicker material.

"Bulletproof?" he asked.

"Perhaps, although I would hate to test it." He set the T-shirt on the table with an odd *clunk*. "Go ahead, examine it."

Mike picked it up and was surprised by the weight and thickness. "The rest of the gems, right?"

Than nodded. "A friend of mine uses these particular garments to smuggle currency into and out of China on occasion. He claims he's never been caught, and gave me one to try. I figured last night would be the perfect opportunity. When I get a chance, I must thank your bodyguard for his assistance. I had no idea it would be that heavy underwater."

"You'll have your chance soon enough." Mike worked on the cloth of the shirt with his knife and extracted one of the gems, a flawless, one-carat diamond. He held it up so the gem gleamed in the sun. "Now that is pretty."

"Plenty more where those came from," Than said. "I would prefer to see what they are buying, if you do not mind."

"Of course, Vanner will be happy to show you the rest of the motherboards. That reminds me, since you and I are both now *persona non grata* in Hong Kong for the immediate future, where would you like to go from here?"

Than sipped his tea. "That is an excellent question. Of course, I am supposed to ensure delivery of that package to its final destination."

Mike frowned. "My intel indicated that you usually didn't get involved in that sort of thing."

"There is payment, and there is *payment*," Than said with a smile. "My personal services are available, although the cost is exorbitant. However, when someone is willing to meet that price, that is exactly what they receive. Since the package's ultimate destination is Myanmar, only a brief step away from my old stomping grounds of Thailand, I would like to make you a proposition."

"I'm listening," Mike said while he kept opening the shirt's interior compartments. Soon the table was littered with glittering gems, which flashed red, blue, white, and yellow in the morning sunlight.

"You have the gems, but have you thought about how you are going to convert them into cash?"

Mike looked up at that. "Oh, I have one or two ways."

"No doubt a man of your means does. However, you will not receive a better rate than in Phuket, Thailand, the gem-smuggling capital of Southeast Asia. I can get you whatever payment you desire, gold, U.S. dollars, bearer bonds, you name it, and at a better price than you would receive anywhere else—even in America."

"I don't know—I know some people who would make me a pretty good deal. But let's say I'm interested—what's in it for you?"

"In exchange for my expertise in this area, you agree to escort me and the boards to their final destination in Myanmar. As I said, we'd be heading there anyway, so we might as well kill two birds with one stone, as it were. Your payment would be the improved percentage I will negotiate on your behalf."

While Than was talking, Mike had removed all of the gems and piled them on the cloth. He tied the ends together to make an improvised satchel and sat there staring at the small fortune on the table in front of him. Leaning back in his chair, he finished his coffee, then looked up at Than.

"Sure, why the hell not?"

Vanner couldn't take his eyes off the shining pile of gems in the middle of the conference room table. "How much do you figure they're worth?"

"At current rates on the international market, these are valued at somewhere between three-and-a-half and four million dollars, given the standard fluctuation," Daria said. "Black market rates would probably be around half to two-thirds of the low end."

"I expect Than will do better than that. Don't forget that he wants us to escort him to Myanmar along with the boards," Mike said. "This is practically falling into our lap."

"Yeah, that's what worries me," Jace said while staring at the gems. "You know the old mission saw: *anything* that looks too good to be true *always* isn't."

"Spoken like a true operator." Mike scooped up a handful of the gems and let them trickle through his fingers. "However, since the winds of fortune are blowing us in the right direction, I see no reason not to let them take us as far as possible."

"I notice you didn't say whether they were winds of good fortune or bad," Vanner said.

"We won't know until we reach the next port, will we?" Mike asked as he rose from the table. "Speaking of which, I'm about to go wake up a man whose good luck has just run out. All of you will probably want to watch this."

"Damn, what is that stink?" Jace asked.

"That is *eau de* Ass-Boy, after marinating in equal parts beer, women, and Hong Kong for the past thirty-six hours." Mike shook his head. "It's a miracle he didn't come back buck-naked with who-knows-what tattooed on who-knows-where."

Mike, Vanner, Jace, Daria, Greznya, and many of the Keldara were all gathered on the rear deck, watching the still form of

Adams as he sawed logs in the bright sunlight. The master chief was dressed in what looked like a pair of battered dungarees, one flip-flop, and a blinding, stained, and buttonless Hawaiian shirt that was missing one sleeve.

"Typically the punishment for dereliction of duty and failure to report would have been a keelhauling during the days of the Royal Navy. However, since the offender did return and attempt to acquit himself somewhat honorably, the following lighter punishment will be administered." Mike held out a hand, and a large bucket was given to him. "The rest of you may want to stand back."

After the proper precautions were taken, Mike poured the entire five gallons of ice-cold seawater over Adams' head. The frigid deluge shocked the former SEAL into a semblance of awareness; he sat up, coughed out about a pint of water and other, less identifiable fluids before falling back onto the deck.

"Master Chief Charles Adams, ten-HUT!" Mike bellowed. That got his second-in-command sitting upright again. "Front and center!" That almost got Adams standing, but he slipped on the pool of liquid and landed on his ass again. The shock was enough to get him oriented toward the Kildar, who was glaring at him with all the vehemence he could muster.

"Master Chief, you are charged with failure to report. How do you plead?" Mike demanded.

"I mad' mov'ment, sir!" Adams pulled himself up, almost overbalanced and fell on his face, but saved himself with much arm-flailing.

"I have heard this story before, Master Chief! May I remind you that we are very far from Las Vegas!" Mike replied.

"Accomp'ished my miss'n, sir!" Adams managed.

"And how—" Mike's dressing down of Adams was interrupted by a strange noise. "What is that noise, Master Chief?"

"Thas—my phone—jus' a minit..." Adams groped for his side pocket and dragged out his smartphone, which looked just as bad as its owner.

"I knew getting him the shock and liquid-proof case would come in handy," Vanner said.

"See! Miss'n... accomp'ished! Goddamn Chinese beer, like screwin' inna canoe..." Adams said. Still swaying, he held the phone out to Mike, who grabbed it and read the screen.

"What did Master Chief mean by that last part?" Greznya asked.

"He meant it is fucking close to water," Vanner replied with a straight face. "What's the word, Kildar?"

Mike read everything on the screen, then thumbed up to the top and read it again. "If I wasn't seeing it right here, I wouldn't believe it. Listen to fucking this: '*Dear Mr. Adams: We were very impressed by the materials you had given Mr. Lau regarding the Mountain Tiger Brewery. The follow-up meeting with you last night was also very remarkable—*'"

"Given what he looks like, I'm surprised anyone even remembered there *was* a meeting last night," Vanner said.

"Wait, there's more." Mike continued reading: "'*We look forward to further discussions, and to entering into a mutually beneficial business partnership between your company and ours. Sincerely, Mr. Liu Chen, Vice-President of European Imports, Xìngfú Distribution International.*' Got his goddamn business card attached to the e-mail and everything."

Mike raised his head to stare at Adams. "You told me it was a meeting with your buddy, in and out. Just who the hell else did you meet with in Hong Kong?"

"There was... lotta singin'... karaoke..." Adams slurred. "Lotsa beer and wha'd they call it... bye-joo?"

"Oh, shit. No wonder he's been flat on his ass ever since he got back," Jace said. "Russians have vodka, Irish have whiskey, and the Chinese have *bái jiǔ*. It's an alcoholic drink distilled from rice in the south, and from sorghum, wheat, or Job's tears in the north. It starts at eighty proof, and goes up to one-twenty, although I've heard rumors of a one-forty-proof variety that can strip skin off your tongue and paint off a car. Since he was an honored guest, I'm sure they served him the more potent varieties, as those have the least impurities."

"Now *that* I would have paid to see," Vanner muttered.

"Well, despite his deplorable condition, I cannot argue with results," Mike said. "In light of this new evidence, all charges are hereby dropped." He tossed the phone to Vanner. "Forward all of this information to Mother Mahona, have her secure a translator from Jace's recommendations, and begin negotiations on the contract."

"I would advise retaining an Asian law firm for the contract as well, sir. It will make things much easier in the long run."

"Do it." Mike turned back to Adams, who was still swaying back and forth, despite the fact that they were at a full stop on a calm sea. "Master Chief Adams, get the hell off what was my nice, clean deck and clean yourself up!"

"Yes, sirrr . . ." Adams came to attention, saluted . . . and pitched headlong toward that same deck. He would have broken his nose if not for Mike grabbing him and shoving him back into the waiting arms of Oleg and Vil.

"Get him cleaned up and racked out. I want him ready to go when we reach Phuket." Mike shook his head. "If even half of what I've heard is true, I am going to have to put him in a straight-jacket when we go ashore."

That night, Vanel couldn't sleep. The Kildar's training regimen didn't slack off while in the field (it included cross-overs *under* the stationary yacht). That, combined with four-hour duty watches, prep for upcoming missions, *and* a shift learning how to pilot and navigate the boat itself, meant he should have been lights out as soon as he hit the mattress, but something was keeping him awake.

It wasn't the action they had seen already, or the near guarantee of more to come in the next few days. Indeed, he was looking forward to the next time he would enter combat and win more honor for his house and himself.

Vanel had also received praise in his AARs from both Adams and Yosif. The side mission assisting the Chinese police out of their sinking vehicle had gone very well. He'd even overheard the Kildar himself mention his name in the same sentence as the term "a natural" while talking to the master chief. It wasn't any of that at all.

And it wasn't their destination that was keeping him up either. So far, the landfalls they had made had either been large cities or jungle-filled islands. They were about twenty hours away from Phuket, and had just entered the Strait of Malacca again.

The truth was, Vanel did not know why he couldn't sleep. He just knew he wasn't. After tossing and turning for long minutes, he rose from his bed and padded to the door. He was almost outside when a throat quietly cleared on his left.

Freezing in place, Vanel slowly looked over to see Yosif staring at him from his bed. "Going somewhere, Inara Four?"

"I—cannot sleep. I thought a walk on deck might help."

"Five minutes, then you return."

Vanel nodded. "Yes, sir."

Before his team leader's head hit the pillow, the Keldara was asleep again.

With an envious grin, Vanel headed topside. Walking into the balmy, rainy night, he took a deep breath of the salty air and immediately started to feel better.

Even the rain here is opposite from our homeland, he thought, raising his face into the warm drops as he walked to the railing. Back home, the rain was almost always cold, even in summer. Instinctively he looked left and right for the floating guards that made their irregular rounds, but could scarely make them out in the darkness. They, however, wouldn't have the same problem, as they'd be wearing night-vision goggles.

A shadow fell across him, and he turned, expecting to be challenged by the night guard. Instead, one of the last people in the world he expected to see out here at this hour appeared.

"Kildar!" Vanel stiffened to attention as his leader stood before him, a bottle of Mountain Tiger in his hand.

"At ease, Vanel. The regular rotation is still on. I'm just out for a stroll."

"Yes, Kildar, as am I."

"Can't sleep?"

Vanel shrugged. "Yes—I thought fresh air might help."

"What do you think of our trip so far?"

Vanel's tongue was momentarily paralyzed. He hadn't had a lot of one-on-one time with the Kildar, although Oleg had said the man was like this; utterly dedicated while on mission, and pretty laid-back when off. "It is very enjoyable."

"Oh? Which part have you liked the best?"

"The underwater parts, sir."

The Kildar chuckled. "Half-fish, just like Yosif and the rest. Let me guess, you've been so busy with mission prep and other duties that you haven't had time to get to the sundeck?"

If a Keldara elder—or, All Father forbid—a Mother had asked that question, the right answer would have been, "What sundeck?" Of course, the elders wouldn't have allowed the existence of the sundeck in the first place. However, when the elders were away, the children would play. The girls had all discovered the pleasures of lying out on the upper deck for hours—after enduring a lecture from Greznya regarding sunscreen, of course.

It had already become a game among the various teams to manufacture the best excuse to show up there during shift change. The winner so far had been Marko, who'd stayed there for two hours during the trip to Hong Kong, claiming he'd been instructed to test the lotion the girls were using to make sure it was the proper "SOF." The fact that he'd gotten the acronym wrong hadn't lessened his victory in the slightest.

Vanel had not had a chance to go yet, but he was working on a damn good reason to get himself up there. Therefore, his reply was confident. "I have heard of the place, but have not been there myself, of course." The "*yet*" was added only in his head.

"Of course you haven't." The Kildar grinned as he clapped him on the shoulder. "Keep up the good work, Vanel. And don't stay too late out here. My Inaras have to be rested and ready for whatever Thailand might throw at us."

"Yes, sir." Vanel watched the man head down the middle staircase below deck. He exhaled only when he was sure the Kildar was gone. Still, now he felt a hundred times better than when he had first come topside. Humming quietly, he decided to take one lap around the huge boat, then head back down.

Rounding the stern of the *Big Fish*, he had just started down the port side when he heard an odd noise. Vanel stopped in place, then soundlessly crept to the nearest wall, disappearing into the shadows there. He snuck forward, one step at a time, moving heel-toe, heel-toe as he had been trained. Hearing the noise again—almost like a muffled sob—Vanel peeked around the corner, his eyes widening in surprise.

"Xatia?"

Hearing her name spoken from three feet away made the tiny girl squeak and jump into the air, whirling around to glare at him with tear-streaked eyes. "Vanel! Are you trying to scare me to death?" she hissed, smacking him on his broad chest.

"I—I am sorry to have disturbed you." Even in his embarrassment, he couldn't help noticing that she filled out her two-piece bikini—which was soaking wet—extremely well. Although she was short, her lush curves were straining the bright scraps of cloth. Along with his sympathy, Vanel felt something else stirring a bit further south, and shifted his weight so he could adjust himself and make sure she didn't notice.

"What is the matter?" he asked, to keep her attention from wandering as well.

The small girl shook her head miserably. "I—oh, this is so embarrassing, I mean, I have just arrived here, but I am homesick already!" She waved her hand at the endless ocean. "The ship is great, and the girls are fun too, but I simply cannot take all this water!"

Before he knew it, she had thrown herself into his arms. Even with the very pleasant sensation of all that female skin on his, Vanel still glanced around to ensure no one else was observing them. No matter what the circumstances, the elders would *not* look upon this at all kindly.

He patted her back awkwardly while clearing his throat. "There, there—"

She looked up at him, and although he tried to fight it, he stared back into her eyes. "I feel ever so much better now that you are here, Vanel."

"Uhh..." Even almost losing himself in her deep brown eyes, and with those lush, pouty lips mere inches away from his own, Vanel was still able to retain his situational awareness. Therefore, instead of kissing her, which he wanted very much to do, he clamped a hand over her mouth and drew her into the shadows with him.

"Shh," he hissed into her ear. To her credit, Xatia didn't squirm, squeal, or try to bite his hand. Instead, she waited for his next words.

For a long moment, the two Keldara just stood there, waiting. Then Vanel heard the noise that had put him on alert again.

A faint *clink* that could only come from an anchor chain. But it shouldn't be making any noise, as they were up and secured fast. Which could only mean...

"Find the nearest guard and let him know there are tangos incoming on the port bow." Releasing Xatia, Vanel didn't check to make sure she was going to do what he had told her to do. He was already heading forward to intercept whoever was stupid enough to try to sneak aboard a Keldara vessel.

CHAPTER THIRTEEN

These guys are crazy, Somchai Chaisukkasem thought as he guided the small skiff across the ocean water toward the majestic yacht. *No way am I going up there.*

Fortunately, he didn't have to. A former fisherman, he had turned to rice farming five years ago, but the floods in his native land had wiped out his crop, so he had no choice but to return to the ocean and try to catch enough to sell again.

Since then, his days had been filled with nothing but water, water, and more water, starting before dawn and ending after dusk. The fish he caught was barely keeping his family fed, and Somchai found he had to go farther and farther out to catch them every day.

So, when a man he had never seen before walked up to his boat and offered him a month's earnings to take five men out onto the Gulf of Thailand for one night, Somchai had not thought too hard before agreeing. He figured they were probably criminals, but by that point he was too tired and desperate to care. They had paid the half of the outrageous price up front, and he had made sure his wife and three children had received it before he left. They had also brought a brand-new electric motor for his boat, which they said he could keep after the job was done. Somchai had his doubts that he'd ever see land again, but he was still willing to take the risk.

Now, however, he was having second thoughts about the whole

thing. The night had started with him coming down to the pier to see a half-dozen masked men with wicked looking guns waiting for him. The forty-foot cigarette boat they rode in for the first thirty miles with his fishing boat lashed to the stern was the next clue.

When he saw exactly what they were asking him to do, however, he almost backed out right then and there. But the only way out now was with a bullet to the back of his head. Therefore, Somchai had aimed his boat through the rain toward the fast-moving white yacht in the distance, concentrating very hard on the masked man's insistence that they approach the *bow* of the immense pleasure craft. Fortunately, the electric motor worked perfectly, propelling his eighteen-foot skiff toward the superyacht in near silence. The plan had been to have the cigarette boat distract any one who might be on deck with a pass to the rear, making sure to show up on their radar, while the skiff approached the bow and allowed the boarding party to come aboard.

"You will have only one chance," he said when they were less than a minute out. "I will pass in front of the yacht only once. How you get aboard is your problem. I won't be coming back for anyone."

"Just get us there and we will do the rest." The leader had replied.

Even with his fifteen years of piloting, they had almost gone down anyway. Somchai thought the yacht was doing about sixteen knots, and had come in on an angle to the bow, hoping to give these men enough time to throw their grapples and get aboard before he passed the ship completely.

The boat was moving faster than he had thought, however, and his skiff came dangerously close to the sweeping bow. Wanting to veer away, he'd felt the cold circle of a pistol barrel pressed against his neck. "Get us close to the boat, and you won't get shot," the leader had said. Somchai had done as ordered, sending up a silent prayer for himself and his family and preparing himself for a short swim before drowning in the middle of the Gulf.

He had come as close to the gleaming vessel's port side as he had dared, and the two men had thrown their grappling hooks, then the six had scrambled aboard. One of them had hit the anchor as he climbed, making the chain clink in the quiet night. Somchai didn't care if they made it aboard or not, he only had eyes for the huge yacht bow that was about to crush his skiff into flotsam.

Jamming the rudder hard to port with all his strength, Somchai felt his skiff rock wildly back and forth under him as he hit the swells rolling out from the yacht. He took on a good deal of water, and thought he was going to sink before the skiff righted itself and kept going, although now riding low in the water. Once he was stable, he twisted the throttle and sped off into the night, wanting to get as far away from those pirates as he could. Rowing back to the shore once the engine gave out would be a small price to pay for escaping with his life.

The last man on deck, Daniel bin Suleiman, scrambled over the railing of the yacht, anticipating an easy subdual and looting. Even though his cousin Issako had warned him about the dangerous people he was going up against, the former Malaysian Army corporal thought if they could maintain the element of surprise in the first few minutes, then the battle would already be half won. And recovering the package and getting it back to Sunia would set him up in the tongs for good this time.

That was why he had rounded up a couple of army buddies who weren't doing jack-shit after their discharge, grabbed a couple of Sunia's boys, and hopped a plane to the southern tip of Thailand. Sunia had supplied them with all of the information they'd needed and seed money to pull off the plan. He just wanted the green box back. Anything else they found on the boat they could keep or sell. And that had been poor Daniel's marginally thought-out plan.

He was reaching for his submachine gun when a form charged him from the shadows. Daniel tried to bring the weapon up, but the man closed too fast and shot a palm heel strike to his chin. He move his head aside so the blow only grazed him, but the man kept moving, trapping his gun so that he couldn't fire with one arm, and grabbing the back of his neck and bringing his head forward in a vicious head-butt.

The intruders might have had more success with their infiltration, except for two problems. One, they had made enough noise to attract Vanel's attention.

Second, they were trying to come aboard just after the guard rotation. The new man was awake, alert, and very large. Like every member of each team, he shouldered his share of more mundane duties along with leading his fellow Keldara.

Fortunately, Oleg had very large shoulders. So, when he saw Xatia's small form round the aft corner of the yacht's superstructure, he didn't even raise his carbine, having identified her the moment after he caught her movement.

"What are you doing up, little one?" he asked.

She pointed across the boat to the front port side. "Men coming aboard on that side. I do not know how many. Vanel is over there already."

"Get inside now," Oleg said, then hit his mike. "All guards, tangos on front port quarter, repeat, tangos on the front port side. Move to intercept now."

As he spoke, he climbed a ladder that took him up to the raised portion of the bow that flowed into the bridge. Moving silently, Oleg stepped across the reinforced fiberglass cowling, sinking to his elbows and knees and low-crawling the rest of the way. When he reached the edge, he could hear footsteps, and then the sounds of a scuffle.

Peeking his head over, he saw a half-dozen men beginning to fan out along the railing, heading in both directions. Not one of them was looking up. Oleg heard the bow and stern guards report in as they closed from those directions. He raised his rifle and sighted in on the nearest man when one of the men was tackled by a figure that leaped on him from the shadows.

"Eliminate the rest," Oleg said as he squeezed the trigger on his silenced rifle, dropping one of the intruders just as he was about to shoot Vanel. "Leave the one Vanel is subduing alive."

Four more shots sounded in the next five seconds. Four more tangos dropped to the deck, dead.

The blow to his nose made Daniel see stars, and by the time he recovered, his weapon was gone and he was face down on the deck, his arm hammerlocked up between his shoulder blades. He looked over for the rest of his team, but only heard a series of silenced shots and the thuds of bodies falling.

He barely had time to think that maybe Issako had been right about these guys when his hands were zip-tied and he was flipped over, finding himself surrounded by a half-dozen men. One of them, a shorter guy with brown hair and cold, brown eyes, stared back at him.

"Now what the hell do we have here?"

Mike was disappointed in the night's work, though not in his men.

He'd barely gotten started on the ringleader of the pirates when the man had spilled everything he knew, including that he was working for Sunia. A team had gone out and recovered the fisherman who had brought them aboard, but the cigarette boat that had passed astern of the *Big Fish* several minutes ago had gotten away.

But all wasn't lost. While the fisherman skipper had been useless, a patsy induced by poverty to ferry these so-called pirates to the *Big Fish*, their leader had coughed up the one bit of information Mike had found interesting.

He sighed, and tossed his knife on the tray beside him. "Give me a fucking Armenian any day—they last longer. Hell, I'd go another round with Tony, if he were still here." True to his word, they had dropped Tony and his henchman off in Malaysia to be bound over for trial there.

He straightened up. "Time to go ask Soon Yi a few questions again. Keep our new friend on ice 'til we reach Thailand—we'll clean ship when we dock."

"Adams will have the AAR reports so we can find out what happened with the guards. I want to know how the hell these amateurs managed to get aboard."

Vanner nodded. "I expect it will be what we already know. Night vision isn't the greatest in rain, and they chose the best, if riskiest, attack vector by going for the bow. Even if Vanel hadn't been there, they wouldn't have gotten much farther, but we might have taken casualties."

"Exactly. So, everyone will run the numbers and make sure all bases are covered. I'm going below. Unless more pirates come over the bow, don't disturb me."

"You got it."

Mike headed below deck to Soon Yi's room. Vil was on duty outside the door, and he nodded as Mike let himself in as quietly as possible.

The clouds and rain outside ensured that there was no moonlight to see by, and he took a moment to take in the room. A shape was huddled under the blankets in the middle of the bed. As soon as he could see, Mike moved toward it like a stalking panther, intent on not being surprised. Sneaking to the bottom of the bed, he grabbed the whore's foot.

The moment he did, the blanket flew up toward his head and the foot slipped out of his grasp. As he batted the sagging cloth away, he saw a dark form come in low and piston a foot squarely at his crotch. Mike shifted and took the rock-hard sole on his thigh. He tried to grab the leg to push her onto her back and control her that way, but she used the rebound and drew it back before he could get a firm grasp on it.

Soon Yi crouched on the bed, then sprang at him. Mike was prepared for her attempted rake to his eyes. He blocked the attack with all of his strength, whipping her arm away from him and riposting with a straight arm to her chest, propelling her backward toward the closet.

Mike followed up immediately, expecting her to try to use the closet door either as a shield or a feint to lure him in and block with it. She did neither, however, grabbing the edge of the door and lashing out at him with a foot at his knee. He dodged, and this time grabbed her foot and pulled her off the door. Even as she came forward, she lashed out with her other foot while in midair, coming within a hair of hitting his face. Only Mike's superb reflexes and training kept her from connecting.

She landed on the floor with a bone-jarring *thud*. Following up his advantage, Mike used his superior weight to pin her down. However, as he dropped to one knee, she jammed her free foot against his thigh and shoved herself away with everything she had while sitting up and lashing at his face again. As Mike reared back, he felt the wind from her fingers as they passed less than an inch away from his face.

Despite her ferocity, Mike hadn't let go of her foot, and now he twisted it one hundred eighty degrees. She was forced to roll with it, otherwise he would have crippled her by tearing the ligaments in her ankle and knee. However, she didn't try to get away from him, but slid toward him, free leg cocked to attempt to hit him again.

This time Mike was ready, and snaked out his free arm to grab her other leg before it could connect. Getting his feet under him, he lifted her off the ground and dropped her before she could get both arms underneath to protect her head. The top of her skull smacked into the carpet. Mike repeated the blow, then swung her into the closet door, the last smack knocking her half-senseless.

Mike dropped her back on the floor. He knelt down and got her in a choke hold, applying enough pressure so that she was on the edge of blacking out.

"I was going to simply have another little chat with you about some people you might know who came on board tonight, but since we've both gotten all sweaty, we're going to clean up first."

He lifted her up and dragged her into the bathroom's shower stall. Mike pushed her inside, grabbed her hands, and forced them up to the showerhead pipe, lashing them to it with his belt. The shower had been designed for Americans, and she had to stand on her tiptoes to reach the ground.

Mike hit the w ater, letting the stinging cold spray play over her, making her come to with a splutter and cough. She moved her head out of the stream, but he forced it back under, prying her mouth open so the jet got inside. "Something's not right with you, and we're staying in here until I find out what it is!"

"I swear—" she said between coughs and choking. "I don't know anything!"

"Wrong answer! Earlier tonight that fat fuck Sunia sent men to board my ship. I am sure they were trying to steal that box. The only way they could have even found us is if someone was transmitting them our coordinates, and the only person on board who could do that—who would do that—is you."

"How—could I—do that?" She spluttered. "I'm always—locked in here—!"

"I don't know yet—but I am going to find out before we're through here. You're like no whore I've ever met, even Katya. You fight way too well and you haven't gone to pieces like a normal hooker would have by now."

"That's 'cause—I don't take shit—from any man! I'd rather die first!" She tried to bring her knee up into his groin, but Mike easily batted it aside.

"If you don't start talking, you will wish you were dead before I'm through with you." he tore off the soaking wet T-shirt and cotton panties they had given her for clothes, then spun her around to face the wall, heedless of her pained groan as the belt cut into her wrists.

Turning the handle to hot, Mike grabbed her jaw and forced her face up to the cascading water. "Again, telling me what I want to know might make this easier on you—then again, you're pissing me off so much that it probably won't."

A moan escaped her gritted teeth, and she tried wrenching her head away from the water to spit in his face, but Mike forced her back under, until she was choking on the stream again.

She tried to head-butt him, and he slapped her so hard that when he grabbed her head and lifted it to see if she was conscious, a trickle of blood leaked from her nose.

"*Tsk-tsk.* That should knock some sense into you. Now, I'm still waiting for you to tell me how you communicated with Sunia's men!"

"I don't—know what—you're talking about!"

"Bullshit!" Mike changed the shower spray to freezing cold water again. "I'll stay here all night if I have to."

"It had—to be—something else! Maybe someone bribed a port guard to give up your route," she gasped.

"Impossible, since we change course every hour, regardless of what we tell the harbor. Try again!"

"I—don't—KNOW! The case itself—maybe it's—bugged!!"

The words made Mike stop right there. He untied her and let her slide to the shower floor, trying to rub some feeling into her bruised and swollen wrists. Breathing hard, he stepped out of the shower. "I'm going to go check on what you just said. Who knows, maybe you're right. If not, I'll be back."

Soaking wet, he walked out of the room, earning a raised eyebrow from Vil at his appearance.

"No one can say that I'm not willing to go to any lengths to get what I need from an interrogation," He started to walk down the hall, then turned him Vil again. "Remove the closet doors—all of them—and no male is to be left alone with her in the room. Pairs only. Katya can go in unescorted if she wishes."

On his way back to his room, Mike sent a quick text to Vanner to check to see if there was any kind of transmittal device on the box. He then toweled off and fell into bed, where he slept dreamlessly for the next eight hours.

"Exactly how in the hell did you know that?"

The next morning, Mike was enjoying a three-cheese omelet with steak, home fries, toast, and coffee on the aft deck when Vanner strode up to his table and set a photograph in front of him.

Munching a slice of buttered sourdough, Mike leaned over to see a shot of the dissected case, with what looked like a small transmitter hidden inside the lining. "Huh. Is it still working?"

"Yup, transmitting a microburst pulse about every six hours. The funny part is it only transmits its coordinates when prompted, otherwise it's damn near inert. It wouldn't show up on any sort of electromagnetic scan, and of course, a lot of those would be out of the question due to the cargo in the first place."

"It's still able to transmit, right?" Mike asked.

"Yes, Creata made sure it was still powered during her examination." Vanner frowned. "So, this means that we pretty much have eyes on us the whole time we're doing this."

"Until we get rid of it, yeah." Mike nodded while staring at the photo. "She was right."

"Who. Soon Yi? You're shitting me!"

Mike leaned back in his chair. "No, we discussed it at length last night. You never came up with anything on her from the databases, right?"

The Marine intel chief almost looked insulted. "No. And we ran her every which way we could in every country in the region. Even in such backwoods places like Mongolia."

Mike forked up some home fries. "Do they even have an intelligence service?"

"We're still trying to figure that out. Bottom line, she's definitely not from there. I had Greznya and the girls run everything they could think of everywhere. I swear, if they had the epicanthic fold, we checked it out. She's got half a dozen priors in Pontianak, the capitol city of West Kalimantan province, Indonesia. For all intents and purposes, she's a working girl who decided to leave the capitol for greener pastures. She wound up near Pemangkat, where she met Tony, and the rest we know. Bottom line, if she is a spook, she's so deep undercover her own agency doesn't keep a jacket on her."

"Or you haven't found it yet." Mike smiled as he said this—he was sure Vanner and the girls had done everything they could, but he also liked to keep the stocky Marine on his toes.

"If we haven't, that's 'cause it doesn't exist to be found."

"Maybe so, but how in the hell did she know about that?"

"Lucky guess pulled out of her ass?" Vanner guessed.

"Nope. Besides, there's some other things about her that don't add up." Mike summarized his encounters with her. "First she takes a waterboarding, but has the stones to still come on to me the next day. I don't care if she flew all the way to Stockholm—no way is that normal. She's been trained by someone. You searched her clothes, right?"

"Every which way before locking her up, and then again while she was sleeping. Took the damn things apart this time. Nothing but cloth." Putting his hands on the back of a chair, Vanner leaned forward. "You think she's shadowing the box?"

"Perhaps, or maybe she's gone rogue or got burned by her agency, and is looking for either revenge, or to make a profit off this—and us."

"Now that's an interesting theory," Vanner said

"Maybe, but I'd prefer some facts to back it up." Mike thought about this while he sipped his coffee. "Maybe we can put out some feelers in the merc world, see if anyone knows about a female Chinese operative who got burned or double-crossed."

Vanner frowned. "We're good, but that will take some time. Everyone working in the shadows is always ultra-careful about who they friend and who they foe. Even with our bona fides, that doesn't mean they're just going to open up to us."

"Well, I guess you'll just have to persuade them—that, or break into some serious top-secret files."

"Let's try the web first, see what we can scare up."

"Okay. Want some breakfast?"

"No thanks, I already ate." Vanner straightened up and turned toward the stairs. "I should head back down anyway, see how Creata's doing with putting that damn box together again. I'll let you know if there's any trouble."

Mike nodded. "Works. We should make Phuket in a few hours. Make sure everything's ready to go by then."

"Can do."

CHAPTER FOURTEEN

Six hours later, Mike, Adams, Jace, and Arun were riding through the streets of the city of Phuket, in the Muang Phuket District, on the island of Phuket, Thailand.

Midway off the western coast of the Kra Isthmus, Phuket had been fiercely contested by the English, French, and Dutch for its lucrative tin resources in the seventeenth century. The victorious French established a brief monopoly until 1688, when they were expelled from the country during the Siam Revolution.

A century later, the Burmese attacked the island in 1785. They were repelled by the heroic actions of two women, Than Phu Ying Chan, the wife of the deceased governor, and her sister, Mook, both of whom achieved their victory by dressing as male soldiers, and dressing other women as male soldiers to swell the numbers of their army. Afterward, the local heroines were awarded the honorific titles Thao Thep Kasattri and Thao Si Sunthon, respectively.

When the tin market collapsed in the twentieth century, Phuket and the rest of Thailand turned to other exports and imports to survive, mainly, exporting rubber and importing tourists. After the tsunami of 2004, which killed tens of thousands, many of the island's resorts and buildings had to be repaired or rebuilt, all of which was swiftly done.

Now, as the party drove through the streets, they found no evidence of the terrible disaster. The streets were clean and well-lit, the buildings were modern, and even the palm trees were thick and lush. Tourists mingled with locals everywhere, and the city looked, and even more importantly, *felt* prosperous and thriving. The island had also escaped the massive flooding that had inundated most of the mainland, including the capitol city of Bangkok, and was definitely open for business.

The four men were all dressed in tourist casual, with loose-fitting, short-sleeved shirts and linen sport coats that could hide much underneath them. Adams had left his coat behind, preferring a brightly colored Hawaiian shirt covered with palm trees and bright parrots that Mike had said looked like Thailand had thrown up on him.

"Man, you guys sure are into economy—naming the city, province, and island the same thing." Adams said. "How does anyone tell where they're going?"

"Oh, we get around well enough. People's names around here are hard enough to say, so we try to make it easy on the foreigners," Than replied with a smile.

"Maybe so, however, your name is a model of brevity," Jace said. "I assume that it's a nickname, like most Thais?"

"More like a professional alias, if you must." The black marketer shrugged. "My true name is not as—renowned in certain circles. Therefore, I conduct most of my business under my nickname, as is common in our country. But, I am sure you would find the local women to be more than enough variety for you, Mr. Adams," Than said from the SUV's front seat.

"I definitely agree with you there." The master chief said as he turned to ogle a pair of bikini-clad women walking down the street.

"Eyes front, Ass-Boy. You're staying within sight of me at all times on the ground," Mike said without looking back.

"Even after what I got done in Hong Kong?" Adams asked.

"We shouldn't be here long enough even for you to get into trouble. Than's set up the meeting to convert our gems, and then we're back on the water to Myanmar. The sooner we get these boards out of our lives, the faster we can go back to busting pirate heads."

"That should not be a problem—I have been doing business with Khun Chal for years. Everything should be in order, and we will complete your transaction swiftly and be on our way."

"Yeah, I just keep remembering the saying about best-laid plans," Mike said, staring out at the nightlife around them.

"We should be fine. Just remember those pointers I told you about," Jace said.

"I've got them," Mike said.

"Hell, at least here we can go around strapped," Adams said. "That should make you feel better." Besides pistols, the three men all had their earpieces that linked them with Vanner and his girls on the boat.

"That it does," Mike said. "Let's just get in, sell the gems, and get out."

Jace followed Than's directions to a street a block off the main thoroughfare. They drove past a bar undergoing obvious remodeling, with soaped over windows and scaffolding covering the outside. Jace parked the SUV on the next block, and the three men scoped the area before they all got out and headed to a side door leading into the club.

With Jace and Adams casually sweep-and-clearing the way forward, Mike and Arun walked up to the metal fire door that looked bolted shut. Arun hit a button on his phone, said a quick phrase in Thai, and the door clicked open a few seconds later.

The inside was in the midst of being transformed from a dingy tropical dive into something decidedly more upscale. The walls had been patched and primed, the bare wooden floor had been sanded and was ready to varnish, and the old, rattan furniture was stacked along one wall, probably awaiting the junkman to cart them away. A marble-topped table and five chairs sat in the middle of the otherwise bare room.

"Come on." Than strode toward the table and pulled out a

chair, with Mike, Adams, and Jace following suit. They were all just about to sit down when a door behind the bar opened, and a small, wizened old man with a fringe of white hair came out. He was simply dressed in a loose, white linen shirt and matching trousers, with sandals on his feet.

Than immediately rose and clasped his hands together in front of his chest, fingers pointing up, and bowed until his face touched his fingertips. "*Sawasdee khrap*, Khun Chal."

The older man mirrored the gesture, bowing not quite as deeply as Than had. "*Sawasdee khrap*, Khun Arun."

"These are my associates that I had told you about." Than indicated each person as he introduced them. "Michael Jenkins, Charles Adams, and Jace Morgan."

The old man gave each American a slighter bow, nodding as he saw all three men return the gesture before sitting. Jace had instructed Mike and Adams about the greeting, saying it would be polite to return it if someone used it to greet them. It was especially important to do so for an older person, as Thai culture particularly venerated its elders.

"Welcome, gentlemen, to what will soon be the most popular bar on Phuket," he said in Thai as he took his seat. Chal was at twelve o'clock, with Than sitting across from him. Mike and Adams sat to the right of Chal, with Jace on the left.

"Thank you for seeing us on such short notice, Khun Chal," Than said, with Jace translating for Mike and Adams.

The old man waved off his thanks with a stubby brown hand. "For you, it is no problem, Khun Arun. Do any of you require anything. Drinks? Smoke? Something stronger?"

The three Americans demurred, and Arun asked for mineral water. A henchman brought a bottle of Perrier, as well as a hookah for Chal, who prepared the water pipe, lit it, and puffed contentedly. After a few puffs, he offered the pipe around the table. Than took it first, then Mike, Adams, and Jace. The smoke was smooth, sweet, and minty. As the last one to use the hookah, Jace passed the pipe back to Chal, who nodded with satisfaction.

"Very good, Khun Arun, very good indeed. Shall we get down to business?"

"As you wish." Than nodded again to the old man, and handed him the same small pouch Soon had given him. Chal brought out his own loupe and examined several of the gems under a small lamp that was brought to him. Then the two Thais began a rapid negotiation that Jace could barely follow. He tried letting Mike know the numbers being bandied back and forth, but they changed too fast for him to keep up with. There was much arm-waving and head shaking and Chal even waggled a wrinkled finger in Than's face at one point while saying several derogatory things about Than's ancestry, appearance, and the terrible deal he was being forced to make. Than, however, stuck to his guns throughout the entire tirade, citing the quality of the gems and Chal's expertise in selling them for an even higher price elsewhere.

After several minutes of this, Than turned to Mike and mopped his lightly sweating brow with a linen handkerchief. "It has cost me a favor, however, Chal says he will pay two million, nine hundred and fifty thousand U.S. dollars for the gems in international negotiable bearer bonds, not one penny more."

Mike did the rapid calculation in his head and nodded—they were at least a half-million to the good on the deal thanks to Than. Besides, the gem sale was technically all profit anyway. "Tell him that it is a pleasure doing business with him."

"For you, maybe." Than fired off more rapid Thai, and the old man smiled, making his seamed face break out in wrinkles. He addressed Than again. "It will take a day or so to get the bonds in order. We should meet again in thirty-six hours to complete the transaction."

Adams' face broke into a shit-eating grin. "Hell, yeah—looks like we'll get that chance to sample the nightlife after all."

"Not so fast. We all need to stay on our toes here, so shore leave is going to be severely curtailed—" Mike was about to issue marching orders to his second when the main doors flew open.

Before anyone could move, six armed men burst in through

the front doors. Each one was waving a pistol, while their leader shouted angrily in Thai.

"Hands on the table! Everyone stay where you are! I kill the first one who moves!"

Although the drawn pistols were dead giveaways to the threats the men were shouting, Jace was also watching the Chal's reaction to the armed intruders. Despite Than's reassurance, he had been concerned about a double-cross from the start. The old Thai had a well-known and deserved reputation for ruthlessness, although he'd never heard of the man double-dealing with any customer before.

He'd discussed the possibility with Mike, hoping his answer wouldn't be to bring an entire squad of Keldara with them, as that would sink the entire deal. Mike had agreed with his assessment, and said that they should all simply stay alert. "Unless Chal brings a small army, Adams, you, and I should be plenty to handle whatever these guys might try," the Kildar had said.

However, Chal looked anything but comfortable at the intrusion. The old man sat stiffly in his chair, hands on the table, glaring at the invaders with steely black eyes that had been warm and inviting just a minute ago. *Either he's a hell of an actor, or he's not in on it*, Jace thought.

Satisfied for the moment, he turned back to their assailants. Two men were covering the group from a distance, one at the back door, and one at the front entrance. Three of the other four ringed the table, all of them holding weapons on the group. They all looked like low-level street trash, each one showing signs of some kind of addiction to something or another, most likely heroin or meth. The entire group was thin, pale, and sweating, with dark circles under their eyes and armpits and stained, rotting teeth behind chapped lips.

The sweating ringleader had strutted over to Chal and stuck his pistol in the old man's face while talking rapidly. The old man shook his head and muttered something, which made the leader smack him hard in the face with the barrel of his gun. Chal glared at him, making no move to wipe the blood off his split lip.

"What's going on?" Mike whispered.

"Looks like a rival gang's making their move... they want Chal's territory... they're gonna kill him and all of us... make it look like a deal gone bad."

"Yeah, like that's going to happen—" Mike began.

A pistol muzzle was placed to Mike's temple, and a guttural voice snarled. "Shut mouth, *yet mae!*"

Mike slowly raised his hands, making eye contact with Jace and Adams and indicating their targets. Adams caught Jace's eye and pointed to Than, who was sitting calmly with his hands on the table. Jace got the message and gave him the barest nod of confirmation.

"What'd he just call me?" Mike asked through clenched teeth.

"Motherfucker," Jace replied.

"Oh, hell no!"

In most armed confrontations, the longer the assailants think they have the upper hand, the sloppier they tend to become. This is particularly true if the gunmen are poorly trained. They think simply holding a gun gives them all the power, and that that their hostages are either shocked or scared into not retaliating.

Against highly trained, professional operators, this is a deadly miscalculation, even taking into account the potential hazard of getting shot by a nervous or high gunman. This group was about to find out just how wrong they were in trying to take Chal down on this particular night.

While it is true that no battle plan survives first contact with the enemy, there are several measures that can be taken to ensure that a plan is executed as well as possible before things go to hell. The importance of gaining the element of surprise and a coordinated first strike by all participants cannot be understated in such a situation.

In the few seconds before Mike moved, he, Adams and Jace

had roughed out their plan to kill all six of their attackers without losing Than or Chal.

All they needed was the go signal. That came when Mike grabbed the pistol of the thug standing next to him, pushed it over, and pressed the man's trigger finger, shooting the ringleader in the stomach.

At the same time, Jace and Adams drew their pistols and took out the two men closest to them. Adams put two shots into his man, hitting him in the throat and face. The angle of his bullet coming out of the top of the thug's skull made a geyser of blood spatter against the ceiling and the blades of the lazily turning fan overhead.

Jace double tapped his nearest target in the center of the chest, the .40 caliber rounds shattering his sternum and destroying the man's heart in a second. Before the man hit the floor, Jace slid to a crouch behind Than's chair and fired twice at the man covering the front door. The man shot his pistol uselessly into the ground as he tried to staunch the bleeding from the four bullet holes that had appeared in his chest. Glancing over, Jace saw Adams with his pistol also aimed at the door guard.

As quickly as the violence had exploded, it stopped. The three men fanned out to clear and check their victims. There was one more gunshot from the back of the room, which Adams and Jace both recognized as Mike's .45.

"Back clear!" Mike said.

"Left clear!" Adams said.

"Right clear!" Jace said. His ears were ringing from the shots, and the room was hazy with smoke and thick with the odor of blood, but all of that was far more preferable to taking a bullet.

"Check Than and Chal!" Mike said.

Jace had already come back to the two men, who were still sitting at the table. While he was there, he took a look at the Kildar's handiwork. Adams' and his own work had been impressive, but Mike had taken out half of the invaders by himself. After shooting the leader, he'd disarmed the man beside him and used him as a human shield. Then he had killed the man at the back door, eliminated his protection, and finished off the leader with a shot to the head—all in under three seconds.

Eyebrows raised in admiration, Jace talked to both men, who nodded in answer to his query. Chal bowed deeply to all three. "He is very grateful for our saving his life tonight, and thinks we should adjourn to more comfortable quarters to discuss what will happen next," Than said.

Mike exchanged puzzled glances with Adams and Jace. "If he insists," the Kildar replied.

After confirming that his own security had been killed by their assailants on the way in, Chal had called in more of his own people for protection. He accompanied the four men to a modern, two-story house surrounded by a landscaped yard and garden in a planned complex. Although they could see security guards, they drove into a private entrance to Chal's house. The white and tan home was airy and inviting, with a red, tile roof, bright, tiled floors, and a large, second-story outdoor balcony overlooking an artificial lake.

Chal had Jace park the rented SUV around back. As they walked back toward the house, Adams remarked, "Not exactly where I expected a crime lord to live."

Than shook his head. "Don't be fooled. Chal owns the entire neighborhood. He likes living here because no one has any idea who he really is or what he does. They just think he's a retired business-man. Plus, the neighborhood security keeps the undesirables out."

"Not including us, obviously," Jace said with a smile.

Than nodded. "Not at all. You have all impressed him greatly for him to invite you into this home. Other than myself and now you gentlemen, I can count the number of people who are aware of it on one hand."

Chal met them at the door and brought them into the open living room. "Please, gentleman, as my honored guests, I insist that you have a drink with me. I have a full bar, and my man can make virtually anything you require."

Mike requested Elijah Craig if it was available, or Maker's Mark if not, straight. Adams joined him, while Jace asked for Mekhong, a native Thai liquor distilled from sugarcane and molasses, over ice. Than requested a Sabai Sabai, otherwise known as the Thai Welcome Drink.

As the drinks were being made, Jace walked over to Than. "Is there going to be any trouble with the police?"

Than shook his head and chuckled. "Chal's arrangement with the local constabulary has existed for more than thirty years, back to the current chief's father. If we do have a visit from them, it will be to inform Chal of the unfortunate accident that occurred on his property, that's all."

Once their drinks had been brought over, with Chal apologizing for only having the twelve-year small-batch Elijah Craig on hand, the old man raised his glass. "To the gentlemen who saved this aged one's life tonight. *Chon!*"

The other men raised their glasses as well and drank. Chal set his glass of Samuel Adams Infinium down and regarded Than and the three Americans.

"Due to this evening's events, I find myself in an unusual position. You see, I recognized the leader of the men who tried to kill us. He was the nephew of my former business partner, who recently passed away—from natural causes, I assure you," Chal added at seeing Adams' raised eyebrows. "Unfortunately, his nephew is associated with some less-than-reputable characters. More than likely he convinced them that they could muscle in on the territory of a feeble, old man...me."

Chal sipped his beer as he regarded Mike, Adams, and Jace. "Thanks to you gentlemen—" he raised his glass again, "—that is no longer an issue...for now. However, I cannot suffer the rest of these *hua quay* to live. If word was to get out that I did not retaliate against them, my reputation would suffer, and then it would be nothing but work, work, work all the time again. That is where you come in."

Mike sipped his bourbon. "I'm listening."

"Before we go any further, I must clear my already-incurred

debt with you, as we cannot have that clouding these discussions. I will increase my payment for the gems to an even four million U.S. dollars. It seems a small price to pay, considering that I still breathe this evening, but I trust that it will be satisfactory."

Mike appeared to give it some thought, while Jace leaned close to him. "This offer is *extremely* unusual, and it would be bad form to try to negotiate a higher price now," he whispered.

"I'm sure it would be—however, I can't just give the impression that I'm willing to take what he's offering right away, now, can I?" Mike let the silence drag out for a few more seconds before nodding. "Tell him his generosity is appreciated."

Jace did so, inwardly sighing with relief. He followed that up with, "And as to the matter regarding these insolent devils?"

Chal nodded, his dark eyes sparkling. "I wish that they be removed from this earth—tonight. Unfortunately, I cannot use any of my men to move against them. Although the police and I do have an arrangement regarding my business interests, I cannot simply have my people executing others in the street. The reason I have thrived for so long on my island is that I keep a low profile. That is where you gentlemen come in."

"I thought this was sounding like some kind of sales pitch," Adams muttered into his drink.

"I know where their headquarters is, and can provide you with suitable weapons, equipment, and vehicles to eliminate them, and will do so at no cost. In return for removing this thorn in my side, I offer three things. First, anything you find at their headquarters—and you should find quite a bit—is yours, provided you can remove it from the island. Second, when you begin your operation, my people will provide a suitable distraction for the police, to ensure that none of them cause you any trouble as you're going about your business."

"And the third thing?" Mike asked.

"Word of the package that you gentlemen are assisting Khun Arun with has reached me. I can smooth the way for you into Myanmar, as well as provide a personal recommendation to the gentleman who is moving that particular package. I think he will be very interested in doing more business with you. You see, he has been assembling a large shipment of weapons for transport into the north country, and will be looking for men with your particular talents to escort it. With my word accompanying you, the job is as good as yours."

Jace exchanged an incredulous look with Mike, who shrugged. *Everything falling into place? What is he, a mind reader?*

The Kildar locked eyes with the old Thai crime lord for long seconds, then abruptly nodded. "All right. You've got a deal."

CHAPTER FIFTEEN

"God*damn!* This place is like a one-stop crime shop!" Adams exclaimed.

After accepting the job of eliminating Chal's competition, Mike had contacted the ship and requested Teams Jayne and Inara, along with Lasko, to come ashore with an urban combat load-out. While waiting for the Keldara, Adams, Jace, and he had borrowed a battered, rusty Toyota 4Runner and driven over to the target site for a preliminary recon.

Adams' comment wasn't too far off the mark, either. The gang was one of many urban ones that existed in every major city: groups of disenfranchised, poor, and uneducated youths banding together to survive. This gang was called *Mạngkr då*, the Black Dragons, and resembled many other street gangs all over the world.

Their HQ was an old, three-story brick building in a section of town where every standing wall was covered by graffiti and gang signs, and garbage littered the dirt street. The structure, probably a tin factory or some kind of manufacturing facility in the previous century, took up the entire block. The gang also looked to have taken over the area as well, with their headquarters the center of all crimes occurring throughout the neighborhood.

Scantily clad women with heavy make-up and effeminate boys in short-shorts and tank tops strolled up and down the street. The main entrance had two young gang members serving as de facto doormen and protection for the hookers. A steady stream of men, women, and children arrived and left; running numbers, drugs, stolen goods, whatever anyone was willing to buy or sell. Prostitution was also a thriving market, with the girls and boys flagging down every passing car or propositioning any man—or woman—that walked by. However, this part of town didn't get a lot of accidental traffic—the people who stopped by did so for one thing.

Mike, Adams, and Jace were parked a block up the street, checking the scene out through a pair of pocket binoculars Chal had supplied. After a briefing by Mike on what was happening, Vanner and the girls were downloading maps of the area along with whatever history they could find on the building itself.

"Certainly an active target zone," Mike said, while peering through the glasses.

"Active? You've got unknown tangos inside, multiple entry points, unknown armaments and who knows what kind of defenses in there." Adams said. "Don't know 'bout either of you, but I have no desire to waltz in and find myself staring down the barrels of another Quad .50."

"Don't worry, we won't," Mike said.

At the same time, Jace asked, "When was that?"

"I'll tell you later." Adams said, then looked sidelong at Mike, along with Jace. "What do you mean, 'we' won't?"

"I'm sure the three of us won't find anything like that inside. However, I am confident that we'll find everything to make this a very profitable op," Mike said.

"Really?" Adams grabbed the glasses and scanned the building again. "All I'm seeing is probably a fuckload of drugs, which we aren't into, and a few hundred thousand bahts, which at current market rates is, Jace?"

"From the looks of these bottom-feeders, we'll be lucky to find a hundred grand U.S. And we haven't even begun to discuss how we'd smuggle any pistols inside." Jace pointed at two johns being admitted. "They may be street punks, but they are smart enough to use hand-held metal detectors. And check that out—he's hitting a safe button behind him to let in the johns. Probably someone manning a camera inside to keep an eye on things."

Mike shook his head. "That's the trouble with both you guys—a distinct lack of imagination. Remember what I said about Asian women during the pirate op, Ass-boy?"

"What? Wait...oh yeah." Adams' mouth curved into a devilish smile. "Well, Chal *did* say we could take anything with us that we could get off the island..."

Two hours later, Mike, Adams, and Jace rounded the corner of the gang headquarters and staggered toward the entrance. Dressed in off-the-rack clothes and passing a bottle of cheap whiskey back and forth, they all reeked of booze and talked loudly at and over each other.

"—then I said, then I said, then I said—you can take that goddamn TPS report and shove it up yer ASS!!!" Mike bellowed, making Adams and Jace both howl with laughter. They hadn't gone a dozen more steps before they were surrounded by clouds of cheap perfume, brought their way by the half-dozen Thai, Korean, and Vietnamese whores surrounding them. The girls all giggled and screamed as they mock-fought over the three Americans.

"Hey, ladies! Guys, I think we found the place we're lookin' fer!" Mike said.

"—Ohh, you have big muscles!" A lean Thai hooker exclaimed as she felt his arm. "You come inside and party!"

"Damn straight!" Adams seconded the idea.

"Your friends come too! We show you all good time!" A tiny Vietnamese whore had snuggled up to Adams and was vigorously rubbing his crotch.

"Yeah, we got everything inside—booze, smokes, weed, coke, whatever you need. We party all night long!" An unusually tall Chinese prostitute had gotten her lacquer-nailed hands on Jace, and was rubbing his chest while alternating whispering into and licking his ear.

"I think we jes' found that party we were lookin' fer!" Mike slurred, to fresh cheering from the other two. He looped his arm around the girl. "Come on, swee'heart, and show me a good time!"

Whooping and hollering, Adams and Jace also selected one or two of the streetwalkers and brought them to the brothel entrance. There, two of the enforcers stopped the trio and held up their metal detectors. "Must scan before enter," one said in barely understandable English.

"Do what you gotta do, bud! Jus' as long as it don't keep me from doin' what I'm gonna do!" As he said that, Mike grabbed a handful of his whore's tit, getting more shouts and catcalls from the other two. "Let's go, boys!"

Each man dutifully managed to stand upright long enough for the metal detector scan. While fondling his chosen whore, Jace was listening to the conversation between the girls and their protection.

"More drunk Americans. Probably have money. We fuck them, drug and rob them, dump them on main road again," one said quickly.

The man she spoke to nodded. "Just don't kill them this time," he replied as he pushed a button beside the door. It opened, and Mike, Adams, and Jace walked inside the gang's HQ.

"All right, they are in." Oleg said. "Everyone watch their tablets, map out as much of interior as you can. When we go in, I do not wish to do so blind as a bat."

Beside him, Givi shook his head. "I know the Kildar has balls, but they must be as large as an ox's to go in to a place like this with nothing but that little pigsticker."

Oleg didn't take his eyes off his tablet, having split the screen so he could keep an eye on what Mike was doing as well as the door of the building. "The Kildar knows what he is doing. Just be ready when he gives the signal."

The entire team was clustered in the back of an old, surplus deuce-and-a-half M35 Army truck, sold off after the Vietnam

Conflict and converted to civilian use. Chal had bought it simply because he liked the way it looked. Having seen several on the road already, Mike and Oleg knew the moment they saw it that they had found the perfect vehicle to keep Team Jayne onsite yet out of sight.

The video feed on Oleg's tablet jerked and faded as the pinhole button camera on Mike's shirt was occasionally obscured by his jacket or couldn't draw enough light to function, forcing it to occasionally recalibrate. Even so, he got a rough idea of what they would face if they had to make a hard entrance. "Does not look difficult…not much small arms visible…mostly men getting drunk or stoned. Lasko will eliminate outside pair, we make sure the ice packs are secured on our helmets, then proceed to entry and meet with the Kildar and the others."

Oleg hit his mic. "Are you in position, Blue Hand?"

"Affirmative."

Four hundred yards away and eighteen stories off the ground, Lasko sat in his climbing harness. It was hooked securely to the supports of a radio tower, the only place where he could get the necessary elevation for the field of fire he might need to traverse. Since it was at a diagonal to the left front corner of the target building, Lasko could cover the front entrance, the entire street in front of it, and the intersecting street on the left side of the building too, which was where Team Inara would make their entrance.

Tonight he was using the Barrett .50 caliber with a BTX8 reflex suppressor, which he threaded onto the end of the barrel after removing the muzzle brake. Although the suppressor wouldn't completely eliminate the sound of the shot, it would reduce it from deafening thunder to a more moderate report, like that of a 7.62mm rifle. More importantly, it would also hide his muzzle flash. While Lasko wasn't concerned about any gang members seeing him, civilians calling the police was another matter entirely.

He was looking through an ATN Thor-320 4.5x thermal sight, as some of his targets might be behind doors, or even solid walls.

He had loaded EBR antiricochet frangible rounds for tonight's operation, ensuring maximum knockdown power with minimum risk of collateral damage due to over-penetration or fragmentation.

He was watching the two men out front when he heard two clicks over his radio. The Kildar was authorizing the start of the operation.

Lasko settled in, snugged the Barrett to his shoulder and peered through the thermal scope at the killing ground below him.

Mike, Adams, and James walked into what could be best described as a sexual smorgasbord.

The large room they entered looked like a tacky Las Vegas strip club had been airlifted over and dropped on a South Pacific island. Loud K-pop wailed from a 55-inch plasma television on a wall, the incomprehensible lyrics matching the equally frenetic music video playing. Rows of dusty mirrors lined the plywood walls, and glitter and tinsel was strewn everywhere. Stained, sagging couches and chairs lined the walls, mostly hidden under the working girls. The hot, still air was thick with cheap perfume, sweat, smoke, and of course, the promise of inexpensive, available sex.

Girls and boys of all descriptions were hanging out, dancing, getting high, talking to potential johns, or sizing up the new arrivals. An older, hard-faced madam with iron-gray hair lacquered into place, wearing a red, satin high-collared Chinese dress, and smoking a cigarette in an ivory holder, was watching over everyone with hawklike eyes. Jace spotted a live monkey smoking in the corner, to the stoned amazement of a man and two underage whores who were all pointing and giggling at the animal. He also could have sworn he heard a donkey bray from somewhere farther inside the building.

"Recognize the tune?" Adams shouted.

"What—?" Jace focused on it for a second, hearing a familiar guitar riff cut through the wail of over-sweetened synthesizers. "Is that 'Welcome to the Jungle'...?"

"You got it!" Adams shouted, draining the rest of the watered-down whiskey and tossing the bottle aside. "Let's get to FUCKING!"

he bellowed, making the whores and customers all around them cheer.

A beaded curtain hung on the back wall, flanked by two more skinny, armed gangbangers. Their whores escorted them through it while whispering all kinds of promised delights into their ears. On the other side was a long hallway with curtained-off doorways every several feet, and two more bouncers at the far end, with what looked like the entrance to the second floor stairway between them. The smell was even ranker back here, and the sounds were of one thing only, although once Jace heard the slap of a hand on flesh, From another booth came a woman's hard voice ordering her john to lick her shoes in Thai, followed by what sounded like the *crack* of a riding crop.

"Don't take anything they offer. They plan on drugging and robbing us," Jace subvocalized.

"Now there's a surprise," Adams growled.

"Stick to the plan," Mike said. "Ten-count once we're alone. And don't forget to hit your cold pack."

"Roger that."

The three men were each led to their own empty booths and the curtains were pulled shut behind them. Jace counted off the doors and steps he had taken and radioed that to Vanner. He let the girl shimmy past him and start to pour a drink. As she did, he drew his EOD ceramic fixed-blade knife and came up behind her just as she was about to turn back to him.

Wrapping an arm around her neck, Jace made sure her mouth was covered as he pressed the tip of the ceramic blade to her throat. "Do as I say, and you will get out of this alive. Nod if you understand," he whispered in Thai.

Her eyes wide, the woman nodded.

Hearing the command to begin their portion of the op, Yosif checked the street one last time. "Let us know if anyone's coming, Blue Hand," Yosif said as he gave the go signal to his team.

"I will," the sniper replied.

One by one, Vanel, Edvin, Marko, and the rest of the Inara squad ran to the rear of the building. All intel gathered had indicated that there was no surveillance or guards on the rear of the building, but all it would take is one hooker or john or gang member to come out in the next few minutes, see the heavily armed and armored assault team, let out a yell, and their advantage would be blown. They had considered executing an insertion from the roof of a nearby building, but couldn't locate a suitable launch site, so they had gone in from the ground.

When the rest of his team was in place, Yosif ran over and found the grapnel was up and secure. The first two team members had hauled themselves to the top and established a perimeter. Two more followed, then Marko and Yosif ascended last. Once everyone was on top, Yosif hauled the rope up and secured it, then hustled to the old metal fire door. There he radioed to Vanner.

"Team Inara ready."

"All right," Jace said, feeling the girl's rapid pulse flutter in her neck like a trapped butterfly. "Stay calm, and you will be all right. We are going to the curtain, where you will call for help. You think I am having a heart attack. I can understand every word you will say. No warnings or hand signals, or you die. Nod again if you understand."

As he spoke, he grabbed the portable cold pack from his pocket and crushed it in his hand, making sure the chemicals mixed completely. When the pack was cold, he shoved it in the breast pocket of his shirt, grimacing as the chill spread to his chest. *Sure hope this works*, he thought.

At the woman's second nod, Jace moved her over to the curtain and carefully removed his hand from her mouth, keeping the knife point at the base of her neck. "Remember, call them in and no tricks, otherwise I cut your throat."

She nodded and swept the curtain aside. "Chaiya! Han! Come quick! He not getting up! I think he dying!"

The moment he heard approaching footsteps, Jace hauled her

backward and put her in the corner parallel to the door. "Stay there." Palming the blade, he lay down on the bed. A second later the curtain was shoved aside and two Thais rushed in.

Jace trembled and clutched his chest. "My heart..."

"Get him up and out of here!" the first man said, going to grab Jace roughly by the arm. As the thug bent over him, Jace brought his hand up and uncovered the three-inch blade, sinking it into the man's throat. He stiffened, then opened his mouth to cry out, but nothing was heard but a gurgle as his throat filled with blood.

Pulling the blade out, Jace sat up and shoved the dying man aside. The second guard froze at seeing his partner suddenly fountaining blood and falling over. He grabbed for the pistol on his hip, but Jace got there first.

Pinning the kid's hand on his gun butt, Jace slashed the ceramic blade through his throat, spraying a dark fountain of blood across the room. His target vainly tried to stem the warm tide gushing from his neck. Jace plucked the pistol from his belt as he sank to the floor in the middle of a growing red puddle. The punk's mouth opened and closed in a hopeless effort to draw a final breath.

Drawing the curtain closed again, Jace snatched the first dead guard's pistol and quickly patted both bodies down, finding an extra magazine on each. The two pistols the guards had been carrying couldn't have been more different; an ancient M1911 .45 and a Spanish Astra 600 9mm. Jace glanced at the prostitute, who was huddled in the corner with both hands over her mouth. "Do you want to leave here?" he asked.

She stared at him until he repeated the question. Then she nodded. "All right. Stay right here. Do not come out no matter what you hear. I will come back for you."

Keeping her in his peripheral vision, just in case she tried to stab him in the back, Jace went to the curtain and peeked out. He saw Mike in the doorway across the hall and nodded.

The Kildar checked left and right for observers, then quickly crossed. "What you got?" Jace presented both guns, and Mike took the .45 and quietly checked the action. "It'll do." He took the spare mag and tucked it under his shirt. "Anything else?"

"No radios." Jace jerked a thumb at his whore. "She's coming with."

"Yeah, so's mine. Hopefully Adams kept his mind on why we're here, and isn't knocking boots right now," Mike replied.

"Hey, where the hell is everybody?" Adams asked over their short-range comms.

"In Jace's room," Mike answered.

The master chief burst in a moment later, brandishing a chrome-plated .357 Magnum revolver. "Check this shit out!"

"Damn, guess you win the arms race. Where in the hell did you get that?" Jace asked.

"Bitch tried to get the drop on me, can you imagine that shit?" Adams asked. "She could barely hold the damn thing. Stole it from a john on the street and smuggled it inside. I did *not* ask where she hid it. She was just staying here 'til she could squirrel away enough to get out for good. I took it and told her she's leaving tonight with us."

"All right, now we take out the front hall guards while Lasko hits the doormen and Jayne rounds up anyone still outside. Try to avoid shooting until you have to—" Mike glanced toward the main entry room. "Although the music might cover it, so do what you have to do. When the shit goes down, Jace, tell the whores to stay in their rooms. Jayne and Inara, move on my signal. Let's go." Mike walked out of the room and headed down the hallway, with Adams and Jace right behind him.

When he heard the prelaunch signal, Oleg made sure his team was ready to go. He checked his HK416C, then turned back to his tablet as a blaring engine could be heard getting louder.

"What is—Blue Hand, do you have visual on what is coming?"

"Yes," Lasko answered. "And you are not going to like it."

The pickup truck's engine glowed like a white-hot incendiary as Lasko watched it turn onto the block and roar down the street.

It was packed with men, at least a dozen of them in the bed and three more in the cab, all shouting and waving fists, machetes, and a few pistols in the air.

"Looks like they got the news," he said.

Mike had also asked Chal to have his men spread the word that he was dead, so the gang would lower their guard, thinking they had accomplished their mission.

"The bad news is that they have returned here to celebrate," Oleg said in his ear.

"Bad for you, perhaps," Lasko replied as he watched the pick-up screech to a halt outside the doors and the men pile out. He smiled as he surveyed his suddenly more target-rich environment. "Is looking very good from where I am sitting."

On the *Big Fish*, Vanner was coordinating every aspect of this op, working with Chal's people and their own.

"The traffic accident has just occurred at main intersection in Phuket City—every street is backed up for four blocks in all directions, and chickens are going everywhere," Xatia reported.

"All police units in area have been called in to secure the area, direct traffic, and assist with recovery of escaped animals," Greznya said.

"Nice," Vanner replied.

"Teams Jayne and Inara are in place and ready to begin operation," Martya reported.

"Kildar, Master Chief, and Captain Morgan have reached their first objective, and are ready to execute second phase," Irina said.

"All right, we are ready to go. All teams stand by—"

"Team Jayne to Firefly," Oleg's voice rang loud over the comm.

"Go for Firefly," Vanner said.

"At least twelve more tangos have just arrived at target area, and are entering the building now."

"Kildar, what are your orders?" Vanner asked, making sure the vital answer would be transmitted to all teams.

▲   ▲   ▲

"All teams execute NOW!" Mike said, brushing aside the beaded curtain and putting a round into the head of each guard as they started to turn and see who was yelling. He pushed forward, covering the left, with Adams taking the right side of the room.

Meanwhile, Jace covered their backside while grabbing the pistols from each of the dead guards and shouting orders to the hookers in Thai, Chinese, and Korean. The dragon lady opened her mouth to scream, but Adams crossed to her with one giant step and laid her out cold with the barrel of his Magnum across her skull.

The whores and customers hadn't even registered what was really going on. For all intents and purposes, the heads of both guards had just exploded, splattering everyone in the room with blood, bone fragments, and brains.

The nearest drenched whore let out a piercing scream just as the first group of gang members crowded inside, laughing and bragging about how they were going to expand their territory. They walked right into Mike's and Adams' blazing pistols, which cut down the first three before anyone else even knew what was happening.

At the same time, muffled detonations and automatic weapons fire erupted outside, audible even over the blaring rock music.

The charge was set, and Yosif had made sure every Inara member had their cold packs out and secured to their helmets before he blew the door.

The lock disintegrated, but the door didn't move. "All Father's Sight!" Yosif cursed as he reached forward with two other team members to pry the rusted door open. Forcing it ajar with a loud screech, they began sweeping the old, dusty stairwell leading down to the third floor of the building.

When they reached the small hallway that ended in a warped, wooden door, Yosif held up his clenched fist to halt his team. Shouts and screams, along with the thud of what sounded like many running feet, could be heard from the other side.

Finger on the trigger, Yosif nodded for their point man to open the door. Marko pulled on it, and the rest of the team spilled out, weapons tracking everywhere—

—Only to find themselves facing a charging horde of prostitutes and half-dressed johns stampeding toward the staircase across the way. Yosif immediately activated the plan they'd worked out in case they encountered innocents along the way.

"Block the stairs! Blue Hand, do not shoot at third floor, repeat, do not shoot at three!" Shoving his way to the front, Yosif reinforced his men there, funneling the people in the corridor into their hallway and the stairs leading to the roof. "This way, up, everyone, go go go!"

Although he didn't speak the native tongue, the sight of a half-dozen black-clad men in full face helmets and masks and carrying automatic rifles was enough to get the point across to the frightened herd, which immediately followed Yosif's motions and began heading to the roof.

Lasko was in his element. His first two rounds cored the guards on either side of the door, making the whores outside run for cover as the guards dropped.

Many of the newly arrived gang members tried to take cover behind the truck, but to no avail. The frangible rounds Lasko was using gave him plenty of penetration power, even through the stamped metal of the truck, while minimizing the risk of fragments hitting unintended targets. Add the thermal scope to the mix, which let him spot anyone who wasn't hiding near the engine, and every time he squeezed the trigger, a gang member died.

After the fifth man's chest was shattered by a .50 caliber round, the rest tried to dash into the building, thinking they would be safe there. At the door, they met the remaining survivors of the bloodbath inside, who were just as desperately trying to get out. The two sides hit in a frantic collision that resulted in at least two men getting shot by their fellow gang members.

Leaving that mess for Jayne and the Kildar to mop up, Lasko turned his attention to a fleet-footed guy who had taken off from behind the engine, zigging and zagging in the desperate hope of outrunning a bullet. The Keldara sniper ended that idea and the rest of his life with a shot that tore through his chest, knocking him into the wall just before he reached the corner of the building.

Reloading the Barrett, Lasko turned to the second floor, pleasantly surprised to discover that Vanner's idea about the cold packs was working perfectly. Each member of the Keldara team had a large, blue-black spot on their helmets from the freezing pack. The packs would last at least ten to fifteen minutes, and clearly designated each team member as a friendly. Although Lasko was under strict orders not to engage any targets on a floor that also had Keldara on it, they had decided to use the cold packs, just to be sure.

Anyone else was fair game unless otherwise directed from the boots on the ground. Seeing that none of the Keldara had reached the second floor yet, Lasko sighted in on a group of scrambling figures there and went to work.

At the rate he was knocking them down, he would be finished long before those packs grew warm.

"GO GO GO!" Oleg shouted the moment they got the word.

Team Jayne burst out of their hiding place and leapfrogged toward the target area. As they covered the block, they could hear shots fired from inside, along with the loud *crack* of Lasko's Barrett steadily going off in the distance.

By the time they had reached their first staging point, the group in front of the building had been whittled down to less than a third of their original number. Oleg counted at least four bodies with missing chests or heads lying in the street. One took off running away from them. He sighted in, but before he could pull the trigger, blood exploded from the runner's chest and he crashed to the ground.

"Damn it, Blue Hand, leave some for us!" he radioed.

"Move faster," came the laconic reply.

"Securing the front entrance," Oleg said.

"Roger that. Acquiring targets on second floor."

Waving his team forward, Oleg's men cut down the remainder before they knew what hit them. They took the backside of the truck, which now sported several holes in its body. Its windows were shattered, both driver's side tires were flat, and it was leaking radiator fluid and oil all over the street.

"Sweep forward!" Oleg ordered. His point men leaped to the stairs and kicked in the door, about to toss in two flash-bang grenades.

"Hold on front door!" A familiar voice shouted from inside. A moment later, Mike poked his head out. "Get in here and sweep forward past the beaded curtain at the back!"

Oleg's team pounded inside and headed through the room to the doorway just as the first wave of hookers and johns came barreling down the stairs and into the hallway. Givi and the rest of the men had their weapons online, but held their fire as the panicked men, boys, and girls ran through them to the front door.

Through all the panic and confusion, Oleg heard the Kildar shouting, "Women to the right, men to the left. Keep moving! Two lines now!"

Vanel watched the parade of naked women and half-dressed men and boys stream past and bolt up the stairs. When the flood slowed to a trickle, he received the go signal from Yosif and headed down the hallway to the end, which faced the street.

Setting his shaped Semtex charge on the wall, Vanel double-timed it back to the center of the room. There he joined with Marko and Edvin, both of whom had planted their charges on this floor as well. Getting a boost from his teammates, Edvin stuck one more on the ceiling. Then they moved to regroup with their team at the back stairwell leading to the second floor.

Yosif motioned for Vanel and Marko to head down first, with the rest providing cover. With their element of surprise gone, the stairwell could turn into a death trap in moments. Adding the impossibility of hearing what was going on below due to the gunfire everywhere, Team Inara could walk into an ambush before they knew it. While all team members were wearing Type III rifle body armor with trauma plates, neither Vanel nor Marko had any desire to get caught in hail of bullets.

"Blue Hand, can you give us a sitrep on the second floor, over?" Vanel whispered.

"Yes." Lasko's voice was interrupted by the suppressed *crack* of his rifle. "I am killing many of them."

The Barrett cracked again in Vanel's ear and outside. He looked at Marko and nodded. "Let's go."

The two men crept down the stairs as quietly as they could, hearing shouts and screams from the level when they reached the ground.

"Inaras Three and Four, be aware that Blue Hand has engaged the enemy on Floor Two," Vanel heard. "Tangos may be coming your way."

"Roger," Marko said. "Tell us something we don't know," he muttered to Vanel, not into the radio. Meanwhile, Vanel pulled a flash-bang off his LBE harness and grabbed the pin with his teeth when the door was yanked open. A blood-spattered gangmember appeared in the doorway, and was shredded by two short bursts from the Inara members.

The man behind him scrambled sideways while bringing up a sawed-off hunting rifle and firing wildly into the stairwell. Vanel tracked him through the wall and let off two three-round bursts, hoping to wound him, or at least make him stop shooting. Right after, he pulled the pin on his M84.

"Fire in the hole!" He shouted as Marko readied his own flash-bang. They tossed both grenades outside the stairwell and pulled the door shut. The one-million-candlepower bursts of light and 170-decibel reports, intensified by detonating in an enclosed space, brought a new chorus of screams and *thuds* of bodies hitting the floor outside.

By the time the grenades stopped, the rest of the team had advanced to join Vanel and Marko. They pushed the door open and hit the room, spreading out and killing anyone still alive and holding a weapon. A flurry of single shots rang out. In less than a minute, Team Inara was surrounded by dead bodies. They had not taken a single casualty themselves.

"Second floor clear," Yosif said just as Oleg and Team Jayne emerged from the stairs to the first floor. "Sorry, guys," he said, his wide smile indicating he wasn't sorry at all.

"Plant the rest of your charges," Oleg grunted.

"Oleg, since you're here, and we do have to set our charges," Yosif said with an even wider smile. "There is a matter up on the roof you could handle for us."

"Yes, about forty of them," Edvin said with a matching grin.

With a frown, Oleg took his team up to the roof. They returned a minute later, escorting the rest of the whores and customers through the second floor down to the first. Oleg brought up the rear, his face impassive, except for the glower he threw at Yosif and the rest of his team.

Yosif's smile didn't fade until after his team had finished their work and filed out behind him to the wrecked first floor and into the street.

CHAPTER SIXTEEN

"Now *that* is a suitable haul of booty."

Mike surveyed the group with a satisfied smile. The johns had been allowed to slip away into the night once the Keldara had relieved them of their cell phones—not that they would be in any hurry to call the police after where they had been.

The girls were grouped by the side of the M35. Around thirty all told, they were dressed in whatever clothes they could scrounge from the building.

A thorough search of the premises had come up with several small caches of bills and jewelry. They had also discovered a four-foot high safe. It had been blown open to reveal stacks and stacks of baht, along with around one hundred thousand U.S. dollars, a shoebox filled with jewelry, a collection of gold coins, and about ten kilos of heroin, which Mike had left on the floor in front of the safe. They had also found several sets of identification papers, which Mike held in his hands.

For this part, Mike had brought Soon Yi with him to translate. He stepped on the bumper of the truck and held both hands up. "Ladies, all of you, please listen to me!"

Every girl turned to him, and Soon Yi began translating in Chinese, while Jace repeated the same message in Thai.

"My name is Michael Jenkins, and I am the one responsible

for what has happened tonight. Now, I don't know each of your situations, and I don't really want to know. However, since your previous place of employment no longer exists—"

He nodded to Oleg, who hit the radio detonator for all the charges inside the building. With a loud report and a huge cloud of dust, the three-story building collapsed on itself, reduced to a pile of rubble in seconds.

"—You can now choose what you wish to do with the rest of your life. So, here's the deal. Anyone who wants to leave right now, step forward," Mike said.

There was a pregnant pause, then one girl meekly stepped forward. When she wasn't slapped, beaten or shot, several more joined her. In the end, roughly half of the girls wanted out.

"All right, when one of these two—" Mike handed half the stack of IDs to Soon, and the other half to Jace. "—call your name, come and collect your papers."

Soon called out the first name, and a tiny Korean stepped forward. Soon gave her the passport, and Mike handed her a thick stack of baht worth at least two thousand dollars. Tears streaming down her face, she hugged Soon, Mike, and even Vanel, who had been holding the money, before tucking the bills away and starting to walk down the street.

"Jesus—Soon, go get her and tell her we'll take her to a hotel to rest and get cleaned up and dressed first," Mike said. "Okay, who's next?"

They went through the rest of the group that were leaving while Mike called Chal. By the time all of the departees were set up, a small bus had arrived, and the driver recited the arrangement Mike had made with Chal word for word.

"Good. And if I find out any of these girls end up back in the life, both you and the old man will be seeing me again, and I guarantee neither of you will like it," he'd told the driver, who nodded so hard Jace thought he was going to sprain his neck.

"What about rest of us?" The tall Chinese girl asked once the bus had left.

"You have a choice," Mike replied. "You can go back to the streets and keep trying to earn a living that way ... or you can join us."

"Doing what? Same thing we did in there?" She pointed at the ruined building.

"For now, yes. However, there will be several changes. First, you will be paid much better than you were working for them. Second, you will have a small stipend to replace whatever you may have lost. Third, you'll have the chance to get an education ..." Mike went through the entire harem pitch to the girls, ending with. "... Anyone agreeing to accompany us will be leaving Thailand."

To his surprise, the majority of the girls burst into laughter. "We fucking hate it here!" said a willowy Japanese girl with a detailed dragon tattoo crawling down her arm.

"Well then, are you coming or staying?" Mike asked.

The girls all hudded together to confer about the offer. In the end, three more decided to leave, and Mike gave them their IDs and severance pay. That left an even dozen prostitutes filing into the M35.

Jace looked at the bevy of girls packing into the truck and turned to Adams with a befuddled look on his face. "Does this happen often?"

The master chief shrugged. "More often than you would think. Don't look so surprised. What Mike's offering them is a damn sight better than anything they'd find here. Come on, get on, we're getting the hell out of here."

"What about her?" Jace pointed at the unconscious dragon lady lying by the side of the road.

"Too ugly to fuck, and we got enough managers already." Adams didn't even glance at her as he climbed in the back of the truck. "I say let that sleeping dog lie."

The rest of the night was mostly clean-up. Mike had radioed ahead to have the ship prepped for their new arrivals around tomorrow afternoon. Then he had taken them all to the Hyatt and put them up two to a room, telling them to get cleaned up and rest before shopping for replacement clothes and other essentials later that morning. He requested Katya and three of the intel girls to come ashore and help oversee the new girls' excursion to the mall and answer any questions they had. Soon Yi agreed to serve as an interpreter, and Jace agreed to go along as both back-up translation as well as escort. Mike let him do so with a strange smile and a knowing shake of his head.

It was a decision the former Marine soon regretted. The girls, while separately charming and delightful in their own way, devolved into a group of fashion and appearance-obsessed little girls the second they hit the mall. It also didn't help that they saw him as their personal valet, piling bag after bag onto him until he made arrangements to collect all of the purchases from each store at the end of the trip.

Jace's morning passed in a grinding blur of women's clothes shops and perfume and makeup counters. They walked from one end of the large shopping center to the other and back again. By the time they were finished, he had a headache from all the scents he'd been subjected to, and was still so loaded down with department store bags, he could hardly see—things the girls didn't trust the stores to hold for them.

"Holy shit!" he said as he collapsed into the bus seat. "I'd rather do a thirty-klick march in full ruck than go through that again!"

Sitting across the aisle from him, Soon Yi smiled. "Surely you knew what you were getting into when you signed up for this?"

Jace ruefully shook his head. "I've been with this outfit for less than a week, and already I've seen more action than in two full tours of duty as a Marine. Don't get me wrong, I'm not complaining. I'm just not sure if this Kildar is a tactical genius, insane, or some combination of the two."

Soon Yi's smile faded as he spoke. "It is very likely that he is the latter."

"I'm sorry, did I say something to offend you?" Jace asked.

Soon shook her head. "No—it is a private matter." Her smile was more hesitant this time. "Do not worry about it. It is nothing that should concern you."

"Oh. Well, if you don't mind my asking, how'd you sign up with these guys?"

She looked at the rest of the chattering, squealing whores with a sad, knowing smile. "I was also a prostitute at a pirate den that the Kildar and his men attacked and shot up. I was taken as a spoil of war, and now service the Kildar exclusively. Oh, and provide translation on occasion. Does that answer your question?"

"Yes, ma'am."

They were both quiet the rest of the way back to the dock.

"Damn, it was bad enough to be tripping over the intel girls on their way back and forth from the sundeck—now we've got these other women running every which way!" Adams' complaint would have been more believable if he hadn't been wearing an ear-to-ear-grin while saying it.

"Yeah, you look like you're dying over this. Everyone settling in all right?" Mike asked.

"The new girls seem to be, though Morgan looked a bit shaken when Soon and he came back from their shopping trip."

Mike chuckled. "I was going to warn him, but decided experience would be the best teacher."

"So, other than having to squeeze past barely dressed hotties every time I leave my room, things are great." Adams stared at Mike. "Tell me again why you didn't bring any of the harem with us on this trip?"

"That smile on your ugly mug is your answer," Mike replied. "Besides, there's always Daria if you're so inclined."

Adams shook his head. "Not my style. Don't get me wrong, she's a looker, and she can act the part, but I know her heart's just not in it, that's all. Kinda takes the fun out of it for me."

Mike's jaw dropped. "Damn, I never thought I'd hear you say that."

"Hey, just 'cause I get my rocks off doesn't mean I don't want the girl to have a good time too, if possible."

"And here I thought you were all about hitting it and quitting it. You best watch it, buddy—I might start thinking you're a man of unsuspected depth."

"I try to learn from the best," Adams said.

"But getting back to your original question: the other reason is that this is a *training* mission, remember?" Mike mock-frowned at him. "And mostly because then I wouldn't have to worry about you dipping your wick every chance you got before they came aboard—like I do now."

"Hey hey hey, they have to get a full health clearance from our medic before they get to sample my wares. Momma Adams didn't raise no fool, you know." Adams managed to return Mike's deadpan stare for a few seconds until they both burst out laughing.

The humor was interrupted a knock at the door from Daria. "Kildar? Am I interrupting something?"

"If you mean two braying jackasses, then yes you are, Daria, but come in anyway," Mike said.

Walking to his desk, she handed him a tablet. "Here is the cost breakdown and profit figure for the trip so far."

Mike ran down the numbers. "Chal's payment put us back in the black, and about two-point-five million to the good so far, even with scrambling Kacey, Tamara, and the girls down here by our private airline." He stared at the screen again. "With all the running around we do, you'd think we could figure out some way to lease a used jet, or time-share one at least."

"The cost versus availability window has never worked out, but I'm still looking for a program that might work for us," Daria said.

Adams drained his Mountain Tiger and belched. "At least all this—" He waved his empty at the yacht. "—is on the house, thanks to Uncle Sam."

"Yeah, don't remind me." Even with his investments in the valley of the Keldara, Mike was comfortable, to be sure, but the money they'd gotten from the "sale" of the boards was certainly welcome. Mountain Tiger beer was steadily gaining market share in the U.S., but it was slow going. If Adams' contact paid off in China—hell, throughout Southeast Asia—they'd probably have to expand their brewing operation to keep up with the demand. But that would cost money in the short-term before starting to show a profit. *All in good time...* Mike thought.

"There is one more thing." Daria hit the screen to bring up an e-mail. "Chal has set up the initial phone call with your contact in Myanmar."

"No rest for the wicked, eh?" Mike pulled out his satphone and dialed the number. With Vanner bouncing any communications off several area satellites, he wasn't concerned about being traced. *Besides, I'm on a motherfucking boat...*

The phone rang four times before it was picked up. "Hello."

"This is Mike Jenkins. I was told to call this number regarding a job."

"Call this number in three minutes." The voice repeated an international number twice, then hung up.

"Very careful," Mike said as he finished jotting the number down and committed it to memory. When the allotted time had elapsed, he dialed the new number and waited.

Six rings later, it was answered. "Yes."

"This better be who I am supposed to be talking to."

"Who gave you this number?"

"The first guy I spoke to three minutes and—" Mike checked his chronograph. "—eleven seconds ago."

"You are Mr. Jenkins?"

"Yup."

"And you are currently sailing off the west coast of Thailand."

"Around there, yes." Mike was getting impatient. "I heard you have a job you need doing, right?"

"I have many things that need doing. However, for this one, I require specialized personnel."

"Well, if you've been watching the news out of Phuket, you should know what we're about." After delivering video of their op, as well as a few heads in a bag to prove they'd done what Mike had said they could do, he had spent a pleasant hour with the old man. Chal had ended up buying the gems and jewelry for a nice price. However, despite Mike's polite fishing, the old Thai would not say whom he would be meeting regarding the computer boards. All he would say is, "You probably wouldn't believe me." He did, however, tell Mike two things. First, not to use any official currency conversion places like banks in Myanmar, but to exchange any money on the street, as he would get a much better rate. Second, to look him up again the next time he came to Thailand.

Mike had kept an eye on the news reports as well, and watched as the local media described the remains of the deserted building as being destroyed by a fire of unknown origins. The reporter did say that the police were checking on whether clashing gangs might have been the culprits, but there was no mention of any foreigners being involved.

Mike had smiled as he'd watched the report. He'd made sure both teams and Lasko had all used brass catchers on their weapons, ensuring no telltale casings were left at the scene. Chal had also assured him that the official report would say that the building was destroyed by fire, with arson suspected, but never proven.

"Yes. From what I have seen so far, you may be acceptable. Be at the Mandarin Oriental in Bangkok at eleven tomorrow morning. You will be contacted there." With that the speaker hung up.

Mike set the phone down and shook his head. "Why do I have the feeling that I am not going to like this prick very much?"

Bangkok, Thailand is a glittering jewel among the great cities of Southeast Asia. Established on the Chao Praya River in the Ayutthaya Kingdom in the fifteenth century, the port town quickly became a vital shipping point for foreign traders. It saw its share of ups and downs over the years, including coming under siege in 1688 during the expulsion of the French from Siam.

The city survived the eventual downfall of Ayutthaya to the Burmese Kingdom in 1767, and the modern city was founded in 1782, when King Buddha Yodfa Chulaloke moved the capitol to the eastern bank of the river. Since then, Bangkok had thrived and grown over the centuries, and is now at the heart of a regional megalopolis of twenty million people. Despite its often rapid industrialization, the city always retained links to its past, with centuries-old architectural wonders such as the Grand Palace, Vinmanmek Palace Complex, and Wat Arun still drawing tens of millions of international tourists each year.

The origin of the city's name is lost to history. The word "Bang" in Central Thai means "town on a riverbank." The word "ko" means "island," which may refer to the area being divided by rivers and other waterways. Given the constant stream of foreigners in the area, the corruption to Bangkok was inevitable. The city's ceremonial name, bestowed by King Rama IV during his reign in the nineteenth century, is listed in the Guinness Book of World Records as the longest place name in the world. A combination of Thai, Pāli, and Sanskrit, it takes more than ten seconds to say, and translates to: "The city of angels, the great city, the eternal jewel city, the impregnable city of God Indra, the grand capital of the world endowed with nine precious gems, the happy city, abounding in an enormous Royal Palace that resembles the heavenly abode where reigns the reincarnated god, a city given by Indra and built by Vishnukarma."

Of late, however, it seemed that the gods had turned their backs on the crown jewel of Thailand. The widespread flooding of 2011 had caused billions of dollars of damage across the country, and Bangkok had suffered its share of rising water as well. The local government had dithered as to the best way to handle it, infuriating many citizens and merchants who found their streets blocked by lines of sandbags. Protests had swiftly developed, and the police had been called out to handle them. This was not what a city that depended on tourism wished to show to the rest of the world. Eventually the waters receded, and the city cleaned up and got back to its regular swing of things.

Mike, Jace, and Arun, however, had no time for enjoying the city's history or splendor when they came ashore the next morning. They had motored through the night to ensure they would arrive at the Mandarin Oriental early. Judging by Mike's dour expression, Jace figured whoever they were meeting was already rubbing him the wrong way.

The two Americans were dressed in sport coats, button-down shirts, and chinos. Jace was carrying the case that held the vital motherboards. Arun had gotten outfitted in Phuket, and was dressed in a fawn silk summer suit, complete with a woven straw fedora, ascot, and matching handkerchief.

Overlooking the Chao Praya River, the one hundred-thirty-five-year-old Mandarin Oriental's most recent incarnation consisted of three buildings. The main structure was a modern, thirteen-story white building that housed the majority of the guests. A smaller, eight-story structure had been built at a ninety-degree angle to the main building, farther from the river. Lastly, in front of that was a small, two-story building containing many of the hotel's famous Author Suites, named after great writers that had stayed there, including Joseph Conrad, Somerset Maugham, Noel Coward, and James Michener.

While the hotel had modernized its exterior, it had retained and updated its elegant interior. The three men walked through the opulent, hardwood-trimmed lobby to the Authors' Lounge, a large, bright, white room decorated with palm and bamboo trees, with a grand staircase that led to a large second floor balcony. Selecting an empty set of wicker furniture around a low table near the center of the room, they sat and waited.

When a young woman dressed in a traditional silk dress approached and offered them tea, Jace thanked her and said that they were meeting their party there. She nodded and walked away.

Less than a minute later, a hard-faced Chinese man with crew-cut black hair, dark sunglasses, and wearing a black suit and a corded earpiece approached the table. He looked directly at Mike. "You are Michael Jenkins."

"Last time I checked," Mike replied, ignoring Jace's slight wince.

The bodyguard didn't move a muscle. "The general will see you in the Royal Oriental Suite. Follow me." Without waiting for a reply, he turned and headed deeper into the hotel. With an eyebrow raised, Mike glanced at Jace and Arun as they all rose to follow him.

The security man led them to a private lift and rode with them up to the hotel's top floor. There he escorted them into a foyer that opened up into a large living room with hardwood floors and floor-to-ceiling windows that revealed a magnificent view of the river below. It was decorated with modern furniture, including a writing desk in the corner, next to a teak round table and four chairs. A sitting space was bordered by a subdued, blue and brown striped couch with two white easy chairs to its left and another teak table, this one square, in the middle, all resting on a beautiful Oriental rug. Soft classical music could be heard throughout the large suite.

Another suited, sunglasses-wearing man who might have been the first man's twin walked up to them. Their escort's demeanor didn't change as he picked up a handheld metal detector from the side table. "Spread your legs shoulder-width apart and raise your arms to each side."

Mike did so, allowing the man to perform a thorough check of his person, as did Jace and Arun. None of them were carrying weapons. Mike was still using the button wired for video and sound, however; no sense in wasting a perfectly good surveillance set-up.

The first man started to move the detector toward the metal case, but stopped when he saw what it was. He nodded to the other man, who walked deeper into the suite. "The general will be with you shortly," the first man said. "Come with me." Turning on his heel, he led them to the sitting area.

Mike nodded and followed him. They were just about to sit down when a loud, British-accented voice made everyone look up.

"Mr. Michael Jenkins!" It came from a short, trim Chinese man dressed in a three-piece navy silk suit. He looked to be in his mid-forties, with the beginnings of crow's feet at the corners of his clear, cold brown eyes. The rest of his face was either surgically retouched or strangely untouched by age. A full head of black hair was combed straight back from his forehead. "I am General Zháo Cong, of the Army of the People's Republic of China."

Mike shook the proffered hand and nodded. "May I introduce Arun Than, whom we are currently working for, and my business associate, Jace Morgan."

Jace nodded at the general. He noticed that the two bodyguards had taken stations in opposite corners of the room. Another man dressed in the hotel's livery had come in, and now stood by the round table with his hands clasped behind his back. The general snapped an order to one of men and gave a curt nod toward the bedroom. The man headed back there, while Cong turned back to his guests.

"Sit, gentlemen. Something to drink? Brandy? Cognac? Perhaps a cigar?"

"Elijah Craig for me. We will see about that cigar once we've concluded our business," Mike replied. Jace and Than both asked for water.

Cong nodded, his smooth face breaking into a smile that never came close to his eyes. "Of course." He snapped out another order in Chinese to the hotel's man, who bowed and headed out the door. Meanwhile, Cong went to the white chair farthest from the couch and sat down. Mike chose the other white chair, and Than selected the left end of the couch, leaving Jace to sit on the right end, with the case on the floor beside him.

"That is for me," Cong said.

They had agreed to let Than handle this part, and the Thai nodded. "As promised."

"Put it on the table," the general ordered.

Than nodded to Jace, who set the case on the table, turning it so the locks faced the general, who had removed a pair of tubular keys from his inside jacket pocket.

Jace swallowed when he saw them. Mike had assured him that no one would be able to tell that the case had been tampered with, and he sincerely hoped that was still true.

Cong inserted both keys and turned them at the same time.

Two barely audible *clicks* were heard from inside, and the general nodded after he opened the case and reviewed its contents.

As he was doing so, the bodyguard emerged from the bedroom behind him, holding a limping young woman by the arm. She was silent, but from her short, tight, disheveled dress, it was obvious what her occupation was. The ripening black eye, split lip, and bruises on her arms and legs made it obvious what Cong had been doing last night.

The general didn't even look up as she was escorted out of the room. "Very good, Mr. Than. The payment will be transferred to your Swiss account as agreed."

"That is satisfactory, General." Than sat stiffly on the couch, with his hands on his knees. As Jace glanced at him, he noticed a small bead of sweat at the Thai's hairline, despite the air-conditioning in the room. *He'd better not be pulling a fucking double-cross*, he thought, gauging the distance to the fixer's throat, and then to the door if necessary.

Cong picked up the hotel's cordless phone and dialed a number. When he was connected, he had a short conversation with the person on the other end, then handed the phone to Than. "Just follow their directions."

"If you all will excuse me for a moment." Than walked over to the desk, speaking quietly into the receiver. Meanwhile, Cong had summoned one of his bodyguards, who closed and removed the case. At that moment, the butler returned with a tray, bottle of whiskey, and four glasses. He showed the bottle to Cong, who nodded, then leaned back in his chair. "You and your people are now free to consider other contracts, correct?"

Mike nodded. "Depending on the nature of the assignment. And the payment, of course." He made no move toward his drink yet.

"But of course. Why don't you tell me a bit more about these—Keldara, is it?—of yours."

"Georgian mountain people. Sturdy and tough, they take to military training and discipline like ducks to water. They are exceptionally capable and exceedingly loyal. I give them an objective and point them in a direction, and they do not stop until the mission is accomplished," Mike said.

"Apparently. You also come highly recommended from our mutual acquaintance in Phuket. I did catch some of the satellite footage of that business in the Caucasus Mountains last year— very impressive. The Russians must be very pleased to have you keeping the Chechens in their place, yes?"

"They don't mind." Mike leaned forward. "But we're not here to discuss the past, General. What can I and my people do for you?"

Cong was unfazed by Mike's directness. "I am in need of professional soldiers to escort a convoy of light and medium weapons into the north of Myanmar. With the continued rebel activity up there, I am concerned for the safety of my shipment. However, I hesitate to ask the local military to assist, as they are already stretched thin across the country."

"Surely your own nation would provide an escort for a military shipment of arms?" Mike asked.

The general's eyes flashed. "If that were an option, I wouldn't be speaking to you, now, would I? Your only concern is whether your people can do the job I need doing."

"Of course. How far, and for how long?"

"The trip covers seven hundred fifty kilometers. Depending on climate and the road conditions, it should take us from between two and four days."

"What is the final destination?"

"I prefer to keep that to myself, to prevent intelligence leaks. You will receive that information at the appropriate time. I require a minimum of twenty-five men able to maintain watch twenty-four hours a day. Extraction from the delivery site is to be provided by you. Expenses will be factored into your final total."

"When would you prefer to leave?"

Cong shifted slightly in his chair. "There is a small matter that needs taking care of here in Bangkok. Part of my shipment has been held up in customs. The first task for your people would be to get it released, however you wish, as long as it is done quietly.

Once that portion is transported to Yangon and offloaded, we would leave within the next twelve hours."

Mike didn't bat an eye. "The price is one-point-seven-five million for my team, plus expenses. It is not negotiable. We maintain our own radio equipment and comm channels. My men answer to me, not to you or anyone else in your chain of command. We are to liberate your shipment portion and guard the convoy to its final destination, nothing else. We will have authorization to use deadly force if attacked."

The Chinese general's expression turned grave. "As long as you understand that you answer to me."

Mike's jaw worked, but his reply was level. "As our employer, of course."

"Of course. Your terms are accepted." Cong picked up his glass and saluted Mike with it. "To a very profitable relationship."

Mike raised his glass too. "I'll have the standard contract sent to you this afternoon. One-half of the payment will be due on signature." He knocked back the contents in one gulp.

"Of course. I will have the funds wired as soon as I have approved the contract." Cong stood, signifying the end of the meeting. His bodyguard had appeared again, and gave the Chinese general a flash drive, who handed it to Mike. "Here is the information regarding the shipment here in Bangkok. Let me know your planned schedule so I can have the trucks prepared accordingly." He extended his hand again. "I am looking forward to working with you and your people, Mr. Jenkins."

"And I you." Mike nodded to Jace and Than, and the three men were escorted back to the lift and down to the main lobby again.

"Contact information is also on the drive," the bodyguard said. "Be sure to use the correct pass code per day as indicated."

"Okay," Mike said as he turned and headed for the entrance, with Jace and Than right beside him.

Only when they were outside and safely in a cab did Jace break the silence. "Are you as concerned about a rogue Chinese army general peddling arms into Myanmar as I am?"

"Well, the thought never crossed my mind until a few minutes ago. Now that you mention it, however, I can think of a few people who might consider that to be a problem," Mike said. "However, I think I'll wait until I'm back on the boat to break the bad news."

"You agreed to do *what*?" Pierson asked four hours later.

Despite having heard Mike perfectly clearly the first time, he had asked the question on the off chance the former SEAL was pulling his leg. The problem was that Mike never kidded about mission parameters. If the POTUS *had* wanted him and the Keldara to infiltrate China and assassinate the Premier, Mike would find a way get it done.

"I accepted a job to guard a convoy of weapons under a Chinese general's control into the heart of Myanmar. Oh, that's after I recover part of the shipment that's stuck in customs here in Bangkok."

"Yeah, that's what I thought you said. And this General Zháo Cong, he actually gave you his real name?"

"Vanner's sending you the video footage from our meeting earlier today, so your analysts can confirm his identity. He sure sounded like a lot of generals I've met—pompous, self-important, and with a huge stick up his ass. Likes to beat his women, too."

"That'll get some priority at the Pentagon, I'm sure. First nuclear reactor boards, now arms deals in Myanmar? Are you ever going to take a real vacation someday?"

"Maybe, but not today. I figured I'd better kick this up the chain, in case someone had a problem with it."

"Yeah, but didn't I say to let us know if you got involved in China?"

"You keep saying that. Look, I thought I'd be dealing with another South Asian criminal, maybe a local warlord. The Chinese angle was a complete surprise, especially since the boards came from there in the first place. Besides, as I recall, you said to let you know if this took us into China, not if we spoke with one of them. The guy was ready to deal right then and there. If I had said I needed to think about it, he might have gotten cold feet or gotten someone else."

"Okay, I hear you. The only problem is that this takes the mission in an entirely new direction. If the brass scrubs this, how are you going to back out?"

"Easy," Mike replied. "I'll just turn my boat around and head in the opposite direction. But you know as well as I do the Old Man's going to want this followed up."

"Yeah, I do." Bob sighed. "I'm off to get my ducks in a row over here. I'll be in touch as soon as I have the orders."

"Talk to you soon," Mike said. "I've got an extraction to plan."

"And just plan it for now, okay? Remember what time it is over here? I probably won't be able to get everyone together for a couple hours. Just sit tight, and I'll get back to you ASAP."

"Are you telling me that China is involved in this Myanmar situation?" the President asked.

"Not exactly. All available information indicates that this is the act of a lone Chinese army general who has been using his contacts throughout the region to both foment unrest and line his pockets at the same time."

Having assuaged the POTUS, the director of the National Security Agency activated the hastily assembled PowerPoint briefing, bringing up the first slide of their potential enemy. "General Zháo Cong was born in 1963 to Bolin and Daiyu Cong. Bolin was a senior Party member who schooled his son in the Communist doctrine from an early age. Zháo entered the military on his eighteenth birthday, and swiftly ascended the chain of command. It is unknown whether his rapid ascent was due to his family's status or simply natural talent. Assigned to the Department of Military Intelligence in the General Staff Department, he was promoted to the rank of general by age thirty-four."

The NSA director advanced the program, showing a breakdown of China divided into its various military districts. "Six months after his promotion, General Cong was reassigned to the Chengdu Military Region for an unknown reason. Despite its proximity to India, Myanmar, and Thailand, in Chinese military circles the region is considered a backwater for officers whose careers have stalled. When he was unable to transfer out, Cong apparently decided to capitalize on his new assignment. He was still a hard-core Communist, but got onboard fast when the capitalist movement swept the nation in the '90s. Since then, rumors have circulated that he's been using his military connections to facilitate shipments of arms, drugs, and even people in both directions between China and neighboring countries for whoever's willing to meet his price. We've heard from more than one source that he is involved in Myanmar's heroin trade, but he's very good at keeping his hands clean. Two separate investigations both failed to connect him to any of the major players in the area. However, in the past few years, the general has been living a lavish lifestyle that would be impossible on any normal army general's salary, even one who was taking bribes inside the Chinese system."

The director brought up the next slide, a close-up of the border between Myanmar and China—much of it adjacent to Cong's military region. "Lately he's been seen hobnobbing around with several of the Myanmar's old guard. All career military men who are known to be against the democratic government established in 2010, although there's no way to prove that. There is a legitimate concern that these men, if given the means, would do whatever they can to return the nation to what they would consider the good old days of military dictatorship."

"And a large convoy of weapons would go a long way toward achieving that goal." The President merely said what everyone in the room was already thinking.

"I suppose it's too much to ask that Mike simply dispose of this general and ensure that those weapons never make it to their destination?" The CIA director asked.

The President studied the map and border between the two countries. "Tempting as that option is, I need every bit of leverage over the Chinese that I can get. Taking Cong out and telling the

Chinese we cleaned up a mess in their own backyard isn't bad, but if we can link him to the parties actively trying to destabilize another country . . . well, that could almost be seen as an aggressive act on China's part now, wouldn't it?"

"Mr. President, you can't possibly be thinking of trying them in the world press, would you?" The NSA director asked. "First, they'll deny the hell out of it and claim he was acting on his own, which he is, so I don't see what that would gain us by making it public. Hell, they'd probably try to find some way to say we had made up the whole damn thing to discredit them. Then they stop buying our foreign debt, and the economy goes even more in the crapper than it is already."

The President waved off the man's protest. "I'll settle for aiding and abetting. I've been considering having the secretary of state visit China later this year or early in the next. Having conclusive evidence that one of theirs was involved in a military coup would be a great thing to have in our hip pocket for that trip . . . just in case."

He turned to Bob Pierson, who had remained quiet during all of this. "Let Mike know to continue the operation. Tell him to ingratiate himself with this General Cong as much as he can stomach, and gather as much information on him as possible. Video identifying him actually involved in the transfer for the weapons would be great, if possible."

"He wants *what*?" Mike asked.

"Look, his exact words were, 'if possible.' You're already doing enough over there, I'm sure the Old Man doesn't expect miracles."

"No, but . . . well, it's not necessarily impossible—"

"Really?"

"Yeah. We've been working more surveillance on this op than usual, and it's gone pretty well so far. That file we sent to you was taken with a hidden pen HD camera we ordered over the Internet, if you can believe that. Plus, I've got another way that's practically undetectable. If you tell him that, he'll know what I mean. Probably have to disguise her to make sure Cong doesn't get his hands on her..."

"What was that last part, Mike?"

"What? Oh, just thinking out loud. We'll get on the job. Will let you know more when there's more to know."

"Okay, and be careful out there, will you? The jungle can hide a lot of secrets—or bodies."

"I know." Mike said. "I'll just have to make sure they're all the other guys', that's all."

CHAPTER SEVENTEEN

"So, that's what we're looking at. Any questions before I continue?" Mike had assembled his officers, Daria, and Katya together to brief them on the operation as well as continue planning it.

"Is no one else concerned that Cong is being so secretive about the final destination?" Neilson asked from the monitor. "Taking a guess by the sketchy information he provided, you could be heading to Pyin U Lwin or Mandalay—"

"—or any one of a number of other towns nearby. I saw the map," Mike interrupted. "Your point is noted, David, but we don't have a huge choice. Washington wants us to both find out if there is a reactor somewhere in Myanmar *and* get hard evidence on Cong, so right now we have to play his game by his rules."

"Perhaps, but the point I wish to make about Pyin U Lwin is that it is a training site for the Myanmar military. If you really are driving into there, it could be a problem," Nielson said.

"Not if Cong will live up to the agreement that we sent to him. As we are working for him, under the terms of the contract, no foreign military should be able to impede us or prevent us from leaving when we have completed our assignment," Mike replied.

"Assuming that this dirty Chinese general is going to play fair with you, too," Neilson said.

Jace raised a hand. "Colonel Nielson brings up a good point. How certain are we that he's even going to adhere to the terms?

I mean, he's certainly not acting on behalf of the Chinese government here, so what incentive does he have to play fair with us?
I mean, besides the fact that we would shoot him full of holes
if he doesn't?"

Mike smiled. "The typical rule of thumb when dealing with men
with guns is that you do not want to stiff them—on anything. We
signed a piece of paper, but that doesn't mean I trust him. We are
simply going to have to stay on guard even more than usual, not
only from outside forces, but also from Cong and his own people."

Jace nodded. "Works for me."

"Anyone else with questions?" When no one spoke up, Mike
kept going. "All right. We'll need reliable transportation for the
Keldara teams, as well as the command and support staff. Even
if Cong allows us the use of his vehicles, I don't want to rely on
him any more than necessary. Daria, we'll need two transports
able to hold twelve men plus gear apiece, as well as three of the
toughest off-road SUVs or pickups you can find. You know my
preferences, but whatever's available will have to do. Get the best
deal you can, and try not to let them know that we are in a hurry.
Coordinate with Jace and Vanner on any issues about foreigners
purchasing vehicles. Hopefully the amount of cash we're plunking
down for these will remove those obstacles before they become a
problem. Before I turn to the customs issue, a couple more things
to address. First, Patrick, how are the contract negotiations going?"

Vanner pushed a manila folder toward him. "What negotiations? He signed the base contract as is, even with our built-in
escalators for extended time in the field and heavy combat. Drag
your feet a little and pop some caps at the trees, and we could
be looking at another half-million in fees before we're done. This
guy must really be in a hurry to get these weapons on the road."

"He certainly seemed impatient when we met him," Mike said.

"Probably couldn't find what he needed around here without
alerting the locals," Jace said.

"Good thing we just happened to be in the neighborhood,"
Adams commented.

"Indeed." Mike finished flipping through the boilerplate agreement. "What about the down payment?"

"Already deposited in a bank account opened specifically for that purpose this morning." The intel chief shrugged. "Like I said, dude's in a hurry."

"Probably coming out of some Chinese army slush fund anyway, although he'd be crazy to use any cash that could be traced," Mike said.

"Hell, the U.S. has spent billions on PMCs and outside contractors in the past decade, why shouldn't other countries get in on the fun?" Adams asked.

Mike shrugged. "Point. I guess we could consider this doing our part to address America's trade imbalance with China. All right, one last thing on the agenda. I've been advised that certain parties on the other side of the world would like to have video evidence of General Cong and his misdeeds. That—" he pointed at Katya. "—is where you come in."

"Not that I am complaining about another job, but surely you have other methods of doing this," she said.

"We do, and they probably wouldn't cost as much—" Mike exchanged a thin smile with her. "—but none of them are as undetectable as you. Besides, we might need your other assets, too. There is one thing that, to be honest, I'm not sure if you'll care about or not. I think it will be best if you go in dressed as a man."

Katya cocked her head. "Why?"

"Two reasons. One, a blond woman will be too distracting to the other men out there, and prevent you from being able to do the job you are there to do. Two, General Cong has some unusual hobbies in the bedroom, and I don't want him getting any ideas around you. Bottom line, you are in my employ, not his."

"You are too kind," she said.

"I have my moments. All right, how are we fixed for the customs job?"

"Team Inara has reviewed the operations documents and is

sacked out right now, pending the 0100 mission launch time. However this turns out, I would suggest that we try to stay off this Cong guy's shit list, 'cause he is fucking thorough." Adams held up a thick sheaf of papers. "The jacket on the customs guy who's holding up the shipment has everything in it but how he holds his dick when he pisses, and I'll bet if we asked for it, he'd find out and get it to us. We've got his daily schedule, family intel, house blueprints, security plans, neighborhood maps, the quickest route from there to the warehouse and from there to the rendezvous point, everything we need. We've even got the proper forms that this jackass needs to approve, stamp, and sign. You give the word, we'll be up and running it within twenty minutes."

"Works." Mike frowned. "Do we have any idea why this shipment is being held up in the first place? We don't need any foreign entanglements if we go in to get this and find out it's in quarantine or some shit like that."

Daria answered this one. "According to the documentation on the drive, this shipment of 'televisions' is currently pending a 'supervisor's inspection' because the 'special duty payment' offered was not enough."

"Just can't make a living on a public servant's salary any more, can you?" Mike asked. "Is the paperwork in order?"

She nodded at Jace. "With Captain Morgan's assistance, we were able to make sense of it. Everything is in order except for the final inspection and sign-off by the official."

"Okay...so why don't we simply make our own customs stamp, process the paperwork ourselves, and go pick up the shipment without ever getting this guy involved?"

"Just because Daria and I think we've got this done right isn't the same thing as getting someone who knows it inside out and backwards putting their seal of approval on it to make it all nice and pretend legal," Jace said. "Besides, if we tell him we know his little game, there's no way he would blow the whistle on us. He won't want to destroy the comfortable life he's made for himself and his family."

Mike nodded. "Roll Inara out at oh-dark-thirty hours. I want plenty of time for you all to pay this guy a visit."

Six hours earlier, Senior Customs Official Prasopchai Maneerrattana had left his office at the Central Administration Sub-Division of the Import Cargo Examination Division, Bangkok Port Customs Bureau, at the end of another workday. He smoothed his thinning brown hair, loosened his handmade, purple pindot English silk tie and unbuttoned the French cuffs on his Charles Tyrwhitt Black Label oxford button-down shirt as he walked to his silver 2012 Jaguar XJL supercharged sedan with tinted windows.

Pras drove home, skillfully avoiding the seemingly endless traffic jams on the freeways around the city by virtue of knowing which side roads to take and cut a half-hour off his normal ninety-minute commute to his sprawling house in the upscale Huai Kwang neighborhood on the northeast side of the city. There he had dinner with his lovely second wife, Araya, and his two daughters, Vipada, aged eight, and Sunsia, aged ten. He played with the girls afterward, then the family settled down to watch television before sending the kids off to bed at 9 PM. With nothing planned for the rest of the evening, Pras and Araya relaxed for a couple of hours before going to bed themselves—the perfect end to another perfect day.

This was nothing new to Pras, however, as he had truly led a charmed life from the moment he entered this world. Born to a comfortable merchant family in a middle-class suburb around Bangkok, he had been educated in the best schools his family could provide—including being sent to Eton on a partial scholarship—and had never known want, or any sort of hardship, really. He had played cricket in college, and being better than average looking, dated more than the average number of young women before falling for his first wife, whom he had been with for several years. She had caused the only interruption of his otherwise harmonious life when she had left him after five years, primarily for what she claimed was a "lack of ambition."

That had rankled Pras at the time. He had just completed his second year at the Bangkok Port Customs Bureau, where he was doing all right. The job came easy enough to him; the only problem was that there didn't seem to be anywhere to go in terms of upward mobility. And Pras had expensive tastes that were getting more difficult to finance. But when the Asian financial crisis of 1997 hit, he found ways to make his position more lucrative.

Customs agents were often approached by foreigners, businessmen, or criminals attempting to bribe them to let certain packages pass through the port with little or no inspection or interference. Even with money tight, people would ironically spend large amounts to get whatever they needed shipped wherever it needed to go. When a man who appeared to be a legitimate Singapore businessman came to him with an offer that would net Pras a cool one million baht just to look the other way, he decided to go for it. Why shouldn't he partake in the rampant corruption that extended into every part of the Bangkok government? After all, everyone did it.

Pras not only did it, but found he was very good at it. So good in fact, that one of his regular people tipped him off that the government was looking into "irregularities" in the customs accounts. They were working with his superior, a crusty, by-the-book supervisor named Niwat Kadesadayurat, to gather evidence. Knowing the old man would catch him if he looked into things too closely, Pras struck first. He neatly framed Niwat for approving several illegal packages going through customs without proper inspection or paperwork. He even turned the man in himself, knowing the surest way to deflect suspicion was to step up as the loyal subordinate who, although troubled by what he found, knew he had to do what was right.

Niwat was arrested, fired, and spent the rest of his days in abject poverty, dying soon afterward. As a reward for his betrayal, Pras was promoted into Niwat's position. More bribes followed, and even a few more internal investigations, but much like his earlier life, Pras always escaped getting caught. Part of this was due to the extensive network of friends and associates, both legal and illegal, he had built up over the years. The other part was his learning from that first time so many years ago, and keeping meticulous records of his real and fake shipments, so that he could produce authentic, if completely false, documentation when needed.

So things had gone this way for years, with Pras able to provide for his new wife and family, gradually working up to a higher station in life where they were more comfortable. And it all would have kept on being perfect, too. Except for 2009.

The financial panic had wiped out much of Pras's savings, and his overreactions to the market swings had led him to gamble on risky investments, which had cost him even more. With his oldest daughter about to go off to the same prep school he had—at a much higher cost twenty years later—he was scrambling to keep everything afloat. So, when word of the Chinese general who worked in the black market had come to him, and he had verified the shipment for himself, Pras thought he had found the answer to his problems. One big score, instead of waiting and hoping for a bunch of little ones to trickle in over the next year, and everything would be back to normal.

The real beauty of his plan was that the general would *have* to pay. He certainly couldn't go to the authorities and ask that his shipment of illegal arms be released, risking an investigation from both Thailand and China. He also certainly couldn't put too much overt pressure on Pras without risking the whole scheme being uncovered either.

That was why the customs official had enjoyed the relaxing evening with his family, and why he had gone to bed secure in the knowledge that he would be much richer in the next forty-eight hours. That, and the knowledge that the security system in his house was state of the art, and the police were well paid to patrol their neighborhood.

Therefore, it was an incredible shock when Pras was jolted awake in the dark, quiet hours of the morning to find himself immobilized in his bed with a gloved hand clamped over his mouth. Other than his eyes, which scanned wildly in all directions, he couldn't move a muscle. He could only move his eyes enough to see shadows moving on either side of him. He couldn't see his wife, who normally slept right beside him, and he had no idea if his daughters were all right. Panic rising in him, Pras tried thrashing around as he shouted into the gloved hand. His efforts were just as futile as the first time. Whoever or however they were holding him, the grip was unbreakable.

A head out of a nightmare appeared in front of him. The intruder's face was completely covered in a matte-black helmet, goggles, and concealing facemask. This person was the same one who had the hand over Pras's mouth. The person waited until he stopped moving and calmed down.

"Can you understand what I am saying?" he asked in Thai, letting up on Pras's head just enough for him to nod.

"Then listen to me very carefully. Your family is unharmed. They will sleep through the night and have no idea that anything ever happened here—if you do exactly what we say. Do you understand?"

Pras nodded again.

"All right. In a moment I am going to release you. You will get up, get dressed, and gather whatever materials you need to approve the entire shipment being held in Lot Twenty-Seven in Warehouse Seven at the Bangkok Port Customs Bureau. Nod if you understand."

Pras nodded again. The person took his hand away, and the Thai customs official felt the pressure on his body lessen. He looked around to find his bed surrounded by five more people, all dressed in black and holding huge, black guns.

Pras checked on his wife, who looked as if she was still sleeping peacefully beside him. He reached over to touch her, then shake her, but got no response. She was breathing, but unconscious.

"The clock is ticking, Mr. Maneerrattana. Believe me, this is one inspection that you do not want to be late for," the masked leader said.

Too terrified to speak, Pras scurried to his closet. Grabbing the first shirt and pair of pants he put his hands on, he struggled into them. Shoving his bare feet into a pair of Italian leather shoes, he turned to find the masked man right in front of him, holding a tie. "You will need to look professional if you are going into work, won't you?"

With a shaky nod, Pras took the tie and tried to tie it around his neck, the silk slipping through his fumbling fingers. After the third try, the masked person shook his head and moved his fingers away before tying a perfect half-Windsor knot. "Get your jacket, we have to get moving."

Once Pras was dressed, the masked man led him to the garage. "Here is what is going to happen. One of my associates and I are going to accompany you to your office. There you are going to take care of any internal issues with that particular shipment. Then we are going to that particular warehouse. While we are doing that, the rest of my associates are going to stay here and keep watch over your family—"

A pained sob rose in Pras's throat, and he couldn't stop it from escaping. "Please, I will do whatever you wish, just do not hurt them—"

The masked man held up a hand. "They will not be harmed as long as you do what we ask."

"H—how do you expect to remove the shipment? It—it is more than twenty-five large, heavy wooden boxes. No trucks are scheduled to come in tonight."

"By the river, of course. Don't worry, you'll be overseeing the entire operation from start to finish. Once we have everything we need, I will call my associates, who will leave your home and family in exactly the same condition they found them in. If anything goes wrong, or if I do not call them to check in one hour from now, well, I am sure you have a pretty good idea of what will happen to them. Now let's get going, shall we? Make sure you have whatever identification you require for access to both your office and the warehouse."

Pras double-checked that he had everything he needed, then got into his car, with the two men accompanying him both sitting in the back seat.

He drove first to the main customs office, a long, shallow, U-shaped building that faced the river, with two wings branching off the main unit. He had to go into the smaller, F-shaped building in front of it to enter the inspection appointment and falsify the approval for the shipment to go out.

When he pulled into the parking lot, he turned to the men in the back seat. "I must go in alone. It would be suspicious to have anyone with me at this hour."

"Of course." The speaker placed a pen in the inner pocket of his suit jacket, and one in his outer jacket pocket. "The outer pen contains a tiny video camera with sound, so we will be able to see and hear every movement you make, every person you talk to. The inner pen contains an ounce and a half of Semtex, a high explosive that is connected to both a timer and a remote. The amount is more than enough to kill you if you force us to detonate it. Go inside, do whatever you must do to clear the shipment, and return to your car. You have fifteen minutes to comply, starting now."

The next several minutes passed in a terrifying blur for Pras. He was aware of certain things as they happened... activating the door security lock with his identification... dropping the key to his office and hitting his head when he bent to retrieve it while trying to make sure that both pens stayed in his pockets... frantically typing in the clearance and scheduling the inspection for that morning... printing the proper forms and grabbing the correct stamps... walking back to the car, all the while aware of the small, concealed bomb resting in his breast pocket. Pras was petrified that someone would try to engage him in conversation, even at that hour of the morning.

When he reached the car, he was soaked in sweat. Sliding in, he turned to the man, who was now alone in the back seat. "I have everything you will need—please take this thing off of me!"

"Not yet." The person took the printed forms and scanned them for what seemed like an eternity. With a nod, he took the bomb pen back, but left the camera one where it was. "Let's go."

"How do you expect to make it through the main gate?" Pras asked.

"One of us will be crouched in the back seat, the other in the trunk," the man replied. "A pistol will be on you at all times, and, of course, we will be watching through the camera. Try to alert the guard or give any kind of warning, and you will die before your family does. Just stay calm, get us to the warehouse, and we'll handle the rest."

Pras started the car and drove to the white main security gate that led into the customs holding and warehousing area for Bangkok. After clearing the security checkpoint, he drove along a double row of warehouses that had been built back-to-back, facing both the river and the city, until he stopped in front of Warehouse Seven. Unlocking the door, he pushed it open, revealing an interior stacked high with various boxes.

"They are over here." He led the two men to the Chinese general's containers.

The masked man compared the numbers on the boxes with the list Pras had printed on the inspection invoice, then compared both of those with a third list on a smartphone. Only when he was satisfied did he hit a button on the phone and say something in a strange language.

"Stand right here." Pras did as ordered. The first man waited for less than a minute before the sound of multiple boat motors could be heard. Moments later, a long, sleek cigarette boat pulled up to the dock outside, and several more men, all clad in black, got out.

Pres looked over to see the man holding out a sheaf of papers. "Finish your inspection and clear this shipment."

With a shaking hand, Pras did as he was told, marking all of the boxes as having cleared customs on the Import Declaration Form: Kor Sor Kor 99/1. He stamped it where indicated, signed off on releasing the shipment, and held out the papers to the masked man who read them again, then nodded to the other men, who immediately began team lifting the boxes out to the boat.

It took ninety minutes and two trips, but finally all of the boxes were gone. The masked man was the last one to leave the warehouse after handing the customs official his smartphone.

"Go home to your family, Mr. Maneerrattana. They are safe. My people left twenty minutes ago." The masked man watched him as the cigarette boat powered away from the pier.

A shaking Prasopchai Maneerrattana dialed his house with trembling fingers as he felt his bladder finally let go, releasing warm urine that trickled down his leg.

During the mid-afternoon of the same day, Mike met General Cong several miles outside Yangon to hand over the liberated shipment. He'd chosen a deserted beach near sparse rows of palm trees dotting the surrounding terrain, and told Cong to arrange for three trucks and either a forklift or a lot of strong backs to offload his cargo.

Dressed in a double-breasted charcoal gray suit, Cong himself had arrived from the Andaman Sea in a thirty-foot cigarette boat to supervise the transfer. He was very meticulous, examining each box as his sweating men unloaded them, but found nothing amiss. "There were no problems, then?"

Mike shook his head. "Nothing we couldn't handle."

The general nodded. "And there has been no word about any sort of break-in or incident at the customs facility in the press or across military channels. You have performed admirably, Mr. Jenkins. Are your people ready to go?"

Mike nodded. "Just waiting for the word to move."

"I have a few things to wrap up in the city, but there is no reason not to get a head start this afternoon. There is a small shipping company that lies just north of the Mingalardon Industrial Park on Route 3. Take Thu Dhammar Road and follow it all the way out of the city. Meet me there in eight hours."

"We'll be there." Mike said, staring into the Andaman Sea, where an amazing superyacht lay at anchor. At least three hundred feet long, it was a third longer than the *Big Fish*, and was a study in sleek white and black steel. With four decks, it looked like it could comfortably sleep twenty, and uncomfortably handle twice that number.

"You like what you see out there?" Cong asked.

"That is a nice boat. Yours?" Mike asked.

The general nodded. "It was built for one of our real estate billionaires. Unfortunately, he ran into some legal trouble with the government, and all of his assets were seized. I got it for a song, all things considered. When we're finished here, you should come aboard. I'll give you the captain's tour."

"I look forward to it. Until this evening, then." Mike watched the small man get aboard his shore boat and head back to the huge yacht a half-mile away. "Now that's the way to sail." He had made sure to anchor the *Big Fish* several miles away. No sense in letting Cong get any more information on him than the man already had.

"Yeah, if you can afford it," Adams said beside him. "That sucker would wipe out every dollar you got, and not even come close to buying a third of it, I'd bet."

"You been looking into the books again, Ass-Boy?"

"Hell no, I just know what you've put into the place back home, that's all. Come on, buddy, your own superyacht will have to wait for another day."

"Yeah, someday..." With a last, wistful look at the magnificent vessel, Mike turned back to his own boat, and signaled for the others to head back to the *Big Fish*.

They were cruising through the sapphire-blue waters of the bay when Mike got a call from Vanner. "You are not going to guess who just requested permission to come aboard?"

"Lieutenant Fang Gui of the Hong Kong Police?"

"Yeah, how in the hell did you know?"

"Because he *is* the very last person I would expect to see out here." Mike frowned as he pushed the throttle forward, making the sleek boat's bow rise out of the glass-smooth water as it surged ahead. "Have him come aboard, keep him on the rear deck, and tell him we will be there in about twenty minutes. By the way, we are still in international waters, right?"

Vanner snorted. "We haven't even come within ten miles of any territories' nautical border since leaving Hong Kong."

"Good. Oh, and be sure to keep the Asian prostitutes below deck and quiet, will you?" Mike signed off, but overheard part of Vanner's comment to himself.

"Never thought I'd *ever* hear that kind of order..."

"Lieutenant, this is truly an unexpected surprise," Mike said as he climbed aboard the *Big Fish*'s stern. "If I didn't know better, I'd think you were keeping tabs on us."

Fang Gui turned from where he was watching the far-off landscape of Myanmar. He looked just as rumpled as when Mike had first met him, only his suit was a different shade of tan. The two Special Police Unit men with him remained on their boat, but stayed close enough to lend assistance if needed. "The U.S. is not the only one with satellites, Mr. Jenkins. How have you been enjoying your cruise through our waters?"

Waving the police officer to a chair at the table, Mike pulled out another one and sat down. "Considering we're at least five days from Hong Kong, I hardly think these qualify as 'your' waters."

"Of course." Fang smiled. "I merely meant to ask if you are enjoying your time in the South Pacific? You've certainly been busy over the past couple of days since your unexpected departure from our city."

Mike waved a hand at the azure ocean and far-off land mass on the horizon. "Well, there's so much to see out here, I want to make the most of our time in the area."

"Naturally." Fang nodded. "I'm not here about what happened at the shipping dock, in case you are wondering. You accomplished what needed to be done, and in a most spectacular fashion."

"About that, I sincerely hope that none of your men were injured too badly."

"I expect I should be happy that you didn't kill any of them. One has a ruptured eardrum, and another is recovering from a minor concussion, but other than a lot of bumps and bruises, everyone is all right."

"Good. I told my men to incapacitate as harmlessly as possible, but often the best approach is still fairly brutal."

"That is one way of putting it. There is one loose end regarding that incident. I suppose you have no idea whatsoever about Mr. Than's current whereabouts?"

"He left us more than a day ago."

That part, at least, was true. Once Than had made his delivery, he had wished Mike the best of luck. He also said if Mike ever needed anything in this area of the world, to get in touch with him through Chal. Mike said he would do that, and extended an offer to drop by if the fixer ever found himself east of the Black Sea. "Can I get you a drink?"

"Technically I am on duty, but I don't expect anyone to be asking too many questions about what I did when meeting with a confidential informant. A beer would be great."

"Got just the thing." Mike held up two fingers and nodded at Daria, who went below. "So, I'm your CI now? If your visit really is official business, why don't you tell me what I could have possibly done to bring you all the way out here."

"Like I said, Mr. Jenkins, you have been very busy. Everywhere you go, things happen. Your yacht was spotted in the vicinity of Phuket Island off Thailand thirty-six hours ago. Less than twenty-four hours later, the known headquarters of a local gang was destroyed in what the local police described as a 'military-style assault,' leaving no one alive. You wouldn't happen to know anything about that, would you?"

"Phuket is a lovely island. Great beaches, and the nightlife cannot be beat. Ah, here's our beers." One of the girls had returned with a bucket filled with bottles of Mountain Tiger on ice. Mike grabbed one, opened it, and clinked the neck against the lieutenant's. "Cheers."

"We typically say '*suíyì*,' which means each person can drink how they like. If I wanted you to drain the entire bottle, I would say '*gānbēi!*' However, my favorite is *wàn shòu wú jiāng*—to longevity and health." The policeman sipped, then drank deeper, his eyes widening. "What heavenly brew is this?"

"Glad you like it. It's from my neck of the woods, brewed in the valley of the Keldara."

"It is truly unlike anything I have ever tasted." Like most people who drank Mountain Tiger for the first time, Fang had a hard time setting the bottle down.

"We hear that a lot. So, you were about to tell me the real reason you are here in person?" Mike asked.

"Of course. How is your follow-up of the computer boards going?"

"It's progressing. I suppose you are aware of a General Zháo Cong in the Chinese Army?"

"Oh, yes, very much so. Are you saying he's involved?"

"I watched Than hand the case to him in his luxury hotel suite yesterday. I think that counts as involved."

"Ah, that would explain this footage we took of you meeting him earlier today." Fang slid his smartphone over to Mike, who watched as the boxes of weapons were unloaded on the beach where he had just been less than an hour ago.

"You guys sure like keeping tabs on me and mine." Mike's jaw worked. "There may come a time in the future when I am not very fond of that."

Fang spread his hands. "What can I say? Wherever you go, Mr. Jenkins, it seems that you also happen to do a lot of our work for us. That shipment of weapons was under surveillance the moment it arrived in Bangkok. The customs official who was 'persuaded' by an unknown group of masked and black-clad men to release it has been arrested and is being interrogated by the local police. We've been keeping an eye on it ever since that same party liberated it from customs. It is fortunate that I had instructed the customs security to let that particular shipment go, but to notify us when anyone inquired about it or moved it. When I received word that you had taken it, I was unsurprised."

While the lieutenant was talking, Mike was sipping his beer to quell the turmoil in his stomach at realizing how close Jace and his team had come to possibly getting arrested by the customs police. His expression, however, was a study in nonchalance. "And all of that concerns me how?"

"Well, you are still working with General Cong, correct?"

"You would just bring out something to prove I was lying if I said no, wouldn't you?" Mike asked.

"You could try it and see." Fang smiled before draining his bottle.

"Have another." Mike finished his and opened another bottle while filling Fang in on their rest of their assignment for Cong. "Either he has got a big buyer, perhaps a local group up there who has cash and a desire to commit suicide against the army, or someone in country's planning to do something that involves a lot of bullets in the near future."

"Quite. A man like Cong is the worst example of a rank opportunist, exploiting his position and the trust of his nation to line his own pockets. It sullies the reputation of the entire People's Army."

"Yes, but I suppose the torture that your police and prison guards inflict on suspected dissidents and minorities, particularly the practitioners of Falun Gong, is fine for China's international reputation. But I guess truthfulness, compassion, and forbearance don't have a place in twenty-first-century China, do they?" Mike kept his gaze and jaw still as he watched Fang. He didn't really care what the Chinese did to their people in their prisons; he was more interested in seeing how the police officer would react.

The lieutenant stiffened and set his bottle down on the table with a *clink*. "They are opposed to the Communist Party of China and the central government, and spread sedition by preaching idealism, theism, and feudal superstition. The so-called 'truth, kindness and forbearance' principle preached by Li has nothing in common with the socialist ethical and cultural progress we are striving to achieve."

"So, you *are* a good little Communist. That's a pretty good sound bite you've memorized, by the way. Straight out of the Xinhua News Agency." Mike leaned back in his chair. "Cong was in charge of a large military prison outside of Beijing. I only bring this up as it would seem to be a sufficient reason as to why he was transferred to his current position."

"I have no knowledge of whether that was a factor or not." Fang's mouth said "*no*" while his eyes said "*yes*." "Bringing this conversation back to the matter at hand, we would like you to follow up with Cong and find out exactly what he is up to."

"You have got to be kidding me. Surely you've been able to get a man inside his operation?"

"The last one died ten months ago. It was handled so skillfully that even we are not sure whether the man's death was accidental or on purpose. Lately Cong has grown more paranoid about who works with him. You must have impressed him greatly. I cannot remember the last time, if ever, that he worked with foreigners."

"On the other hand, if he doesn't trust other Chinese, which, judging by whom I'm talking to right now, might be a wise idea for him, he would look outside the box to someone like us," Mike replied. "That means that he might just see me and my men as disposable *gwai-lo* labor. In which case we go into the jungle and never come out again."

"There is that, although I doubt that there are many situations that pose that sort of problem to you."

"I have not run into one yet, but there is always a first time," Mike said. "However, that does bring up the question of once Cong has delivered this large shipment of weapons, what am I supposed to do with him? It seems that the simplest solution would be the application of three cents worth of lead accelerated to the appropriate velocity."

"Although you and your fellow American cowboys may prefer

that sort of vigilante justice, we must have the general taken alive. He must stand trial and serve as an example to others in the military and the country that this sort of behavior will not be tolerated."

"And China certainly wouldn't want to be seen as a country that simply 'disappears' its problems, would it?" Mike asked.

Fang didn't blink at that. "We are trying to change certain aspects of how we are viewed by the rest of the world, yes. You may be called to testify on what you saw."

Mike shook his head. "I'm not really big on that sort of thing. How about if I provided you with video corroborating what went down?"

"Would you be willing to sign a statement attesting to what you saw as well?"

"I'll have to think about that. I'm not that up on international law. Hell, would that even carry any weight in your court system?"

"It would at his court-martial."

"Again, I'll have to get back to you on that."

"And once again, it would seem that our fates are intertwined, if I may use a staple of Chinese folklore. This time I cannot make you do as I wish—"

"As I recall, Fang, you didn't the last time we met either. Our goals happened to be mutually aligned, that's all," Mike replied.

"So, I can only ask. Will you do this for me and my country?" Fang asked.

"Throwing in China is a bit much, but I'll give you the same answer I gave back in Hong Kong. I'll see what I can do."

"What more can I ask for?" The lieutenant stood up. "Thank you for the beer."

"If things go well, we may have an Asian distributor who could roll it out in your neck of the world sometime in the next year. That way you won't have to hunt me down the next time you'd like some."

"I will keep that in mind. Hopefully I will have the chance to repay your generosity the next time you're in Hong Kong," Fang said.

"We'll see." Mike saw the lieutenant down to his boat and watched him sail off until the boat was just a speck on the horizon.

Vanner came on deck to join him. "Everything go all right with the Asian fuzz?"

"As good as expected, although one of the girls will need to review how witness testimony works in China, particularly in regards to court-martials."

"How's that again?" Vanner asked.

Mike detailed his conversation with the police lieutenant. "Too goddamn many eyeballs on us every step of the way. Not to mention Fang popping up in the oddest places."

"Yeah, like way the hell out here," Vanner said. "We're not exactly anywhere near his jurisdiction."

"Exactly. He's the riddle wrapped in a mystery inside an enigma that Churchill spoke of. Something's definitely not quite right about that guy, but I'll be damned if I can figure out what," Mike said.

"So, we're still dancing to the tunes of two masters?" Vanner asked.

"For the time being. I expect that to change once we dump Cong, however." Mike turned to head below. "One more thing. About ten miles east of us is the general's yacht."

"Yeah, it's hard to miss on radar."

"Good. I want you to have the captain shadow it. If it moves, stick with it. Try not to be obvious about it, of course."

"Keep your distance, but don't look like you're trying to keep your distance. Should I order the captain to sail casual?" Vanner asked with a smile.

"Something like that."

When the patrol boat was a good ten miles away, Fang Gui went below to report in. Setting a pair of headphones on his head, he called in on a scrambled satellite feed, but not back to the Hong Kong Police Headquarters. Instead, he contacted his own handler at the Third Bureau in the MSS in Beijing.

The conversation was short. "I have just met with the American again."

"And?"

"I believe he will continue to follow our target's trail."

"He told you this directly?"

Fang stifled a sigh. "He can be...obtuse in these matters. As before, he did not come right out and confirm exactly what he was going to do."

"However, he did accomplish what you had asked, even if he made the Hong Kong police look foolish in the bargain."

"Yes. If he is also answering to the U.S. government as we surmise, then I see no reason that he would suspend his investigation now."

"And afterward?"

"Given the instructions I received about this man back in Hong Kong, no matter what happens with the general, unless this Jenkins is killed during the operation, we will be forced to let him go while holding sensitive information about one of our high-ranking military officials." Fang chose his next words carefully. "However, from what I understand, that is the least of the information he seems to possess about our country."

There was a long pause before his handler answered. "Unfortunately, you are more correct than you know, and that is how this matter shall remain. Remain in the area pending the conclusion of the operation."

"Yes sir. One question, if I may."

"Go ahead."

"Is the operative from Second still on site?" In a rare display of cross-Bureau cooperation, the Second and Third Departments were working together on this case. Although he was unable to confirm it, Gui was sure that the Chinese woman who had been apprehended with Jenkins and his group was the mole. After all, she was the only Chinese woman with them, which made the supposition easy.

"Yes, she is. Why? Has she contacted you directly?"

"No, I was just wondering if there were any new directives regarding her. For example, I was never informed about her status on this assignment." Fang was politely asking who was supposed to be in charge of this investigation, her or him.

"There has been nothing new that I am aware of. You are to maintain overwatch of the various shipments tied to Cong and let the American continue his efforts. If a change in directive comes along, you will be informed. Third out."

CHAPTER EIGHTEEN

Seven hours later, Mike, Adams, Jace, Katya, Soon Yi, and the twenty-five Keldara chosen for this mission, including all of Team Jayne and most of Inara, pulled into the driveway of the small trucking company where Cong had told him to meet.

Daria had done an amazing job on short notice. She had picked up two Toyota Hilux Vigo extended-cab pickups with rear bed covers. For Mike's command vehicle, she had found the Thai version of the Ford Expedition, called the Everest. All of the vehicles had four-wheel drive, and were less than a year old. Because of the slow sales season, she had paid just under ninety million kyat for all three. They also all had the steering wheel on the right-hand side, even though Myanmar had switched to the right-hand rule of the road in 1970.

The team vehicles were a pair of olive-green M35A2s, the same ones as those Team Jayne had used in Phuket. Although these were much older than the smaller trucks, the dealer had showed her the maintenance records from the seller, a bankrupt cargo delivery company. They had also provided a written guarantee that the trucks would be good for another five years, although Daria said she thought that might have been entirely due to the short skirt she had worn to the purchase meeting. Initially skeptical, Mike and Adams had taken a look at the engine, transmission, and other visible parts, and they had all looked okay. Plus, the price couldn't be beat—forty-five million kyat for the pair.

They had picked up the vehicles that afternoon and immediately loaded the men, weapons, ammo, and gear. They'd selected enough for a five-night run, figuring two days there, two back, and one extra day for friction. Just getting out of the city took almost three hours—and that was during a non-rush hour time of day. They had just made it to the rendezvous point on schedule.

Cong and his people were ready and waiting for them. He had ten brand-new Mercedes-Benz cargo trucks filled to capacity with the weapons and ammunition. A white Lexus SUV was serving as Cong's private transportation, with another SUV holding the rest of his personal guard. The sun was just starting to set as Mike, Adams, Jace, and Soon Yi met with Cong to discuss the proposed route.

"We're staying on the main roads, all well-traveled highways that shouldn't give us any problems," the general said. "I want a vehicle scouting the road at least two kilometers ahead of the main unit, so they can radio back if they encounter any problem. Any questions?"

Mike shook his head. "My men will travel in four-hour shifts, then break while we switch out drivers at the front and back, which will keep them more alert. I expect you'll want to be traveling from just after dawn to just after dark, not counting today, of course. I've been looking into the conflicts in any areas we'll be passing through, and they seem to be more to the north and west."

Cong nodded. "You are correct, but I cannot be certain that other groups have not gotten word of this shipment. It would be a tremendous prize for any of the various rebel groups in the country. However, we have you and your teams to ensure that that doesn't happen."

"Right. Now that we're all assembled, why don't you give us our final destination?"

"Not just yet. I will notify you when the time is right."

Mike's jaw worked, but he didn't say anything else as they all went back to their respective vehicles.

"You still cool with this?" Adams asked.

"Bit late to back out now," Mike replied. "As I figured, everyone's going to have to stay on yellow alert for the next two or three days. Pass the word down."

Mike and Adams had worked out the driving schedules for their various teams to give just about everyone a chance behind the wheel. The forward vehicle was under strict instructions to report in to him directly every ten minutes.

Mike and Adams did one more walk-around to make sure everything on their trucks was lashed and secure, and that the teams knew to keep their eyes and ears open. Then, with Edvin and Vanel in the lead scout truck, the convoy pulled out onto the road.

In the Toyota's passenger seat, Vanel sat very still, trying to keep an eye on everything around them at once. Away from the city and after sundown, the night was deep, with a three-quarter moon providing scattered silver light in between the heavy clouds.

Vanel's job was to navigate using his tablet and its turn-by-turn directions. He flicked at the screen with his finger, following the oddly named roads to their destination. "What do you think of this country?" he finally asked Edvin.

His teammate shrugged. "Hot. Damp. Flat. This rain every day... I could not put up with that for long."

"Strange, isn't it?"

Edvin didn't look over, just grunted. "I'm sure the people who live here would think our own valley just as strange."

"I suppose." Vanel stared out the window at the dark landscape whizzing past. He made sure his weapon was at hand before calling in for the first time. "Inara Four to Mal."

"Go, Inara Four," the Kildar replied.

"All clear."

"Roger that."

And that was that. Vanel leaned back in his seat, mentally counting down the time to the next check-in.

Even on this main road, the farther they got from the city, the sparser the traffic got, until the only other vehicles on the road were large tractor-trailers and the occasional car or truck. Vanel was prepared for anything, even crazed guerillas on elephants charging them, for he had seen the huge beasts while driving through the city. But except for the six radio checks, the next hour passed in mind-numbing monotony.

Well, I guess everything is not guaranteed to end in a firefight, he thought.

Edvin glanced over at him. "You might as well relax. Nothing is going to happen this evening."

"How do you know?" Vanel asked.

"We are still too close to Yangon. Any rebel forces would strike farther away from the city. That way they protect themselves from the army, as well as delay the response from the army forces if they do strike us."

"Oh. Of course." Slightly nettled that he had not thought of that himself, Vanel took a deep breath. "I just do not wish to disappoint the Kildar, that's all."

"Do not worry, Vanel, you are not doing that. Your skills are fine, all you need now is experience. Soon you will be able to feel how a situation is going to play out simply by trusting your instincts. Sometimes they can tell you more than all of the training in the world."

"Yes, but ... how will I know which to rely on?" Vanel asked.

"As I said, experience will teach you that. Don't get me wrong, nine times out of ten your training will win out, and it will be correct. But every once in a while, your gut will insist on something. When it does, you would be wise to heed it, or at least take another look at the situation you are in, for the belly does not often lie."

"I will remember that, Edvin. Thank you."

"You're welcome, but I tell you this as much for me as you. If knowing these things helps keep you alive, then it helps you to keep the rest of the team alive. It is simple as that."

The next two days passed in a blur of tropical scenery and a lot of collective sitting on asses. Mike's take on the route had been right; the main highway was simply too open a target for anyone to risk assaulting a convoy on it. And even if someone had wanted to take on the large convoy, they would have been spotted by the point vehicle in enough time for the others to mount a preemptive strike. Other than a roadblock caused by an overturned lumber truck, there was a distinct lack of danger.

Passing unmolested through the country, they reached the small city of Pyin U Lwin by late afternoon of the third day. As they approached the outskirts, Cong radioed Mike to call back his scout vehicle and pull off to the side of the road before entering the city.

"I will take the lead from this point forward. Your vehicle will follow me, and the rest will trail behind the convoy. I will lead you to where we'll offload the cargo."

"All right." Mike radioed the orders down the line. Along with the men on site, every word was heard by Vanner and the girls back on the *Big Fish*.

"Hey, Kildar, am I seeing your position correctly? You're near Pyin U Lwin, right?" Vanner asked.

"Correct. Cong is taking us in right now. We're almost done here. Just have to get the handover on film, and we're out."

"Okay, we'll be watching." Vanner wasn't kidding either—they were tied in to Katya's remote viewing system.

She, however, was less than enthusiastic. "Should put out sign: no hitchhikers."

"Hey, you're getting paid very well just to stand around and watch this time," Mike said.

Katya smiled at that. "Is true. Much easier than usual."

"All right, then. Just make sure you have your eyes on the transfer, and once it's done, we're out of here."

Mike, Adams, and everyone else saw Cong's SUV pull back onto the road again. "All right, here we go."

On the *Big Fish*, Vanner had taken Neilson's concerns about the mission to heart, and had been tracking communications around the convoy and any possible destination for the past two days. They had come up empty so far; just a lot of commercial truck driving chatter and everyday military communications that weren't pertinent to what the Kildar was doing.

Now that his boss was so close to what was basically a large, potentially hostile military encampment, Vanner and his team were all on high alert this evening. "Anything yet?"

"Nothing of interest, Patrick," Greznya replied. "Is it possible that this is just a simple drop-off, and that the Kildar will be able to head back without any difficulty?"

"Possible, but not probable," Vanner replied. "Think about it. Would you leave an American and his very foreign entourage who had just seen you deliver a large cache of most likely stolen arms to a foreign country leave in one piece?"

His beautiful Keldara wife cocked her head. "Probably not, but not necessarily for that reason. If he is dead, then I do not have to pay the other half of the money, for who is going to argue about it with me?"

"That is the other thing," Vanner said. "Along with never get involved in a land war in Asia, a good rule of thumb is to never, *ever* trust a crooked military general."

"The convoy is moving again," Xatia said.

"What was the conversation between Cong and the people at his destination?" Vanner asked.

"Just that they are coming in with the complete shipment, and to expect them within ten minutes."

"Everything seems to be proceeding according to plan," Vanner said. "So why do I have a bad feeling about this?" He looked over at another console. "Where's Cong's ship?"

"Maintaining a steady distance of eight nautical miles ahead of us, sir," Martya reported. "The nearest port city to them now is Sittwe. We've been altering our course to plot an 'S' across their trail. Hopefully that will make them think there is more than one boat out here."

"All right, keep it up." Vanner tapped the arm of his chair in nervous anticipation. "Damn it, what am I missing—other than the fact that we're working with a double-dealing criminal?"

▲   ▲   ▲

Adams drove the command vehicle, following Cong's SUV through the town to a fenced-in site north of the city. It looked fairly innocuous, consisting of several concrete buildings with metal roofs, all of various sizes, spread out over about four acres. Several construction vehicles were scattered around the site as well.

Cong's bright white SUV pulled up next to the largest building and stopped. Adams pulled up next to him. "You'd think they'd have a forklift or two for unloading—" he began.

Vanel had also taken his recent conversation with Edvin to heart, and was looking around as they drove into the facility. "One access point, closed-in area, no maneuverability. This would be a good place for a trap, Edvin."

His team mate looked out the back of the M35. "Yes, it would—"

That was when the high-pressure sodium arc floodlights went on all around the perimeter, throwing the vehicles in the middle into sharp relief. At the same time, the sound of diesel engines growling to life reverberated throughout the compound. Seconds later, spotlights from the armored cars driving out of the buildings and coming up behind them lit everything up even more.

"Communications have increased exponentially across all channels, sir," Martya said. "At least a company's worth of men have been ordered to move out."

"There are also vehicles moving all around the Kildar and the others."

"They don't need that many people to unload those trucks—shit!" Vanner hit his mike. "Kildar, it's a trap!"

In seconds, the convoy and smaller vehicles were all surrounded by EE-9 Cascavel IV armored cars, their turret-mounted 90mm cannons and 12.7mm machine guns of the six-wheeled vehicles all pointing toward the group.

"Acknowledged, *Big Fish*. Cong should be handling this already. Will advise as soon as possible." Mike switched over to the team frequency. "All units, this is Kildar. Do not engage, repeat, do not engage. Stay where you are and await further orders." Next he contacted Cong even as a voice blared at them through loudspeakers.

"Unauthorized vehicles, you are on restricted military property! Turn off your engines and step out with your hands up!"

"General, what is going on out there? This is not the reception I expected," Mike said.

"Do not worry. I am sure it is just a bit of confusion on their end. I am going to talk to them right now. I will straighten this all out. Just stay where you are."

"I am so not liking this," Adams said, his hands still on the steering wheel. "This better not be one of those, 'what happens in Pyin U Lwin, stays in Pyin U Lwin' situations."

"Just sit tight. Right now we have to wait and see what side Cong is going to come down on, theirs or ours," Mike said.

"I got fifty bucks that says he'll come down on his own goddamn side," Adams replied.

"Not much we can do against those armored cars anyway. The only thing we got that could penetrate that armor is Lasko's .50 caliber, and one gun wouldn't do a hell of a lot against everything out there."

"That makes me feel *so* much better," Adams muttered.

Mike turned to Katya, who had spent the last two days with her hair tucked under her hat and making sure that absolutely no one ever saw her go to the bathroom. "No matter what happens, don't let Cong discover you're a woman. When I give you the high sign, however make sure these soldiers do."

Katya frowned at first, then nodded. "We will discuss fee for my additional services later."

"Glad to, assuming we all live through this," Mike replied.

"Here he comes," Adams said, drawing his pistol and holding it below the window.

Flanked by two bodyguards carrying compact Steyr MP 69 submachine guns, the diminutive general walked up to the Mike's window and pointed for it to go down.

He did so. "What's the good word, General?"

"The good word is that I am receiving the rest of my promised payment and will be leaving shortly." He pointed a pistol at Mike, resting it on the sill of the door as his two men also aimed their weapons at the people inside. "The confusion, I'm afraid, was on your part. You will not be getting paid the rest of your money, and you definitely will not be leaving here."

Sun Tzu's adage, "he who knows when he can fight and when he cannot will be victorious," ran through Mike's head as he ordered his men to file out of their vehicles and surrender their weapons and to the barely-bearded soldiers holding MA-1 rifles on them. They could have tried to fight their way out of the ambush; Mike had considered the option. However, against the firepower surrounding them, the fine, hard steel of the Keldara would have been smashed against the blunt, crude anvil of their captors.

Also, the fact that they hadn't simply opened fire once General Cong was out of the way meant that the Myanmar soldiers wanted them alive. And where there was life, there was possibility.

The possibility of vengeance.

Cong was as satisfied as the proverbial cat that had just caught thirty canaries. "It is very simple, Mr. Jenkins. How in the world do you expect a country as poor as Myanmar to afford these weapons? They pay me in gemstones...many, many gemstones. Although I know the U.S. embargo is lessening, many countries are still unwilling to traffic in their quite lovely gems. I, however, have no such restriction. With my connections, I can move them for a very nice profit...especially since I never bought the weapons I am selling in the first place. Along with the motherboards, this has been one of my most profitable endeavors. And I have you to thank for assisting me in bringing it off so perfectly."

The general had been walking around Mike while he was talking, and now stopped in front of him. "However, the mines here are always short of labor. When I found you and these Keldara of yours, I knew I had also found the perfect work force. It should make you happy to learn that you were not sold cheaply." He nodded at Oleg. "The big one alone garnered me fifty sapphires. Pity about the leg, though. Altogether, you and yours have made me a very rich man."

"Enjoy it while you can," Mike said evenly.

"Ah yes, here is where you Americans bluster or threaten or some such nonsense." Cong shook his head. "You are in the middle of nowhere, with no communication to the rest of your people, and surrounded by several thousand Myanmar soldiers. Soon you will be taken to another location, where you will work in the mines until you die. That is the reality of your situation."

Mike shook his head. "Since you do not seem to understand, I will say it again more slowly. Enjoy. It. While. You. Can. Because you will be seeing me again, Cong," was the Kildar's only reply.

Cong snapped out orders in Chinese. The men were herded to one side, while Soon Yi was brought to the general. He grabbed her chin and forced her head up, examining her critically. "She will do. She is coming with me." Cong gave her to his men, who forced her into his SUV. He, however, walked back to the line of Keldara, stopping in front of Oleg.

"Occasionally I like to take mementoes of my time in certain places. I do have the gems, and your woman already, but I desire something more personal. This man's artificial leg."

"What—fuck you! How is he supposed to work?!" Mike snapped.

"That is hardly my problem," Cong said. "I do not like his attitude. He needs to be humbled." He signaled to four of his men, who advanced on the blond giant.

"Wait!" Mike said. "If they come any closer, they are going to be killed, and then the others will shoot him. Let me talk to him first."

Cong looked from Mike to Oleg. "You have one minute."

"Then back the fuck up." Mike walked over to stand in front of his team leader. "There is no easy way to say this, Oleg. Cong wants your leg."

The big man frowned. "As a trophy of battle? He has not defeated me. He would have to kill me first to take it."

"I know, and I don't think he would hesitate to do exactly that. Is there any way to do this without you dying over it?"

"You could order me to do it, Kildar. I would not have a choice then."

"I'd rather not, as I know it is an insult to the honor of both you and your house."

"That it is. There is only one way to erase such an insult."

"I'm listening."

"When someone lays claim to a trophy they have not earned in righteous battle, yet the trophy is still given to them, the only way to remove the stain is to personally kill the one who took it and reclaim the item."

"You and I are definitely on the same page, Oleg."

"Time's up, Jenkins!" Cong called from his vehicle.

"Just a second, goddamn it!" Mike turned back to the big man. "To lessen the shame of this, as your Kildar, I am ordering you to surrender the leg. That way no one can say it was done of your own free will."

Oleg nodded curtly. "Thank you." He unfastened the titanium-and-plastic prosthetic and held it in his huge hands. "It is good that you did not order me to give *you* the leg. It would be a shame to have to defeat you to take it back."

"Wrestling you at the Spring Festival was enough for me. And after the training you've done, I don't even want to think about taking you on again." That actually brought a small smile to Oleg's face.

Mike reached up and clapped his Jayne Team leader's shoulder. "As Kildar, I swear that you will have the chance to avenge this insult."

"By the word of the Kildar, so shall it be." Oleg handed the leg to Mike, who took it and walked over to Cong.

"Take it and get the fuck out of here."

"Thank you, Mr. Jenkins. As I said in Bangkok, this has been a most profitable relationship." He got in his SUV, which took off in a cloud of dust.

Everyone was separated and thoroughly searched. Everything that could be taken, including identification papers, watches, boots, smartphones, and other personal items, was removed, and their hands zip-tied behind their backs.

During the search, Mike caught Katya's eye and nodded. When her turn came, she slapped the soldier groping her so hard he fell to the ground. As she cursed him in halting Chinese, Katya made sure to get so worked up that her cap fell off.

Three soldiers immediately covered her with their rifles. The commanding officer, a sergeant who looked only a few years older than the men under his command, ran over and shut Katya up by backhanding her across the face. That was before he saw the blond hair framing her face. Tearing open her shirt, he hiked up her T-shirt to reveal taped breasts. He grabbed her by the arm and dragged her over to Mike, his translator hurrying to keep up.

"Why do you have a woman disguised as a man in your group?"

"She is my personal assistant. Because Cong likes women. I did not wish her taken by him."

"Too bad. She is going with us now." He turned and said something in Burmese that made the rest of the solders laugh.

"What did he say?" Mike asked.

"Something about how Cong wasn't the only one who found a prize," Jace answered.

"That's right, just keep thinking that, buddy," Mike said with a grim smile.

"You do know they're planning on raping the shit out of her, then probably killing her if she's lucky, right?" Jace asked when he saw a similar smile appear on Adams' face as well.

"Yeah, but they don't know that they just found the one woman in the world they do *not* want to do anything like that to," Mike said, watching as she was hauled off to one of the armored cars. "Oh, please, just try and touch her in one of those. If they do, we'll be out of here in a half-hour."

Unfortunately, that Cascavel started up and headed into town, while Mike and the others were loaded back onto the back of their Chinese-manufactured Aeolus 4x2 six-ton utility trucks, along with a half dozen armed guards as escorts, which also started up and headed in the opposite direction.

"Keep that translation feed coming—isolate any information on where they're being taken. I want five-minute updates on the tracking bugs in the trucks. Irina, where's my personnel report on who we've got left?"

From the moment the trap had been sprung, Vanner had been pulling together a back-up plan, but it was looking very weak at the moment. With the majority of the Keldara having just been captured, and with no local air support or any quick way to get a rescue team mobilized for at least forty-eight to seventy-two hours, Vanner was stuck on the boat with nothing to do but watch.

Well, that wasn't quite true. One of the first things he had done was contact Neilson, who was scrambling a team out of Georgia. That, however, was going to take some time. "And you know Mike's not going to take this lying down." Neilson had said when Vanner had told him what had gone down.

"You know that and I know that, but I'll be damned if I'm going to sit on my thumbs and wait for him to bust out of there," Vanner had replied.

"I hear you," Nielson said. "The reinforcements should be wheels up in ten hours, and we'll do everything we can to get them over there sooner. I'll notify you when we're en route."

"You're coming, too?"

"With our command officers behind enemy lines in the field, that leaves you and me. As you'll be heading up the rescue op, I'll remain at command HQ to coordinate from there."

"Works," Vanner had replied.

The one good thing that had come out of this—if indeed it could be called that—was that the stupid son-of-a-bitch Chinese general had been both arrogant and dumb enough to take Oleg's *leg* from him. When they had seen that through Katya's eyes, the girls had all stopped what they were doing and stared, with Grezyna slowly placing both hands over her mouth.

"I'm assuming that's a bad thing, right?" Vanner had asked.

"There is almost no worse insult than to take a personal item from a Keldara and leave him alive," Greznya said.

"The only thing worse than that would be to defeat one of our warriors in battle and not kill him," Martya said.

"That man has just guaranteed his own death," Greznya said.

"I guess that will save the Chinese military the expense of a trial." Vanner sighed. "Speaking of higher ups, I'd better contact Pierson. He will definitely want to hear about this." He conferenced in Neilson again before picking up the secure satphone. "Hello, Bob, go scramble..."

"How can we help? What does Mike or any of the Keldara need?" were the first words out of the President's mouth an hour later.

"While we thank you for your generous offer, Mr. President, there is every indication that Mike will most likely have the situation under control shortly," Nielson replied. "Also, he had mentioned to us that it could be politically dangerous to put U.S. assets in the area. Therefore, we are currently getting our own locate and extraction mission up and running. That said, if there is any way to commandeer a C-130 Hercules anywhere near Tbilisi and get it to that airport, that would be a godsend."

"We can scramble one from Incirlik Air Base in Turkey. Where do your men need to be dropped off?"

Vanner had just brought up the map of the country with major airports listed. "Holy shit—sorry, sir. If you can get them to Mandalay International Airport, they'd be less than a hundred fifty klicks away from Mike's last known location."

"Consider it done." The President pointed at an aide. "Get me the Air Force Chief of Staff on the phone *now*."

Any effort at talking among the prisoners was met with a stern reprimand, and, when Jace persisted in trying to whisper one more thing, he had taken a rifle butt to the chest. They all remained quiet for the remainder of the trip, the trucks stopping only once to refuel. After three days of mostly air-conditioning, it was swelteringly hot in the back of the trucks, although the Keldara bore the discomfort with their usual stoic expressions.

After what Jace estimated was about three hours of travel over rough, dirt roads, the trucks stopped at a large, abandoned city. Getting out, he saw buildings that could have easily housed hundreds of thousands of people filling both sides of a large valley. Scattered lights shone on the far side, and a cluster of lights in the windows of buildings they were in front of showed where the inhabitants were clustered.

A row of armed guards stood ready to greet them as they filed out of the back of the trucks. A watchtower rose thirty feet into the air, and was manned by a pair of guards behind a light machine gun. If there was any surprise or puzzlement about their new prisoners, it didn't show on their captors' faces.

Jace found himself next to Mike, who was also looking around, sizing up their opposition. "Probably split us up to isolate the groups," the Kildar said. "Have to assess our situation and make contact with others, then find access to a radio."

Jace nodded. "Should I offer to translate or hang back?"

"Help the rest as much as possible. Adams and I will have to tell the others in Keldaran anyway."

As the guards herded the Keldara into two lines, a thin Burmese man with a lean face and a shock of gray hair strode forward to stand in front of the line. He was dressed in a gray uniform with his hand resting on the butt of the holstered pistol on his hip. "Does anyone here speak Burmese?"

Jace stepped forward. "I do."

"Good, translate what I am saying to the rest."

"Ah, sir?"

"What is it?"

"The majority of these people come from Georgia—the nation, not the American state. I can translate into English, but these two"—Jace pointed at Mike and Adams—"will have to translate your speech into their native tongue, as I do not speak it."

The man stared hard at the Kildar and his second-in-command for a few seconds. "Proceed."

Jace waved both men forward. "He told me to have you guys translate into Keldaran as I translate his words into English."

"Oh, hell," Adams replied. "My Keldaran is not the best, by the way."

"You certainly swear like one. Just do your best. You know what to tell them anyway," Mike said.

"You may begin when ready," Jace said to the camp commander.

"My name is Warden Sein. That is the only title you will address me by. You are in the mining city of Mogok. All of you will be working in the gem mines here for the foreseeable future. Work hard, and you will do well. Do not work hard, and you will be punished with time in the box." He pointed at a small metal box, about three feet by three feet by four feet high. With a frown, the warden waved one of his subordinates to him. With a whisper, the other man ran to the box and opened it.

A sweat-soaked, barely-conscious man tumbled out, his leg muscles twitching uncontrollably from being forced to squat for hours. His cheek was red and blistered, burned, Jace thought, by coming in contact with the hot metal. Two guards dragged the limp, unresisting man toward one of the barracks.

The warden continued. "We supply you with clothes, meals, and a place to sleep. Destruction of any of these items will result in time in the box. Fighting with the other men will result in time in the box. Smuggling of items into the labor camp from outside will result in time in the box. Does everyone understand these rules?"

Mike and Adams repeated the statements from the warden, adding that the Keldara should stick together whenever possible, protect themselves if attacked, and wait for word from the Kildar, who would be contacting each group shortly.

As he spoke, the warden was walking up and down the line,

inspecting the new men. When he reached Oleg, he looked down at the man's single foot. "Why have I been brought a man with only one leg?"

"Jace, tell him his prosthetic was only recently taken from him, but as you can see, he's very strong. He will work hard," Mike replied.

Sein drew his pistol. "How, if he cannot walk?" He took a step back and started to raise the gun. "All he will be is a drain on our already limited resources."

"STOP!"

The vehemence in Mike's command actually made Sein look over at him, while the guards all around the group raised their rifles. Catching Oleg's unasked but obvious question of whether or not to go for the warden, Mike shook his head once while talking. "Just give me until the start of the next work day. I will present a solution then that will satisfy everybody."

Sein's gaze flicked to the massive Keldara, who hadn't reacted in the slightest to what was happening around him. He looked at the heavy-set man's brawny, corded muscles, then lowered his pistol. "Very well. You have until muster later this morning."

The warden turned on his heel to face the entire group. "You will now be assigned to your various bunkhouses. You had best get whatever rest you can, because there is a full day's work ahead, in just a few hours." This last was said with a vicious smile at Mike. "Guards!" With that, the warden strolled off toward a larger house higher on the hill.

The head guard, a large man with his MA-1 slung over a shoulder, addressed Jace. "You speak Burmese?" At his nod, the man continued. "All right, divide this group into four groups of seven men apiece. You have thirty seconds."

Jace relayed the orders to Mike, who called out to the assembled men. "Teams, casually fall into your squad assignments."

In less than ten seconds the men were grouped in four clusters. Mike, Jace, and Adams were about to join two other groups when the guards stopped them. One pointed to another large hut that looked like it was somewhat better maintained. "No. You three stay there for the time being. The trustees will educate you on how things run here. It will be your job to teach these other men and make sure they do their job. If they do well, you do well. If they do not, you will be punished, as well as them."

Nodding, Jace explained the situation to the other two, ending with, "This ought to be interesting."

Mike and Adams gave the men their last-minute marching orders, and the four groups of Keldara headed off to several gray, dilapidated barracks farther down in the camp.

The guards escorted the three men to the trustees' hut, unlocked it, and led them in, turning on the lights as they did. Bleary-eyed, sullen-faced men roused from sleep to stare daggers at the newcomers. Other than being sleep-deprived, they looked fairly healthy, which surprised Jace.

"New arrivals. Show them how things work," the head guard said. Then he walked out, leaving Mike, Jace, and Adams facing a dozen unhappy Burmese and Thais.

One of them, a muscular man dressed in pajama bottoms, held a wooden club in his hand and thwacked the end into his palm as he spoke. "Who speaks Burmese or Thai?"

Jace raised a hand.

"All right, here's how it goes—"

Mike held up a hand. "Tell him to shut the fuck up."

Jace interrupted the trustee leader, making the leader's eyes widen. "What did he say?"

Mike was already talking as he walked over to stand in front of the leader. "Tell him my name, and that we are in charge as of right now. Tell all of them that they will be taking orders from any of us at any time."

Jace translated all of this. His announcement made all the men laugh, with the leader laughing hardest of all. "And who the fuck are you to come in here and tell us you are the leader now?"

Jace translated that for Mike, who casually shifted his weight. "Say, 'I'm the Kildar,' and be ready to move."

Jace translated Mike's words, saying "Kildar" in English, since there was no Burmese equivalent. While he spoke, he took in the measurements of the room, the height of the ceiling, and the position of the nearest three men to him.

The moment the leader frowned and cocked his head at the unfamiliar word, Mike lashed out with his foot, sinking it deep into the man's crotch. As he jackknifed forward, his face slammed into Mike's knee as Mike simultaneously relieved the dropping man of his club.

"About fuckin' time!" Adams said as he whipped a front kick into the chest of the man closest to him. The powerhouse blow drove the man back into two other, tangling them up for a few seconds while the master chief took on the next guy nearest to him.

Jace had also moved in the same instant as Mike, using the exact same combination to drop a tall Thai to his knees, rendering him unable to do anything but bleed and vomit. His next two targets were marginally more on the ball. They charged him, one going high, one going low. Jace sidestepped the low one and caught the man's foot with his own. Shoving him forward, he sent him sprawling to the ground. Blocking the high attacker's punch, he jabbed the heel of his palm into the other man's nose. The shot made the man's eyes water and sent a sharp stab of pain through his head.

As the man clapped his hands to his face, Jace followed up with a kick to the knee, dropping the man to the floor. As he whirled to meet the next one, he had the oddest thought.

I wonder what Katya's going through right now...

CHAPTER NINETEEN

Two hundred kilometers away, Katya was escorted out of the armored car and into a barracks. All the while, she looked around as much as she could, trying to give Vanner and the girls as much intel as possible.

She couldn't understand a word the soldiers were saying, but their stares and the tone of their comments and laughter to each other told her volumes. *They plan to rape me, probably as a group, and when they are finished, they will probably kill me.*

A few years ago, this situation would have scared her, although she would have hidden it behind a cold, bitter veneer. Now, she was able to recognize the fear and divorce herself from it. Above all, she refused to let it hamper her current mission, which was not only to get out of this alive, but to commandeer weapons and a vehicle, then try to find Mike and the others.

"Katya, we're here. Is there anything you need to tell us?" Vanner asked.

Katya barely resisted rolling her eyes. *"If you want to find out what it's like to be gang-raped, just keep watching,"* almost came out of her mouth, but she restrained herself.

"Just let me work. Will call when free." The subvocalization was still hard, but getting better. Katya had been practicing with some of the girls back home, and she could now make herself understood most of the time. She hoped this was one of those times.

"Understood. Vanner out."

Katya almost breathed a sigh of relief at not having the intrusive voice in her head. Instead, Jay's training came back to her, almost as if she could hear the spymaster's calm voice in her mind:

"When it comes to sex, most men are not that far removed from animals. In a group, there is a leader, just like in every unit or pack in nature. Whether you're dancing at a bachelor party in Las Vegas, or stripping for the Joint Chiefs of Staff, there is always a leader among men. Identify him. Make him yours. He will keep the others in line. Only then, when you are commanding him while still letting him think that he is calling the shots, that is the time to do what you must, whether it is seduce him, fuck him—and there is a difference between the two—or kill him."

Fortunately, she had already picked the leader out. The sergeant who had "discovered" her exercised discipline over his men without any trouble. When one of the enlisted men had tried to lift her shirt again, The NCO had slapped him across the face and dressed him down in front of the others. Apparently the fun wasn't to begin until they were back at quarters.

At the doors, two of the men opened them for the sergeant and the new woman. When he brought her inside, the rest of the men, all Burmese, and all getting ready for bed, came alive immediately, talking loudly and jostling for a chance to get close to her.

Spotting a six-pack of what she assumed was beer on the table, Katya shrugged her shoulder free of the sergeant's hand. Grabbing a bottle, she climbed onto the improvised platform. One of the men started climbing after her, but was halted by his superior.

Running the cold bottle across her sweating forehead, Katya dragged it down the valley of her breasts. *That reminds me...* She reached under her shirt and unwound the gauze and tape holding her breasts down. *Thank God that's over with!*

The moment she finished removing the tape, her breasts began expanding, as if performing a stripper's magic trick. The men were all over this, shouting and reaching for her. Katya evaded their hands, even slapping a few away from her. Striding to the other end of the table, she tossed the gauze to the sergeant, which brought an entirely new round of catcalls and shouts. *Enjoy it, pig—it's filled with two days of sweat.* He didn't seem to mind, picking it up off his shoulder and smelling what had to be a fairly noxious odor of sweat, body odor, and maybe a little musk if he was lucky.

The men were going crazy. *Time for stage two.* Selecting what she thought was a private from the crowd, Katya subtly shook the bottle, then bent over and held it out to him, indicating that he should open it. Goaded by the comments and smirks of the other men, he produced a bottle opener and popped the cap off. Immediately golden-white foam started flowing down the sides. Katya put on her best "oops" expression and began licking the foam off, ending up with her mouth completely over the top and neck of it and sucking down the weak liquid. *What disgusting swill.*

The crowd went absolutely fucking crazy. Even the sergeant had trouble getting the men back into some semblance of order. Partly because they were getting too riled up, and partly because he was too distracted by Katya's show.

"Katya, what the hell are you doing? They all look like they're about to riot!" Vanner said.

No shit, that is exactly what I am going for, she thought, but didn't say. *Time for stage three.* Katya began slowly removing her button-down olive drab shirt. She eased it off her shoulder, then back on, then back off. After teasing them like this for a minute, she slipped out of one sleeve and dangled it in front of the men, whipping it out of their reach whenever anyone grabbed for it. Her coy act was riling the men up even more; she now had all of them in the palm of her hand. *They must be really repressed here—I haven't even shown any skin yet.*

Katya slipped the shirt completely off. Sashaying across the table to the sergeant, she draped it around his shoulders like a scarf while still holding on to the ends of both sleeves. She slowly drew him in for a kiss, but released the shirt ends at the last second and turned away. She strutted back to the middle of the table, leaving the man dumbstruck. The rest of his men pounded the table while shouting and catcalling even more.

Now dressed in a stained, wrinkled white T-shirt and fatigue pants, Katya thrust her hip out and threw her shoulders back. The pose drew every eye in the room to her splendid breasts straining against the flimsy cotton. All of this made the men even crazier. Spotting a chair at the end of the table, Katya motioned for it to be brought up onto the table. She watched with concealed glee as a fistfight nearly broke out over who would have the honor of performing the simple task. After a few clumsy punches and another chewing out from the sergeant, the chair was set on the table.

Katya turned it so she could sit in profile to the men. As part of her research, Jay had given her specific films to watch, regardless of when they had been made. He had assigned her to study the women and their interactions with others, particularly men. *"While understanding the psychology of how and why a woman strips is important, it is also important to understand the fantasy that the media, particularly in America, has always portrayed about women. To sell your role as the party girl/stripper, you're giving your audience something that is twenty-five percent reality and seventy-five percent fantasy. You, however, have to portray it one hundred percent, all the time, every time."*

Katya had struggled with most of them. The one about the girl who had hitchhiked to Las Vegas to become a showgirl had been particularly awful. However, there was one film from the 1980s about a woman who was a welder by day and a dancer at night, It had intrigued her, despite being as unbelievable as anything else she had seen. The bottle in her hand wasn't a cascade of water, but given how she had already got this group's blood boiling, it would probably do.

Arching her spine over the back of the chair so that her proud breasts stood out in relief, Katya raised the beer over her chest and tipped the bottle down. A golden river poured out over her chest and legs, making the T-shirt transparent and revealing her magnificent tits for everyone in the room to see.

Katya thought she might go deaf from the whooping and hollering that erupted around her. After that, they were putty in her hands. Well, except for certain parts of them.

Finally the sergeant couldn't take it any more. He pushed his way to the table, grabbed Katya's hand, and pulled her off the table so roughly that she almost twisted her ankle on the way down. She just managed to get her feet under her, or she would have landed on her ass, and that might have been the end of it. However, he pulled her toward a door near the entrance that led to a smaller room in the building. Katya hoped it was the one she had noticed with a window in it.

The man pushed her into a small kitchen, complete with dirty tables, greasy counters, dusty cabinets, and a secondary exit on the side wall. The room smelled of burned rice and spoiled fruit. It was even better than she had expected.

The only problem was the three other men, all with one or two similar downward pointing black stripes with red edging around them on their shirt sleeves. *Fantastic—the senior men get to fuck me before throwing me to the others.* But she could work with this just fine.

Besides the exit, there were two more pieces of good news to this scene. The first was that one of the men had brought a rifle with him, and had set it down in the corner in preparation for the show. The second was that the other men were continuing the loud party she had gotten started outside, so anything short of full torture would be masked by the noise in the other room.

The sergeant pushed Katya toward the nearest counter, banging her hip painfully. She whirled around to see him drop his pants. Masking her pain and anger with a come-hither pout, she took stock of the position of her targets. The other three men were ranged around the room, too far apart for her to take them all out without one sounding the alarm first. She needed a way to bring all of them close to her. And when the sergeant dropped his drawers, revealing his thick, erect dick, everything fell into place.

Crossing her arms at her waist, Katya slowly drew her beer-soaked T-shirt off over her head. When she could see again, every man's eyes were on her. She would have to be very careful when poisoning the sergeant, as she needed him to live for about a minute afterward.

She ran a finger around her lips, then put her hand on his stiff cock. He nodded, grabbing the back of her head and shoving her toward his crotch. Katya took him into her mouth and began vigorously fellating him. While doing that, she also kept one hand stroking his shaft while she manipulated the valve at the base of her finger on her other hand to ready the poison. When that hand was ready, she began massaging his firm balls, slowly increasing the tempo of all three movements in a pattern guaranteed to make a man come in minutes.

Curious about the toxin she could inflict on others, Katya had done enough research to get a pretty good idea of what it was. The doctor who had installed the system had said it was modified cobra venom. Katya had learned that different venoms of various cobras had one or more deadly effects. Some were neurotoxic, attacking and incapacitating the nervous system to cause paralysis in the victim. Some also had a cytotoxic element as well, causing swelling and necrosis in cells near the bite area. And lastly, some venoms also had a cardiotoxic effect, weakening the heart muscle and causing it to be unable to pump blood efficiently, causing general weakness throughout the body.

Katya didn't know exactly what kind of poison cocktail they'd given her, but she did know it was seriously neurotoxic, which was exactly what she needed. Increasing her pace on the sergeant's cock, she felt him about to climax, which was the last thing she needed to go to work.

He threw his head back as he spasmed into her mouth. Lost in the climax, he didn't feel her stab a fingernail into the base of his testicle and inject the toxin. As his semen squirted into her mouth, Katya was careful not to swallow any of it. After all, she needed all the weapons she could get. She kept the injector right where it was, pumping the man full of poison while sucking him dry.

When the first full-body spasm hit, Katya pulled away, making sure to look puzzled. The man jerked again, lurching against the counter while stammering to his subordinates for help. Katya backed away while activating the other chemical reservoir inside her body, the one that heightened her strength, speed, and reflexes.

The three men all came forward at the same time.

Perfect.

As they moved to their stricken leader, Katya looked the nearest one right in the face and spit the mouthful of semen into his eyes. Caught by surprise, he staggered back, wiping at his eyes and saying something she assumed was a curse.

The drug kicked into full speed, and Katya saw everyone around her slow down while her own vision, movement, and reactions remained swift and crystal-clear. She had carefully trained herself to ride the heightened rush the drug gave her and channel it into devastating attacks against one man or a group. The training had been remarkably effective. Even Mike, the only one who would take her on while in this state, had suffered bruises and muscle sprains through his padded suit. This was the first time she would be trying those methods in the field, however.

With one man temporarily distracted, she was already moving to the other two. Both were still trying to help the sergeant, who had started convulsing as he slid to the floor. One turned his head toward the door and opened his mouth to call for help. Katya drew her foot back and kicked him in the   apple, crushing his larynx and trachea. The blow was so powerful it knocked him off his feet and onto his ass. Both hands clutched at his swelling neck as his face began turning red. His mouth opened and closed silently, like a fish trying to breathe out of water.

The last soldier was just turning to her, one hand dropping to the pistol on his hip while he also opened his mouth to yell for help. Katya fired the heel of her palm into his jaw, slamming the lower mandible into the upper maxilla hard enough to fracture both and splinter a few teeth. The man grunted through a spray of blood as Katya pistoned the same palm heel into his solar plexus, paralyzing the large bundle of nerves there and sending him crashing to the floor.

Hearing a footstep behind her, she whirled to find the first man charging her. To Katya, it looked like he was running against a strong wind. Grabbing his closest outstretched hand, she pivoted and used his momentum to flip him over her hip to the ground with a breath-stealing *thud*. Katya followed up with a ram's-head punch to the temple. She hit him so hard that his head bounced off the tile floor. The blow crushed the temporal bone, creating a hemorrhage in the temporal lobe directly underneath. Immediately knocked unconscious, the man would never wake up again as he slowly bled to death inside his skull.

Checking the man with the broken teeth, she found he had managed to draw his pistol and pull the slide back. Before he could aim it at her, she was on top of him, grabbing the gun and wrenching it free hard enough to break three fingers. He clutched his injured hand and opened his bloody mouth to scream. Katya prevented that by clubbing his jaw with the butt, breaking it again and knocking him out.

She looked around to see all four men incapacitated or dead. Just then the drug wore off, and Katya steeled herself against the muscle spasms that sometimes followed the strenuous activity. They subsided in a few seconds, and she quickly began stripping clothing and equipment off the four bodies.

When she was finished, she had the rifle and two extra magazines; four pistols and four extra magazines; four combat knives; and four grenades, two smoke and two tear gas. Most important, she had found a set of keys in the sergeant's pocket.

Weapons first. Katya dressed herself in the cleanest shirt she could find. Then she tucked a loaded pistol into her waistband, hiding it under her shirttail, but still available for a fast draw. Wrapping up the other three pistols and extra magazines in another shirt, she tied it into a pouch. When she was done with that, she slung the rifle over one shoulder and the gun-filled bag over her other one. Taking two canteens, she rinsed her mouth before filling them with water at the sink. In the small refrigerator she found moldy chicken curry and curdled goat's milk, which she skipped. There was a container of cold, plain rice and an unopened mango drink of some kind. She grabbed both; every extra calorie would help in what she had to do.

Someone pounded on the door from outside, making Katya almost drop the canteen as she drew the pistol and aimed it at the door. The soldier outside shouted something that sounded like a question. *What the fuck is he asking? Wait—that has to be it!*

Katya moaned loudly as if getting fucked. A loud cheer went up from the other side of the wall. She kept going, varying her cries of simulated pleasure as she pulled the pins on a tear gas and smoke grenade. Tipping a chair over, she wedged the top of it against the grenades, placing them with the spoons held against the door.

Still groaning, she changed the tone so it sounded like she had her mouth full before slipping out the side door, making sure to lock it behind her. The Cascavel armored cars were parked right outside. Katya shook her head. *The Kildar would never allow such sloppiness . . .*

Inside, the party was going on in full force. She could hear the men singing drunkenly even from here. Checking the cars until she found the one her keys fit, Katya dumped the stolen gear into it and drew one of the knives. Going to each vehicle, she punctured three tires on each one. It was hard work, and her fingers and wrists were sore by the time she was finished, but all of the nearest vehicles were disabled when she was done.

Climbing back into the Cascavel, she locked the outer hatch and took a moment to familiarize herself with the controls. Everything seemed fairly basic; steering wheel, gas and brake pedals.

It was an automatic transmission, which made Katya breathe a sigh of relief, as she wasn't that great with manual. Its gas tank was also almost full. Finally, she located the headlight switch and flipped it on.

Taking a deep breath, she turned the key, making the 190-horsepower Mercedes Benz diesel engine rumble to life. Shifting into gear, she depressed the gas pedal, taking off as men began spilling out of the barracks to see one of their armored cars being stolen.

Over the rumble of the engine, Katya could barely hear the shouts and screams as the men found the surprise she had left for them in the kitchen. She found what looked like a main road leading out of town and took it, making the armored car leap forward to put as much distance between her and the barracks as possible.

Once sure she was safely away, she called the *Big Fish*. "Vanner, this is Katya. Tell me how to find Mike and the others."

"So, you don't know shit about what's going on either?" Copilot Major Jonathan Wolfe said as he completed the preflight checklist for the C-130J-30 Super Hercules cargo plane.

"I know exactly the same things you do. Get our asses in the air and get to Tbilisi airport with all due haste." Aircraft Commander Major Alan Timmons ran through his checklist as well, then lowered his voice. "But the scuttlebutt on the tarmac says the orders came straight from the top."

"The Joint Chief?" Wolfe asked incredulously.

Timmons shook his head and pointed upward.

"The POTUS himself?!"

Timmons shrugged as he strapped himself in. "Take that for what's it worth, but everyone who mentioned it so far said that's who gave the order."

Wolfe didn't mind in the least. He had been finishing up his rotation at Ramstein Air Force Base in Germany. They had just completed a supply run to Incirlik the day before, and were about to head back home when the orders had come in diverting their aircraft northeast to Tbilisi instead. It would be about a two-hour hop, and that was only the start of the mystery.

"What are we supposed to do once we get there?" Wolfe asked.

"Orders said we will be contacted by a party on the ground, and that we are to give any and all aid and assistance possible. That's what the Old Man told me, and that's exactly what I plan on doing, regardless of any secret squirrel stuff going around." He hit his mike. "Sergeant, prepare for takeoff."

"Yes, sir," Tech Sergeant Sandra Wilcox replied from the cargo hold.

Wolfe nodded and concentrated on his duties as Timmons contacted the tower and got clearance. As far as he was concerned, anything coming down from the President had to look good when the promotion boards came up, right?

Mike, Jace, and Adams stood in the middle of the trustees' quarters, which now looked like a hurricane had gone through it. Several of the rough bunk beds had been smashed to pieces, and the dozen prisoners lay scattered among the wreckage.

Injuries were light among the three operators. Adams had dislocated three knuckles, which he had popped back into place. Jace had received a split lip from a lucky punch, and Mike had suffered a graze from a swinging board off one of the beds that had come a hair's width away from beaning him.

"Any more questions?" Mike asked.

"Yes." The leader pushed himself up into a sitting position on the floor. Gingerly probing his swelling jaw with scraped fingers, he spat out a tooth. "What the fuck are you going to do with us now?"

After getting the translation from Jace, Mike replied. "Well, as attractive as digging gems for the fucking military for the rest of my life sounds, my friends and I are going to break out of here tomorrow morning. All of you can either stay here, or you can join us."

Those trustees who were still conscious broke out in ragged laughter. "Man, you must be crazy, and not just by taking all of us on," the leader said. "Don't you think others have tried to escape? Where do you think you are going to go? There's a hundred kilometers of jungle between us and any place larger than a village. We can't count on the surrounding villages to help, not since the warden put out a five-hundred-thousand-kyat reward for any information about escaped prisoners. We can't even smuggle out gems to try to pay our way to freedom, since the guards strip search us every day—every goddamn inch."

Another prisoner spoke. "The last two times someone tried to escape, the guards hunted them down like dogs, running them through the jungle until they dropped from exhaustion. They shot them and brought the bodies back for us to bury. No one's been stupid enough to try since then."

"Then it's a good thing I have an ace in the hole. How many people are held prisoner here?" Mike asked.

"At least three hundred," the leader said.

"And how many guards?"

"About fifty," came the reply.

"Don't you see?" Mike asked. "Our enemy has already given us enough energy for victory." He pointed at each one of them. "All of you and the rest of the prisoners are a force powerful enough to overcome twice as many guards."

"Oh yeah? And what about their guns?" Another one asked.

"Before morning, I will eliminate that advantage," Mike said. "However, there will be plenty to do in the meantime. Look, either you all accept what you think is your fate here, and work until you die, or you take a shot at being free men again. Me, I would rather die than live under another man's boot. None of you really look like the kind to do that either. Now, what's it going to be?"

"Do you swear you can take care of the guards?" a prisoner asked.

"I guarantee it," Mike replied.

"We need to talk about this," the leader said. "Give us a few minutes."

"You've got five. Master Chief, Jace, with me."

Jace followed Mike over to a relatively unspoiled corner of the room to huddle with Adams.

"Okay, now I know you can pull off some crazy shit, 'cause I've watched you do it, but how in the hell do you expect to do this?" Adams asked.

"Because Katya's coming to find us," Mike answered.

"And just how do you know that?" Adams pressed.

Mike shrugged. "The practical answer would be that she hasn't gotten paid yet." He tapped his chest. "This part that knows she's coming would say, even though she would never admit it, that we're her—"

"You're not going to say family, are you?" Adams asked.

"I doubt if she would go as far as that, but yes, that's the general idea. We, or I, if you prefer, have given her a home, a place to belong. That is something she has never had, not even as a child. Call me sentimental, call me soft if you want, but deep down, I know that counts for something with her. Trust me, she's coming."

"And if she's not?" Jace asked.

"Then we go to Plan B," Mike replied.

"Which is?" Adams asked.

"General prisoner revolt. Ideally, through, we'll be able to combine both of them. Right now we've got to establish communications with the other groups, and to do that, we need a way out of here. Let's rejoin the others, see what they say, and figure out how we're busting out of this building."

"You know that if some of them don't go along with this, they'll have to be put down so they don't rat us out to the guards," Jace said.

"I think they'll all go along with it. I know I wouldn't want to stay here a day longer than I had to." Mike looked over Adams' shoulder. "Looks like they've come to an agreement. Come on."

He walked back to the center of the room, where the deposed trustee leader was waiting for him. "You talk a really big game."

"I'll deliver on it, too," Mike said.

"If we throw in with you, everyone here goes free, not just some of us."

"I can get you all out of the camp. Getting anywhere else is your problem. But at least you'll have a fighting chance."

The man stared at him for a few seconds, then thrust out his hand. "We're in, all of us."

Mike shook it. "All right, we've got a lot to do, and not a hell of a lot of time to do it. First assignment is to find us a way out of this building that isn't visible from the yard out front."

That proved easier than expected—the boards on the back wall had already been modified to provide a secret way out. When Mike frowned at the leader, who identified himself as Maung, the man said, "I said people tried to escape, I didn't say that the guards found every bit of work that had been done on each plan."

The trustees' building, along with the rest of the prisoner barracks, had been built along a high cliff of rock. Mike, Adams, and Jace used this cover to sneak from building to building, where Keldara were already waiting to talk. Mike filled them in on the plan, which all hinged on one thing; that Katya really was coming to find them.

"*Nabozvaro! Bozis shvilo!*" Katya cursed as she retraced her route for the second time. "Son of a bitch! Son of a whore!"

When she had set out to catch Mike and the others, Katya had figured she was only about forty-five minutes behind them, an hour tops. But that was before she had had to navigate the Myanmar jungle in the dark with no readable maps and only voice directions from the *Big Fish* command room to guide her. Exhausted and pissed off, she was worried about getting lost, of running out of gas, of running into more soldiers, and of failing most of all.

"You are almost there. Just a few more kilometers," Greznya said in her head.

"Easy for you to say. You are sitting on boat while I am driving circles in goddamn jungle!" Katya took a deep breath. "I am sorry, Greznya. I do not mean to be so harsh. I could not be doing this without your help."

"That is all right. I am not sure I could do what you are doing right now."

Katya snorted. "I bet you would do a better job of not getting lost!"

That made the Keldara girl chuckle. Katya grinned at hearing the other woman laugh, then chuckled, then finally laughed at the absurdity of it all. "Damn it, girl, do not make me drive off the road!"

"Is not *my* fault, you made me laugh first." Greznya took a deep breath. "Okay, are you back on Route 312?"

"Yes, finally! Main road, my ass! Is barely better than the dirt roads you all had before the Kildar."

"You are doing fine. If you are where I think you are, you have only about twenty kilometers to go," Grezyna said.

"If there is a prison camp there, I certainly do not want to just barrel in, even in this thing," Katya said.

"True. Are you planning to try to sneak all of the weapons inside?" Greznya asked.

"Depends on what I find when I get there. I am sure that the Kildar and the others will need everything they can get to break out. I am driving a vehicle with a big gun, but it is not as if I know how to use it."

"True, but the guards at the camp do not know this," Greznya replied. "That may work to our advantage later. Best to concentrate on the here and now. The rest is something to figure out once you find where the Kildar and the men are."

"Right." Katya drove in silence for several more kilometers, then slowed when she saw a road sign covered with gibberish. "Please translate this and tell me how far I have to go."

Greznya had the answer in seconds. "That is the sign for Mogak ahead. It says the town is about seven kilometers away."

"Good. Another five, and I will stop and walk in the rest of the way."

Eight minutes later, she reached what she estimated was the

proper distance away from the city. It took another ten minutes to find a side road and drive down far enough to hide the Cascavel. She turned it off, removed the keys, grabbed one of the pistols, and headed back to the main road.

"If you are not sure how far away it is, count your steps as you head in. That way you will have an estimate of the distance, give or take one hundred paces," Greznya said.

About to retort with a snide comment, Katya stopped herself and thought about the other girl's words. "That is a very good idea," she replied, starting the count at fifty to include how far she had already gone.

One thousand, eight hundred and sixteen steps later, she came upon the valley of Mogok, and the city inside it.

"This actually looks easier than I thought it would be. There is no fence or guards or anything," she said after observing the grounds for fifteen minutes through a pair of binoculars she had found inside the car. "No one is patrolling even. It almost looks deserted except for a few lights here and there. There is a guard tower, but I'm pretty sure the men inside are asleep. Infiltration will not be a problem."

"Great, but there is still one problem. We do not know where the Kildar or the other men are," Greznya said.

"I do not think they will be hard to find. The Kildar is probably still awake, planning his escape. All I will have to do is look for the building that still has people moving around or talking inside, and that will be the one."

It took her ten minutes to get to the mining camp compound, and another five to scout out the drab gray building that had people talking inside. Katya snuck around to the rear, where she found a large hole covered with a mattress.

Pistol in hand, she gently knocked on the wood. "Kildar?"

Silence fell over the interior of the building, then the mattress was whisked away to reveal Mike standing on the other side with a big smile on his face.

"What kept you?"

CHAPTER TWENTY

Not only was Mike very happy to see Katya, he was overjoyed when he found out what she had brought with her.

"You stole one of their fucking *armored cars?!*"

"It was the nearest vehicle, and no one has taught me how to hotwire yet, so, yes."

"*That's* my girl! What other presents did you bring?"

Katya handed her pistol to him. "Three more and a rifle, one extra magazine apiece. I left them in the car, in case I was caught coming in, but that doesn't seem to be a problem here."

"Smart thinking anyway." Mike turned to the trustees to find them all gaping at what was going on. First this Kildar and his two men beat the shit out of all of them not three hours ago. Then, out of nowhere, a blond, teenage girl snuck into camp and not only handed him a loaded pistol, but brought him an entire armored vehicle.

"What are you, a magician?" one of them asked.

"Nope, I just work with really great people," Mike replied. "As I said, I have nullified the guards' guns, and with this vehicle, I will now eliminate the guards themselves. The plan has changed, gentlemen. Here's how it will go down..."

Major Timmons came in on his final approach to the runway at Tbilisi International Airport. The Super Hercules landed gently, the cargo plane settling onto the tarmac like greeting an old friend. As they headed toward the terminal, they received instructions to head to the cargo loading and unloading section, specifically the warehouses owned by Georgian Air Gate, one of three cargo companies that operated out of the airport.

When they pulled up, Timmons saw a man in neat digicam fatigues and sunglasses, with high-and-tight black hair, standing in front of the open hangar. His MOLLE gear was simple; a basic harness with a pistol on his right hip and a radio and two extra magazines on his left. Inside the hangar were three black Ford Explorers and a cargo truck. Next to the vehicles were at least twenty very large men, also dressed the same way. Among them were two gorgeous women, both dressed casually with their hair pulled back.

"Remember, if you or any member of your team is caught or killed, the U.S.A.F. will disavow any knowledge of your actions," Wolfe intoned. "This guy screams operator, or I'm a fiddler crab."

"What the hell have we been dropped into?" Timmons asked. He made sure the aircraft was secure before getting out of his seat.

"I guess we're about to find out," Wolfe said, falling in right behind him.

Sergeant Wilcox joined them as well. "Best see what I'm gonna be loading up."

Exiting out the forward crew hatch, Timmons walked down the stairs and over to the man in fatigues. "Major Alan Timmons. By the looks of things, you must be the man we are supposed to meet."

"Colonel David Nielson, former U.S. Army Special Forces, and that is correct. What was your briefing on this hop?"

"Get here and talk to you. Extend any and all assistance that we can."

"Excellent. Let's get your bird refueled, and then get the vehicles and operators loaded. While that's happening, you can plot our flight to Mandalay International Airport."

"Mandalay, Myanmar?" Timmons asked.

"The same."

"We're gonna need to avoid Iran and refuel. Do you care if we go over or under?"

"Whichever gets us there faster."

Timmons calculated altitude and weather conditions in his head. "Over will probably be faster, but refueling is a problem, unless you can get us a tanker over Kabul about five hours from now. If we go south, we skirt more of Iran, which adds miles and we'll need to stop at Mumbai, which will definitely take more time to get in and out of their flight pattern."

Colonel Neilson nodded. "The tanker is not a problem. Time is, however. When can we get wheels-up?"

Timmons turned to Wilcox, who jumped in. "Should take about twenty minutes to secure your vehicles. We can take all three Explorers, or two and the panel truck."

"The latter configuration is fine. The truck is holding our gear right now, so it has to go regardless."

"Let me get started then. I'll load the men once the vehicles are secure."

"Talk to the woman named Vanda inside. She'll be your translator if you need to direct them."

"I will tell them to bundle up. It can get a bit chilly at angels thirty-five." With a nod, the tech sergeant headed into the hangar.

Timmons took over. "Our tanks are almost full, so we just need to top off. Refueling will probably take a half-hour if we're lucky, since these guys aren't known for their speed..." He trailed off as a fuel truck pulled to a stop nearby.

Neilson smiled. "It helps to know people. Let's get that flight plan and the necessary clearances taken care of, shall we?"

The next morning dawned bright, sunny, and humid—just like every other day in Myanmar.

Just after sunrise, Mike joined the rest of the men at the morning formation. Just like Maung had said, there were at least three hundred men assembled on the hard ground in front of the row of barracks. They were a mix of Burmese, Chinese, and a fairly large group that Mike thought might be Nepalese, judging by their broad faces and the epicanthic fold of their eyes. He made a mental note to check on that later. It was easy to see the Keldara among them; each one typically stood several inches taller than the rest of their group. Oleg was there as well, leaning on a bedpost he had fashioned into an improvised crutch.

The plan had been explained in detail to everyone, and mostly involved the prisoners getting to cover before everything went to hell. Strategically placed personnel had been assigned key duties for the escape to go off successfully. Not the least of which was Katya, who was already in position and awaiting the go signal.

Warden Sein came out to inspect the men. He walked down the line, hands clasped behind his back, then came back up it, stopping at Mike.

"The two men who were with you last evening, where are they?"

Of course, with Jace gone, Mike didn't understand a word the other man was saying, but he replied anyway. "If you're asking about Jace and Adams, they left."

Sein frowned at the English until one of the prisoners translated what he had said. The warden blinked several times, as if he didn't understand the answer. "What?"

"I said, they left. They weren't thrilled about being here, and decided to bug out. They should be back soon, however. Oh wait, here they come now!"

Mike pointed at the road behind the warden, who turned and looked just as the Cascavel roared over a small hill and headed straight for the man.

"*Ko may ko loe!*" the Burmese man swore as he dove out of the way. "Motherfucker!" He scrabbled to draw his pistol when he saw the armored car skid to a stop and the turret swivel toward the guards' barracks.

Then the world exploded.

▲   ▲   ▲

When she heard Mike's shout, Katya ran to the shack containing the base's radio communications equipment. Her shirt hung open, revealing her bare breasts, and she had tried to make herself look as attractive as possible under the circumstances. As she headed for the door, she kept repeating the two short Burmese phrases Jace had drilled into her to throw the guard on duty completely off his game.

She reached the door and threw it open, making the man spin around in his chair and reach for his pistol. Taking a deep breath, Katya said—

"—I am so lost. Do you want sex?"

Of all the things Chankrisna Salai Kyi expected to see in this prison camp, a half-naked teenage blond woman coming on to him didn't even *make* the list.

He was totally flustered by her appearance, and even more confused by her second question. All he could do was slowly rise out of his chair as she walked toward him, staring at him with those odd blue eyes...

The next thing Kyi was aware of was a sharp pain in his stomach, followed by coldness radiating out from his belly. Looking down, he saw a dark stain on his shirt and realized that blood was seeping from his abdomen. Even more in shock now, he looked back up at the woman, who was thrusting a bloody knife at his throat—

In the commander's seat of the Cascavel, Adams watched through the panoramic day sight as their gunner, a man called Thant, aimed the 90mm main gun at the guards' quarters.

"Hope everyone outside's eating dirt right now!" the master chief said as the high-explosive fragmentation round shot from the barrel. It covered the hundred yards between the car and the building in an eye blink, penetrating the wall and detonating less than a second after firing.

The entire structure blew apart. The explosion launched the roof straight up into the air, only to crash back down on what was left of the place a few moments later. Mixed with the fragments and splinters was a rain of body parts and blood, which came down in a fifty-foot radius.

A machine gun started up outside, and Adams heard the sharp *ping ping ping* of rounds ricocheting off the armor plate outside. He glanced at Thant, who was reloading the 90mm. "I take it he's going to do something about that!" he called to Jace, who was driving. The cannon roar a few seconds later answered his question, and Adams put his eye to the sight again to see more body parts and chunks of wood rain down over the far side of the yard.

Thant started working the 12.7mm guns next. He mowed down the remaining guards trying to stand after being blasted off their feet by the twin concussions. The prisoners had all hit the ground the moment the vehicle had appeared. Small groups of them were belly-crawling back to their individual barracks. The Keldara, however, were heading toward the various guards. As their remaining captors struggled to their feet, they were quickly taken down again. Oleg proved particularly formidable at this, with his improvised crutch becoming a limb and skull-crushing club in his huge hands

In the forward driver's seat, Jace was ready to take directions as to where they should be going next. Thant, however, had complete coverage of the field of fire from where they were. Less than a minute after the destruction of the guard quarters, only the prisoners, Mike, and the warden were still alive in the yard. All of the other guards had either fled or were dead.

On the radio inside the Cascavel, Adams heard: "Master Chief, this is Katya."

He grabbed the microphone. "Go ahead, Katya."

"Radio room is secure."

"Roger that." Adams turned to the other two. "Okay, I think the zone is secure, too."

Half-deafened by the blasts from the 90mm, Sein rolled over onto his back to find a smiling Mike standing over him, pointing a pistol at his face. He was joined by the prisoner who had translated for him earlier.

The warden raised his hands in surrender. Mike said, "Told you I would find a suitable arrangement for everyone. I just didn't include you in that group."

Sein couldn't understand the man's words, but his next action was unmistakable as he pointed his pistol at the warden's knee and pulled the trigger.

The warden's world exploded again, this time in agony.

"Figure we've got maybe six to eight hours before someone in the army notices there's no communications coming out of their little mining operation and sends someone up here to check it out. So we have to unass in a hurry."

Mike was talking to Vanner on the guards' radio system, with Adams, Jace, and Katya listening.

"Right. Listen, since you had never been captured before, we went into serious rescue mode. Neilson's on his way over with an entire team in case we needed to spring you," Vanner replied.

"Good to know I'd be missed. Where are they now?" Mike asked.

"I heard from them an hour ago. If everything went as planned, they're just leaving Afghanistan airspace. They're going to edge around the top of Pakistan and shoot the border between Nepal and India. The plan is to land at Mandalay International in about three hours," Vanner said.

"Works. In fact, that might be perfect. Depending on what's going on down here, the reinforcements will probably come in handy. When they touch down, have them hold at the airport for further orders."

"Roger that. What's your next move?"

"I've got to find out what is up with the nuclear reactor around here. If there even is one. We're trying to figure out a way to find it, or find someone who knows about it here."

Mike's conversation gave Jace an idea. He tapped Adams on the shoulder. "I'll be right back."

Heading outside, he walked among the prisoners, most of whom were outfitting themselves for the trek through the jungle. Finding Maung, Jace told him what he needed. The Burmese man nodded. "I know exactly who you should talk to. Come on."

A few minutes later, Jace entered the radio room with a short, older, Burmese man in tow. "Hey, Kildar, I found the guy you needed." He waved the small man forward. "Khin here actually worked on the damn thing."

"Really? And you know where it's located?" Mike asked.

Khin nodded. "It is not far from here. Can take you there if you want to look at it. There is not much to see, however, since it has not gone online, as far as I know."

"Jace, did you tell him about the boards?"

"No, because I didn't have that information."

"Then get ready to translate a lot, 'cause we're about to have an in-depth conversation about them."

"Let me get this straight. Poor-ass Myanmar teamed up with North Korea to create a nuclear reactor in the middle of the jungle? Where did Kim get the plans and the technology to do this?" Adams asked ten minutes later.

"Apparently the one constructed here is an Economic Simplified Boiling Water Reactor," Jace translated. "Since the deal with the Russians fell through back in 2007, the military had been looking around for a feasible replacement with whoever was willing to deal with them. Before he died, Kim reached an agreement with the ruling junta to supply material and personnel to build a test facility in the middle of the jungle out here."

"Makes sense, especially since Myanmar is already on most countries' ignore list, so no one would be watching it so closely. Also, it has plenty of thick jungle for cover. North Korea, on the other hand..." Mike said.

Jace continued. "The Generation III+ ESBWR was the most suitable choice for several reasons. First, it has no recirculation pumps, associated piping, or heat exchangers, nor the various control systems associated with those, greatly simplifying ongoing maintenance."

"Wait a minute. What prevents a meltdown if there's no heat exchangers or pumps or any of that shit?" Adams asked.

When asked the question, Khin launched into a long monologue, complete with gestures, that Jace attempted to boil down. "That is the other reason this particular reactor system was chosen. It has three redundant safety systems to prevent a reactor breach. First is the Isolation Condenser System, a passive heat exchanger located above the containment unit in a pool of open water. Excess decay heat produces steam, which is piped to the condenser, which does what its title suggests. The heat enters the atmosphere and the condensed water falls back into the pool, which is slowly boiled away, and must be refilled periodically. Next is the Gravity Driven Cooling System, which are large pools of water inside the containment unit above the reactor itself. If this system is initiated, the water flows down into the reactor, taking on the decay heat and also transferring it out in the form of steam, which is released after the reactor has been depressurized. Lastly, there is the Passive Containment Cooling System, another series of passive heat exchangers in the upper part of the reactor building. Container steam from the reactor rises to these exchangers, where it is condensed, with the heat escaping again, while the water flows back down to the GDCS pools and back to the reactor pressure vessel."

Jace took a deep breath. "Both the ISC and the GDCS pools are large enough to maintain a cooling cycle for at least seventy-two hours, even in the event of a power loss. The pools can also be easily refilled through pipes to local water sources, or even trucked-in water if necessary."

"Like the Irrawaddy River, right?" Mike asked.

Upon hearing the English name of the major river in Myanmar, Khin pointed at the Kildar and nodded.

"Okay, great. And the military wants to keep it under wraps not only because North Korea is subsidizing it, which wouldn't go over well in the nuclear community, but there is also all that increased scrutiny about whether any nuclear plant in a foreign country could be used to process waste into material for nuclear weapons," Adams said.

"Got it in two," Mike replied, then turned back to Khin with a frown. "Wait a minute. He sounds like an engineer. How did he end up here?"

Jace asked, and the small man's face darkened as he spat out a stream of words. "He is a safety systems engineer with a degree in nuclear engineering. He says one day he overheard a conversation between one of the military leaders and the lead engineer that he wasn't supposed to hear. It had to do with the safety precautions, and more importantly, how they could be circumvented. When he inquired about it later to the lead engineer, he was told that the general was merely asking about precautions in the event of a local terrorist action against the plant. But it didn't sound like that's what they were talking about at all. It sounded like the general was asking about ways the reactor might malfunction from *inside* the plant. When the reactor was completed, except for the fuel rod delivery and the master control boards, the lead engineer died in a car crash. The next night, Khin was taken from his home and brought up here, with no papers or any way to contact the outside world. That was two months ago."

"So, why haven't they killed him too?" Adams asked.

As quickly as his face had darkened, Khin smiled again. "He says they killed the lead engineer too soon. The reactor still has issues. However, they are desperate to get it online. They've been keeping him here in order to break him so he'll go back to work for them. But after seeing what happened to the last guy, he'd rather work up here and live than go back down there and die."

"Really?" Mike thought for a moment. "Ask him how he would feel about gaining his freedom and sticking it to the guys who put him in here?"

Jace had barely finished translating when Khin nodded so hard he thought the little man was going to give himself whiplash. "He's in. What does he have to do?"

"First, we have to get word to the commander of the plant

that you're ready to make a deal. And I know just the guy to make that call."

An hour later, they were heading down the NH 31 highway toward the site of the nuclear facility. Mike had filled in Vanner and told him to pass the information on to Bob Pierson while he went to personally investigate the site.

Jace, Khin, and he were riding in the armored car. In a truck behind them was Katya and half of Team Jayne, with Oleg at the wheel. Accompanying them were several prisoners who had volunteered to help take over the facility while Mike got to the bottom of what was going on there. The rest were busy loading up the other Aeolus truck and scrounging whatever other vehicles they could find so they wouldn't have to walk to Mandalay. Before he left, Mike promised that he would send something back for the rest of the men if possible. As he watched the road, he wondered just how in the hell he was going to keep that promise.

"This is the sign for Chaunggyi. Here's the turnoff," Jace said as he turned right onto a rough dirt road. Khin had said they had set the plant about nine kilometers off the main road so it wouldn't be immediately detectable from above. They had found a suitable site near a stream that emptied into the Irrawaddy as their coolant source.

After putting a tourniquet on his leg, Mike had "convinced" Warden Sein to make the call to the head of the nuclear facility and tell him that Khin was ready to discuss the terms of his returning to work. The colonel, one Ront Ohnmar, was all too eager to have Khin come to the reactor immediately. Mike had Sein confirm that he was sending the engineer over under heavy guard. Mike also had Khin change into a guard uniform so he could talk them past the guards at the gate.

Several kilometers later, they came to a nine-foot-high chain-link perimeter fence with an electric gate. The barrier was topped with razor wire, and Jace spotted the conductors that indicated it was electrified. A guard checkpoint was on the right side of the fence, and a uniformed soldier came out to watch the two-vehicle convoy pull to a stop.

Khin popped out of the turret hatch. "I have Safety Engineer Khin to see Colonel Ohnmar," he said.

The soldier immediately saluted and ran back inside the gatehouse. The gate trundled aside on wheels as Khin disappeared back inside. The second the opening was wide enough, Jace drove through.

"You're sure it's just a skeleton crew?" Mike asked.

"The reactor isn't operational yet, so there isn't really a lot to guard here," Khin replied through Jace. "They keep a rotating staff on three eight-hour shifts. From what I saw, the fence does a lot of the work."

The site looked pretty much like someone had built a standard power plant in the middle of the jungle. The main building, a dull gray, concrete structure, was straight ahead, with a parking lot in front holding about thirty vehicles. To their left was what looked like a large row of metal building blocks.

"Just park in the lot there." Khin pointed to an asphalt lot next to another dull concrete building. "We'll be heading to the administration building to see the colonel."

"Where's the cooling towers?" Adams asked as he looked around.

"They decided to go with a series of crossflow cooling towers, in which the hot water is piped in and flows perpendicular through the flow material to the bottom where it is collected. At the same time, air is drawn in and is heated, then the moist, hot air is expelled through the top of the tower by the fan."

"Convenient that it also doesn't look like the typical 'nuclear reactor' design. Hell, with the right containment unit, you guys could probably pass this off as some kind of manufacturing company, as long as no one gets inside," Mike said.

"That had been discussed more than once," Khin admitted as they got out of the Cascavel. "Come with me."

"One second." Mike and Jace went to the back of the large truck. "Everyone knows their assignments, right?" The mixed group of Keldara and Burmese all nodded. "All right, everyone head out."

Joined by Katya, who was transmitting the video of the site

back to Vanner, and Adams, Mike, Jace, and Khin headed toward the administrative building. They were only a few steps away when the door was opened by a soldier. They all walked inside, the guard frowning at the three Americans dressed in Myanmar army uniforms. As he started to say something, Mike nodded at Adams, who was the last man in.

The master chief took one step past the door guard, then drew his pistol, pivoted, and whipped the butt across the man's face. His cheekbone and nose shattered, the guard hit the floor and didn't move while blood flowed down the front of his shirt.

The door led into a large, open office with four desks, two of which were occupied by a man and a woman. Both stared in shock at what had just happened. Pistol drawn and a finger raised to his lips, Mike motioned both of them to raise their hands. He had them get up and stand near the wall, away from any telephones. Quickly patting all of them down, Mike found a cell on the man and pocketed it. Assigning Adams to watch both them and the front door, he joined Khin and Jace at the door at the back of the office. About to burst in, Mike stopped as a moan was heard on the other side, along with the familiar sound of someone getting blown.

"Guess there really isn't anything to do here but bang the secretaries." Mike gently twisted the handle, only to find it locked. Shaking his head, he put his boot into the door just below the lock. The door flew open hard enough to crash into the wall next to it.

Mike walked in to see exactly what he thought he would see. The stacked brunette who had been on her knees behind the desk was frantically trying to cover herself while the colonel, dressed only in short-sleeves, yanked up his boxers and shot out of his chair.

"What is the meaning of this—" was all Jace could translate before Mike rounded the desk and smashed the butt of his pistol into the man's face. Blood squirted from his crushed nose, and the man clasped his hands to his face with a strangled scream as he fell back into his chair.

"Tell Khin to get her dressed and outside," Mike said. "Let the master chief know he's got another person to watch." He brought the pistol butt down on the colonel's hand, which had been inching toward the desk phone. The man screamed again through gritted teeth and clasped his broken fingers to his bloody chest. "Katya, close the door while Jace and I have a chat with the colonel."

Vanel had been assigned the job of clearing the crew out of the main reactor building. With him was Marko and a young Burmese named Bourey who had worked on building the exterior of the reactor building. He had been exiled to the gem mines when he was caught stealing construction materials to try to fix the roof on his parents' house. Between the three men, they knew just enough English to make themselves understood to each other.

"Control room here," Bourey said as he led them around the side of the reactor building to a smaller structure that jutted out the side. He tried the door, but it was locked, with an electronic keypad next to it.

"Too bad Mouse is not here," Marko said.

"Why do you not just shoot the lock off?" Bourey asked.

"Because we still have surprise on our side. Also, do not wish to cause undue alarm to other teams," Vanel replied.

"I have idea." Stepping up to the door, Bourey banged hard on it with a fist. Behind him, Vanel and Marko exchanged puzzled glances.

To everyone's surprise, the door opened. "Htun, I've told you a thousand times that you cannot keep banging on the—" the radiation-suited worker, complete with full-face helmet and independent air supply, looked as shocked as Vanel and the others did at seeing him. "You're not—"

Vanel and Marko both pointed their pistols in the man's face and advanced on him, forcing him to backpedal into the room. Three more people, all dressed in the same outfits, looked up in surprise as the group marched into the small control area. Marko and Bourey swung their guns over to cover the rest of the group. What really made Vanel's eyes widen was the fully operational control panel, with glowing monitors showing incomprehensible readings and lights blinking and on all across the board.

"Tell them to get their hands up!" Vanel said, motioning at the ceiling with his pistol. Bourey rattled off some Burmese, and the other three slowly began to comply.

"Hey, what's with leaving the control room door open—" said a loud voice behind them. Marko turned to cover the new arrival. "Hey, what's—who?"

Seeing the pistol, the man turned and bolted back outside. With a curse, Marko took off after him, leaving Vanel and Bourey to cover the other four.

Spotting one of them slowly moving toward a console, Vanel said, "Don't—"

The man lunged toward a red button, leaving Vanel with no choice but to fire. The shot was loud in the confined space, making his ears ring.

A small black hole appeared in the middle of the man's suit, just below his heart. He collapsed where he was, his hand inches from that button, breathed one last time, and died. The other three didn't move a muscle, just alternated between staring at their dead co-worker and the man who had just shot him.

Vanel was already on his radio. "Inara Four to Kildar."

"Go for Kildar," Mike replied.

"What the hell is going on here?" Bourey asked. "The only time you are to be in the suits is . . . when . . . there is leak . . ." He whirled to Vanel. "We have to get out of here right now! There is leak in reactor!"

Khin hustled the semi-clothed young woman through the door as Jace called out, "Another one to keep an eye on, Chief."

Meanwhile, Mike sat on the dark wooden desk and set the pistol on his leg, the muzzle casually pointing at the colonel's head. Jace closed the door and walked over to stand in front of the desk. The army officer started to turn to look at him, but was stopped when his jaw hit the slide of Mike's pistol.

"No no no, you really want to keep those watering eyes on me right now," Mike said, tapping the man's face with the muzzle for emphasis. "Now, you've already seen what I do when I stop in to say hello. So you can imagine how much worse I get when I ask a few questions and don't like the answers I hear, right?"

Colonel Ohnmar nodded, his eyes on the black muzzle of the 9mm pistol inches away from his face.

"All right then. You have received the motherboards for the reactor, correct?"

The colonel nodded.

"Where are they right now?"

"In the main reactor building, undergoing a final inspection before being installed," Jace translated.

"Good. Since the rest of the crew has been rounded up, have Adams and Khin go and collect the boards. Lock the officer personnel up with the rest of the crew." Mike turned back to the colonel. "Where were we? Ah, yes. You were about to tell me the military's true purpose for this reactor."

"I don't know what you are talking about—" was all the farther the officer got before Mike placed the muzzle of his pistol on the man's lips and slowly shook his head.

"See, that is exactly what I am talking about. You tell me something that I do not want to hear—" Mike increased his pressure on the gun, forcing it into the man's mouth. He gagged as the slide scraped past his teeth, tears trickling down his face as Mike shoved the pistol in farther. "—and that really upsets me. Now let's try it again, or I am going to shoot your other hand."

Squirming in the leather chair, the colonel tried to speak around the metal filling his mouth.

"I can't understand anything he's saying with his mouth full," Jace said, then wrinkled his nose. "Is that what I think it is?"

"Yes, he pissed himself." Mike withdrew the pistol fast, chipping Ohnmar's upper front tooth. Grabbing the man's undamaged hand, he slapped it on the desk. Setting the muzzle on top of it, he said, "I am going to count to three, and I'd better hear something better than 'I don't know!' One..." He stared at the colonel, whose sweat was trickling down his forehead to mingle with the blood on his jaw and shirt.

"...Two..." Mike thumbed back the trigger. "...Th—"

The officer started babbling in a torrent Jace could barely follow. "God damnit, get him to slow down!"

Mike pulled the pistol away and held it up in front of the man's face. "Once more, from the top."

"Okay, okay, I will tell you! Several high-ranking military officers are planning to manufacture a large-scale nuclear event at this plant in order to take over the country. They needed the control boards to get the reactor running so they could create a meltdown scenario and release a large cloud of radioactive steam—"

"But Mandalay is only about forty miles south of here. They are going to release radiation that could affect their own people?" Mike asked.

"That is not the real target. We were supposed to wait until a southern wind came up and then cause the criticality accident. The goal was to get a cloud of radioactive material heading toward Nay Pyi Taw—"

"The country's new capitol city," Jace interrupted his own translation to add.

"—and force a city-wide evacuation. The men in charge of managing the evacuation would remove the government staff and hold them prisoner in an undisclosed location until the military can launch their *coup d'etat* and reestablish their control over the nation. Afterward, they would use Yangon as a base of operations until they can decontaminate the central area of the country."

"Okay, but if they're the military, why did they need to buy all those arms from China?" Mike asked.

"Because not all of the upper officers are in on the plan. The group couldn't draw that much weapons and equipment and send it north without it looking suspicious, especially with most the insurgent activity occurring in the west and the south. The weapons are to arm a large contingent of loyalists who are waiting for its arrival in Mandalay right now."

"Shit! I thought Cong might have been selling them to the

insurgents, not the fucking army itself!" Mike's radio buzzed, and he snatched it up. "Go for Kildar."

"This is Inara Four, we are evacuating the control room. Have found men in radiation suits working inside, and control panel is operational."

"What the fuck?" Mike's head snapped up. "Khin, I thought you said the control room wasn't working yet."

At Jace's translation, the engineer's face paled. "It shouldn't be—" He yanked the door open and ran out of the office.

Mike grabbed the colonel, whose face was also draining of blood, by the shirt collar. "Come on, we're going to see what the fuck is going on out there."

"Wait—what are you talking about? No one should be working in there right now. They are just supposed to be doing final adjustments to the reactor before installing the boards."

"Well, we're gonna find out one way or the other." Keeping the man in front of him, Mike marched him out of the office. He instructed Adams to maintain his position as he went by.

Leaving the administrative building, they walked over to the control room, where four people in heavy radiation gear were standing with their hands on the wall. The last member had dirt stains on his knees, chest, and arms, as if he had been tackled. A fifth suited body lay on the ground beside them.

As Mike and Colonel Ohnmar walked up, Khin burst out of the room, holding both hands up. "It is okay. There is no danger, the fuel rods are secure." He put his hands on his knees, breathing heavily.

"What was going on in there?" Mike asked.

"Don't get me wrong, if your people had been a couple minutes later, these guys would have initiated a countdown to a criticality accident."

"Meaning?" Mike asked, although he had a pretty damn good idea what the short engineer was talking about.

"A core meltdown and release of radioactive steam—a lot of radioactive steam—into the atmosphere."

CHAPTER TWENTY-ONE

"Cargo hold, this is your captain speaking. We are about to begin our final approach into Mandalay International Airport in the oppressed nation of Myanmar, and should be landing in approximately six minutes. Please make sure that you are in your seat with your seat belts fastened. You've probably already noticed that there are no tray tables, so no need to concern yourself with returning them to an upright position. In the event of one of the vehicles breaking loose and careening around the cabin—not that that would happen under our excellent tech sergeant's watch—however, if that were to happen, we'd probably be heading straight into the ground, with only enough time to stick your head between your legs and kiss your ass goodbye. On behalf of the pilot, tech sergeant, and myself, we'd like to thank you for flying the United States Air Force Super Hercules, the loudest, most uncomfortable flight in the air."

"Really, Major Wolfe?" Timmons asked as he did one final check of his flaps, landing gear, and airspeed. Everything was nominal. The 14,000-foot runway stretched out before him like a concrete road into infinity. He took a moment to admire the design of the access paths to and from the main terminal. They were at forty-five-degree angles to both the runway and the road next to the boarding bridges, allowing easy access both to and from the main runway.

"Hey, I never get the chance to do any of that with our cargo runs."

"Yes, but you know probably none of them heard you."

His copilot shrugged. "The opportunity was there. Besides, it's not like I had anything to do like watch for other flights out here at the ghost airport."

"Yeah, it is a bit off-putting, isn't it?" Timmons checked the radar one last time. As before, he found it amazingly empty for a major international airport. The Super Hercules came down onto the runway perfectly. With so much space ahead of him, he didn't even have to work the brakes, but could let the Herc coast to a stop using less than half of the available runway.

This was Timmons's first time to Mandalay, and he marveled at the clean, neat lines of the main building with its pair of twin tiered pagoda-style roofs. Everything, from the terminal itself to the huge runway, was less than fifteen years old. And the whole place was pretty much barren.

Built to handle one thousand passenger arrivals and departures every hour, or three million passengers a year, with a flight leaving or arriving every eight minutes, the forlorn Mandalay airport now looked exactly like the white elephant government critics had labeled it when the decision to build it was first announced. There were only a handful of aircraft from lesser-known flight companies like Air Bagan, Air Mandalay, Asian Wings Airlines, China Eastern Airlines, and Yangon Airways at various boarding gates. There was certainly no line waiting to take off on the huge runway.

Feathering his turboprops, Timmons taxied to the end of the runway and found a parking area that looked like a good place to sit for a bit while their passengers and cargo got themselves sorted out.

Wolfe was staring out his side window. "Looks like we're about to have company. That didn't take long."

Timmons looked over to see an unmarked sedan plus an airport security car speeding in their direction. "Sure hope our mystery leader can work his magic on these guys as easily as he did at Tbilisi and Kabul. I'm going to head down to see if he needs any assistance."

"Hey, count me in." His copilot was right behind him as Timmons went down the stairs leading to the cargo area. The twenty men were still sitting facing each other in the red seat webbing Sandra had rigged for them. The vehicles were still secure, as expected, and took up every available inch of the bay remaining.

Colonel Neilson was up, however, and greeted the pilots with a smile. "Thank you for the excellent and speedy flight, gentlemen."

"Our pleasure, sir. However—" Timmons jerked a thumb in the general direction of the approaching car. "What looks like a security car is approaching outside. I imagine they want to have a word with us."

The colonel's smile grew even broader. "I'll take care of them, and see if I can get you refueled at the same time. Meanwhile, let's get the men and vehicles offloaded, all right? Do you need anything else while I'm out there?"

Timmons exchanged a puzzled glance with his copilot. "Not that I can think of."

"Okay, see you in a bit." By this time Sandra had lowered the rear loading ramp, and Nielson walked down. He headed straight for the cars, which had stopped about fifteen yards away.

Timmons walked down just far enough to see the man conversing with three men who had gotten out of the cars to meet him. One was in a suit jacket and the other two were in security uniforms. They spoke for several minutes, and at one point Nielson pulled out a satphone and began dialing a number. This made the jacketed man raise his hands and shake his head. Nielson put the phone away and pointed at one of the engines. The airport suit's shoulders slumped, but he nodded and pulled out a radio mic from his car and began talking into it.

As Nielson walked back to the aircraft, Timmons glanced at Wolfe again.

"Who the hell are these guys?"

▲   ▲   ▲

"Well, that was interesting," Mike said.

"That's one way to put it," Jace replied.

They had just spent the last twenty minutes interrogating the control room crew. All of them had been very willing to talk after seeing their team leader get shot to death right in front of them. They had put together a disturbing picture of what had been about to happen if Vanel and his team hadn't interrupted them.

With the control boards in place and the nuclear fuel loaded, the control team had been about to scram the reactor while it was only partially covered with water. That would enable the safety systems to engage, but at nowhere near maximum efficiency. Also, they were going to override the activation of the Isolation Condenser System and the crossflow cooling towers. According to Khin, the result would have been catastrophic. The metal cladding around the uranium fuel pellets would have melted, releasing a lethal amount of radiation into the surrounding area. If the meltdown wasn't contained in time, it might have even led to the theorized "China Syndrome" of the late '70s, where superheated nuclear material would have melted deep into the earth's crust.

"Can you remove those boards again, intact and undamaged?" Mike asked when he was through.

Khin nodded.

"Get to it."

The best part was that Colonel Ohnmar had heard for himself how the leaders of the coup had considered him to be an expendable sacrifice. He would have been killed in the meltdown, along with the rest of the unprotected personnel at the nuclear facility, to help create the illusion of a real accident happening. He had been so surprised by the betrayal that he hadn't even offered a token protest about the boards being removed. The range of emotions on his face, from surprise to shock to anger to resignation, said it all. Although Jace got the impression he could give a flying fuck about the others, the fact that his fellow officers thought so little of him had demolished the man's self-esteem and *esprit de corps*.

Fortunately, this revelation also made it very easy for him to give up the rest of the details about the operation with only a little prodding from Mike and Jace. Unfortunately, that led to other complications.

He called Vanner immediately. "Patrick, what's the word on David and that back-up team?"

"They just touched down about twenty minutes ago, and are ready to rock and roll. What's going on?"

"The good news is that the potential reactor meltdown has been averted—"

"*What*—where?" Vanner's question made Mike realize that he hadn't had time to fill the intel chief in on what they had learned.

"No time to go into it, just know that the reactor's safe. I'll fill you in on the details later. Can you conference David in right now?"

"Sure, hang on." Thirty seconds later. "You should have both of us now."

"Good to hear your voice, Kildar," Nielson greeted him.

Mike wasted no time. "It's good to be heard, David. Get your team into Mandalay and over by the Kandawgyi Pat Road, on the east side of Tet Thay Pond. Look for a cluster of warehouses about a thousand feet south of the Gold Star Hotel, which is at the intersection where Kandawgyi intersects with itself. Google Maps will give you a good satellite view of it for quick reference. When you get there, do a light recon only. The arms convoy is supposed to be in holed up one of those buildings. The problem is that local units are supposed to be dropping by later today to be issued their weapons before they spread out to other cities up here. I'm coming down from the north, and will be driving a Cascavel armored car. It worked in a bluff earlier today, so I am hoping it will work again. What vehicles did you bring?"

"Two Explorers and a panel truck rented on short notice for an exorbitant price."

"How did you get here so fast?"

"Your Uncle Sam pulled a few strings and got us a U.S.A.F. C-130J-30 Super Hercules from Turkey. When we're through here, I'll remind you to thank a certain gentleman who lives in an alabaster house. He instructed them to give any and all aid and assistance to us, which they have done admirably."

"Excellent. Right now we have to stop these arms from falling into the wrong hands. If we don't, the entire country is in danger of being taken over in a military coup."

"We're on it," David said. "If you don't need me at the moment, we'll call in once we've located the warehouse facility."

"Go. Vanner, stay on for one more question. Are you still tracking Cong's yacht?"

"Like white on rice. He's ten miles off the western coast of Myanmar, parallel to a port city called Sittwe, and seems to have dropped anchor, since he has not moved in the past twelve hours. Guess he needed a break after running guns and nuclear motherboards to crazy military officers who want to overthrow their government."

"Stick with him. If the boat moves ten feet, I want to know. If he takes a swim around that yacht, I want to know what color Speedo he's wearing."

"You got it, although that is not a picture I want in my head," Vanner replied.

"I will contact you once I've met up with Nielson at the arms cache. Hopefully we will all get there in time. Kildar out."

Mike walked around the side of the truck to the group of former prisoners there. As he'd thought, at least half of the volunteers were those he thought might be Nepalese. "Jace?"

"Yes, Kildar?"

"Refresh my memory. Did you list Nepali as one of your languages?"

"Not so much. Visited the country a couple times, but never stayed long enough to pick it up."

"All right, we go to plan B." He faced the group and pointed at his suspects. "Any of you speak English?"

"I do," said one with an odd mix of a British accent underlaid with that of his homeland. He was a general prisoner who hadn't lost too much muscle tone from his time in the mines. His head was shaved, most likely to avoid lice. He had the prerequisite Indo-Tibetan-Mongolian appearance, with piercing black eyes that settled on nothing, but still took in everything around him.

"What's your name, soldier?"

The man smiled and nodded. "That obvious?"

Mike nodded back. "We know our own."

"Lance Corporal Himal Chanda, of the Shree Naya Gorakh Battalion. I did UN Peacekeeping operations in Africa—Somalia, to be precise—and the Balkans."

"Gurkha military, right?"

Himal nodded.

"We just might be able to pull this off after all." Mike raised his voice. "Okay, Himal, please translate this to the rest for me. This goes for anyone here with military experience. I am hiring freelance soldiers for one to two days. Payment is five hundred U.S. dollars a day, but you will be earning it, as we will probably be seeing action from this point forward. Are there any volunteers?"

Every prisoner except Khin and two others stepped forward. With Himal's and Jace's help, Mike got the particulars of each man's experience and confirmed whether he was in or out. In the end, he had swelled the men under his command by a solid dozen. He turned back to Himal. "Do you know anyone else in Mandalay with that kind of training?"

The wiry man nodded again. "Since the abolishment of the Nepalese monarchy, many of the soldiers whose army term is up have gone into private security work. I'm sure I can scrounge up a few more in the city, and they probably know others I don't."

"Great. While we're securing the weapons, I need you to contact as many as you can find. Same terms as you are getting, but they have to be available immediately—like within an hour after your call."

"If you would lend me a phone, I can start contacting some of them on our way in," Himal replied.

Mike handed his over. "Works."

▲   ▲   ▲

An hour later, Mike sat beside Nielson in the Explorer, which was parked on the street a block down from their target, watching the warehouse complex through binoculars. They'd stashed the Cascavel outside of the city, although Mike was aware of the minutes ticking away. Still, he'd be damned if he was going to go into an unfamiliar situation without doing at least some kind of recon.

"You sure you don't need something to keep your focus up?" Nielson asked. "Got plenty of Modafinil—"

Mike had wolfed three energy bars and drunk two bottles of water. "See if any of the men want some. I'm good."

"As your XO, I feel compelled to remind you that you haven't slept in what, a day?" David said. "And you've been all go since early this morning. None of us are as young as we used to be. That includes you, you know."

Mike kept scanning the cluster of buildings. "I will not rest until Oleg and I have killed that prick General Cong. Then I will sleep."

"Yeah, Vanner filled me in. What the fuck's up with that?"

"The man likes collecting trophies. Be interesting to see how he likes it when I cut his fucking nuts off and mount those on the wall. The good thing about that is that he will still be alive for Oleg to kill."

"How'd he take it?"

"Like a Keldara. He has to kill the one who dishonored him and reclaim the trophy. I ordered him to give it to me so that Chinese fuckhead didn't shoot him like a dog and take it anyway."

"Jesus."

Mike lowered the binoculars and looked through Neilson with a thousand-yard stare. "It's probably a good thing he's not around here either. He wouldn't like what's going to go down in the next hour."

Himal's calls had paid off. By the time he was through, Mike's force had swelled to thirty-five Gurkha soldiers. All of them looked like they had seen the elephant, and each one carried his personal kukri on a ring sheath at his belt.

Mike was thrilled, since he considered them the equivalent of his Keldara. After arming as many as he could with the weapons he'd seized at the nuclear facility, he explained the current mission, finishing with, "If there are no questions, let's take the warehouse."

They got into the back of the troop truck again, and Nielson led them to the Cascavel, where he dropped Mike off to rejoin Adams and Jace in the armored car. With it leading, the truck wound its way back into town again, heading directly for the warehouses this time.

"Have you thought about how exactly you're going to get inside? It's not like we've radioed ahead or anything," Adams said.

"From what I could tell, it didn't look like the main door was locked. Himal can just jump out of the truck and open it. Since he's dressed for the part, they'll probably figure someone showed up early. We drive inside and point the big guns at everyone, and they give up."

"Works. Let's do it," Adams said.

They arrived at the warehouse a few minutes later, and sure enough, Himal jumped out of the back of the truck and ran to the door, which was another one that slid open horizontally on a top-mounted rail. Grabbing the handle, he pulled with all his might, yanking the door aside. Again, as soon as the space was wide enough, Jace drove the armored car inside.

The five soldiers in the large room all whirled and raised their rifles when they heard the door open, but relaxed when they saw the Cascavel pull into the building. The trucks were packed in here like sardines, and there was barely enough room for Jace to pull in. The truck behind them pulled up tight to the entrance, blocking it from the street so no one could see what was about to happen.

Shouting and waving angrily, one of the soldiers put his rifle up on his shoulder and tried to wave the armored car back out of the building. He froze when Adams popped up on the 7.62mm machine gun and aimed it at him. By that time Himal had reached the man. Grabbing the MA-1 rifle from his unresisting hands, he covered the others. One of the soldiers, hidden from Adams' view by one of the trucks, tried to unsling his rifle, and was immediately stitched with a short burst from Himal. Three more ducked for cover, with at least one trying to escape out the back of the warehouse.

"Surround the building! Make sure no one escapes!" Adams called out. Himal signaled the others, and a squad immediately peeled off and split up, with a group of three men going around each side of the warehouse.

Himal was reinforced by a second squad of Gurkha riflemen, who disarmed and searched the other soldiers before tying their hands and feet. One of the three-person groups that had circled the warehouse returned with a disheveled, limping soldier who had obviously been taken down hard. He was also searched and secured.

"Okay." Mike and Jace jumped down from the car and walked up to the captured men. "We know what you are up to, and what you were supposed to do here. That is not going to happen today. Tell me who is behind this, and you guys can all walk. Don't talk, or try to lie to me, and you won't even crawl out of here."

One of the men shouted something at Mike and spat on the floor at his feet, ignoring the other men's demands that he be quiet.

"What did he say?" Mike asked.

"You can't stop the movement. Nay Pyi Daw will be ours soon, and after that Yangon, and then the whole country!"

Mike pointed at the loudmouth. "Bring him over here. The rest of you, please come outside for a minute. Himal, with me, please."

Once Mike was sure he was out of earshot of the Myanmar soldiers, he addressed the group through the Gurkha soldier. "I need two things from all of you right now. One, I need you to contact anyone else from the service that you know is available for this kind of work immediately. Two, I need ten volunteers to drive these trucks. Nine of you will go directly to the port city of Sittwe and find a spot as close to the harbor as possible. I will have someone meet you there. You will unload the trucks as they direct. Pay rate is the same, and you probably don't run the risk of getting shot on that job."

The group looked at one another, then one shrugged and said

he would drive a truck. Once one said it, others followed suit, until Mike had his ten drivers. "Okay, the tenth guy—you," he pointed at the last volunteer. "Grab one of the trucks that has rifles and ammo in it and get to the Mandalay Airport south of town. Find the C130 there and break out the weapons. I will call ahead and let them know you're coming. Get moving, right now!"

The last man took off to the trucks, and Mike addressed the rest. "I'd suggest you get started out of town immediately. Soldiers are going to be here any minute looking for the weapons they've been promised. Make your calls on the way out, send anyone who is available to the Mandalay International Airport. *Do not* tell them any particulars of the mission over the phone. I don't want the local army intercepting any of the calls. Tell them they should reference a family reunion if they need to speak about it. They have sixty minutes to get there, then we are wheels-up."

When they heard that, the Gurkha drivers all ran to their trucks, all of them pulling out cell phones on the way. Mike turned to Himal and Adams. "Himal, get that truck out of the way. Adams, back the car up."

While they were jockeying for position on the street, Mike walked back over to his selected soldier, cut his feet free, grabbed his shirt, and dragged him outside toward the pond.

A frown crossing his face, the soldier asked what Mike was doing. When Jace translated, Mike replied. "Tell him he's going for a swim. Except that I'm lying about the swimming part."

Jace dutifully translated, and the man frowned again. By then they were at the pond's edge, and Mike kept going, marching out into the brown water. The man began to protest, but as soon as they were waist-deep Mike kicked his legs out from under him and plunged him under the surface. There was a bit of thrashing, and many bubbles, but with his hands tied, there wasn't a lot he could do except eventually suck water. Mike held him under for a forty count, then brought him up, spluttering and gasping.

"Tell me everything you know about what's happening in Yangon."

"Fuck...off!" Jace translated.

"Wrong answer." Back he went, this time Mike kept him under for a full minute. When he brought the soldier up this time, he was much weaker, and a mixture of water and bile streamed from his nose and mouth. "Care to try again?"

"You cannot stop it. It is already in motion—" was all the man said before Mike dunked him again, letting another minute go by before bringing him back up. This time the man sagged in the Kildar's arms, half-drowned.

"If I cannot stop it, then there is no reason not to tell me what is going to happen. If you do not tell me, however, the next time you go under, you will not come back up alive."

As soon as Jace finished translating that, the soldier shook his head, gasping out words. "Bring him out, I can't hear from here," Jace said.

Mike dragged him to the bank, where Jace had him repeat what he'd said. When he was finished, the Marine glanced up at Mike. "We didn't get all of the weapons. Part of the shipment was held back in Yangon for the forces there to take over the City Hall building to prepare it for the officers to set up their temporary headquarters there. It's their secondary plan, in case the nuclear event doesn't go off as planned. He says the timetable is already in motion, and supposedly cannot be stopped by anyone, not even the coup leaders."

"Determined little fuckers, aren't they? We have to get there ASAP." Mike pulled out his radio. "Nielson, this is Kildar."

"Nielson here."

"Is the plane you rode in on still at the airport?"

"Yes, on the tarmac right now."

"Great. Get in touch with them and tell them to have the plane ready to go in sixty minutes. We are coming down there right now."

"Not a moment too soon either. My outlying scouts are saying military convoys are coming from the east. They are hitting the outskirts of town right now."

"Son of a—" Mike ran up the embankment to see a truck

rumble out of the warehouse. Running inside, he saw that all ten of them were on the road. "Okay, pull your men back and get to the airport. We will meet you there, and then it's back to Yangon."

"What, the weapons aren't all of it?"

"Nope, I will fill you in when we get there. Also, if you see Gurkhas arriving at the airport, they're with us. Collect them and bring them to the plane as quickly as possible. We will leave the vehicles here in exchange for personnel. From what I saw of Yangon, traffic would be a nightmare, and I have a feeling we're going to need every trigger finger we can get."

Fifty-six minutes later, Mike, Adams, Jace, and the rest of the men pulled onto the tarmac of the Mandalay International Airport. What he saw made him smile.

At least forty more Gurkhas stood in several rows in front of the plane, which had its turboprops already warmed up. Dressed in a mix of blue jeans, cargo shorts or pants, and T-shirts and short-sleeved button-down shirts, each one had an MA-1 rifle slung over his left shoulder and basic web gear on. All of them looked ready for action.

Mike brought Himal with him to address the group. "Have 'em all gather round."

Instead of trying to bellow the order, the Gurkha waved the rest of the men in. When they were all clustered around him, Mike started talking.

"First, thanks for mustering out on such short notice. Before we go any further, you need to know the details of the mission, in case anybody wants to back out. We're heading to Yangon to stop a rogue Myanmar army unit of unknown size from taking over the city's capital building. We will most likely be outnumbered, probably heavily. All we have going for us is the element of surprise, and about seventy-five of the finest warriors on the planet. Are you with me?"

As one, every man in the group shouted, *"Jai Mahakali, Ayo Gurkhali!"*

"What was that?" Mike shouted to Himal.

"The Gurkha battle cry. 'Glory be to the Goddess Kali, here come the Gurkhas!'" Himal grinned. "We are all with you."

"Then let's move out!"

CHAPTER TWENTY-TWO

Every day, Mya Soe stared with undisguised envy at the throngs of people hustling past her souvenir kiosk. Men, women, couples, families, all coming or going somewhere much more interesting than this stupid airport. Meanwhile, she was stuck here every day, hawking cheap candy, T-shirts, and duffel bags; forever grounded, while everyone else got to fly away.

Ever since she had been a little girl, Mya had dreamed of seeing the rest of the world outside Myanmar. But her family was poor, and life was expensive in Yangon. So, she had dropped out of school at thirteen, and been working to help her family ever since.

The seventeen-year-old had lucked into this job four months ago through one of her friends. She was supposed to work there, but preferred to roam the streets with her boyfriend instead. When she heard of the girl's problem, Mya had offered to work in her place.

The next day, she had gone to the airport with her black hair pulled back in a tight ponytail, wearing her best skirt and blouse. With her heart in her throat, she reported in at the beginning of her shift, waiting to be thrown out. But the manager's face hadn't even changed expression when she said she was the new girl. He had just given her an hour's instruction on how to open and close the kiosk and use the register, and left her for the first of many eleven-hour shifts.

Mya had quickly mastered the process of selling the products. But once that obstacle had been conquered, she soon realized that this job was worse than hell for her. It wasn't so much the long hours, boredom, or standing on her feet all day. It was having to watch people coming and going every single day. Knowing that each one was coming from or going to something, moving forward, living their lives. And every day, all she could do was watch them while she remained here, trapped.

What made her feel even worse was that the pittance she brought in was really helping her family. They had just managed to scrape together enough to move out of their leaking, rotting apartment deep in the slums to the edge of it. They had found a relatively clean, quiet place that welcomed families without asking too many questions. If she were to lose or quit her job, it would send her mother, father, and two younger brothers right back into the filthy, decaying neighborhood they had just escaped. So she worked and watched the people going by every day.

At first, the airport had been exciting and strange, with so many different kinds of people passing by. Mya had even hoped that some rich businessman might see her and sweep her off her feet, maybe even marry her and take her away to exotic lands. Or maybe a talent scout or modeling agent would spot her and offer to represent her while she became a model or a pop star. But after a few weeks on the job, she realized that to the thousands of travelers passing by her booth, she was only slightly more visible than the cleaning crew. It had gotten so bad that she barely acknowledged the customers anymore, just rang up their purchases, made change, handed them the bagged items, and watched as they walked off.

She also thought she had seen everything there was to see go by her in the airport. But when a young man carrying a double-armload of quadruple-large T-shirts in a variety of neon pink, green, and yellow, and at least thirty of their largest duffle bags staggered up to the desk, her eyebrows raised in surprise. "Can I—help you?"

The bearer of the majority of her stock dumped all of it on the counter and flashed her a bright smile. "Yes, I'll take all of it, please. And I'm afraid I'm in a hurry, so I'll just pack the shirts into the bags, if you don't mind."

Mya glanced up at him and saw a handsome Nepalese man, maybe around thirty years old, looking back at her. "All right."

She began scanning the tags of the bags through the OCR reader on the cash register, hoping he wouldn't notice the small price discrepancy between what was on the tag of each bag, and what each one was actually ringing up as. She had figured out how to short-change the register every few transactions, yet make it appear as though the sales were still being made properly. Of course, she was pocketing the difference. On the rare chance a customer complained, she would claim it was a pricing error and give them the lower amount.

While she rang up his purchases, Mya kept stealing glances at the man, who was efficiently packing the shirts into several of the duffels. "Can I ask you a question?"

"Sure."

"Why are you getting all of these? I mean, they're not even in your size."

Her customer looked up at her and smiled again. "I'm surprised you'd even care."

"I'm just curious, that's all. Will you resell them elsewhere?" Mya didn't know why, but she wanted to keep talking to this man.

He shook his head. "No, these are actually going to be used to save your country from itself."

She cocked her head as she finished ringing up the last of the shirts. "What's that supposed to mean?"

He waved a hand at her. "Never mind, it's not important. Besides, you'll probably find out later today anyway."

"Oh. Okay." She gave him the total, and he handed over a thick wad of kyat, much more than was necessary.

"Keep the change. I don't imagine that you make a lot doing this."

"You'd be right." Mya put the correct total in the register and pocketed the rest. "Thank you, and good luck with whatever you are doing."

He stared at her for a moment, then nodded. "Thank you. And please, do not take the gift your country is about to receive lightly. Freedom is always something to be prized."

"Yes, but only if you know what it is," she replied without thinking.

He nodded. "I hope someday that you do." Gathering up the loaded duffel bags, he disappeared into the crowd.

Mya watched him go, her feeling that she somehow had to get out of this dead-end job suddenly reinforced, although she could not have said why.

"All right, everyone wrap your weapons!"

The flight from Mandalay to Yangon had taken about an hour, but getting into the city was proving much more difficult. First, they'd had to circle the much-busier Yangon Airport for a half-hour while waiting for a landing window to open up. Once they were finally on the ground, Mike had Jace dispatch several men into the terminal to buy concealing materials for their rifles, in order to prevent a panic in the streets. He figured there would be enough once the fighting started, no need to start it early.

Finally, everything had been prepared, and the men were moving out. Himal had suggested renting a couple of private buses to get the men into the heart of the city, and Mike had agreed. The buses had been fairly easy to procure, with large handfuls of kyat smoothing the way. Unfortunately, the congested traffic in the city proper had slowed them to a snail's pace, even on the fifty-meter-wide streets, the cars, trucks, and buses all came together in an interminable snarl, miring them in a thick cloud of exhaust. After forty-five minutes of snail's-pace progress, they were still almost a mile from the City Hall building. The only good thing was that everyone had had plenty of time to conceal their rifles in the duffel bags or wrap them in the colorful T-shirts.

"I thought you guys had a lot of street vendors here?" Jace asked as he looked out through the front window.

"We did, but the government has been cracking down on them

more and more lately, restricting their hours of operation and limiting where they can sell things," Himal replied.

"So much for one of our insertion ideas," Mike said. They had discussed buying outright any carts or food stands to use as cover to get close to the City Hall, but that option was gone, since there was no one to buy the carts from.

"All right, we have to get there faster than this. Vanner, plot me the best route to the Hall by foot." Mike said as he got on his radio. "All teams, this is the Kildar. We are going the rest of the way on foot. Unass from your bus and follow my lead."

He turned to Oleg, who was sitting behind the driver, a pair of crutches resting beside him, and a dark glower on his face. "I wish we could have found a way to have you come with us, Oleg."

The Keldara accepted his fate with a stolid nod. "I understand. Will remain here to make sure he—" he jerked his head at the driver, "—does not decide to leave early."

"Affirmative." Mike and Jace both stood to address the thirty men in his bus. "Everyone, we are getting off now and heading to the target on foot. Let's move out!"

Leading the way, he pulled the door lever over the incensed protests of the driver. Stuffing another handful of kyat into the man's hand, Mike hit the street, the men piling out behind him. "How far away are we, Patrick?"

"Okay, you've just hit Phone Gyee Street. Follow it south for 550 meters, then turn left onto Maha Bandoola Road. Follow that for 1.4 kilometers, take the first exit onto Sule Pagoda Road, and the City Hall will be on your right."

"Got that, Himal?" At the Gurkha's nod, Mike waved the group forward. "Let's go!"

As they trotted through the crowds, Vanel looked around at the wide thoroughfare filled with traffic, cars, trucks, and buses, all teeming with innocents. While he knew the Kildar and team leaders planned their operations carefully to avoid civilian casualties, this time there might not be a choice once the bullets started flying.

They kept moving as best as they could through the mix of locals and tourists, clearing a path while trying to stay as inconspicuous as possible. In a few minutes, the *pyatthat*, or traditional tiered roofs of Yangon City Hall came into view.

The sandstone-colored building had been designed by Burmese architect U Tin and completed in 1936. At the time, it was considered an excellent example of blending traditional and modern architecture into a pleasing whole. The building had been the site of many political demonstrations throughout the last several decades. These included a rally by the People's Peace Committee in 1964, which brought more than 200,000 people together before it was dispersed by the Socialist regime led by General Ne Win. Recently bombings had supplanted demonstrations, with the building coming under attack three times in the last ten years alone.

As they rounded the corner onto Sule Pagoda Road, Vanel caught sight of a flurry of activity ahead. Several BTR-3U eight-wheeled armored personnel carriers escorting a half-dozen troop transports had assumed defensive positions on the road in front of the City Hall. The doors opened on the sides of the APCs, and soldiers began exiting, joining the men streaming out from the back of the troop trucks.

"Sniper teams, disperse! Find the highest ground you can and take your positions!" Himal translated for Mike. "All other teams, move forward!"

Cars were beginning to jam up behind the blocked road. Unable to see what was stopping traffic, the confused drivers in the waves behind the first vehicles furiously honked their horns. While the noise was useful for sowing confusion and concealing their approach, it also made it hard for the various teams to communicate. Although Mike and Himal did their best to keep the teams together, they began to spread out as they approached the growing mass of soldiers that were about to move on City Hall.

Of greatest concern to Vanel were the 7.62 machine guns on the BTR-3Us, which could quickly scythe through the smaller force in a few seconds. He resolved to keep an eye on them, and go at them the moment they started turning toward the Kildar and his motley crew. What exactly he was going to do once he reached them would be decided once he got there.

Jace had also noticed the weapons on the APCs, and was about to ask Mike what, if anything, they should do about them when about ten Gurkhas abruptly turned left and began moving toward the far side of the vehicles through the crowd of people that had started to gather near them.

Guess he's got that handled, Jace thought. By now the main force of insurgents was almost on the group of soldiers. The enemy force, perhaps two hundred strong, had organized itself in the road outside City Hall and was about to move up to the main entrance. Expecting no resistance, the soldiers hadn't even unslung their rifles yet. The commanding officer, a colonel, walked to the front of the line, and had just raised his arm to give the command to move forward when another voice shouted from the side of the street.

"All soldiers of the Myanmar Army, lay down your weapons and place your hands above your heads!"

The order was accompanied by the sight of sixty men popping out of the crowd and pointing automatic weapons at the assembled soldiers. The crowd behind them, seeing rifles appear, began to scatter, their shouts and screams rising above the noise of the idling engines and the confused bellow of the general. The turret of the nearest BTR-3U swung over to point at the interlopers as the general yelled for the others to surrender to the soldiers immediately.

Himal repeated the order, making the soldiers, with their rifles still on their shoulders, look at the determined, well-armed force on their left, and the colonel and their armored vehicles flanking them.

Toward the back of the assembled soldiers, Myanmar Army Lance Corporal Sanda stared at the men who had come out of nowhere and were now aiming rifles at him and his fellow soldiers.

This was not how it was supposed to happen!

His commanding general had told him and the rest of his men that only they could help stop the insidious spread of antination-alist forces that were conspiring to take over the government under their so-called "democratic" demands. Sanda had believed this, much as he had believed everything any military man had told him, beginning with his own father, a second lieutenant in the army.

Sanda had been perfectly schooled in the might and right of the military since he was a toddler. It had been only natural that he follow in his father's footsteps and join the army as soon as he came of age. In many ways, he was the perfect military candidate; strong, relatively unthinking, and blindly obedient to the idea of the military state.

With all that in mind, there was no doubt that he would resist any enemies that tried to stop their progress toward bringing the nation back under its rightful rulers. He did not even need an order to do what he knew was so obviously right.

Using the cover of his fellow soldiers, Sanda unslung his weapon, chambered a round, and stepped out to aim at the attackers. He was just about to squeeze the trigger when—

Upon spotting one of the soldiers pointing his rifle at them, a Gurkha killed him with a single shot.

That was when the 7.62mm machine gun on the nearest APC opened up, and all hell broke loose.

Of all the groups, the Myanmar soldiers were caught in the worst position possible. Out in the open, with the nearest cover several meters away. More than a third of them went down in the initial volley from the combined force of Keldara and Gurkha soldiers. The rest scrambled for whatever cover they could find, some running back to the nearest BTR-3U, others diving behind the dead bodies of their former compatriots. The range was so short that almost all of the victims of the first volley had been killed outright.

Even with the chattering machine gun, the Keldara and Gurkhas had a much easier time falling back to cover. The cars littering the road made good, if not perfect, barriers, depending on the type of round the Burmese were using; even the engine block wouldn't provide sufficient cover if they had gotten their hands on 7.62mm NATO rounds. Fortunately, with the APCs lined up in a row, there wasn't any way for more than the turrets on the first two vehicles to draw a bead on the attackers.

Most of the nearest drivers stuck between the two groups of fighting men either got out of their cars and ran like hell or hunkered down in their vehicles, hoping their cars would protect them.

Against the 7.62mm machine gun, the runners were doomed, with the rounds punching through them like a hot knife through butter. Those who stayed put were better protected, as the gunner was primarily focusing on moving targets, not stationary vehicles.

The Keldara and Gurkhas had already been going for cover when the turret started to move. The majority of them had ended up behind the cars as rounds whizzed by, shattering windows, flattening tires, and punching holes in hoods and fenders.

A few, including Vanel, had even swept forward. They had ended up under the nearest APC's slanted front end, which provided plenty of cover from the turret weapons as well as protection from the men in the road. Even the couple of army men who came around the corner of the tall vehicle were quickly shot and killed.

Now all Vanel had to do was come up with a plan to take out that machine gun . . .

Phen sat in the driver's seat of his idling bus and cursed his luck. Even with the large payment the foreigners had given him, he could be making even more money on a run back to the airport. Times were still tight, and if he wasn't moving, he wasn't earning. It had taken him four years of bribery and working his fingers to the bone to secure a bus driver job, and he wasn't about to lose it because some damn fools were going to keep him from working.

Glancing in his wide rear-view mirror at the huge, one-legged man with bright white hair sitting behind him, Phen repressed a shudder. He had a pretty good idea of why the big man had been left behind—beside his missing leg, of course.

The *pop-pop-pop* of gunfire sounded in the distance, making the bus driver sit up in his seat and crane his neck to try to get a look at what was going on. Sensing a shadow fall over him, he looked up to see the white-haired man towering over him. Staring at Phen, he pointed in the direction of the firefight just as several bursts from what sounded like a machine gun echoed all around them.

"*Lee sok pay!*" the driver exclaimed. "Suck my dick—I'll be damned if I'm driving toward that—"

The huge man didn't give any sign that he understood what Phen was saying. He just reached out and grabbed the collar of his shirt with one massive hand. Hauling the shouting, smaller man out of his seat, he opened the door, and tossed him out onto the road.

Phen landed on his ass, scraping skin from his palms as he tried to break his fall. He looked up at the giant, who was wedging himself behind the wheel with one of his crutches poised to work the clutch. As Phen scrambled to his feet, the white-haired man reached over to close the door.

With a grinding of gears, the bus lurched left. Smacking into a small truck, it shoved it out of the way as the man drove Phen's prized bus onto the sidewalk.

Vanel was now crouched with Marko and a pair of Gurkhas in the shadow of the BTR-3U's angled snout. While the APC didn't seem to be going anywhere, its chattering machine gun kept spitting rounds and pinning down the Kildar's forces. Along with the screams of the wounded, the loud bursts, along with the return fire, made it almost impossible to talk.

Suddenly they were faced with a trio of Myanmar soldiers who were trying to take cover in the same space Vanel and his teammates occupied. Three short bursts from the Gurkhas and Keldara made quick work of the retreating soldiers. As the bodies fell, the smoke grenades on their web gear gave Vanel an idea.

Exchanging his standard magazine for AP rounds, he grabbed three grenades and shouted to Marko, "Boost me!" while pointing up. With a puzzled look on his face, Marko did just that.

Bracing his HK 416C in the crook of his arm, Vanel fired a short burst into the APC's front viewport, punching a hole in the bullet-resistant glass. Before the crew could return fire, he pulled the pins on two of the grenades and tossed them inside. He followed both with a few more shots to make sure no one tried to throw one back out. Dark gray smoke immediately began pluming from the open hole, and coughing and panicked shouts could be heard inside.

"Down!" he said to Marko, who set him back on the ground. Vanel ran around to the right side of the vehicle in time to see the first crewmember climb out of the side hatch, coughing and wiping at his eyes. Vanel clubbed him with the butt of his rifle the moment his feet hit the pavement. By the time the second crewman had come out, Marko and one of the other Gurkhas had joined him, and they captured the rest of the crew as they stumbled out.

Grabbing another trio of smoke grenades, Vanel pointed at the next APC, which was one of the ones firing its machine gun. He was heading toward it, assault carbine at the ready, when a Myanmar soldier came appeared around the back corner of the one they had just disabled.

Vanel and the private both fired at the same moment. The Keldara's target fell back, blood bursting from his chest as his rifle fired into the sky.

Vanel felt something punch him in the stomach, beneath his body armor, and suddenly he found himself sitting on the ground, feeling lightheaded and numb around his waist. He fell backward as his hand went to his stomach and came away bloody.

"Vanel! What happen—" Marko said as he cleared the corner

and crouched by his teammate's side. Then he looked back toward their forces and yelled, "MEDIC!"

Beads of sweat dotted Oleg's forehead as he wrestled with the balky bus. The vehicle had been indifferently maintained, and it showed in the stiff clutch and loose transmission. Oleg had to jam the crutch down on the clutch pedal while letting up on the gas as he forced the bus into second gear. At the same time, he leaned hard on the horn to clear the sidewalk of anyone either deaf or stupid enough to still be in the area.

With a resigned groan, the bus began picking up speed. Oleg smashed the clutch down again and forced the stick shift into third gear, making the thirty-year-old vehicle lurch up to maybe forty miles an hour.

Judging by the louder gunfire, he was getting closer. Now he just needed a bit of the All Father's luck to get him near enough to his target to make a difference.

"No go, Mike! We are fucking pinned!" Adams shouted after almost getting his ass shot off during a brief recon to see if they could somehow flank the machine gun that was keeping them under cover. "What we could really use right now is some air support!"

"What about the snipers?" Mike yelled back.

"Watch!" Jace shouted. The three men peeked around the corner of their battered cover to see a series of sparks flash off the top armor of the second APC. "They don't have anything powerful enough to penetrate it!"

The main force of soldiers had been killed, driven to cover, or scattered by the initial attack, but the APC machine guns were causing a huge problem. Every time anyone showed even a flash of movement, the guns zeroed in and tried to shoot through their cover to get the man behind it. Three cars were on fire from rounds piercing the engines and gas tanks, and it was only luck that none of them had exploded yet.

Mike, Adams, and Jace were hunkered down about twenty meters from the second APC, which was firing at anything that moved. "We have to disable that weapon!"

"Short of getting in the first one and unloading on the one behind it, we don't have a chance in hell of taking it out!" Adams shouted, just before his eyes widened as he looked beyond Mike's shoulder. "What the hell—?"

Mike and Jace both turned to see the bus they'd been riding in barreling toward the stopped military convoy, picking up speed. "No way that's the driver, which means—" Jace began.

"—Oleg's doing a fucking suicide run!" Mike finished.

But the moment the bus lined up on the second vehicle, the door flew open and a large body tumbled out. He rolled over and over on the road as both of the turrets traversed to take out this new threat. The 7.62s shattered the windshield and began walking rounds across its front grille. But before the 30mm main gun could begin firing, the bus slammed into the side of the APC, right where the turret was—just as it shot its first shell.

Detonating right outside the muzzle, the blast rushed back down the bore as the second shell came out, making it detonate early as well. The barrel was next to go, rocking the turret as it exploded. Smoke started pouring out of the vehicle, and the side hatch flew open as the crew evacuated.

"We just got our distraction. Move in now!" Mike ran around the front of the destroyed car he'd been hiding behind and headed for the first APC. Adams and Jace followed right behind him. Seeing their leaders sweeping forward, the rest of the warriors followed, covering the three men as they reached the first BTR-3U.

Gray smoke was still billowing out of the viewport and open side hatch. Mike spotted a Keldara medic working on one of their downed men. He ran over to find Vanel lying in a spreading pool of blood. "What's the situation?"

"Gut-shot, bleeding badly. I've got him stabilized, but we have to get him to a hospital right now!" the medic shouted back.

"Commandeer a car and make it happen!" Mike shouted as

he pulled out a handkerchief and doused it in water from his canteen. "Adams, Jace, Himal, follow me!"

Wrapping the cloth around his head, Mike took a deep breath and held it as he climbed into the smoke-filled interior of the APC. His vision was cut to nothing, and he crouched on the floor and crawled forward, listening for the hiss of the grenade. It sounded like it was coming from the forward compartment, so he headed that way, arm outstretched to ward off any obstacles. Along the way, he was starting to think this might have been a really bad idea...

The hissing was louder in here, and Mike unwrapped the bandanna from his head and wrapped it around his hand. His lungs were just starting to feel tight as he groped along the floor until his hand contacted round, hot metal.

"Got one!" Hoping he remembered where the broken viewport was, he wrapped the grenade in the wet handkerchief and stood up, remaining bent over. Groping along the front until he felt a breeze from outside, Mike shoved the grenade out just as his hands started to blister from the heat. The volume of smoke lessened, but it was still thick in here. Smothering a cough, Mike put his face to the window and sucked in a relatively clean breath of air, then went back after the second grenade.

"I've got the other! Move move move!" Adams said. Mike sat in the driver's seat as the master chief lunged past him and tossed the second grenade out the window. The smoke still hung over everything, but Mike slapped the air conditioning switches on the master control panel, and fans began blowing the smoke away from the driver's compartment.

"Someone get on the thirty millimeter!" Mike said as he revved the engine. Sirens could be heard in the distance. "We've got to take out the other APCs and unass before reinforcements arrive!"

"Thirty mike-mike is locked and loaded!" Jace called from the turret.

"Seven point six-two ready to rock and roll!" Adams called from the machine gun.

"Fire at will!" Mike said, putting the twenty-ton vehicle into gear and pulling around in a huge U-turn, either shoving cars out of the way or running them over.

With the second APC disabled, the commander of the third BTR-3U thought the lead vehicle was repositioning itself to press the attack against the enemy soldiers on the ground. He couldn't have been more wrong.

As soon as they had a line of sight on the enemy vehicle, Jace and Adams opened up on it with both guns while also laying down a thick cloud of smoke from the six 81mm smoke dispensers. The 30mm rounds chewed through the front of the target APC, shredding the driver. The rounds continued into its turret, finding the ammo and cooking it off.

Faced with the confusion of one of their own vehicles attacking them, the other 8x8s tried to face it down, but Mike and his crew weaved among them and the huge smoke cloud like a huge, camouflaged ghost, there one moment, and gone the next. Using the dense haze as cover, Mike swung around to the rear and attacked the rear APC next, disabling its tires and its turret. Soon smoke and soldiers were pouring out of it in equal measure.

The last APC pulled away from its dead brethren and took off down the road, smashing through cars in its way as it cleared a path away from the chaos.

"All right, we are done here," Mike said as they evacuated the APC. "Jace, Himal, make sure everyone gets the hell out. Master Chief, you're with me. We've got a team leader to recover."

CHAPTER TWENTY-THREE

Ten hours later, Vanel awoke in a hospital bed, surrounded by beeping machines. There was an IV attached to his arm, and a cool bag was strapped to his thigh as well.

Colonel Nielson stood at his bedside, along with Daria and Xatia. Vanel's head was fuzzy and his abdomen ached dully. The Keldara tried to speak, but all that came out of his dry mouth was a wheeze. He did manage, however, to raise his hand in salute to his superior officer.

Nielson snapped off a crisp salute in return. "At ease, Vanel—you just came out of surgery an hour ago. How about some water?"

Even as Nielson spoke, Xatia was there, offering Vanel a sweating bottle with a straw in it. He drained half of it before she removed it. "Good, but would prefer... beer instead."

"That'll have to do for now. You have to give your intestines time to heal first," the colonel said.

"What... what happened? Last I remember I was trying to reach... second APC—"

"You did fine, Vanel. You were shot through the lower intestine, with the bullet grazing your colon before exiting your lower back. You were fortunate, an inch more to the left, and it would have hit your spine. Not a bad place to get shot, all things considered, although it does hurt like hell. Our medic stabilized you and got you here to Witoriya General Hospital, where they operated for the past six hours to patch up your insides. You're missing about three feet of small intestine, but that's a small price to pay, considering what could have happened. As soon as you can be moved, we'll be transferring you to a hospital in Singapore to complete your recuperation."

Vanel nodded. "Was the coup stopped?"

Nielson smiled. "Yes, Mike, Adams, and the rest stopped the plotters from accomplishing their goal. We lost a few men, but overall the mission was a complete success. Marko told us what you'd done during the op. They couldn't have completed the mission without your help. Now you rest up," The XO leaned close to Vanel's ear. "We'll see how you're doing in the morning and whether you can be transferred to a *real* hospital."

"Yes, sir. Thank you, sir." Vanel sucked in a breath, despite how it made his stomach flare with pain, and slumped on his pillow.

"Ladies, we should let Vanel get some sleep," Nielson said.

"Sir...may I have a moment with Xatia, please?" Vanel asked.

An odd look passed between the Keldara XO and the two young women, then Nielson nodded. "Yes, but keep it brief. Daria, let's go make sure our boy gets the care he needs." The two walked out of the room, leaving Vanel alone with the petite blonde.

"Xatia, I—" Vanel began, but was stopped by her finger on his lips. With an effort, he moved his head aside. "No, I have to... say this... After almost dying today, it has given me the courage to...declare my feelings for you. I—I love you...and I want to marry you."

She smiled, a cute dimple appearing in one cheek. "Oh, Vanel... I know that you love me. I always have."

"You...do?"

She leaned over and patted his cheek. "I've known ever since you first looked at me, back when we were children. There was never going to be another boy for me, not after I saw you. When you are better, and we are back in our homeland, we will begin the discussion between our two families regarding the bride-price."

Vanel's already dizzy head was spinning even faster now. "You already knew? But...but...what about your mother?"

Xatia smiled. "It is true, your family will have to bargain hard to best Mother Mahona. I believe that she is aware of how I feel—not that that will make a huge difference, I think. But I believe they will eventually come to terms." With a quick glance at the door, Xatia leaned over and kissed Vanel on the forehead. "You should rest now. I will see you in the morning."

"Okay..." Exhausted yet exhilarated, Vanel felt sleep begin to claim him. However, he did have one more question. "Xatia?"

She turned at the door. "Yes, my love?"

"Where is the Kildar and everybody else?"

She smiled again, this one as cold and hard as her previous one had been warm and soft. "They are just taking care of one last piece of business."

Three hundred and thirty miles away, and several miles out to sea, General Cong's superyacht, lit up like a Carnival cruise ship, floated peacefully in the Bay of Bengal.

Two miles due south, with their lights dimmed and running as quietly as they could, Mike took one last look at the boat through his night-vision binoculars, then pulled his mask down over his face. "All teams, move out."

Slipping into the water, he made sure his rebreather readout was in the green, then grabbed the handles of his matte-gray Seabob Cayago F7 water scooter and hit the throttle, taking off at almost ten miles per hour on the surface. Nearly silent and practically invisible on the water, with a one-hour operation time, the scooters were the perfect insertion vehicle for this mission.

Behind him were Adams, Jace, and the entire Inara team, except for Vanel. Instead, they had included a very special addition to tonight's strike force.

Five hundred yards from the *Big Fish*, Mike slipped ten meters beneath the surface. When submerged, the F7 slowed to a very decent 8.7 miles per hour. Mike kept the throttle on maximum as he made minor adjustments to his course.

Nine minutes later, he slowed to a crawl and ascended just enough so he could just see out of the water. His navigation had been dead-on—the stern of Cong's yacht was twenty meters ahead.

"Firefly, this is Mal."

"This is Firefly, go Mal."

"Is Blue Hand in position yet?"

"Affirmative, and waiting on your word."

"Begin insertion on my mark. Blue Hand may begin acquisition and termination immediately afterward. Three ... two ... one ... mark."

One thousand yards south, Lasko sat on the roof of an Ocean Master 336 Sport Cabin fishing boat they had found for sale in Yangon. Raising him nine feet above the water, it was the perfect platform for the Keldara sniper to do what he did best.

Being a big fan of the "if it is not broke, do not fix it" rule, he was using the M110 again, with the Leopold scope rigged for night vision. The difference this time was in his ammunition. Lasko had loaded twenty rounds of 7.62 NATO Precision Bonded Subsonic bullets from Engel Balistic Research, out of Smithville, Texas. When the Kildar and he had tested various subsonic rounds to find the one that offered the best range and penetration versus the lower velocity, the PBS rounds had won hands-down, able to penetrate eighteen inches of ballistic gelatin at one hundred yards. The effects on similar targets at longer ranges were just as devastating, and in the rifle of a sniper as good as Lasko, they defined the term "whispering death."

When he got the go signal from Firefly, Lasko fired two shots. He compensated high on the first one, due for the tendency of the cold rifle barrel to sap energy from the first round out. However, the second shot left the barrel at its standard 1,090 feet per second.

On the yacht, the pair of guards at the rear of the boat both crumpled to the deck, their lifeblood leaking out of the new holes in their hearts. Less than five seconds later, a neoprene grappling hook arced up onto the railing and the Kildar, followed by the Inara members, began climbing aboard.

By that time, Lasko had moved on to the bow of the boat. Caressing the trigger twice more, he dropped the front pair of guards in their tracks. He kept his eye to the scope, looking for more targets as the invasion team swarmed aboard.

. . . Four-Mississippi, five-Mississippi, six-Mississippi . . .

While removing his face mask and positioning his night-vision goggles on his forehead, Mike kept a silent count going in his head as the team members came aboard. Their monitoring of the guard rotation on Cong's ship gave them a three-minute window between check-ins. They had to get on board and take out as many of the guards as possible in the next one hundred seventy seconds.

With the Inara team aboard and spread out to cover the entire stern of the yacht, Mike checked on the last team member coming aboard. Hauling himself up hand over hand, Oleg reached the railing and swung himself over with the peculiar grace of the very large man. He was wearing his back-up leg, but the fire in his eyes as he swept the aft quarter of the boat with his suppressed 416C made it very clear what he was after tonight.

"Mal, this is Firefly. Four tangos confirmed down, repeat four down, two front, two rear."

Fifteen-Mississippi . . . "Roger that, sweeping forward." Mike motioned for the two Inara squads to sweep forward, one going up the starboard side, the other going up the port side.

When they reached the door leading below, a three-man team split off and began moving to the engine room. The plan was very similar to how they had taken the pirate's freighter. However, they were expecting much heavier and more organized resistance this time. Therefore, it was a surprise when the trio reached the engine room with relative ease, only having to take out one more bodyguard and the three crewmembers in the room itself, whom they captured rather than killed.

Twenty-eight seconds later, Mike heard: "Mal, this is Inara Leader, we are ready to cut power."

Here's where it gets tricky, Mike thought as he prepared to bring his goggles down. "Go."

The yacht was instantly plunged into darkness. With the FLIR secure over his face, Mike led Oleg, Adams, and Jace along the starboard side of the boat until they reached the door leading to the main salon floor. Remembering the blueprints they had gained by hacking the shipbuilder's computers, he led his team below, heading for Cong's personal quarters.

From the moment she had entered the SUV as Cong's prisoner, Soon Yi had entered a nightmarish world of pain and degradation. In the past forty-eight hours, she had endured tortures that would have broken many men.

General Cong had turned out to be a rarified sadist of the highest caliber, using physical and sexual abuse the likes of which even she had never even heard of before. He had installed her in a torture room that he had built in a space adjacent to the master bedroom suite. Electrocution, gang rape, genital mutilation, severe bondage; the list went on and on, until the entire room reeked of sweat, blood, and burned flesh.

She had thought she could withstand it.

She had been wrong.

If she had had any idea of what was going to happen to her, she would have used the poisoned needles hidden in her slippers to kill the general. But those had been taken from her, along with every other stitch of clothing, the moment she had set foot on the yacht.

Cong had broken her after twenty hours of continuous torment, dosing her and himself with speed to keep them both awake. He would also snort lines of cocaine from time to time, alternating that with swigging glasses of chilled Dom Perignon champagne. When she passed out from the continuous abuse, he would dump ice-cold water on her to awaken her again.

Currently, she was suspended upside-down, with her bloody, swollen ankles chained to a rod that kept her legs spread-eagled. Cong had taken great pleasure in informing her that this technique was called "hip-splitting," and after several hours in the device, she knew why. Her entire body from the waist down had been in unrelenting agony for hours until her legs had gone numb. During this time she had been repeatedly sodomized in both her vagina and her anus. Cong had poured hot pepper oil on her genitals, then rammed the end of a police baton into her. After that, he would insert ice cubes into her vagina and leave them there until they had melted, making her shake uncontrollably with the cold and pain.

Clamps had been attached to her nipples, and electric shocks had been administered as well. Cong also delighted in using a variety of whips, including a cat-o-nine-tails with small barbs woven into the leather. He had taken great joy in whipping the palms of her hands and soles of her feet until they were reduced to skinless, bloody pieces of meat.

As hard as she had tried not to, Soon Yi had told him everything she knew; the fact that she was an intelligence agent, that she had been tracking the computer boards, even everything she knew about the mercenaries he had hired. The information had flowed out of her in an endless babble as she offered up anything to try to stop him from hurting her any more. But the pain just kept coming, until she was nearly insensate.

He had finally wound down, and had spent the last thirty minutes walking around her. Occasionally he would slap her lightly with the scourge before sitting on a metal chair that was bolted to the floor in front of her. In the dark recesses of her mind, Soon Yi was terrified that he would begin whipping her face, then kill her.

Dimly, the part of her that was still an agent noted an empty champagne bottle on the floor, near her bloody hands. But she was too cowed to try to reach for it, not with him so close. If she failed, he would certainly kill her.

And would that be so bad now? she asked herself. No one was coming to rescue her. No one even knew where she was at the moment. Cong had stripped her of every scrap of clothing, and the implant didn't have a long enough range without the antenna in her dress.

No, she thought just as strongly. *If I am to die, I will take him with me.* That thought was the only one that sustained her through the hours that had followed.

Suddenly Cong stood again, and Soon Yi tried not to react as he approached her. But when he was just a step away, the lights went out.

"What the fuck?" He muttered in the sudden darkness before stomping off toward the door.

It was now or never.

Stretching out her abused muscles, Soon Yi reached for the champagne bottle with her maimed hands. She felt the slick glass slip under her questing, bloody fingers, and bit back a sob as she tried to keep it from rolling away. Her hips, thighs, and chest felt like they were going to shatter under the pressure. Still she reached out with every remaining bit of strength she had, the cool glass bottle so close to her, yet still so far.

Just one more inch . . .

With Mike in the lead, the four men swept through the lower deck of the ship like a bullet-spraying whirlwind. With their silenced weapons, body armor, and night vision giving them an almost unassailable tactical advantage, they mowed down a half-dozen of the general's guards before they even knew what had hit them.

The only snag had come when one of the men had managed to shine a flashlight down the corridor, nearly blinding Mike and Adams. A quick three-round burst had taken him out and shattered the flashlight too. From that point on they had been careful to approach corners and doorways cautiously, in case someone else had gotten that bright idea.

Sporadic gunfire could be heard elsewhere in the ship, but the Kildar and his team were focused on their specific target. Turning down one more corridor, they leap-frogged toward the door at the end of the hallway. Cong's personal bedroom.

The door was locked, but Mike fixed that by putting two three-round bursts through the lock. With Jace flattened on the wall to his right and Adams on the left, he slid the pocket door open and covered the right flank. Mike stepped into the room and moved right, with Jace taking the left side and Adams going up the middle.

The room was empty, except for another door beside the bed that was also closed. This one, however, was slightly ajar, and when Mike stood to one side and touched it, two shots rang out and bullet holes appeared in the teak wood.

"Son of a bitch is ruining my boat," Mike muttered.

"Anyone comes in here and they die!" Cong shouted from inside. "I have an agent from the Ministry of Security in here as my hostage! She will die first if anyone comes inside!"

Jace translated that, adding, "He sounds unhinged, like he's been up for a while. If he does have Soon Yi in there as a hostage, he'll try to bargain his way out."

"Fuck, I don't have time for that. Keep him talking." Mike went around the bed and up to the wall separating the two rooms.

Meanwhile, Jace took his position near the door. "All right, just calm down, and no one else has to get hurt. What do you want?"

"No one comes in or the bitch dies! I want my cigarette boat prepared, and all of my gems put aboard. Then, I will take this bitch and cast—"

That was as far as he had gotten before Mike put two bursts through the wall, aiming for where he thought the general was standing.

Soon Yi had just gotten her fingers around the bottle neck when Cong fired twice and scurried back to stand near her, shouting at the intruders in his bedroom as he did so.

By now her eyes had adjusted somewhat to the darkness, and she could sense exactly where he was standing. The chair was also nearby, and she rallied her battered, exhausted body for one more try.

As someone—she thought it might be Jace—shouted from outside, Cong began angrily shouting back. Suddenly she heard the sound of cloth ripping, and six holes appeared in the far wall, the bullets making them flying high and smacking into the other wall of the torture room.

However, the shots had distracted Cong just long enough. As he twisted and returned fire, Soon put everything she had into smashing the champagne bottle against the leg of the metal chair. The glass shattered at the blow, leaving her with the neck and a jagged ring of sharp glass at the end. She had been terrified that the entire bottle would smash to pieces, but fortunately that hadn't happened.

Shouting and shooting wildly, Cong hadn't even heard the bottle break. Sucking in a deep breath, she curled her upper body up and stabbed at where she thought his crotch was, twisting as hard as she could with her mauled hand.

The high, piercing scream he let out told her she must have gotten pretty close.

When Cong had started returning fire, everyone in the outer room had ducked for cover. Then they all heard a loud shriek of someone in mortal agony.

"Go!" Mike said.

Jace shoved the door open and leaped inside, covering the right side of the room. Adams was right behind him, going left. Mike went up the middle, and Oleg held the doorway.

When he reached the corner, Jace shouted, "Clear!" and turned toward the center of the room. The stink had hit him right before he saw what had been done to Soon Yi. "Jesus Christ..."

"Get her down *now!*" Mike stood over the general, who was sobbing as he clutched both hands over his privates. "The general is cleared."

Jace had slung his weapon and was unshackling Soon Yi from

the restraints. "Sorry about this," he said as he ran an arm around her back and supported her while releasing the last shackle. He took her to the bed outside and wrapped her in the silk comforter.

"Oleg, bring me a sheet from the other room. No sense in getting blood all over my floor," Mike said.

The big man grabbed a burgundy silk sheet from the bed and stepped into the torture chamber. Moments later, he reappeared with Mike. Both of them were dragging the Chinese general, who was wrapped in the sheet, out onto the floor. Mike looked over at Jace and Soon Yi as they headed to the bedroom entrance. "Bring her, she will want to see this."

Jace picked up the Chinese woman and followed them. She trembled in his embrace, and he didn't blame her—right now, he guessed the last thing she wanted to be near was any man.

Cong had gotten his wits about him on the way to the aft deck, and was pleading in Cantonese to anyone who would listen. "What the fuck is he saying?" Mike asked.

"He says he can make us all rich beyond anything we could imagine if we just let him live. This boat, the gems, all of it is ours if we let him go in the smaller boat."

Mike's smile was a wolf's-head grin. "Is that so? Oleg—" He motioned at the huge Keldara, who stepped over and picked the smaller man up by his neck. He walked to the stern of the yacht and held the general over the water, letting blood drops from his injured genitals drip down his legs and into the water.

Cong wheezed and grabbed at Oleg's huge fingers, trying to pry them away from his throat. He might as well have tried to bend steel.

"Here is my answer. There's nothing he can offer me that I have not already taken from him. His boat is mine. His guns are mine. His gems are mine."

Mike got up and leaned out so that his face was only inches away from the other man's. "I told you to enjoy this while you could, you son of a bitch, because you would be seeing me again. And now you have."

He nodded at Oleg, who slowly tightened his grip around Cong's throat. The Chinese man tried to scream, but the sound was choked off as the huge Keldara crushed his larynx and trachea. Cong's face turned red, then purple as the oxygen was cut off to his lungs first, and then his brain. Oleg gave his crushed windpipe one final squeeze, then dropped him overboard, where the hungry sharks were already waiting.

The general didn't make another sound as the sharks thrashed and fought over their prize.

EPILOGUE

Lieutenant Fang Gui sipped his coffee and set the cup back down on the table.

"So, let me get this straight. You tracked Cong to the middle of the jungle, where he betrayed you and left you as slave labor in Myanmar's gem mines. You promptly escaped and followed his trail to the nuclear facility near—Chaunggyi, right?—and learned that a cabal of military generals were about to cause a nuclear accident to throw the country into turmoil and use that to launch a military coup?"

"Right so far," Mike replied.

"Then, you found out that the weapons being used in this *coup d'etat* were in Mandalay, so you went there and took them back. *Then* you rounded up a group of out-of-work Gurkhas and managed to fly them and your men down to Yangon in time to stop a contingent of the same army from taking over City Hall?"

"I know it sounds crazy, but—"

"If it wasn't for the intelligence we've been getting out of Myanmar over the past twenty-four hours, I would have said you were insane to even try to feed me this story." Fang sighed and shook his head. "However, given what we have heard, I have little choice but to accept your version of events."

Mike sipped his coffee. "It doesn't matter whether you like it or not, that's the way it went down."

It was thirty-six hours later, and the two men were enjoying a late breakfast at Sky on 57, on the 57th floor of the Marina Bay Sands Singapore. They were the only ones on the terrace, since Mike had reserved the entire place for his meeting with the lieutenant. He figured the eight billion-dollar hotel, casino, and entertainment complex was a fitting place for his team to stay for a bit of R & R after everything that had gone down.

Vanel and Soon Yi were both getting the best medical care he could find in the country, although Yi's injuries were far more extensive. Mike couldn't help wondering if she would ever be herself again after what Cong—and he—had put her through. He had considered going to see her, but decided against it, figuring that paying for her care here for as long as it took would have to be apology enough for what had happened.

The rest of his people were enjoying the luxurious rooms, sightseeing, or, in Adams' case, gambling and partying almost nonstop. Mike had approved that on the condition that the master chief not leave the complex. Adams had just grinned and said, "Leave the building? Hell, I'm not sure I'm going back with you when you leave the *country!*"

"That, however, does leave a few unanswered questions, Mr. Jenkins..." The police lieutenant's voice brought Mike back to the present, and he looked over to find the other man steepling his fingers as he regarded him. "For example, there is the matter of the computer boards."

"I'm afraid that in all the running around, I never got the chance to get them back from Cong. If they're not still in the facility, then I have no idea where they are." Unlike what he had told the police officer earlier, only some of this statement was true. Specifically, the part about not knowing where they were. The rest was pure bull—Mike had made sure that the Super Hercules crew had taken the boards back with them, and let Bob Pierson know that they were inbound. The U.S. government would have all the time in the world to look them over, and then, at some future date, they would be "recovered" and returned to the Chinese government.

"I see. And the whereabouts of General Cong?"

"Also unknown. After I got done preventing that coup, I got the hell out of Myanmar and laid low for a couple of days to make sure the government or the army wasn't coming after me next." Most of that was true, including his statement about Cong's whereabouts. *Besides, those sharks should be halfway across the Bay of Bengal by now.*

"Well, you do not have to worry about that. Representatives from my government have already been in touch with the Myanmar government regarding this matter. They have been informed that any attempt to arrest you or otherwise hold you accountable for anything that happened will bring severe repercussions from my government." Fang smiled. "We didn't even have to mention the unlawful reactor they have in their possession. That will be kept for another time."

"Well, then, sounds like everyone's happy," Mike said.

"Under the circumstances, I would say yes." Fang pushed his chair back and stood up. "However, and I hope that you will not take offense at these words, once you have left this area of the world, it may behoove you to let a few years go by before returning."

"Oh, believe me, I've had enough mai tais and tropical flowers to last me for a decade, at least." Mike stood up and extended his hand. "Have a safe trip back to Hong Kong, Lieutenant."

Fang shook his hand and nodded slightly. "And may you have a pleasant journey home as well." He walked to the door and left, leaving Mike to finish his coffee and stare out at the calm, blue-green waters of the port.

Overall, it had been a *very* profitable voyage. Mike had already contacted Chal about an even larger load of gems he had to cash out, and the preliminary estimate was that he'd be clearing about ten million dollars. That was in addition to the payment they'd received from Arun Than on the previous gems. Then there was the ten truckloads of weapons, ammunition, and equipment that he'd "rescued" from the army. The weapons and ammo had been cached in a hidden location—the former pirate base—until Mike could secure a ship large enough to haul all of it away.

And that is the best part of all, he thought as he picked up his coffee cup and sipped again.

About a mile offshore, a very distinctive black and gray super-yacht lay at anchor. If he squinted, Mike thought he could see the workmen busy making repairs to the boat. He smiled at the thought of sailing that beauty wherever his heart decided to take him—once a few niggling details were worked out, of course.

His smartphone rang, and Mike leaned back in his chair as he answered it.

"Hello? Arun, my friend, how are things?...Yes, I know you weren't expecting to hear from me so soon, but I am sure that the matter I am calling about is a trifling one for a man with your skills...You see, I seem to have come into possession of a rather large yacht...Yes, it was quite a deal—the previous owner couldn't wait to be free of it...

"As a matter of fact, the papers are somewhat nonexistent at the moment, and that's where I thought you might be of some small assistance..."

▶ END ◀